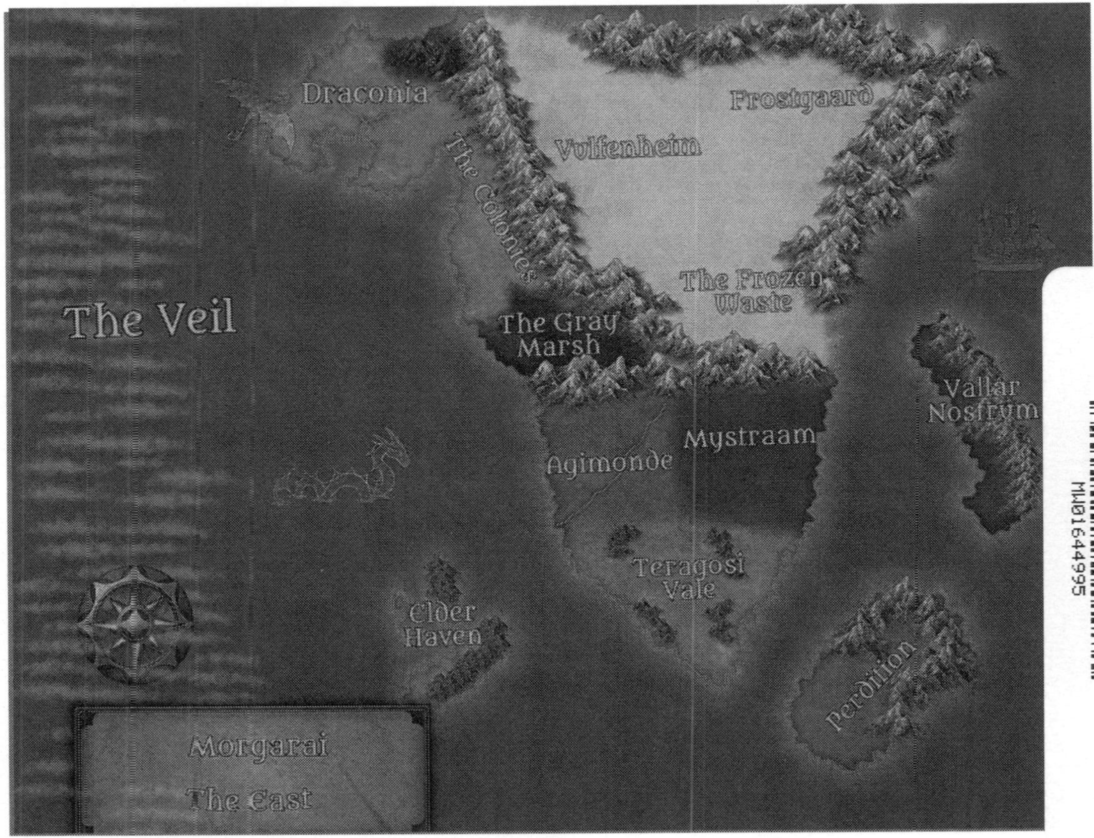

The Veil

Draconia

Vulfenheim

Frostgaard

The Colonies

The Frozen Waste

The Gray Marsh

Vallar Nosfrym

Mystraam

Agimonde

Teragosi Vale

Elder Haven

Perdition

Morgarai

The East

This is a work of fiction. Similarities to real people, places, or events are entirely coincidental.

SIX-GUN SORCERY

First edition. February 17, 2021.

Written by Andrew Slinde.

To Sarah, My Queen of Darkness

And to absent friends, those lost along the way.

Author's Note

There are many stories told throughout the Parallels: tales of bravery and honor, valorous and virtuous warriors, and of horrible things beaten back into the Void. Countless holy writings tell us of demigods and prophets spreading the word of the gods, martyrs who died for their beliefs. There are stories about flawless heroes – paragons of their races – who could do no wrong.

This is not one of those stories.

Just as the brightest light casts the darkest shadow, so too can the best of us fall, and the fallen rise.

It starts, like any story, in the beginning...

In the beginning...

...There was the Source, the center of all life and magick. It was from the Source that the Ethereals (some called them gods) emerged – Ylvey, god of substance; Ordo, god of law; and Pandaemonia, goddess of chaos.

It was then that Ylvey looked into the Void and gave it form. He crafted the earth, the water, the heavens from the fires of creation, forging each with care. The light of the Source bathed it and there was Life.

Jealous of what her brother had made, Pandaemonia formed her own sphere: a cold mass of pitted rock, but the Source's light could not reach it leaving the frozen surface devoid of life. Enraged at her failure, she cast her orb into the orbit of her brother's. The world of Ylvey tilted on its axis, the earth cracked and soured, the seas boiled, the heavens fractured, and the fire of creation was nearly snuffed out.

When Ordo saw this, he lamented. His brother's sphere was built in perfect balance, but his sister had thrown it into chaos. So Ordo took in his hands a mighty flame that shone incandescent in the Void, bathing the world in its light. Ordo sent the flame chasing the cold orb that belonged to his sister, restoring balance once more.

Thus, the earth, the moon, and the sun came into being.

Afterward, having seen their capacity for both creation and for destruction, the Ethereals were filled with remorse. They agreed that each would sleep and dream the world they saw fit. So they slept, and for each dream, a Parallel was born.

The dreams of Ylvey and Ordo have many names, but Pandaemonia's world bears only one name: Morgarai.

-Librum ex Genisi, 1:1-20

Chapter One: Ordo's Call, Perdition

The island nation of Perdition was an inhospitable place, even as far as places in Morgarai are concerned: the land there laid to waste by years of warfare between the Sapiens and the half-daemon race the Cythraul. Some scholars say (usually after a few drinks) that the Daemon Wars ended thousands of years ago, but the news never reached Perdition.

Ordo's Call was an academic establishment, a university of sorts that trained Peacekeepers in enforcing the Unbound Law – a code signed and upheld by all governing bodies of Morgarai. The Call stood on the Barrowlands, a massive stone structure with walls pockmarked from engines of war. The founders placed it at the battlefront so up-and-coming Peacekeepers would be reminded of the consequences of failing their mission. Since then, the front advanced, but Ordo's Call remained, its spires rising to the ashen sky.

Newly-minted Peacekeeper Esther Triad sat on a bench outside the Magister's Hall, looking over the desolate Barrowlands. Outwardly calm and collected, she nervously counted the cairns in the field and tried not to think about why she was being summoned.

Esther, an unassuming, fresh-faced young woman, wore the uniform of the Peacekeeper: a cassock and broad brimmed hat with a domed crown, both black, and a golden medallion depicting the Scales of Ordo, her badge of office. She kept her straight black hair plaited in a tight braid over one shoulder; she idly fingered it now.

After what seemed like an eternity, the heavy steel doors ground open with the rasp of gears and pulleys. Two Peacekeepers exited, one an older man with lines and scars on his face and a younger initiate, probably in training. They gave Esther a brief nod of acknowledgment in passing. Behind them, Secretary Morgis came for her, a big man, nearly as wide as he was tall, walking with a pronounced limp from his time serving in the Brigades; his face was kind, albeit sour, as if he'd just finished eating a lemon that he found delicious.

"My, you make a fine Peacekeeper indeed," the old man said.

Secretary Morgis had once been an instructor of Esther's, a favorite. She had been an apt pupil and he a proud teacher. Esther smiled and shook his hand. "Thank you, Secretary," she said.

Falling into step, he escorted her into the hall. Esther found being summoned before the Magister much less daunting with her teacher at her side. The enormous hall had a high, vaulted ceiling and stone benches lining either side of the wide center aisle. Gilded columns around the edges depicted various aspects of Ordo: the Sun, the Scales, the Lion. At the end of the hall loomed the High Seat, a great judiciary bench carved from stone. Behind it sat Magister Pontus.

The Magister's stoic and severe features chilled the already chilly room. The burned side of his face left little expression save for one cold, dead eye glaring out. The other eye, still alive and as sharp as ever, wasn't much better. Esther *felt* his piercing stare before she saw it.

"Presenting Peacekeeper Esther Triad," Secretary Morgis announced. He left Esther's side and took his place behind the Magister's seat, leaving her feeling alone and exposed. She glanced down at her feet standing squarely in the center of Ordo's Seal, round and gold with two hammers crossed behind the scales – one for Order, the other for Law.

How many people have been sentenced to die in this very spot? Esther thought, feeling a cold stone settle into her stomach. *They call this place Gallowschurch for a reason.*

"Esther Triad," Magister Pontus said, looking over the sheaf of papers in front of him. "Daughter of Zeks Triad and Gilyana Marshall."

"Yes, Your Honor," Esther said, the phrase mechanical and well-rehearsed.

"Your mother was a Peacekeeper as well?" the Magister asked, again consulting his records.

"Yes, Your Honor," Esther replied, "until she was killed in the line of duty at Naxis Rock."

The Magister nodded, his expression darkening. "I remember Naxis Rock. We lost many good Peacekeepers that day."

Esther soured at the Magister's gross understatement. Before his days of teaching and politicking, the old man had been a commanding officer in the Brigades. Hours of studying that particular battle led her to two conclusions: one, Naxis Rock had no strategic significance; and two, Pontus had given the order to the take the Rock dooming twenty-eight Peacekeepers to a fiery death in the process. Naxis Rock was volcanic and rigged with magicks to explode on command. In other words, it had been a colossal failure.

Magister Pontus kept going through his papers. "Good marks in all your coursework, skilled in combat – including a commendation for valor during your service in the Brigades. You possess a knowledge of the Unbound Law that surpasses your fellow initiates. A remarkable student."

"Thank you, Your Honor."

Pontus turned that dead eye on her again asking, "Are you prepared for your first assignment, Peacekeeper?"

Esther visibly started, then collected herself: according to tradition, the newly minted Peacekeepers would gather in the Court of the Penitent to receive their assignments en masse. None of the graduates she'd known over the years had ever been summoned before the Magister to receive theirs individually. Unless they needed someone for a special assignment.

"A special assignment, Your Honor?" Esther couldn't help asking.

Pontus cleared his throat. "Indeed," he said, "if you like."

Morgis stepped forward, handing her a leather-bound file. "There has been a disturbance in the Colonies," Pontus explained. "An arcanist, formerly in the employ of the governor to bring rains to ease their long-standing drought, appears to have gone rogue. Governor Avalos of Estrella Nova reports that the rains have gone unbroken for days, flooding the fields and destroying this year's crop. He has asked that we investigate and put a stop to this dissident."

"With respect, sir," Esther interjected, "why do they need a Peacekeeper? The Colonies are an extension of the kingdom of Kairal. Wouldn't a military response be more appropriate?"

Pontus cleared his throat again. Too late Esther recognized it for what it was: a sign of irritation. "Kairal is busy fighting their endless wars; they cannot spare any men. The Governor's security forces are busy keeping the peace among the frightened people. The arcanist in question is also of Gigan descent, making this an international incident, thus falling into our jurisdiction."

Esther nodded her acknowledgment but said nothing out of deference for the Magister's throat.

"You will depart for the Colonies tomorrow morning. The details of your mission are in the file, as is a check for five hundred royals to cover your expenses. Peacekeeper Triad, you are tasked with seeking out this arcanist and bringing him to justice under the Unbound Law." Pontus raised his gavel and slammed it down, marking the end of their meeting. "Ordo be with you."

"And also with you," Esther replied mechanically.

• • • •

IT ISN'T SNOW, IT'S ash, Esther reminded herself as she stepped out of Ordo's Call.

The great stone building overlooked the village of the same name. Esther could see the tile roofs and rough-hewn stone of the structures below, smoke and steam rising from their chimneys. The constantly overcast sky dusted them with gray-white flakes – the ashes of war. Though the sun peeked over the horizon, the only indication was the vague lightening of the sky on the western horizon. Esther wondered briefly how she would cope in places where she could see the sun. She also mused at the irony that, although Ordo created the sun, it seldom shined in the place of his worship.

She needed to report to the sky harbor by ten o'clock, which gave her time to cash her check, purchase a few supplies, and maybe stop for a coffee at her favorite cafe. Trudging down the long stair that wound down the hillside to the village, she could see the streets were nearly deserted this early in the day. A few early risers passed her by – laborers at the black iron mine and the foundry. Most were Sapien, but she recognized a few Agi artisans by their red hair and orange-tinted skin. With their remarkable craftsmanship and the ability to fold spellcraft into steel, the Agi were essential to both the manufacturing industry and the war effort. Were it not for them, the wards and protective capabilities of the village walls wouldn't exist.

The artisans gave her a sideways glance, speaking their melodic language in low tones. Part of training as a Peacekeeper included having a tentative grasp on world languages. What the Agi said about her couldn't be repeated in polite company, and Esther reminded herself that they weren't talking about her, they were talking about the uniform. Even in Perdition, the Peacekeepers were looked upon with wariness – upholding the Unbound Law didn't make one popular.

Shrugging off the slight, Esther crossed the high street to the bank. Central Counting became ubiquitous in Morgarai thanks to the expansion of the Wraithbane Empire centuries before. The Unbound Law curbed their conquest; universal currency presented an unexpected benefit. The bank's large, ornate structure made it the only white building among the otherwise dismal gray of the village.

Solid marble columns flanked the gilded doors, circling the building. Armed guards gave a little color with crisp blue uniforms and finely polished rifles. Esther stopped for a moment, admiring the cut of their uniforms and the beauty of their steel. One of the guards, the younger one, blushed. After passing them, she heard the older of the two guffaw at the younger and smiled in spite of herself.

The tellers inside were also dressed in those sharp blue uniforms, although Esther had to admit that they didn't wear them as well as the guards. There were a few affluent customers inside – men in waistcoats and trilbies, women in corsets and petticoats, hats with plumage – getting a jump start on their day. They gave Esther a wide berth as she crossed the bank's green marble floor.

She recognized the first teller to catch her eye. Leiyara also waited tables at the cafe Esther frequented, creating a moment of dissonance in seeing in a vibrant blue Central Counting uniform. The very moment Leiyara registered Esther, her big brown eyes lit up with excitement. Each time Esther encountered the girl in the past, Leiyara bombarded her with questions about life in the Call and about being a Peacekeeper.

"I always wanted to be one," the girl gushed one day while refilling Esther's cup, "but I don't think I could pull off the look. Also, I'm terrible at firing a pistol."

The "look" and the pistol were Leiyara's chief concerns. That sort of naivete usually irritated Esther to no end, but at the same time, something about the girl's wide-eyed innocence endeared her to the Peacekeeper. Esther had continued answering Leiyara's questions and nursing the girl's hopes that one day she could be accepted at the Call. Now, Esther lingered a little too long before stepping up to the counter, amusing herself watching the energetic girl battle between her excitement and her professionalism – practically *vibrating*.

Another teller, a man sporting what he probably mistook for a stylish pencil mustache, cleared his throat. "I can help you, Miss," he intoned.

Leiyara practically jumped out of her skin. "No! I can help her – help you! Let me help her!"

The mustachioed man rolled his eyes and assumed that disdainful demeanor perpetuated by all men who thought pencil mustaches were stylish. Once again smiling in spite of herself, Esther stepped to Leiyara's window.

"How can I help you, ma'am?" the red-haired girl asked, brushing the curls out of her eyes. In the same breath, she noticed Esther's knapsack and duffle bag. "Are you going on a trip? Is it far? Will it be dangerous?" Leiyara's eyes glowed like brown embers with tiny flecks of red in the irises – flame-flecked, they called it.

Esther set down her gear and produced her check for five hundred royals. "I'm really not supposed to talk about it," she said.

One of those things that made people wary of Peacekeepers, especially in a small community like Ordo's Call: no one knew their business. Even in a village that bred and trained them, a community was only as safe and secure as its network of gossips and busybodies. Still, Leiyara's eyes widened in fascination and delight. There was truly no deterring this girl.

"Matron's name! It must be dangerous. And important. And secret. And dangerous!"

The way Leiyara said "dangerous" likened it to a picnic, further betraying her innocence. *Someone has read a few too many ha'slip dreadfuls*, Esther thought. "All of the above," she replied, handing over the check.

Leiyara hardly noticed, instead her countenance shifted from excitement to concern. "Matron's name! I hope you don't get hurt. Or dead – I mean, killed!"

The Matron again. Esther reminded herself during Leiyara's fawning that she'd be hearing that honorific a lot in the course of her investigation. Leiyara's family came from the Colonies when her father got work at the foundry. An extension of the kingdom of Kairal in the west, they practiced Elderism – a reverence for the fabled immortals who traversed the Parallels and brought the Sapien race to Morgarai. The sainted Matron, Aisha, was a stand-in for any god because, according to legend, she was tasked with the care and protection of Morgarai. The culture and traditions of Elderism were very different from the doctrines of Ordoism. Still, Esther remembered her sensitivity training and just went with it. Intercultural relations were important to maintaining the Unbound Law, after all.

"It's a routine investigation," Esther said. "I'm sure I'll be fine."

Leiyara nodded, looking at Esther doubtfully, then finally realizing she held the check. "Five hundred royals!"

The exclamation reverberated off the bank's marble walls while her co-workers – Pencil-mustache especially – stared at her in derision. "That's almost half a gold imperial!" Leiyara whispered, overcompensating for her outburst. "Do you want it all now because I don't have the cash in my drawer and I'd have to get the manager."

Esther shook her head. "That's alright," she said, keeping an even tone – this exchange took up more of her time than she liked. "I'll take two hundred for now, for travel expenses."

Leiyara nodded emphatically, bouncing her fiery curls. As the enthusiastic little teller went to work on the check with her stylus, Esther idly wondered if the girl didn't have Agi blood somewhere in her ancestry. It would explain the red hair and flame-flecked eyes.

"Do you want this in slips or silverbacks?" she asked after finishing her documentation.

"I'll take half and half," Esther decided. The traditional form of currency, a thin slip of silver- or gold-plated nickel, still served as the standard currency, although more places in Morgarai were accepting paper money. The silverbacks and goldnotes represented the royal and imperial respectively, the bills displaying faces of dead Wraithbane emperors (considering some of those heads were lost to the ax, it was a rather controversial feature).

Leiyara counted out the money in a mix of denominations, seeming to understand that Esther would need smaller increments. Once finished, the red-haired girl pushed two stacks – one heavy silver, the other thin paper – to Esther. The Peacekeeper felt the urge to count it herself, but considered how adept and attentive Leiyara laid it out and didn't want to hurt the girl's feelings. Instead, Esther loaded the silver into her side pouch and stuffed the silverbacks unceremoniously into her pocket.

"I wish I was going with you," Leiyara chattered. "Boy, to see the world and travel by airship, and meet all kinds of people. I bet you even get to meet a Draconian! That would be amazing!"

Suppressing a chuckle, Esther took back her much scribbled-on check. Mystery and mysticism surrounded the Draconian race, mostly because their lineage traced back to the dragons – those former rulers of Morgarai's skies. Draconians also garbed themselves in silks and veils, showing their faces only to people with whom they were intimately familiar. The joke, however, was on Leiyara. Two years ago a Draconian student, the fifth son of his house, joined the Call. Fifth children didn't inherit and, traditionally, didn't have a place in any of Draconian society, so he came to the Call. Peacekeeping attracted a lot of society's rejects.

"It would certainly be something," Esther replied. "Have a nice day."

She turned to leave before Leiyara could chatter at her anymore. When she looked back over her shoulder, she caught a glimpse of the poor girl looking miserable while Pencil-mustache bawled her out.

• • • •

AIR TRAVEL, A RECENT addition to Central Transit's repertoire, caught on quickly as a fast and convenient mode of travel. Once the department of the Wraithbane Empire responsible for roads, bridges, and collecting tolls, the organization was able to come into its own with the advent of the steam engine and the growing popularity of the railway. Few places in Morgarai were not accessible by a locomotive, and now that airships sailed the skies, Morgarai became a much smaller place. This area of modern living didn't pass Perdition by: Ordo's Call had their very own sky harbor, a tower of steel scaffolding hastily welded to scrapmetal platforms. The harbor found its home on one of the island's many craggy cliff faces.

After her fourth flight of rickety metal stairs, Esther stopped to catch her breath. She looked out over the village and at the Call on the edge of it. It sat imperiously atop the bluff, a shining gilded beacon in the otherwise dismal setting. Esther wondered idly if she would return anytime soon, but had remarkably few feelings about the matter. Even though she'd spent her entire life in the village, most of it studying at the Call, she found herself nursing a growing sense of detachment to the place. Most people cited getting off that dismal rock as a reason for becoming a Peacekeeper. Esther could barely contain the spark of excitement to see the places she'd only ever read about in books. She'd been expecting some pang of regret for leaving it behind, but as she looked over the wasteland she was only grateful to leave it behind in the dust and the ash.

Earlier, Esther had stopped for supplies at the general store – jerky, beans, water, a bedroll, and other such provisions; she sprang for a small cask of wine, too, as a luxury item. They were being delivered to the airship, which meant that the precious few minutes she'd had to make it to her cafe lapsed into nothing; on top of negotiating her airfare, she'd also have to ensure receipt of the goods and make certain the delivery boy hadn't extracted any "carrying charges".

A part-time shop boy would be wary to cheat a Peacekeeper, but Esther refused to begin her first assignment by taking chances.

Business was picking up at the sky harbor. People were ascending the steel staircases while just as many were disembarking and descending. Starting up her fifth flight, Esther nodded to a pair of fellow Peacekeepers on their way down. She didn't recognize them, so she wondered if perhaps they were returning from a long assignment.

And then it happened. Looking back on the events, even through the haze of many years, she couldn't help but believe that Ordo himself had taken a hand.

However, in the present moment, Esther felt deeply annoyed.

"Esther! Peacekeeper Triad! Wait!"

For a moment Esther thought she might have left something at the bank, but when she stopped on the fifth-floor landing – and nearly got trampled by a burly man and his companion – she turned to see the red-haired girl carrying a knapsack. The girl, having changed out of her bank uniform, wore a linen shirt, a leather jacket, and a pair of trousers. The getup looked rather boyish with her slim frame. The girl still called Esther's name when she reached the landing, huffing and puffing, her face a dark shade of pink.

"Leiyara," Esther said warily, "what are you doing here?"

Between panting breaths Leiyara said the words those dreaded words: "I'm...coming...with you."

Esther eyed her dubiously. "Excuse me?"

Gulping in a few huge breaths Leiyara could finally express herself properly. "I mean, I want to come with you. If you'll have me."

The Peacekeeper's expression didn't change, but seeing the glimmer of hope and the possibility of heartbreak on the girl's face did a lot to soften her.

"I can read and write, and I'm good at math, because I'm a teller and all, and I can cook and serve coffee and whatnot, because, you know, I worked in the cafe –"

"*Worked*?" Esther asked.

Leiyara's face flushed again. "I may have...quit my jobs."

Incredulity overtook Esther's expression. "I'm sorry, you did what? What were you thinking?"

Leiyara threw up her hands defensively, as if Esther would to strike her. "I know. It's impulsive and probably foolish but it's a chance to go on an adventure. And I thought...I guess...since you're my only friend..."

Esther rolled her eyes. "And what is it exactly you think you'll do?"

Leiyara didn't even hesitate. Somehow between turning in her notice at both the bank and the cafe and the mad dash to the sky harbor, she'd put a lot of thought into this. "I can be your secretary," she said, sounding rather less sure of herself by the end of the statement.

"Secretary?" Esther's mind still couldn't grasp the reality of it.

Encouraged by the lack of a firm no, Leiyara brightened. "Sure. It's like in the novels: a mysterious and strong character goes to destinations unknown with her secretary in tow. I'll cook and keep your books and tidy things up. You can bounce ideas off me."

Esther leaned against the railing, then when it shifted she thought better of it and stood upright. On one hand, Leiyara had a point: it would be nice to have a traveling companion, something of the old familiar to cling to when she felt out of her depth. Having someone to mind her domestic affairs while she focused on her mission would be invaluable. Still, this chattering ball of fire-haired energy could be a liability if things took a turn. Morgarai abounded with perils, so if Esther had to keep one eye on a threat, she'd have to keep the other on Leiyara.

"I don't know," Esther said, watching the girl's look become that much more hopeful. "It's not going to be like your novels. There are very real dangers out there. People do a lot of ugly things and I may be required to do ugly things back. Furthermore, where we're going is not a good place. There's spellcraft and the arcane, and maybe some very bad people behind it. Are you prepared for that?"

The girl chewed her lip, the sparkle in her eye fading as the reality began to sink in.

"Do you have any money?" the Peacekeeper asked.

Now Leiyara paled. Could it be that she'd come so close only to fall by the wayside because of a light purse? "Fifty-seven royals," she admitted.

Esther nodded. "That should cover your airfare and a few meals, at least." She shoved her bags into Leiyara's arms. *Why not?* she thought. *Ordo teaches us to be charitable, after all.*

She started up the sixth flight of stairs, leaving a bewildered Leiyara in her wake, all open mouth and wide, flame-flecked eyes. "Come along then," she called back over her shoulder. "The flight leaves in a quarter-hour."

• • • •

A WIDE VARIETY OF AIRSHIP existed in Morgarai. Some were just longboats or skiffs rigged with a balloon on top to keep them aloft, their steam engines fed by coal. The ship upon which Esther embarked, however, was a Central Transit liner made from lightweight black iron and aluminum, equipped with boilers fed with *teravir* to power gleaming propellers The CT logo shone in bright colors on the hydrogen balloon. A truly impressive craft.

Granted, taking an independently owned and operated skiff or longboat would have been cheaper, but the crews were less savory, the aircraft less reliable. In Morgarai, finding yourself stranded could be a perilous affair. After haggling with the ship's bursar over the cost of the flight and meals provided (six royals a day for a seven day flight), Esther left Leiyara on deck to admire the other airships and the truly impressive distance between herself and the ground.

She went to their shared cabin below deck to prepare for the journey ahead.

The cabin cramped cabin contained two bunk beds and a cupboard. Esther didn't mind the lack of space but begrudged the lack of private washrooms. Her cell at the Call measured about this size, but at least it had its own facilities. Esther was pleased to find her luggage laid on the bed for her. She'd packed light with only her knapsack and duffel bag, the Scales of Ordo embroidered on both to warn away thieves and busybodies.

She opened the duffel bag and wrestled out her gun belt. In the holsters a pair of revolvers gleamed, their barrels adorned with broad-bladed bayonets. The traditional weapons of the Peacekeepers, they were designed for both ranged and close combat. The weight of them felt good on Esther's hips, as sure and solid as Ordo's visage. She drew one of the revolvers from the specially crafted holster, checked the cylinder, and ran her thumb gingerly over the bayonet's edge. She then did the same with the other. Both were loaded for bear, both blades sharp and true.

According to code, Peacekeepers should have their weapons on them at all times, save for when they sleep, at which point they should still be close at hand. Still, at the Call she never felt comfortable walking around fully armed among a people who already looked at her warily. And she wasn't about to become one of those Peacekeepers who posed just right with one hand on their hip, showing off their piece. No, in a pinch she had a small pearl-handled pistol hidden up her sleeve and her glyph magicks with which to defend herself.

Esther took a moment to examine herself in the closet's mirrored door. In her full regalia – the black-as-night cassock, her wide-brimmed hat, her brace of pistols and her medallion – she looked like a proper Peacekeeper. Even her posture – stiff, upright, confident

– reflected her station. But for the first time after leaving the Call, Esther wondered if she was truly prepared for what lay ahead of her.

Chapter Two:
The Township of Turner, the Colonies

The saloon was about what one would expect from a saloon: dimly lit gas lamps shedding greasy yellow light and casting dark, mutable shadows; smoke from cigars and loosely rolled cigarettes hanging in the air, and men and women of all sorts gathering to drink, gamble, carouse and make mischief. A player piano in one corner plunked out its tinny tones. Toward the back of the taproom, four men played a game of Taro. One player among them stood out.

The man enjoyed quite a reputation, known for tremendous deeds either heroic, unlawful, or self-serving. In some parts, he touted himself the greatest swordsman that ever lived, while in other places he's trailed by the whispered warning to lock up your daughters. And sisters. And wives. And mothers. He was a hulking, handsome fellow with his long blond hair tied back with a flamboyant red bow, compulsively clad in a red greatcoat, and, when standing, was a head taller than most Sapien men. One crooked smile from him betrayed equal parts charm and arrogance. His true name he kept to himself as a matter of habit – in some places, names still had power – but for his purposes, he went by the honorific *Le Valet des Coeurs*.

On this night, the Valet engaged in his Taro game at the back of the smoky saloon. Between his teeth he chewed the end of a fat cigar. His nimble fingers tapped his cards rhythmically as his blue eyes focused on the men around him, a predator spying its prey. It was the thirteenth hand; the deciding hand.

A certain Patrus Winkle sat to his left, an older gent garbed in the robe of a Confessor – a healer and priest who ran the local Eldrist church. "Bid three," the Patrus said, tossing his silverbacks into the pot. The Matron didn't consider gambling a sin, and a good thing too because the old man was a card sharp and no mistake. He'd become the point leader in a clever ruse known as the Fool's Gambit. It had taken the Valet the better part of an hour to catch up.

A telegraph operator for Central Transit called Jenkins still wore his burgundy uniform; he hadn't even bothered to remove his name badge. If there's a sucker born every minute, then Jenkins' time had come. "Three," he agreed, counting out his slips.

Last, but certainly not least, Marcus "Hopper" Monroe enjoyed his own reputation as a known highwayman and killer. He sat to the Valet's right, eyeballing him with a stone-cold glare over a grizzled black beard. Hopper fancied himself a man of class in his cheap suit and dusty bowler hat. He wore a pistol on one hip and a saber on the other, a remnant of some old army. He looked every bit like the sketch on his wanted poster. "That's three, raise two."

He'd beaten Hopper in the last few hands, dropping the Tower on him and relieving him of a hefty sum. Hopper's blood was up and the Valet could practically smell the violence on him, which only lent more to his predatory smirk.

"It's your bid," Hopper growled.

The Valet eyed him, then his cards. "Five, raising seven royals," he said, dropping the silver slips into the pot with an audible clink.

The Confessor ponied up too eagerly. "Twelve, then," he said.

Jenkins dropped his cards. "Retreat," he pronounced, pushing a pair of spectacles up on his nose. A retreat lost a player seven points, putting Jenkins even with Hopper.

Hopper matched the bid with a snarl. The Valet had been haranguing him all night.

With a flourish and a wider grin, the Valet dumped his cards on the table. "Taro!" he announced. The hand, consisting of all the trump cards, was unbeatable and an automatic thirteen point gain.

Hopper erupted. He shot up out of his chair, overturned the card table, and drew his pistol. The activity in the bar - the murmur of conversation, the catcalls, the din of glasses clinking and knocking on wood – died down. Only the player piano was undisturbed, tinkling out its jovial tune.

"You miserable cheat," Hopper growled. "I ought to kill you right now."

The Valet leaned back in his chair, cool and collected. He dropped the smoldering butt of his cigar onto the floor and spread his hands. "I'm unarmed, Hopper," he said.

Hopper took a step closer and cocked his pistol. "Makes it easier."

The Valet looked into the man's smoldering glare, ice on fire. "Think of what that's going to do to your reputation. Does the great Hopper Monroe kill an unarmed man without a fight? And with all these people around to tell the tale that Hopper Monroe is yellow?"

The outlaw clenched his teeth, flicked his eyes over the patrons. "I ain't yellow," he grumbled. "A duel, then, nice and legit. Outside. Now."

The Valet smiled. *Game, set, match.* "You've declared the time and the place," he said, reciting straight from the *Librum Ordis*. "That is your right. I name the weapon: swords."

The Confessor, who'd jumped up from the table when it was overturned, made the Crux of Alastar over himself, while Jenkins, who had hidden behind the nearest support beam, swore an oath to the Matron. Hopper eyed the Valet warily for a moment, and the Valet wondered if the man knew he was being bushwhacked.

A storm brewed outside, kicking up dust devils on the packed-earth street. Lightning illuminated the duelists as they took their places a few paces apart. Hopper already brandished his saber in what he probably thought of as an impressive display. The Valet, however, carried only a rolled bundle of canvasing, half his height and wide as a dinner plate. Above them, storm callers cawed and screeched as they circled the towering nimbus on the horizon.

"Arm yourself," Hopper shouted over the sound of thunder.

The Valet grinned ear-to-ear. He'd set the outlaw up exquisitely; when Hopper went down it would be nice and legal, and he could have his fun. With a deft motion, he undid the slipknot from his bundle, shook the canvas loose, and revealed a horrifying sight.

Legend has it that there are eight Rune Blades that haunt Morgarai, forged from the arachnid avatar of Pandaemonia herself. The Valet possessed *Glaeve Pandaemonia,* the most dreaded of all the Rune Blades. Nearly four feet in length and as broad as a Sapien hand, it bore a resemblance more to an enormous cleaver than a traditional sword. At its hilt blazed a red jewel the size of a fist, cut to look like an eye. The old, scarred flesh of some old, scarred beast wrapped the grip. Blood-red runes traced the side of the black blade, casting a menacing otherworldly light.

The moment Hopper laid eyes on the Valet's sword his knees began to shake, his expression gaping. The realization of who he'd just challenged broke over him in a cold sweat. *Glaeve Pandaemonia* gave off a malicious hum as the Valet took a fighting stance. "*En garde*," he said, his smile fading and his eyes blazing with deadly light.

Hopper swallowed hard, audibly. "So, you're him, huh?"

"I'm him," the Valet confirmed. "You can lay down arms now if you'd like."

The outlaw's eyes flicked away as he appeared to give the Valet's offer a moment's consideration, but reason would not prevail over the prospect of the man's lost reputation. He clenched his jaw and took up his fighting stance, a classic fencing pose. "I don't lay down for nobody," he spat.

I'm counting on it, the Valet thought.

To say that fight was long and epic would be a lie on both counts – a tall tale that would be later told to save Hopper's reputation or to call attention to the storyteller – but in truth, it ended in a blink. Hopper charged, a mad and desperate battle cry on his lips. The Valet crossed blades with him only once and, over the ring of shattering steel, delivered a blow that bisected Hopper cleanly from shoulder to hip. Blood sprayed, guts spilled into the dirt, and Hopper's last protest died in his throat.

By now, the saloon patrons and wait staff had gathered to watch, looking appalled as *Glaeve Pandaemonia* absorbed – or some would say *drank* – the blood from its blade. The Valet blew a loose lock of hair from his face and began to carefully wrap the Rune Blade in its canvas. Behind him, the crowd began to disperse as men were sent to fetch the undertaker and the local constable. Meantime, Patrus Winkle and tapper Jenkins approached, carrying a small bag.

"Your winnings," the Confessor said, a little sheepishly.

The Valet took the bag from the Patrus and looked inside, made an estimate to whether it was all there, then handed it back. "Split it," he said. Then, when the two men went agape, he added, "Your church needs a new roof, and those families of the Central Transit staff he killed deserve some recompense. The reward for Hopper here will be enough for me."

The two men looked at one another, puzzled. At the same time, another burgundy-uniformed man ran from the Central Transit office, waving a telegram in his hands. "Sir!" he shouted to the Valet. "News from the airship, as you requested!"

Strange, thought the Valet, *that ship wasn't supposed to arrive until tomorrow.*

He took the proffered telegram and looked at it. *S.O.S.* A distress call.

"What's happened?" the Valet asked.

"We don't know sir," the CT employee said between gasping breaths. "They were able to use their signal lights, but they've gone dark since. Their last known location was..." he paled noticeably and swallowed hard, "...well, it was over the Gray Marsh, sir."

I'm supposed to meet someone on that ship, the Valet thought. He crumpled the telegram. "Son of a fetch."

Chapter Three:

The CTS K.D. Morrison, just over the Gray Marsh

The days of travel and poor sleep aboard the K.D. Morrison took their toll on Esther, not to mention the bad food. Leiyara's constant chatter didn't help either, but at least she wasn't airsick anymore. So when boots scuffed and men shouted from the deck above them, the Peacekeeper took it as a reprieve. Leiyara paled at the sounds, stopping mid-sentence in some story about...something. The airship gave a nauseating lurch to one side, nearly throwing the girl off her feet. Esther hardly noticed; she was already out the door.

When she reached the deck a gale from the west nearly knocked her off her feet. All around her Central Transit personnel scrambled for rifles and rushed wayward passengers safely below deck. When one of the women approached her to warn her away, Esther flashed her medallion.

"Peacekeeper," she said, a word that opened doors and closed mouths in the civilized world. "What's happening here?"

The woman – Helena, by her name badge – pointed westward. "Storm callers off the port bow. They're coming straight for us, along with their storm." She pointed at another burgundy-uniformed employee and shouted, "You there! Man the signal lights! Send a distress call."

Esther knew that the nearest signal tower lay in the mountains about ten miles to the south (she'd seen it flashing semaphore signals when they passed it), but she wasn't hopeful of any kind of assistance – not this far out. *No,* she thought, *we're on our own.*

Helena rushed off, shouting to a few gawking passengers and hustling a pregnant woman below. Esther looked in the direction of the port bow. Towering storm clouds blacker than the night sky boiled with lightning, surrounded by a vortex of ravens – no, not ravens. These birds flew about in black feathers, but electricity arced amidst their deep purple wings, living embodiments of the primal force of the storm.

Elementals, Esther realized. There were two ways to fight an elemental: one could either bring to bear the opposing elemental force or damage the energy matrix holding it together. Since she had no Runic magicks in her arsenal, Esther drew her pistols and made her way through the wind to the bow. Several Central Transit guards were waiting there as well, rifles at the ready.

The man supervising them bore the bronze tone and jet-black hair of a Kairulian. A tall man with the straight posture of a soldier, the gray at his temples spoke of experience. "Pick your targets," he shouted, "Pair up! One fires, one reloads. I want a constant volley of shot because if one of these things touches this ship she's doomed."

The Kairulian glanced at Esther. “You there, Peacekeeper,” he called.

Esther straightened and tried to look more dignified than terrified. “Yes?”

The soldier made his way to her, grasping the railing to help keep his footing. “Are you combat ready?” he asked.

Esther thought the question rather redundant, but she held up her revolvers to indicate the affirmative.

“Good,” the Kairulian – Riggs, according to his name badge – “you can help us. If any of these bastards make it past our shooters, it's up to you to take them down.”

Esther nodded and Riggs made his way back to the firing line.

“I have seen storms like this before,” a richly baritone voice said.

Startled, the Peacekeeper barely noticed the lilting accent of the man standing next to her. Only slightly taller than her, he was draped head-to-toe in silks of red and purple. The lightning flashed off the silver skin of his hands and shone in his dark amber eyes. A Draconian.

He turned those slit, reptilian eyes on her. “It was the work of a *hrakhalm* – a weather wizard. This reminds me of that time.”

A weather wizard – an arcanist – a wild mage who communed with elementals and wielded the very forces of nature. It sounded suspiciously like the person she'd been tasked with shutting down.

“But why attack us?” Esther asked.

The Draconian appeared to think it over, his silks flapping around him in the gusting wind. “Perhaps not attacking at all, just making the storm. We only happen to be in its path.”

Esther found that hard to believe. It would have been a likely scenario, and she would have given it due consideration, if her mission didn't involve an arcanist who wreaked havoc with conjured storms. She felt that familiar cold stone in her stomach and knew there was more to this than met the eye. *But how can he possibly know that I'm on this ship? That I'm coming to stop him?* It was a sobering thought, equally open to scrutiny.

“Perhaps,” she conceded. Then she switched to *Drakkenspek*, the Draconians' native tongue. “How does one call oneself?” she asked, hoping she'd swallowed the syllables in the right places.

The Draconian's eyes narrowed in delight, he was smiling. "Hrakar Ch'Flakken," he replied.

Hrakar the Striker, Esther translated. A worthy name, and somewhat a comfort if he lived up to it. The long stiletto-bladed spear and the way he held it reassured her.

“Esther!”

Leiyara's voice, shouting over the wind and encroaching thunder. Esther turned to see her new secretary being manhandled by one of the crew. She resisted, trying to force her way back up to the deck. The poor girl looked sick with worry. Esther hurried to Leiyara and the fresh-faced young crew member who barred her path. She pushed the boy out of the way and, as the airship lurched under her, caught Leiyara in her arms. She barely avoided skewering the poor girl on her bayonets.

Tears formed in Leiyara's flame-flecked as she shook.

I tried to warn you, Esther thought. Instead, she shouted, "Get below deck! Now!"

Leiyara shook her red curls. "No! I want to help!"

Esther holstered one revolver and put her hand on Leiyara's shoulder, firm but gently. "Leiyara, it's not safe for you. You can help me by going back to the cabin and staying safe."

Leiyara started to cry, but she obeyed. The girl crept out of sight, just in time for the first rifle shot to pierce the din of the storm. Esther's head snapped toward the sound just as a storm caller burst into a crackle of light and thunder. There were more rifle reports from the firing line; more tiny bursts of lightning and thunder.

"Incoming!" Riggs shouted from the head of the line.

One of the birds evaded the firing line and dove straight at the deck. Esther raised a revolver to fire, but Hrakar's spear thrust was quicker. It arced through the air and burst the storm caller into sparks. The Draconian gave her a nod before turning back toward the clouds and readied his spear for another strike.

Esther set her eyes on the clouds and raised her pistols. *No more distractions,* she told herself.

Another volley of bullets, another sparkling fireworks display, and another round again. This time, three of the ravens escaped their fate. Esther took aim and shot two of them, each crackling and sparking into nothingness. Hrakar's spear made short work of the third.

The storm cloud loomed closer. The vortex of deep violet birds swirled around the nimbus, lightning flashing in their feathers. The airship lurched starboard in an attempt to move away from the danger. The wind hammered the deck so hard that half of the firing line lost their footing. Three of them went overboard and were immediately set upon by the birds, screaming as they were at once pecked apart and electrocuted.

Rifle fire burst in a constant, discordant hymn. The shooters were firing again and again as quickly as they could. Behind them, the re-loaders worked frantically to shove cartridges into magazines and slap them into the rifles. The air off the port bow crackled and burst with light. The gunfire and thunder were deafening, Esther still shooting at the storm callers that escaped the firing line, Hrakar backing her up with a spear that moved like the ripping wind itself.

Then all the Void broke loose.

Screams from the stern of the ship, more from the prow. Esther turned to see the back of the firing line torn apart by a dark, vaguely feline creature. It too had wings crackling with electricity, its claws flashing iridescent as it sliced through the riflemen.

"Sphinx!" Hrakar exclaimed.

He ran to engage while Esther shot down three more storm callers. The airship careened to one side and Esther pivoted with the motion, just in time to evade another sphinx's pounce. She turned on the creature and pulled both triggers. Nothing. She couldn't even hear the dry clicks from the revolvers over the screams and the shots and the thunder. The sphinx turned on her, its eyes the purple and blue glow of lightning. Where its paws met the deck, tiny flames sprang up. It bared its teeth, folded back its wings, and prepared to strike.

Thinking fast, Esther shoved one of her revolvers into its holster. She cricled the thunder cat, her empty hand shaping glyphs. With each one, a small ethereal symbol burned into existence around her fingers, tiny candle lights in the night. When she stopped circling, the sphinx pounced, showing its electric claws and teeth. Esther threw up her hand and released the spell – blinding light ten times that of the lightning flared and the sphinx rolled into a ball, covering its eyes and landing with a thump on the deck. Esther side-stepped and jabbed her bayonet into the thunder cat. Then she thrust again. The creature let out a roar as she stabbed at it again and again, slashed at its throat, kicked, and screamed oaths to Ordo at it.

At last, the energy matrix gave way, and the body of the cat burst. Esther got thrown back by an electrical surge that set the deck alight. Fortunately, a torrent of rain hit the ship just then, extinguishing the blaze. Esther rose to her knees as the ship gave another nauseating lurch. She tried to look around, but the rain was in her eyes.

"Peacekeeper!" someone shouted.

Wiping her eyes on a sleeve, Esther looked to her right, the port bow of the ship, and saw Riggs pointing. She followed his finger and saw a great ball of lightning – or was it another flock of storm callers? - making for the deck. She dropped her empty revolver and drew her pearl-handled pistol from her sleeve. Firing without aiming, the bullet caught the edge of the lightning orb, sending it careening toward the stern of the ship. For a moment, Esther truly believed they would make it. The storm receded into the western horizon and the airship began turning out of its grasp. The orb, however, spun into the tail fin of the ship. It burst into flames and ignited a portion of the balloon above it.

Ordo's name, Esther cursed as the airship dropped into a nosedive. *We're going to crash.*

Chapter Four: The Bogs, the Gray Marsh

"We shouldn't bury them here."

A voice from out of the darkness. A voice that Esther vaguely recognized, although the last time she'd heard it the woman had been shouting. There had been rifle reports, thunder, fire, death. It came back to Esther in a flood and she opened her eyes, shooting bolt upright. The sudden movement blurred her vision, pain exploded in her head. She dropped back down on the ground, a soft, almost clay-like earth; the sky above was a dismal gray.

Am I back at the Call? She wondered. *Am I home?*

The Peacekeeper took a breath, filling her lungs with a dead, dusty musk. She'd visited a museum exhibit once at the Call when they were displaying some old Iyon mummies, and the smell recalled her back to that time – the stink of old rot. She risked turning her head to get a look around and saw dead trees and withered shrubs peppering the landscape to her left, a viscous gray bog beyond it. To her right she saw more dead gray land and knew that what squished beneath her head was not clay but dying soil.

The Gray Marsh. The only possible place in Morgarai she could be. A feeling of dread settled into her along with that cold feeling in her stomach again.

"You're probably right," another voice said. Riggs, the Kairulian. "We'll build a pyre, cremate them instead."

Someone chuckled from the direction of Esther's feet. It was a throaty sound, and though it pained her to do it, Esther gingerly propped herself up on her elbows. Hrakar was there, the source of the low chuckling. He was hunkered by a small cook fire under some kind of shelter – it looked like a metal lean-to.

"The dead wood will not burn," he said to Esther. "Even the life that gives fire is gone from it."

To emphasize the point, he gestured to a bundle of gnarled gray twigs, blackened with soot but unburned. "I used my own tinder for the fire," he added.

Leiyara sat next to him, looking the worse for wear. Her hair was a mess, her clothes were torn and bloodied, and she had a purple lump on her forehead. Still, she was alive, and it did Esther good to see her.

"Esther!" Leiyara called. The shrill note in her voice made Esther's head pound. The girl ran to her as she tried to get up. "You probably shouldn't do that. We don't know the extent of your injuries yet," she explained, even as she helped Esther to her feet. The Peacekeeper wobbled a little, then leaned on her secretary for support.

"My mother was a Confessor back home," Leiyara explained, her voice still cutting paths in Esther's skull. "I've been able to help some with the injured. I even bound your leg."

"My leg?" Esther managed to say, before putting her full weight on her left leg; a shooting pain up to her hip answered. "Son of a fetch!" she hissed.

Leiyara helped her over to the fire and tenderly set her down next to it. Hrakar had a pot on the coals, a dark liquid boiling within. The Draconian crushed some herbs in his silvery hands and dropped them into the concoction. "An old remedy from home," he explained, his voice sounding cheerful. "You think Draconian spices are only good for cooking?" he added, even winking at Esther to punctuate the jape.

Typically, she would have been irritated at a joke during a time like this, but she found it somehow endearing. "I'll take anything that makes my head feel better," she grumbled, then, "*Ordo's Beard!*"

Leiyara fussed over her leg, moving the bandages and the splint around. "I'm sorry," the girl winced, "but the splint –"

"Move!" Esther almost shouted. Even raising her voice that far sent another shockwave of agony into her head.

Leaning forward, the Peacekeeper closed her eyes and drew upon the Source energies stored at the back of her head. She twisted her fingers into the glyphs for the Litany of Mending. Upon releasing the spell, she felt light and warmth fill her wounded leg like the summer sun. The bones eased back into place uncomfortably and mended, the pain vanishing. In a matter of moments, the leg was whole and healed.

Esther felt the Source take its due, sapping an equal measure of energy from her that she had taken from it. *As Ordo gives, Ordo takes*, she thought. The world spun again and Esther lay back down, soothed by the warmth of the fire and the aroma of Draconian spices.

"My home remedy cannot *quite* do that, I think," Hrakar said.

In spite of herself, Esther laughed. Then something came over her, a memory or a thought she couldn't quite grasp. Something steeped in distress, danger even.

"The Gray Marsh!" she exclaimed, her eyes popping wide open. "We're in the Gray Marsh! We have to get everyone back on the airship and – oh." The metal lean-to she looked at had a part of the Central Transit logo stamped on it. At this angle, the Peacekeeper recognized it as the remains of the burned-out tail fin. "Oh," she repeated.

"You mean you don't remember?" Leiyara asked.

Esther forced herself to sit up, to try to get her head on straight. "I remember now," she said. "We crashed. It was my fault."

Hrakar and Leiyara exchanged a glance that confirmed it. "No," Leiyara said, "it was the storm."

"The fault of the lightning," Hrakar added. "The weather wizard."

Weather wizard and the storm my eye, Esther thought. She would never forget that her shot sent that lightning ball into the tail fin and started the fire. She could never forget that lives had been lost and people had been injured because of her. *If only they'd sent a more experienced Peacekeeper, perhaps everyone would be alright and airborne.*

But another part of her mind took over, the cool pragmatist that had been trained on the fields of Perdition amidst the bloodied and the dying, among the gunpowder and the smoke. *Stop. Breathe. Focus. Focus on getting these people out of here alive, focus on the mission. Ordo always looks ahead and so should I.*

"How many of our supplies survived the crash?" she asked, taking stock of their assets. Of the possessions she had on her person when the airship went down, she was out one revolver and her pearl-handled pistol, and her hat. Her medallion and her side pouch filled with money were still intact, not that either would do much good out here. The daemons and mutilated lifeforms inhabiting these places didn't much observe the Unbound Law, and they had no use for silver.

"We don't know," Leiyara admitted. "We were too busy with the wounded. Now they're working on what to do with the dead."

"Preferably before nightfall," Hrakar said. "This place is haunted."

Haunted, or worse. Esther stood and noticed the world around her didn't suddenly spin anymore. "I'm going to speak to Riggs. The longer we stay in this Ordo-forsaken place the more danger we're in."

She needed answers to questions her companions hadn't thought to ask. She found Riggs only a few yards away, where he, the woman named Helena, and a handful of other Central Transit crew were stacking the dead atop a pyre built from scavenged wood from the airship. On the very top of the pile, Esther spied the pregnant woman that she'd seen escorted below deck before the storm hit. The grim sight filled the Peacekeeper with remorse and regret.

Keep looking forward, she reminded herself.

One man stood at the edge of the gruesome funerary site, a young man in a shredded burgundy uniform, his midsection swathed in bandages. He jotted down the names of the deceased in a small notebook. Central Transit would be responsible for notifying kin and compensating for the loss.

Riggs approached the man, counting off on his fingers. "Jack Harlan, Kairal; Stephanie Redding, Leonis; Kra Ch'Ak, Draconia, Gustav Jaeger, no known origin. There are a few more Helena is still trying to identify."

The young man nodded and scribbled down the names as quickly as he could. At last, Riggs acknowledged Esther. "Peacekeeper Triad," he said, "good to see you up and about."

"You, too." Esther replied. "We need to discuss our situation."

Riggs nodded, then gave a heavy sigh. "I suppose as the ranking officer, I'll have to shoulder that responsibility."

Esther gave a grim nod of acknowledgment. That meant the whole of the flight crew was dead, from the captain to the helmsman. She walked with Riggs to the remnants of the airship's cargo hold. From this angle, half-buried in the gray muck, it look like a cave property of Central Transit. Two surviving passengers were hauling out whatever crates and barrels they could salvage.

"Fortunately, many of the supplies survived," Riggs reported. "We'll have food and water, even some wine, for a few days at least, as long as we ration carefully."

At least it wasn't totally hopeless. "How far are we from the Colonies, or any other civilization?"

Riggs looked around as if consulting a map and a compass in his head. "At our last known coordinates, we'd just passed through Agimonde and crossed the Alcon mountains. I'd say the nearest settlement is a few days' journey due south. It's rough terrain, and we have wounded, so tack on an extra day or two to be safe."

At least five days in the Gray Marsh, Esther thought, that feeling of dread setting in again. "Then we should make for Agimonde with all haste."

The Kairulian put his hands up plaintively. "Whoa there, Peacekeeper. We've got wounded to tend, dead to lay to rest, and salvaging to do. We're not going anywhere for at least another day."

Clenching her fists at her sides, Esther had to remind herself that striking someone, unless in self-defense or unduly provoked, violated her code as a Peacekeeper. "Are you aware, Riggs, of the danger that this place poses? This is a decaying gray waste, crawling with daemons and all manner of horrors. We have wounded reeking of fresh blood and nowhere near enough manpower to defend a camp. I insist that we get moving immediately."

Riggs chewed his lip, mulling it over. "One night," he said at last. "Give us one night to lay our people to rest and allow the living some sleep, then we'll be on our way."

It wasn't ideal by any means, but Esther forced herself to compromise. "One night," she agreed. "But we leave at first light and make haste for the mountains."

She and Riggs shook on it, and he went back to his duties. Esther returned to Hrakar's little camp and sat down by the fire, gloomy and ill-tempered.

"What did he say?" Leiyara asked, her delicate hands wrapped around a mug of Hrakar's spiced drink.

"We leave in the morning," Esther replied. "It's going to be a long night."

• • • •

"YOU SHOULD GET SOME rest."

Esther took her eyes off the camp's perimeter. Leiyara waited next to her with another mug of coffee. They had managed to dig out most of her and Esther's luggage from the airship crash, so Leiyara had changed from her soiled and tattered travel clothes and into a plain black frock. Esther had chosen something a bit more practical

– a pair of trousers, riding boots, and a linen shirt; she still wore her gun belt and medallion.

"So should you," Esther replied, taking a long sip from her coffee cup. "I've got to guard the camp."

Behind her, Riggs and the rest of the remaining crew and passengers were asleep under a makeshift shelter built from crates and a piece of the airship's balloon. There were snores and the occasional shifting body from that direction. Each sound drew Esther's alarmed attention, every movement a call to arms.

How could anyone sleep in this place? she wondered, not for the first time that night.

There was a dead silence here that the Peacekeeper found unnerving, interrupted only by the usual night sounds from the camp. Anywhere else in nature would be alive with birds, bats, insects, *something* to break that horrible drone of silence. Even Leiyara became laconic.

Finishing the coffee in three long swallows, Esther scanned the perimeter again. Besides one harmless stilt sloth, nothing came within range. Esther watched with interest as the creature balanced itself on long front and back claws, its shaggy mane covering its head like a shroud.

"It feels like this place just sucks the life out of you," Leiyara said as if reading Esther's mind.

Technically, she wasn't wrong. The gray wastes were ancient battlefields where the Daemon Wars had been waged, leaving the land scarred and broken by some magick, curse, or weapon. The flora was drained dry, the water turned to poison, and the earth rotted. Theories stated that in another hundred years' time the wastes would collapse in on themselves, leaving Morgarai perforated with enormous sinkholes.

Esther was trying not to think about that. "How is Hrakar?" she asked.

"He's unflappable," Leiyara replied. "He hasn't slept since before the crash, he's barely eaten, and yet he's still in a good mood."

Esther smiled. "It must be that dragon blood. I'll check in with him. I could use some good cheer."

Leiyara nodded, shouldering one of the scavenged rifles a crew member gave to her. She had no idea how to use it, but everyone agreed that their party was better off armed. The young clerk who had been taking down the names of the casualties – Luca, his name was – had jumped at the chance to give her lessons. While he taught her – holding her close, the girl blazing red with embarrassment – Esther and Riggs had shared a chuckle.

Patting her secretary on the shoulder, Esther moved to the other side of the camp. She found Hrakar standing watch. He leaned and his spear, chewing some kind of leaf. His silks were tattered and singed in places but otherwise, he was none the worse for wear. Standing on the small rise and peering out with those amber, reptilian eyes, he looked almost regal.

"Anything?" Esther asked.

Hrakar kept those striking eyes on the mists beyond the bog. "Nothing," he replied. "There are no birds or beasts. Even the waters are perfectly still. This place devours all, does it not?" Esther could only nod, a little astonished that the Draconian read her mind. "Still," Hrakar went on with a smile in his voice, "one must appreciate an appetite that large."

Movement in the camp behind her raised an alarm. She wheeled about, her heart leaping, but relaxed when she saw Riggs groggily chewing a piece of jerky.

Is it morning yet? she wondered. *It never seems to get dark in this place, like it even absorbs the night.*

"I have a confession to make," Hrakar said sheepishly, looking at her now. "When we first met, I did not realize that you were a woman."

"Uh...what?" was all Esther could manage.

The Draconian raised a hand as if in surrender. "I mean no offense. It's just that Sapien women dress a certain way – like your Leiyara, in skirts and layers. It was not until I saw your hair down and your shape now that I realized."

Esther blushed, feeling the light brush of Hrakar's gaze down her body. Since changing out of her uniform, she'd let her dark locks fall about her shoulders while acknowledging that the shirt and trousers she wore did less to hide her curves. She didn't know why it embarrassed her. Perhaps because Hrakar noticed, or maybe it was the confession that he noticed.

The Peacekeeper let out a nervous laugh. "I don't know what to say to that," she confessed.

Hrakar turned those intriguing eyes back to the bog. "Say only that you are not offended and forgive my ignorance. I am new to Sapien society."

"Fair enough," Esther replied. "I take no offense, of course." Then, she ventured, "Why are you here among Sapien society?"

She suspected she knew the answer, even before Hrakar responded. "I am paying *echem* – you would say penance, I think? I was dishonored."

Shame coated his matter-of-fact way of explaining, making her regret asking. Hrakar took a shuddering breath and pressed on. "I am – or was – a Lancer in the Legion. With my drake Sigund, we flew high and fought many battles. It was during one of these battles that I was, how you say, revealed to my enemy. Now, I am outcast until I can regain my honor." Hrakar finished by bowing his head, reciting a verse in his native tongue, Esther didn't quite catch what it was.

"I'm sorry," she said. "I shouldn't have asked."

Hrakar just shrugged. "It is nothing. Part of *echem* is to speak your dishonor to any who ask. It is cleansing."

Esther nodded, although she didn't feel any better for the exchange. Then she spotted something – something in the mist – a shuffling movement that was there one moment and gone the next. "What was that?" she asked, drawing her remaining revolver.

Hrakar squinted into the distance, raised his spear, and took up a fighting stance. "Another of those creatures, perhaps?" he said hopefully.

The silt sloths. No, it had been smaller, about the size of a man. The Peacekeeper strained her eyes until she saw it again, a writhing, jerking motion.

"Esther!" Leiyara called from the other side of the camp. "I've got something here!"

Her secretary's shouting raised the alarm. In an instant, the crew got to its feet and armed themselves. Helena and Luca went to Leiyara, Riggs and one of the passengers – an olive-toned woman whose name Esther hadn't gotten – joined Esther and Hrakar. Two others moved off to the flank to check their exposed side.

"Over here, too!" one of them called. Dariana, a Freeholder.

"Maybe they're friendly?" Hrakar suggested, his grip on the spear's haft betraying him.

"Everyone form a circle around the center of the camp," Esther ordered. Riggs and the Freehold woman went to issue the order while she and Hrakar slowly backed away. "Can you see them any better than I can?" she asked the Draconian.

He shook his head. "Shapes in the mist. Nothing more."

They formed up around the camp's center, where Riggs and his crew had been asleep only moments before. As they retreated, the mist seemed to advance around them in a thick, heavy blanket reeking of decay. A noise pierced the endless silence, a squelching, gurgling noise, like something gasping underwater.

With her left hand, Esther formed the glyphs for Ordo's Hammer. She raised the revolver, leveling it into the mist. Beside and behind her, the others took aim, cocking their rifles. Above the sound of her own pounding heart, the Peacekeeper could hear Leiyara taking panicked breaths.

With a strangled shriek – like the sound of metal twisting – the things attacked. Out of the mist barbed tendrils lashed out and snagged the tan woman and Luca, dragging them away almost before they could scream. At the same moment, a fist like a spiked club, rubbery flesh over iron-hard bone, struck out at Esther; dodging it, she released her spell. The glowing glyphs about her hand instantly formed into a hammer of light, slamming into the creature, sizzling against the cloudy air. In the light, Esther could see a hulking beast with its clubbed fist and enormous, needle-toothed mouth on its chest.

She didn't wait for it to recover, firing two quick shots into its center mass. The hulking horror fell with a dull thud.

Beside her, Hrakar swung his spear at another creature. Black ichor spattered the ground, the thing screeching as it fell. Esther glanced back over her shoulder, watching Riggs and his crew wrestling with more barbed tendrils. She sliced at one and shot another, freeing the Kairulian. Riggs wasted no time, working the bolt of his rifle and firing round after round at the source of those revolting tentacles.

"More of them!" Hrakar called.

The Peacekeeper clocked more shapes, five here, three there, two more, bursting up from the surface of the bog and dripping with a viscous fluid. They were the same writhing daemons that she'd first seen in the fog. Close up she saw vaguely humanoid forms within them, struggling and suffocating against gray, membranous flesh. Their hands had long, whip-like fingers covered in barbs, their feet little more than pointed, boney protrusions that pierced the ground. *Bog walkers.* She remembered them from her studies in daemonology.

"We're surrounded!" Riggs shouted as he reloaded his rifle, letting Helena take over firing at the advancing monstrosities.

"Punch a hole!" Esther cried, firing at the nearest daemon and indicating the direction she thought was south (it was hard to tell, with no sun or landmark by which to navigate). "Riggs, you and Hrakar take point. Helena, Dariana, Leiyara, grab whatever supplies you can. I'll hold up the rear. Make for the mountains!"

The firing already commenced during her litany, but the crew moved quickly to follow her orders. Riggs and Hrakar rushed the daemons, cutting through them and ducking under their whips. Helena grabbed Dariana and the two women started collecting whatever they could grab, Esther hoping they were prioritizing food and fresh water. Leiyara lingered a moment, quaking in terror. The Peacekeeper tried to give her a reassuring glance before blasting a walker that threatened to take Dariana.

"Move!" she shouted at her secretary. The fierceness in her voice, which she would later regret, jump-started the girl into action. Leiyara made a rushing grab for a small barrel of jerky, their bags, and the cask of wine Esther had purchased at the Call.

Esther followed Leiyara, casting Ordo's Hammer on one daemon, then skewering another under the chin with her bayonet. When the women were laden with all that they could carry, the Peacekeeper led them back to Hrakar and Riggs, who already punched a sizable hole in the throng. Hrakar's spear arced and whirled and jabbed, deflecting those barbed tendrils and cutting down the daemons. Riggs switched from his rifle to his rapier – a standard-issue Kairulian sidearm – thrusting and slashing as he advanced.

The Peacekeeper hurried the girls ahead, turned, and fired on the walker coming up on their rear. *Last round,* she thought. *Time to get personal.*

Movement from the corner of her eye. She dropped as a whip whistled just inches away from her. Rising, she made an upward stab straight into the bog walker's throat. The black ichor that served as the creature's blood sprayed out over her hand, the walker convulsed, shrieked, then fell limp. In the second that followed, Esther could see the writhing form beneath the outer membrane slowly stop moving; she could perceive a face beneath, twisted with agony.

The others were already on the move, faster now, running along a winding path to avoiding the pools of standing water to either side. *Nearly there*. She started in their direction but halted as she heard a wet cracking sound followed by a voice screaming. It was Luca.

"I'm sorry," Esther said, trying not to imagine what horrible fate had befallen him.

Chapter Five:
The Dust Field, the Gray Marsh

Leiyara ran. She ran and she ran as if those daemons were still on her heels. She knew Esther must be behind her somewhere in the fog – she'd heard a shot just moments before – but that did little to ease her terror. Her lungs burned; her heart beat so rapidly she thought that it would burst at any moment. She clung to the two small barrels she'd grabbed from the wreckage with trembling arms, her back and shoulders aching under the weight of the knapsacks and the empty Kairulian rifle.

She stopped when she realized she could no longer see the other two women ahead of her. There were no footfalls or panting breaths other than hers. There was nothing but the fog, muffling the already droning silence of this dead and horrible place.

Esther warned you, stupid girl, she thought, her mother's voice in her head. *Just like your father, running headlong into trouble. Now you'll die here. You'll die because you were too stupid to be warned and too worthless to help.*

Shaking her head, Leiyara tried to clear her thoughts. If only she could think! What would Esther do? Easy, she'd fall back on her years of training and experience, blazing a trail right through this Matron-forsaken land. She'd find their friends, everyone would get out alive. But Leiyara couldn't do that. If they needed her to count out change or wait a particularly dangerous table, then they were in luck, but surrounded by a choking mist in a dead land filled with monsters? She was worthless.

"What am I doing here?" she asked herself aloud, just so that she could hear something other than the endlessly droning silence. "Why did I insist on coming along?"

She was on the verge of tears when an answer came from the mist. The voice whispered, but it startled her nonetheless, a harsh sound in this otherwise silent place. Faint and distant, she pinpointed its location somewhere to her left. At first, she winced back, thinking it was another one of those *things*; then she remembered they didn't speak – the whispering voice was forming words – brought her to her senses.

"Hello?" she called.

Matron help me, what am I doing? She took a step toward the sound before she could stop herself. The haze parted before her, revealing a small grove of dead trees, their branches skeletal against the gray sky, their roots bulging from the receding ground like thirsty grubs.

Does it ever get dark here? Leiyara wondered idly, a sudden pall falling over her brain to drown out her fear. *It's just gray all the time.*

Her feet carried her toward the whispers despite the protests screaming in the back in her brain. Those, too, soon quieted. Nothing remained but that whisper, that slow melodic chant in words she couldn't understand.

I'm spellbound, she thought. Or was that really her at all? For all she knew she was the whisperer. Her thoughts seemed to be coming from someone else, someone at the bottom of a deep well. In brief flashes, she could see both the trees and herself walking toward them, as if through the eyes of someone else. Somewhere deep inside, she wondered if she always looked so frail. The whispering came from all around her, but also from her own mouth or mind. She perceived both herself and the presence of another, her own weakness and the power of the other.

I'm losing my mind. The other, the whisperer, seemed amused by the thought. Leiyara smiled despite the encroaching madness.

When she reached the tree line, she finally stopped walking. "Who's there?" she asked. To her, her voice sounded like that of a sleep talker while to the other it sounded foreign, alien. It was her voice and she recognized the words, but at once it sounded like another language, something she hadn't heard in a very long time.

I'm two people at the same time, Leiyara thought. *How am I two people at the same time?*

Her new companion (her new self?), the owner of the whispering voice, materialized between two rotted trunks. Beginning as only a shadow, it coalesced into a solid image. It wore a ragged shroud, not black so much as the color of nothing. Wisps of cloth wafted about as if on a nonexistent breeze. The form's head looked vaguely Sapien, but made of smooth bone without a mouth or nose, just two blazing green eyes – like they were filled with the fires of creation. The bone swept up from its brow to form crown-like protrusions at least a foot high. The bony carapace also covered its hands, which were tipped with claws and glowed with ethereal symbols.

Glyphs? Leiyara wondered. *Does it know glyph magicks?*

The whispering stopped as soon as the shape became solid.

"Hello," she said. "What's your name?"

Leiyara was shocked to find she didn't fear this new guest. Her trembling stopped, her terror from the encounter with the daemons receding. Instead, she looked upon it like some wild animal: one more curious than malicious, more afraid of her than she was of it. She even thought for a moment that it was like the stilt sloths that had scavenged in the bog – harmless.

Later, when reflecting on the moment for the thousandth time on the hundredth sleepless night, she would think of it as a change in expression, although those calcified features weren't capable of it. But somehow she knew by some shift in its demeanor that the creature was angry.

It leaped forward at her, one hand digging into the rotted tree for purchase, the other grabbing her frock by the bodice. At the same time, the monster let out an ear-shattering screech. Even as horror filled it, Leiyara's mind cleared as she realized exactly what she was looking at. She screamed, raising her hands, dropping the supplies to the soft earth. She shut her eyes tight, trying not to think, tried not to feel, tried not to *be*.

There was a flash of light, blinding her even behind her closed eyelids. Leiyara felt herself falling, opening her eyes to a world wheeling away from her. Her attacker faded into nonexistence with another deafening scream, the trees moved out of sight, the gray sky came into focus. Falling. She was falling.

A pair of strong arms caught her, helping her back to her feet. Leiyara spun and lashed out at whatever touched her. Esther caught her wrist mid-swing. The Peacekeeper's grip was firm but gentle, reassuring. She wasn't cross that Leiyara had wandered off but seemed relieved to see her.

"Ordo be praised," Esther said. "I thought I'd lost you, too."

••••

THE DUST FIELD LIVED up to its name. According to lore, the place was once thriving farmland that grew a bounty for the first Sapien settlers in the area. Now, however, only an ash-ridden hardpan remained, as devoid of life as everywhere else in the Gray Marsh. Small hills rolled into valleys filled with brackish water, but mostly it was just dust and ash being kicked up after Ordo-knew-how-long of being settled.

Once they were certain they'd lost their pursuers, the party stopped for a rest just uphill from one of the stagnant pools. The position allowed them a panoramic view high enough above the dense fog that they could see any would-be attackers. They couldn't risk a fire – and besides, they had no decent wood or tinder – so the airship crew sat huddled together, mourning their losses over jerky and Esther's cask of wine.

“She had the good sense to grab the wine,” Riggs had said of Leiyara before tapping the cask.

Where Leiyara would ordinarily have blushed or averted her eyes, for Esther was sure she'd taken the cask by accident, the girl only cradled herself, staring into the distance. Esther and Hrakar busied themselves with keeping watch while crafting makeshift baskets in which to carry their supplies. The dead wood might not burn but it could still be woven.

“Perhaps you should talk to your friend,” Hrakar suggested, pointing his knife in Leiyara's direction. He'd been using it to strip the bark from the wood, although based on its serrated edge and nasty hooked tip, the Peacekeeper guessed it wasn't designed for that purpose.

Esther glanced at the red-haired girl absently. "I warned her it would be dangerous," she remarked, trying to keep her stern disposition.

“Do you remember your first time in battle?” the Draconian asked softly.

She remembered it vividly. The Call required all students to serve a term in the Brigades. Theoretical tactics or sparring with other initiates were good practice, but to uphold the Unbound Law, Peacekeepers needed to have real combat experience. She remembered long days of fighting through the intricate webwork of trenches, shots volleying overhead. Cold, rainy nights when you couldn't sleep because of the screechers screaming above you, threatening to drive you mad. There were times she didn't think she'd survive, and times she'd wished she wouldn't.

She was no stranger to seeing men and women die in battle.

“I remember.” From the knowing glance Hrakar gave her, it was all she needed to say. He nodded in Leiyara's direction, indicating what she ought to do next.

After a moment's hesitation, Esther sighed, getting up to tend to her friend. Leiyara still hugged her knees tightly, shaking with her wide eyes staring into the distance. Esther grabbed one of the blankets they'd managed to salvage from the wreckage and wrapped it around the girl's shoulders. Leiyara didn't seem to notice.

"It's hard," Esther ventured, "losing people."

Leiyara just kept staring.

"When I was at the front," Esther continued, "my commanding officer used to reassure us that our comrades died a good death, a brave death, but I never believed that. Death isn't good or bad, really; it's just death. As Ordo gives, Ordo takes."

Her secretary looked up at her now, tears forming in her eyes. "It's not that," she said, her voice little more than a hitch in her throat. "I mean, it's awful and all, those people dying. And those things that came after us..." She leaned on Esther for support now as she started to cry. The Peacekeeper stiffened but held the girl nonetheless. "When I was out there," Leiyara sobbed, "I saw...something. Something that I couldn't have seen."

"What was it?" Esther asked, thinking of all the daemons or monsters that inhabited this place. She was ill-prepared for the answer.

"I saw a Primivite."

Esther went cold. "Primivite" came from the old tongue meaning "First Life". Historians and scholars widely believed that the Primivites were the first indigenous beings to populate Morgarai. They were shadowy, shifting creatures who could tame the world's volatile nature, bending it to their will. It had been the Primivites who waged the Daemon Wars on the other races, employing the twisted monstrosities known as daemons for their armies. When the Elders killed Pandaemonia in her arachnid avatar, they took away the Primivite's power to alter Morgarai. The tides of the conflict turned so completely that everyone thought the race was wiped out in the Sapiens' ensuing victory.

So when Leiyara claimed to be the first person in over two thousand years to see one, Esther was dumbstruck.

"You what?"

A shrill, hysterical laugh erupted from the girl. "I know. It's crazy – I'm crazy! I must be. It's the only explanation."

Esther tried to find words, a comforting phrase, something – *anything* – to ease the girl's mind. She was at a loss.

"You think so, too," Leiyara said, deflating from her bout of hysterics. "Of course you do. You just think I'm weak and I cracked when those daemons or whatever attacked us."

Esther took Leiyara's hand, giving it what she hoped was a reassuring squeeze. "No, I don't," she said. "Of course I don't think that. It's just not what I expected."

Those big brown eyes looked up at her from beneath frizzy red curls, filled with hopeful tears. "You believe me?" she asked.

"If you say you saw a Primivite, then you saw a Primivite," Esther said, praying to Ordo she sounded more sure than she was. "And it certainly bears investigation."

Her secretary gave a little squeak, throwing her arms around Esther to sob into the Peacekeeper's coat. Esther patted her back, stroking her hair; she tried to remember what her mother had done for her when she was a frightened child.

Nothing, she thought, smiling bitterly at the memory. *She'd tell me to stop bawling and be strong.*

Once Leiyara finished her crying, she took a deep breath. "Thank you, Esther," she sighed. Then, she stood, wiped her eyes with a handkerchief, and smoothed her frock. "Now, on to my duties."

She practically marched over to where Hrakar hunkered, pointing at the basket he was weaving. "Pardon me, sir, but I believe you're doing that wrong."

Hrakar shot Esther an expression of muddled amusement. "Perhaps you did too well, Peacekeeper," he remarked, a smile in his voice.

Esther couldn't help but laugh, but the idea of what Leiyara had seen – had claimed to see – preyed on her mind.

Chapter Six: Just Outside of Turner, the Colonies

The town of Turner stood as the last settlement in the Colonies before the road led into the dreaded Gray Marsh. Central Transit still operated that far out to the frontier, but the roads there were overgrown or filled with potholes. It simply didn't fit the budget to maintain a route so seldom used. The Valet, however, used it now, the big man in red riding a big white horse. Instead of the clockwork horses of the modern age, the Valet preferred real horseflesh. The mare named Heartbreaker had been his faithful companion through many perilous adventures. It didn't seem right to trade her in for something more fashionable.

There was a guard post at the edge of the frontier, erected on the very spot where the land went from a fertile green to a bleak, lifeless gray. A last bastion of civilization, the post consisted of a small bunkhouse, an even smaller office, and a guard shack set flush with the trail. It was the sort of place the Kairulian Royal Army stationed their green recruits with no potential or those soldiers too insubordinate to do anything with.

Two guardsmen were at the post that morning, the other two asleep after the night shift. One of the guards, a young blond man, manned the guard shack. The other, a grizzled old veteran, stood by eating a pastry, droning on about some old war story between bites. As the Valet rode up to the post, both men looked at him agape.

"Good morning," the Valet called to them.

The old vet straightened his uniform shirt – the charcoal gray of the Kairulian army – shouldering his rifle. The younger man only waited at his post. "And a good day to you, sir," the vet said. He had the aspect of your average northern Kairulian: dark eyes and toasted skin, black hair shot through with gray. The other boy was pale and fair-haired, a southern Kairulian.

The Valet reined in, stopping just short of the guard shack's boom. "Has there been any news of an airship crash during the night?"

The pair of guards looked at each other. "Oh, that business," the old vet said. "Hertz – he works the night shift – woke me and Paolo up last night, showed us a telegram from the signal tower."

"All we know is that there was a fire," the younger man, Paolo, said. "Since we're the nearest outpost, we got the message first."

The old vet spat. "I always said we should leave flying to the birds."

The Valet, also a strong opponent of air travel, nodded his agreement. "Did they happen to say where it went down?" he asked. "Their last known location?"

The guards exchanged another glance. *The training it must have taken,* the Valet thought, *to have developed this secret language of theirs.*

Paolo answered. "A couple hundred miles or so to the southeast. Probably near the Bogs. Goners, I'd say. What the crash don't kill, the daemons there are sure to."

The vet slapped his young comrade on the shoulder. "Don't be morbid, lad," he said, putting a hand over his heart reverently. The Valet noticed the triquetra insignia next to his pips: the old vet was a chaplain.

The Valet nodded. "Thank you," he said. "Has Central Transit been notified? Are they organizing a rescue?"

Another exchanged glance, more information passing between the pair. "Delacruz sent a wire last night, just after it happened," the old vet said. "We haven't heard back just yet. Might not even, the Central Authorities like to keep things in-house."

"Good enough then," the Valet said. "If you'll excuse me, I'll be on my way."

The soldiers went wide-eyed. "You're going into the Gray Marsh?" Paolo asked incredulously.

"You got a death wish, son?" the vet asked in quick succession.

"I'm afraid I must," the Valet replied. "I was supposed to meet a Peacekeeper on that flight to Turner. It's a mission of some importance."

The two guards seemed satisfied with that. The Valet had learned long ago that invoking the Peacekeepers opened all sorts of doors. This time, it was even legitimate.

"I hope you're armed, friend," the vet remarked. "The Gray Marsh is a dangerous place."

With a sideways smile, the Valet patted the Rune Blade tucked between the straps of his saddlebags, exposed for all the world to see. Then, with a salute and a wink, he rode past the two dumbfounded guards.

"Matron's name!" Paolo swore. "That's *him*!"

The old vet spat again. "Remind me to wire my wife later and tell her to lock up our daughter."

Chapter Seven: Shard Hills, the Gray Marsh

For nearly three days, by Esther's reckoning, they had traveled the marsh. The land sloped downward into a twisting path around several small quagmires, each stinking of putrescence. When they finally crested a rise out of the sodden stench, they found themselves navigating around sharp, blackened rocks like dark glass. They dared not stop to rest longer than an hour or two, only doing so if they could find a defensible position – being surrounded again was not an option. It had left the party exhausted and irritable, slowing their pace even further. Hrakar was the only exception. He still maintained his good cheer, occasionally entertaining the group with a story or a song. One such song – a bawdy limerick about a wine seller's three daughters – seemed to raise everyone's spirits, but this dismal place seemed to devour even good cheer, and their laughs and smiles didn't last long.

As they walked, Esther dug through her knapsack to find the map of the Gray Marsh among her documents. It represented an amalgam of works cobbled together from cartographers who were either brave or stupid enough to hazard the wasteland. As such, it wasn't the most accurate in terms of distance or scale, containing great blank spaces of uncharted areas.

"You see here," Esther pointed out to Leiyara, who had become miserably laconic, "is where the airship crashed. It's right between the Bogs and the Dust Field."

"Is that where the monsters came from?" Leiyara asked, shuddering at the recollection.

The Peacekeeper nodded, suddenly thinking differently about showing her secretary the map. She'd thought it would give her something to focus on other than her encounters with the unknown or alien. "As a matter of fact, they did. They're called bog walkers, for obvious reasons. They feed by –"

Just ahead, Riggs shot her a warning glare. What Esther was about to describe was likely exactly what had happened to his crew-mates.

–digesting their victims alive and slurping up their remains, her brain finished for her. She refused to stop herself from thinking it, her penance for having failed to save them.

"Anyway," the Peacekeeper said, drawing Leiyara's attention back to the map. "We passed through the Underswamp just now –"

"That was the soppy place, right?" the red-haired girl asked, her flame-flecked eyes perusing the page. "The place with all those smelly water holes?"

Esther nodded. "Exactly. They call it the Underswamp because by all estimates it's below sea level. And here is where we passed into Shard Hills – that steep hill we just climbed a few hours ago was here." She directed Leiyara's gaze to where Shard Hills appeared on the map.

Leiyara's eyes widened as she traced the map's path to the south. She brightened a little. "Those squiggly lines there. Are those the mountains?" she asked, practically squeaking with excitement.

Esther nodded, folding up the map. "That's right," she said. "If all goes to plan we'll reach the Alcon Mountains by sundown tomor-row."

The Freeholder Dariana fell in step with them. On her back, she carried the basket containing fresh water and the cask of wine. "Don't get too excited," she remarked. "There's still two days' journey through Alcon Pass and another half-day at least until we see a settle-ment." She dropped the basket at Leiyara's feet, bringing the girl to a halt. "It's your turn to carry."

Leiyara picked up the basket, looking gloomy again.

Hrakar came to the rescue, coming down from one of the glassy crags, nimbly dodging the sharp points and razor edges; he made not a sound. The Draconian had taken to climbing each perch he could find to get the lay of the land, or to watch for pursuers behind or dangers ahead. His lean form and tightly wound silks allowed him to move like the wind itself.

"In Draconia," he said, "we have a word for people like her: *cheizedrek.*" He leaned in closer to Leiyara, putting one hand to his mouth in a stage whisper. "It means the excrement of a drake."

As Leiyara giggled, Hrakar shot Esther a wink. In turn, the Peacekeeper felt her face redden again, that warm feeling spreading through her midsection. She smiled but turned her face away. One of these days, she'd figure out what came over her when Hrakar looked at her, but this was neither the time nor the place. Up ahead, Riggs and Helena had stopped, so she left Leiyara laughing with Hrakar and went to see what as holding them up. She crested a rise to where they waited, immediately sussing out the cause.

"Ordo's hammer," the Peacekeeper swore.

The rocky land leveled off about a hundred yards away where the Shard Hills ended, beyond that a massive grove of dead trees. The trunks crept with a red-black slime, rooted to the ground by a mass of tendrils. The infested forest stretched out as far as the eye could see, right up to the Alcon Mountains and for miles on either side of them. Esther's heart sank, that cold stone dropping once more into her stomach.

"Watchers," Riggs said, then spat.

Watchers were daemonic fungi. They grew from spores into any living thing they could feed on, including Sapiens. Worse than being infectious, the Watchers were capable of what daemonologists theorized as collective thought. They could communicate, plan, and see their prey through the one huge, bulbous eye that grew in their center mass. The creatures, or, if you considered the singular root structure, *creature,* may be malignantly aware, obsessed with spreading its seed.

"What do we do?" Helena was asking.

"We could go around," Dariana suggested.

Esther and Riggs exchanged a look, both knowing the answer. The Peacekeeper produced her map once more, indicating the forest. "The scale isn't for sure," she explained, "but there's a good chance this forest goes on for days in either direction. See? It's covering the entire valley."

She swept her hand across the map where the aptly named Doomwood was drawn. The Alcon Mountains formed a sort of V-shaped valley here, the forest filling in the whole of that space. The nearest access beyond that was the salt flat, a hundred or more miles to the west.

"Well," Dariana scoffed, "we're certainly not going through it!"

Riggs chewed his lip, a nervous habit. "It may be our only option."

Behind Esther, Leiyara and Hrakar caught up. Their good cheer had been replaced with quiet wariness as they reached the top of the hill. Leiyara paled as she took in the writhing masses in the forest ahead. Hrakar became uncharacteristically silent.

"Riggs, you can't be -" Helena began to protest.

Leiyara chimed in, interrupting her. "Are they in season?"

The response from the party came as confounded looks all around...

"Well," Leiyara continued, somewhat awkwardly, "every plant or mushroom has a season, right? Those things look like plants to me, so I assume it has a season for growing or pollinating or whatever."

Esther thought back to her daemonology courses, cursing at herself for not remembering it sooner. "I think she's right," she said at last. She rummaged through her pack, pulling out a small leather-bound notebook, paged through it, and then recited, "'Watchers tend to spread their spores only during the winter months.' It's what? The ninth of Reaping? We should be safe enough."

Hrakar stepped to her side, a reassuring presence to the Peacekeeper. "This is true," he said. "Unless they are threatened or provoked they should remain asleep."

Riggs nodded, chewed his lip, nodded again. "It's settled, then. We'll rest here for a few hours. Get any jitters out of your systems now, because from here on out we move cautiously and quietly."

Chapter Eight:
The Haunted Mines, the Gray Marsh

The Valet had ridden long and hard for three days, only stopping to get a few hours rest or to water Heartbreaker. One only had a basic estimation of time in the Gray Marsh – the gray sky never seemed to lighten or darken – but the Valet stopped at what he conceived of as mid-day. He didn't need to, per se, but Heartbreaker would be glad of a moment's rest, and he needed to think. As with many brawny men of action, thinking wasn't the Valet's strong suit – even *he* knew he better served as a blunt instrument – but this required a moment's consideration. His original plan was to ride to the crash site to see if there were any survivors, maybe find this Peacekeeper he was supposed to make contact with, provided he survived. Perhaps he'd even play the hero, escorting the survivors to the relative safety of the Colonies.

That plan, however, required that the survivors stayed at the crash site. Given that they were in the thick of the Gray Marsh, that would be a senseless and dangerous thing to do – bordering on suicide. If the Peacekeeper was still alive and had any brains, he would have led them out of the waste by the shortest possible route. That route wasn't northwest to the Colonies, but south to the Alcon Mountains to seek refuge in Agimonde. It made sense, but if they were dead at the crash site following a phantom trail would be a fool's errand.

He turned back to Heartbreaker and *Glaeve Pandaemonia*. "I don't suppose you have any thoughts on this?" he said.

The mare only huffed, drinking from the small cook pot the Valet had prepared for her (no way he'd let her drink the filth in the Gray Marsh). The Rune Blade opened its eye, blinked at him, then returned to its slumber.

"Some help you are," the Valet muttered.

He finally settled on heading southeast to try to pick up their trail, choosing hope. If he found nothing by the time he reached the Underswamp he'd make for the crash site. Heartbreaker was reluctant to resume the journey, but with a few kind words, and a coaxing heel, she sprang into a gallop.

He rode past the Haunted Mines with their gaping shafts, puckered like infected sores in the decaying earth. The mining equipment had all rotted away long ago, but the howling and scraping from deep within suggested the place was anything but abandoned. To the east, he could see the derelict oil fields. The machinery used to pump the now rare, obsolete form of fuel still stood like square-headed soldiers, a monument to an age long gone. They say that in the time of the Elders, before the Daemon Wars, there were fields like that all over Morgarai. Looking at them, the Valet imagined the huge mechanical monstrosities that ran off the stuff, smoking with noxious fumes, cruising around the Elders' great glass cities.

By mid-afternoon, he topped a hill, finding the remains of an ancient city, this one predating the time of the Elders. The domed architecture was propped on heavy stone blocks to keep the rain out. The buildings all had small clay chimneys rising out of their sides, empty round portholes for windows. The largest of these was a three-domed manor with spires of crystal that jabbed at the sky. Staircases wound around it to reach the many levels, the rooftops bristled with chimneys. Such grandiose features marked it as a place of great importance, a temple or capitol building.

Settlements like these peppered the Gray Marsh, the remnants of the long-dead race known as the Iyon. According to myth, each race native to Morgarai was created by one of the Prime, the living embodiments of nature's forces. The Agi were born of fire, the Myrian of water, the dragons of the wind, and the giants of the earth. The Iyon, however, were born from a collaboration of the Prime, a complete, elegant creation much favored by their creators. Such adoration didn't get them far: sometime during the Daemon Wars, their lands were laid waste and their race driven into extinction. No one quite knew how or why.

The Valet slowed Heartbreaker to a walk as he passed through the ruins. The ancient, pitted road made for unsure footing. He took a draw from his flask, then lit a cigar to ease his nerves. The silence was getting to him; for hours he'd only heard Heartbreaker's hoofbeats and his blood in his ears. The wine tasted good, the cigar smoke was rich and aromatic, but in the haunting stillness they brought him little comfort.

At his side, *Glaeve Pandaemonia* opened its eye to scan their surroundings. The Valet felt something like an itch in the back of his brain, an inaudible whisper of sorrow, foreboding, of memories long tucked away.

"And how do you know this place, old friend?" the Valet asked, not expecting a real answer and not getting one. The Rune Blade communicated by instinct or sensation, not by mere words. The Valet found dubious comfort with that; he probably didn't want to know anyway.

He rode down a hill out of the ruins, skirting the southwestern corner of the Bogs. In their infinite wisdom, the Iyon had crafted sturdy stone bridges across each of the stagnant pools, probably for fishing off of when this land was still green and living. The whitestone they'd used had an eerie, luminescent quality, showing little sign of wear despite being ancient. The Valet had to slow Heartbreaker to a walk to navigate the occasional crumbling or loose stone, remarkably the bridge still carried their weight.

When he reached the Underswamp at the bottom of a steep gradient, his gamble paid off. There were clear footprints trod in the soft, rotten mud, here or there the cast-off leavings of people who needed to eat – a wrapper from a piece of jerky, an empty canteen.

The Valet took this as a sign of encouragement, nudging Heartbreaker forward.

Chapter Nine:
Shard Hills, the Gray Marsh

The proximity to the mountains coupled with the lack of cover made for a cold night. Their position on the high ground also meant lighting a fire was out of the question. Their stores of ready-to-eat food, like jerky and the meager military-style Central Transit rations, were running low. All this to say that Esther was huddled, hugging her legs, cold, miserable, and hungry.

The party had three blankets between them, fished from the crash. Esther had refused one so that Leiyara could keep warm, Dariana had insisted on having one for herself (her off-the-shoulder shirt and tight, thin breeches, though fashionable in the maritime climate of the Freehold, did little against the bitter cold), while Helena and Riggs took turns with the third.

Leiyara slept fitfully, waking with a start from her nightmares occasionally to ask if it was time to go yet. Esther watched her with equal parts pity and pride. The girl had left the comfort and familiarity of her childhood home for a world she had never known, doing so on a whim. The courage it must have taken – must still be taking – baffled the Peacekeeper. She at least had her training to fall back on, but Leiyara's bravery was rewarded by being dumped in a place like this, a place of misery, blood, and death. And it had been Esther's doing.

No matter how hard she tried to put it from her mind, in every idle moment Esther still thought of that fateful second when she had only winged that orb of lightning; when she had crashed their ship. Everything since then had been a direct consequence of that one mistake: the deaths at the crash site, the miserable trek across the dismal waste, the constant terror, the shortage of supplies, even the blisters on Dariana's dainty little feet. Esther would have cried were it not for the years of training hardening her. When this was all over, when they were safe within the boundaries of civilization, Esther knew it would all find its way to her. But right now she settled for just being cold and hungry.

Hrakar had drawn the first watch. He perched on one of the crags again, surveying the panorama – Esther had taken notice that he seemed most comfortable in high up places, a testament to his life among the spires of Draconia. He came down now, leaping deftly from rock to shiny rock, moving with that silent grace as he approached the Peacekeeper.

"You are cold," he said.

Esther only nodded.

The Draconian unwound a sheet of silk from around his midsection, wrapping it delicately around her shoulders. Esther held the ends shut at her chest, immediately warmed by it. Though light and thin, the silk was remarkably warm.

Hrakar must have read her expression. "There are silkworms that live in my homeland," he explained, "their silk is adapted for both the extreme cold and the heat from the...how do you call it? Vulkhano?"

Esther nodded her understanding. "Volcano," she corrected.

"Ah yes," Hrakar said, "volcano." He took off another sheet of silk, this one from around his wrist, to demonstrate. "You see, as the cold shrinks the fibers, they bundle together to hold in heat, while the heat expands them into tiny strands, allowing them to breathe." He stretched and crumpled the silk as he spoke, emphasizing the point.

The Peacekeeper smiled for the first time since her last interaction with Hrakar. *How does he do that?* She thought, that warm feeling settling into her belly again.

"Do you see anything out there," Esther asked, changing the subject before she blushed like a schoolgirl again.

Becoming very solemn, Hrakar said, "To one side there is gray. To the other, there is more gray." His eyes betrayed a smile while he winked at Esther again.

I do wish he'd stop that! She thought as she felt her cheeks get hot again.

"No imminent threats?"

The Draconian looked puzzled. "What is 'imminent'?" he asked.

"Immediate," Esther clarified, "or close by."

"Ah! No. I see nothing yet."

Esther breathed her relief. The one upside to the gray wastes, she supposed, was that although they were populated by daemons and horrors, they were at least *sparsely* populated by daemons and horrors. Since leaving the Bogs they hadn't seen another living thing until the Watchers. For the first time, Esther felt grateful for the threat, because there was only one of them.

Hrakar appeared to be thinking something over, debating.

"What is it?" the Peacekeeper asked, trying to swallow the panic that rose in her throat.

The Draconian shifted uncomfortably. "It may have been a trick of the light or some illusion or ghost, but I thought I saw a Sapien man on a white horse. He was wearing red and riding across the Underswamp."

Esther almost laughed, recalling a stereotype among her people about brave men riding white horses, saviors or heroes – true paragons. "Likely a ghost," she said. "This whole place is haunted."

Hrakar nodded, visibly dismissing the sight with a shrug. "I must go back to my watch if you will pardon me."

"Of course."

Turning, Hrakar gave her one last look over his shoulder, then returned to his perch. Esther got that warm feeling in her midsection again as she watched him gracefully glide up the rocks, making her believe that the Draconians were truly born from the air.

A faint giggle interrupted her admiration. The Peacekeeper looked over to find Leiyara lying on her side, watching her. She had a hand over her mouth, trying not to laugh.

"What?" Esther asked.

The red-haired girl burst into giggles. "Yooooouuu liiiiiike him," she said in a singsong voice.

Esther felt herself blush, so she turned her head, shiedling her face with one hand. "Quiet," she commanded. "I only...erm...respect him. His abilities and –"

This only encouraged her young secretary. "Yoooooouuu want to kiiiiiiisssss him," she laughed.

"Go back to sleep!" Esther pleaded. "Stop looking at me!"

Chapter Ten: Doomwood, the Gray Marsh

Despite the unnerving gray light, the foul moods from the crew – not to mention the potential suicide run through Doomwood – Esther was in high spirits the next morning. Since she hadn't eaten the night before, Hrakar made her a concoction of spiced wine that filled her belly, invigorating her. The googly-eyed looks and secret smiles from Leiyara also lifted her spirits. Sure, she felt embarrassed to be called out for feelings she didn't have, but something about the innocence of it endeared the girl to her even further.

They set off out of Shard Hills after their meager breakfast, which depleted any of the remaining dry goods. With any luck, they'd be in the mountains by nightfall enjoying a hot meal. Riggs and Hrakar took point, as they were used to doing by now. Helena, Dariana, and Leiyara stayed in the middle lugging the remaining supplies. Esther held up the rear, constantly looking over one shoulder and occasionally suppressing a snicker at Hrakar's vision of a man on a white horse.

No one had to remind each other to remain silent as they passed into the dead wood. A morbid hush fell over them as the first of the infected trees came into view. Up close, the Watchers looked even more ominous: the thick membrane comprising their flesh throbbed and breathed, the bulbous mass of each central eye flickered under a scaled lid, the eyeball beneath darting this way and that in some primal form of dreaming. The thick, root-like protrusions wrapped around the base of each tree, spilling onto the ground like disemboweled entrails. Looking at them made Esther's stomach turn.

The soft, dead earth provided them with stealth, their footsteps made no sound, but in the quiet closeness the sounds of their breathing, of the heartbeat Esther could hear pulsing in her ear, were maddening. It took all the Peacekeeper had not to speak just to break the monotony. But speaking meant dying – or worse, to be host to one of the monstrosities that surrounded them.

Finding no path or road cut through the wood, the party skirted around the trees with an uncomfortable closeness. More than a few times one of them, Leiyara or Dariana mostly, came close to stepping onto one of the roots. The first time it happened to Leiyara. They walked single file, rounding a huge gnarled oak that, in turn, was engulfed by a huge gnarled Watcher. The creature's tendrils were as big around as Esther's thigh, splayed out on the rotted soil to suck in whatever life they could.

Leiyara watched the Watcher, not her step. Praise Ordo that Esther had been keeping an eye on her friend. As Leiyara raised her foot over the root, the Peacekeeper nearly cried out. She managed instead with a quiet, hissing intake of breath.

Leiyara froze, looking down where her foot nearly landed. Her eyes went huge and she covered her mouth to muffle the squeaking noise that came out. The roots stirred. The eye at the center of the infected oak half-raised its lid, the creature's breathing hitched. Esther dropped one hand to her revolver and, up ahead, noticed the others tensing to fight or flee, or both. The moment seemed to last forever. The half-opened eye, the slowly shifting tendrils, Leiyara teetering on one foot, and the others ready to run for their lives.

At last, the tendrils squirmed from under Leiyara's foot, the Watcher closed its eye, then its breathing evened out. Esther breathed a slow sigh of relief and saw the others do the same. At the front of the line, Riggs gave Leiyara a warning glare before starting them moving again. Leiyara reddened, tears forming in her big brown eyes. Esther put a hand on her shoulder to give it a reassuring squeeze. Secretly, though, she was begging Ordo for patience.

The day went on like that, a slow, careful march through the wood, dodging around the tendril roots, skirting past the membranous bodies of the Watchers – sometimes within mere inches – and fighting the urge to break that oppressive silence. The everlasting gray, that dull light that never waned or waxed, pervaded everything, draining even the Peacekeeper's sense of time. It seemed to her she'd been these woods forever and that they would stretch out forevermore. There were moments when she began to entertain the thought that nothing outside these woods existed. That this would be her eternity.

I died in the crash, she thought, *and for my mistakes and misdeeds, I'm now lost in the Howling Void forever. This waste, this gray world, is a reflection of my own desolation.*

No, the rational part of her mind chimed in. *It's the Gray Marsh. It's a wood inhabited by real horrors. There is an end to it and you just need to keep moving forward.*

At what was most likely mid-day, they came to a stream. It spanned about ten feet, its banks covered in the detritus of the Watchers – half-grown spores with blind, dead eyes and sacks of gelatinous fluid. They gathered on the near bank of the shore, doing their best to communicate non-verbally. After some rushed hand gestures between Riggs and Hrakar, the Draconian finally rolled his eyes, holding up one finger. He then walked as far as he dared toward the water and, with his spear, vaulted himself over the wasted spores. He gave a flourish as he splashed down almost silently, then motioned to Riggs. The Kairulian went to the bank, grudgingly allowing himself the indignity of being manhandled into the middle of the stream.

Hrakar did this for each one of them in turn. When it came to Esther, the last to cross, Hrakar held her more delicately. He used his strong hands to hold her hips instead of her waist, she could swear he held her closer than the other women, and when she touched down in the water he held on to her for just a few seconds longer than he had to. Esther looked into those remarkable amber eyes the entire time, seeing something burning there. Perhaps it burned for her?

When the oddly intimate exchange ended – it had taken the span of a breath for anyone not caught up in it – Esther felt that warmth settle into her again. Fortunately, Hrakar turned to the far bank before he could make her blush again. The stream water came up to Esther's knees, just past her boots. The sensation of it felt surreal: neither cold nor it warm, just a tepid nothingness. The water also seemed thin and insubstantial, a lifeless fluid that could hardly even be characterized as water.

Hrakar is right, she thought, *this place drains the life out of everything.*

They followed the same procedure on the other side. Hrakar vaulted himself over the overgrown bank then hauled each member of the party across one by one. This time, however, Esther was deprived of any overly familiar moment. As soon as Hrakar had gotten Leiyara across, Dariana slipped on the slightly sloping bank, her foot landing among the detritus. Instantly the hungry and neglected half-Watchers were upon her. Their tiny, malformed tendrils engulfed her ankle, tiny pustules filled with digestive fluids burst open, and Dariana very nearly screamed.

Riggs and Helena tended to her right away. The Kairulian stuffed a rag in her mouth to muffle her cries while Helena struggled to free her leg. Leiyara hung back, shaking and covering her mouth, her eyes wide in horror. Hrakar hastily carried Esther across and they both ran to the Freeholder who writhed on the ground, screaming into the rag in her mouth. Riggs snapped his fingers at them, pointing at Dariana's ankle. *Do something!*

Esther went down on one knee, putting her hands over the girl's struggling ankle. She drew upon the Source, forming the glyphs for the Lord's Lantern. Blazing yellow symbols circled her nimble fingers to shed a burning light over the half-grown Watchers. The would-be daemons blackened and withered to ash with no more than the sound of crackling flesh.

With Dariana free, Riggs and Helena dragged her up to level ground. Her ankle bled, blistered, and burned. The flesh the daemon's fluid touched bubbled, sizzled, and stank. The wound left a blood trail up the bank and the starved earth took no time drinking it all in.

Having freed her, the Peacekeeper now ran to the Freeholder's side. Once more she put her hands over the woman's ankle, once more forming glyphs with her fingers. Ordo's Mercy shed its light on the wounded ankle, restoring it. The blistering seared flesh knitted together, the spell making it whole again. Dariana stopped crying out and laid back in relief, taking giant breaths. Riggs and Helena were looking at Esther with wide, wary eyes. The Peacekeeper forgot their western homelands forbade the use of spellcraft, a holdover from Wraithbane's dark history of conquest.

Esther took little time to notice or care, for what Ordo gives, Ordo takes. She felt the Source take its due, draining from her already exhausting body. Her vision blurred, her head spun, her limbs turned to rubber. The next thing she knew, she was on her back looking up at the gray sky and a pair of amber eyes. The silence broke now by a thousand whispering voices in some arcane, dead language. At first, Esther thought it might be Hrakar speaking comforting words to her, but it wasn't Drakkenspek.

That cold stone settled into the Peacekeeper's stomach again. *No, it's Daemoniac.*

"*Shayna raba ravi na shap-aye en...*"

She sat bolt upright and, no longer feeling the need for silence, shouted, "They're waking up! Run!"

••••

"*Shayna raba ravi na shap-aye en...*"

The Valet had no idea what those monstrous fungi were saying, but he knew that his Rune Blade luxuriated in hearing its native language. He also knew that was never a good thing. After falling asleep in his saddle on and off for hours, he'd reached the Whispering Wood (some called it Doomwood, but he thought that name was hokey). The trail of the crash survivors had led straight in, making the Valet wonder if they were ignorant of the forest's dangers or just desperate. If the Peacekeeper survived to lead them, he'd put his silverbacks on the latter.

Instead of blazing a trail into certain death, the Valet found a small stream leading into the wood. It had enough breadth that he could keep his distance from the Watchers, with the added advantage of washing away his and Heartbreaker's scent in case something pursued him. Muffled screams erupted from the trees only moments before the Whispering Wood started living up to its name. A vibration followed the screams and a sudden release of energy, causing the desolation around him to sigh as it drank deep. If the screams hadn't woken the Watchers, then that vibration had.

All around him he could hear little popping puffs as the sacks full of the Watchers' spores burst. The noise started behind him, then progressively moved in the direction from which the screams had come. The Valet, newly invigorated by the prospect of battle and heroics, spurred Heartbreaker into a run.

••••

"RUN!" ESTHER SHOUTED.

As soon as the party made a move toward the wood, the first puffing pops of the daemon's spore sacs began. The noise moved rapidly through the trees, the air filling with a reddish cloud of dust. The Watchers nearest the bank of the stream opened their eyes, leveling a hateful gaze at them.

Riggs grabbed Helena, shoving her back toward the stream as the Watcher closest to him spewed a cloud of red spores at him. They covered his whole left side, boring into his flesh and growing at an alarming rate. Dariana and Esther moved to help him, although they didn't know how. Helena lay on the ground at Leiyara's feet, both of them stunned.

Hrakar used his spear to bar the path of Riggs' would-be rescuers. "Stay back!" he shouted. "It's too late for him now!"

He was right, of course. As Riggs lay on the ground he convulsed and choked, frothing at the mouth. A newborn Watcher already grew over his left side; a bulbous, hideous eye gaping out of his shoulder. The one unmarred eye in his head looked at the party, pleading.

"Do something!" Helena cried, rushing at Hrakar. She struggled to get past him, but the big Draconian held his ground.

Esther knew exactly what to do. She drew her revolver, aiming it at Riggs. *One more death on my conscience,* she thought, cocking back the hammer.

Dariana grabbed the gun from her, discharging the shot into the dirt at Riggs' feet. The Peacekeeper wheeled on her without thinking, landing the butt of the revolver squarely on her forehead. The Freeholder fell, shouting curses at her. Esther turned to aim again, but Riggs tangled with Hrakar, struggling for control while skewered on the Draconian's spear; his gnarled hands still clawed at Hrakar's face. It was all the Draconian could do to keep the man-daemon off of him.

Meanwhile, Helena wasn't idle. She aimed her rifle at Riggs' head point-blank. Before she could pull the trigger, the thing that had been Riggs grabbed the barrel and, in a stroke of bad luck, swatted it toward Hrakar. The shot rang out; a hole burst open in Hrakar's side as the impact threw him back. He lost his grip on the spear and landed bleeding in the dirt.

Esther raised her revolver again but Helena's rifle spiraled toward her, thrown haphazardly by the Riggs-thing. She didn't have time to react as the weapon connected, knocking the gun from her hand and bouncing off her left cheek. The pain and the impact left the Peacekeeper reeling.

The daemon that was once Riggs moved with jerking motions, the Watcher growing inside him awkwardly wrenching control away from his brain. The other half of Riggs' face gaped as it stared into nothing, his mouth opening and closing, like the gasping of a fish out of water. He tore the spear from his midsection, then unceremoniously ran it straight through Helena's throat. The woman gasped, her blood sprayed out in sanguine spurts, her fingers clutched at the haft of the weapon impotently.

Pulling the spear from Helena and dropping her like a rag doll, Riggs turned on Leiyara. All the girl could do was watch in horror as the daemon pointed the spear at her. The right half of his face smiled, and it was clear that Riggs was gone now.

The daemon had consumed him.

Esther went for her revolver at the same time as Dariana. The Freeholder, wild in her panic, tried to wrestle the gun away from her.

"What in the Void are you doing?" Esther shouted at her, giving the girl a hard punch to the ribs.

Riggs charged at Leiyara. So Esther gave up on the revolver. She released her grip and went for the pistol in her sleeve...

The pistol was gone, lost in the crash.

With nothing left but her fists, Esther moved to charge Riggs. Leiyara moved now, circling just outside the spear's range, putting Riggs with his back to the stream. At least she wasn't completely useless.

The Peacekeeper's desperate charge was cut short by the sound of hoofbeats splashing through the shallow water. She couldn't believe her eyes as a man in a bright red coat on a huge white horse rode around the bend, brandishing an enormous sword and crying out in bloodthirsty vigor. Before she could register anything else, the man in red planted his blade in Riggs' skull. The menacing weapon went halfway through the daemon's torso before stopping. Riggs' lifeblood, already blackened by the daemon infection, gushed out as his corpse fell limp.

The man in red surveyed the scene, cool blue eyes falling on the four remaining survivors of the crash, three of them wounded. He extended a hand to Esther.

"Come with me if you want to live," he said.

• • • •

THEY SPENT A FEW MORE hours splashing through the lifeless stream. As they walked, Hrakar leaned heavily on Esther, binding his wound with Draconian herbs he'd made Esther chew first. Leiyara sloshed through the water by her side, trembling as she hugged herself. Dariana trudged a few paces behind them, Esther's revolver hanging loosely from her fingers.

I should cite her for assaulting a Peacekeeper, Esther thought. *And obstructing a Peacekeeper in the course of her duties.* She couldn't help thinking it, after all, if Dariana hadn't made that mad grab for her weapon, Helena might still be alive; but the prospect of Dariana surviving this long only to be executed for her crimes seemed a little counterproductive. Besides, the Peacekeeper had yet to carry out any executions in the interest of due process – she'd never even killed another Sapien.

Their mysterious new companion rode ahead of them. He'd offered only Hrakar his horse because of his injury. Propriety in most parts of the world would dictate that he offer it to the ladies, but the man in the red coat was obviously no gentleman.

"Smelly beasts," is all Hrakar had said to dismiss the offer.

So they walked while all around them the wood whispered, chanting in its dead language. Esther, while versed in a more modern dialect of Daemoniac, could only pick out a few words and phrases from the Watchers' dirges. What she heard made her sick to her stomach so it didn't bear repeating. At last, they came to the end of the wood at the base of the Alcon Mountains. As they walked, the ground gradually turned from gray to brown, the water became cold and substantial, the sky began to darken into dusk once more.

Esther almost wept in relief, Leiyara did.

Chapter Eleven:
The Alcon Mountains, Agimonde

They made camp at a rise in the mountain pass, just off the overgrown coach road they'd started to follow. It was nice to have a fire again, though their dinner consisted of mostly beans and some flatbread their new companion provided, to the Peacekeeper it felt like a feast. They didn't speak much that first night, the party still shaken by the events that unfolded in the Gray Marsh and the losses they'd suffered. Instead, they tended to each others wounds and rested.

Hrakar stripped off the silks around his midsection, revealing a lean, smooth musculature beneath his silvery skin. The blood that soaked the silks looked like quicksilver, smelling faintly of heated metal; it was just a shade darker than the Draconian's skin. The bullet hadn't passed through, but the herbs he'd packed into the wound had stopped the bleeding.

"We should get that bullet out," Esther said. Her cheek just below her eye swelled, bruised from the butt of Helena's cast-off rifle. She spread a medicinal salve onto it.

Leiyara, falling back on her mother's skills as a healer, prepped a needle and thread, soaking each in boiling wine. She'd torn off a few strips from her frock's skirts to use as makeshift bandages. She seemed in better spirits now that they were out of the gray waste, fed, and she had something with which to occupy herself.

"We don't have anything to get it out with," the girl said as she threaded the needle.

"Ah," Hrakar replied. He searched about himself, producing what looked like a forceps from his silks.

Leiyara and Esther exchanged a glance. "Do you get shot often?" the Peacekeeper asked.

Hrakar shrugged. “One must always be prepared,” he said. “*Skein racha*!” he swore. Leiyara had already started in with the forceps. “A little warning, perhaps?”

Unperturbed, the red-haired girl only shrugged. "Sorry," she said.

Once she had Hrakar on the mend, he and Leiyara passed out on the ground near the fire. Esther helped herself to a cup of wine (*of all the things to survive this mess!*) checked Hrakar's bandage, and covered Leiyara with a blanket. When she finished, she sat down by the fire with their new companion. He'd been sitting quietly, watching them with what appeared to be puzzled amusement. The Peacekeeper had wondered more than once what he found so interesting about them.

“So, who are you?” she asked.

The big man looked at her incredulously, shaking his blond mane. “You mean you haven't heard of me?” he asked.

“Should I have?”

“Really?” the man asked, though it was not a question. His hands waved about demonstratively as he pointed out each aspect of himself, hoping to ring some bells. “Big red coat? Red bow in his hair? Rides a white horse? 'Lock up your daughters'? Greatest swordsman that ever lived?”

Well, the Peacekeeper thought, *he certainly has a high opinion of himself.* “I'm sorry, no,” she said.

Her new companion smiled a sideways, debonair grin that Esther would later describe as wolfish. "That's refreshing," he said. "It's not often I meet someone who hasn't heard of *Le Valet des Coeurs*."

Esther arched an eyebrow at him. “Luh valay day what?” she asked. “What sort of language is that?”

Now, the Valet looked affronted. He didn't seem comfortable with being interrogated. "An old one, where I come from," was all he said.

“And where is that?”

The Valet reached into his coat, taking out a flask,and took a swig. "Howling Void you ask a lot of questions."

Esther sipped her wine, relishing the warm feeling of it down her throat into her belly. It was almost as good as the warm feeling she got when she was alone with Hrakar. "Well, I am a Peacekeeper."

In response, her new companion almost choked on his drink. "You're a Peacekeeper?" he coughed. "I came here looking for a Peacekeeper."

Esther nodded, taking out her medallion to show him. "Peacekeeper Esther Triad," she announced.

The Valet eyed her now, looking her up and down, taking in her tussled hair, hip-hugging trousers, and plain linen shirt. "You don't look like any PK I've ever seen. The Call must be getting more liberal these days."

His scrutiny made Esther uncomfortable. Something about those cool blue eyes gave her a feeling like being undressed by them. "It's been quite a journey," she remarked. "Why are you looking for a Peacekeeper?"

The Valet took another long drink, then lit a cigar. "I'm on the job," he explained. "I was supposed to meet a PK in Turner four days ago, bound by airship. I got the S.O.S. and came to see if you were still alive."

Esther looked at him blankly.

"You haven't been briefed?" he asked.

"Ordo's foot!" the Peacekeeper swore, shooting up to grab her knapsack. "The file! With everything that's happened, I completely forgot."

She rummaged through her bag, pulling out the leather-bound stack of papers. Sitting down again, she started leafing through them. "Aha! It says here I was supposed to meet with a contact from the Violet Rose in Turner. You're supposed to be helping me investigate?"

The Valet nodded. "That I am," he said, "or at least that's what they tell me."

"The Violet Rose," Esther thought, tracing the name back to her studies. "That's a spy network that operates throughout Morgarai, isn't it?"

The big man stubbed out his cigar, stretching out on the ground. "Morgarai's worst kept secret," he remarked. "And before you ask what an underground spy organization cares about some weather wizard trouble in the Colonies, I'll just tell you that I didn't ask. I'm a sword for hire, nothing more. I go where they tell me to go."

The Peacekeeper nodded her understanding. "Of course," she said. "Does the Call often work with spies and rogues?"

The Valet chuckled. "The better question would be, does the Violet Rose often work with a universal law enforcement agency and their holier-than-thou agents?"

"Fair enough," Esther replied, smiling a little at the intended slight.

Her new companion and apparent partner covered his eyes with one arm. "Now if you'll excuse me, I'm going to get some shut-eye. Days and nights of hard riding take their toll, even on me."

The Peacekeeper said no more. The Valet was snoring before she even thought to press him further. She finished her cup of wine, taking in the smell of the fire, the sound of distant insects and night birds, the stars and the moon in the darkened sky – it was a Shattered Moon (which, on another Parallel might be called a full moon, but Morgarai's moon was broken long ago when Pandaemonia had been summoned; nearly half of it was in pieces, floating in its orbit). These were all the things she hadn't thought she'd missed in the Gray Marsh, the little things that, as a whole, were the signs of life.

Then, she looked at Hrakar, lying on his side, still draped in layers of silk. "Oh, to the Void with it," she said to herself. She went to him to check his bandages once more, being sure to jostle him just enough to wake him. His amber eyes opened and softened when they set upon her.

"Oh, hello," the Draconian said.

Esther's heart raced, but instead of making excuses or backing down, she spat out the real question on her mind. "Can I lie down with you?"

Hrakar's eyes showed a smile. He pulled aside one of the peculiarly warm silks like a blanket, inviting her to be wrapped in it. Esther lay down close with her back against him, feeling the warmth and solid pressure of his body. He wrapped one of his strong arms around her, and, for the first time since the airship crash, she felt safe and warm. As a Peacekeeper, she knew that she was supposed to be strong, level-headed, self-sufficient. But as a woman, sometimes she just wanted to feel protected, so that's how they slept, safe and comfortable in each other's arms.

• • • •

THEY WOKE TO THE SOUND of a gunshot.

At some point during the night, Esther had turned to face Hrakar, burying her head in his silk-laden chest; she barely heard the shot at all, barely remembered sitting bolt upright, reaching for a revolver that wasn't there.

Dariana, she thought as a wave of panic washed over her. *I left it with Dariana.*

Hrakar, already on his feet, held his spear in one hand and that nasty looking hooked knife in the other. Even Leiyara sat upright, holding the Valet's cast-iron cook pot in both hands. The Valet, however, barely stirred, looking over his shoulder with morose concern. Esther noticed, however, that one of his large hands gripped that terrifying-looking great sword.

Getting to her feet, Esther lamented the fact she, a Peacekeeper of Ordo's Call, was the only member of the party unarmed. To make up for her lack she tapped the Source, summoning the glyphs for the Lash of Light.

The mountain pass quieted eerily, the air still hanging with a light mist of morning dew. The sun was coming up, painting everything red. No one moved.

"Well, good," the Valet said, rising to his full height (*he must be at least six foot seven,* Esther thought). "I'm not the only one who heard that."

They moved as one, following the direction the shot had come from. They found Dariana near a spring between two crags. One dead hand grasped Esther's gun, a bloody hole marred the side of her head. The way she had fallen made it evident that she'd been kneeling; there was still a fresh tear on her cheek.

Leiyara uttered a small cry, turning away – somehow this sight overwhelmed her, despite all she had seen in the Gray Marsh. The others just stood in silence.

"Can't you do something," Leiyara asked Esther. "Heal her or bring her back or something?"

The Peacekeeper shook her head. Of course, there wasn't anything she could do. Dead was dead. "As Ordo gives, Ordo takes," she offered weakly.

Hrakar made some motion too, closing his hand, raising it, then opening it again. The gesture looked vaguely like he was releasing a small bird.

"Who were her gods?" the Valet asked.

The party all looked around at each other. During their trek across the gray waste, none of them had spoken to Dariana much. The Freeholder preferred the company of Riggs and Helena, before that she'd only ever been seen with her countrywoman. Their faces flashed across the backs of Esther's eyelids, all the survivors of the airship crash besides Leiyara and Hrakar, all gone now.

Esther felt grief and guilt stab at her heart. *I didn't even know all of their names.*

"She was from the Freehold," is what she said. "All bets are off."

The Peacekeeper went to retrieve her revolver, the professional part of her mind thinking about how it would reflect on her: a woman committing suicide with a Peacekeeper's weapon. A weapon she'd left in the woman's care.

"I think she practiced Elderism," Leiyara volunteered. "She had a pendant of the triquetra around her neck."

Esther swallowed the lump in her throat. She had a duty to protect them – their lives placed squarely in her hands – yet she hadn't even known them. "Say a few words for her, will you?" she asked Leiyara. "Then we'll bury her."

The Peacekeeper turned away from Dariana, starting her trudge back to camp. Her mourning turned to anger, hot in her chest. *You stupid girl*, she thought. *We went through all that trouble keeping you alive and you just go and put a bullet in your head? You did yourself what an army of daemons couldn't. Had I known, I might have shot you myself to save time.*

She didn't mean it, of course, regretted even thinking it, but regret was just something she was stacking up now, putting it away in a corner while telling herself to keep moving forward. By the time she made it back to the camp, she'd already ticked them all off. Dariana, Riggs, Helena, the blond boy (*what was his name?*), the other Freeholder who'd been dragged off into the murk to die alone and afraid. She thought about all of them, something breaking inside her.

And for the first time in what seemed like ages, Esther cried.

••••

"YOU SHOULD NOT BE PUNISHING yourself," Hrakar said, hunkering down next to her.

“That's ironic, coming from a Draconian,” Esther replied. She even tried to smile.

She had lost track of time. Her companions sauntered somberly back to the camp, having finished with Dariana's makeshift funeral. The Valet worked on cooking up a side of bacon, along with some eggs that – she assumed – Leiyara had found. The red-haired girl cradled them in her torn frock, chattering on half-heartedly about what kind of bird they might have come from.

“Let's just hope we don't open them up to find little baby birds inside,” the Valet remarked with a wink.

“Ew!” Leiyara giggled.

So that was what life amounts to, Esther marveled, *a few droned words over your dirt and then getting on with breakfast.* She found something bittersweet in that, but all Esther could taste was bitterness.

Hrakar chuckled a little. “None of what has happened is your doing. As you say – not your fault.”

The Peacekeeper shook her head. “The crash was –”

Hrakar put his hand on hers gently, stopping what would have been a flood of self-loathing. "The crash was the work of a weather wizard, nothing more. If it had not been one thing that destroyed the airship, it would have been another. Another sphinx, perhaps, or storm callers. The magicks were beyond any of us to fight."

Esther tried to believe him. His kindness warmed her heart, but she wouldn't be so easily relieved of her burden.

“As for the lives lost,” Hrakar continued, “I believe it was you who suggested we leave the crash right away. That other, the man in charge, insisted on staying the night. It was then we were set upon by horrors. If we had moved on as you said...” he spread his hands, “...who knows. Everything after that was the work of the *chatahn* – the daemons, as you say. The responsibility is not yours, and if it is, it is not yours alone.”

Esther fought back more tears as his hand squeezed hers.

A delicate clearing-of-the-throat sound interrupted them. Leiyara stood nearby, once again looking at them all googly-eyed. "There's coffee, and we'll be having eggs and bacon soon." She skipped off back to the campfire where the Valet heroically brandished a spatula.

"Thank you, Hrakar," Esther said.

Hrakar gave her those smiling eyes. "Now, let us have coffee. I have a spice that will make it taste not like campfire coffee."

They moved to the fire where two steaming cups were waiting for them. *Because that's what life is,* Esther thought, deciding this wasn't such a bad funeral after all. *They say some words over your dirt and then have breakfast.*

Chapter Twelve: The Arami Desert, Agimonde

They came down from the Alcon mountains at mid-day and were met by the hot, dry air of Agimonde's Arami desert. Low scrub and small trees peppered the hardpan among enormous red rock formations. A hot sun blazed in the metallic blue sky so Esther understood why Agimonde, home of the Agi, was referred to as the Fireland.

"It's beautiful," Leiyara remarked, scanning the landscape with renewed wonder.

"And hot," Hrakar replied, loosening the silks around his throat and chest.

They stopped for a brief lunch, eating the local bloodfruit – not unlike an orange, except with purple skin and dark crimson flesh. Esther and Hrakar spent quite a bit of time close together during their journey through the mountain pass, so today was no exception. They sat together a ways off, talking about trivialities and enjoying the sweet crimson fruit that came at a premium anywhere else in the world.

Leiyara had bonded with Heartbreaker over the last couple of days, doting on the horse every chance she got. She had even taken up the Valet's duties of brushing her down, feeding her, and saddling her. Having given up entirely, the big man had just left his horse to the girl, even allowing her to be Heartbreaker's primary rider. Now, the girl fed bloodfruit to the animal delighting as the horse nuzzled her affectionately. It became ever rarer in the age of steam, airships, and clockwork to see live horses anymore, so Leiyara seemed immersed in the novelty of it.

"Just great," the Valet grumbled. He shrugged out of his red greatcoat and flopped down it, basking in the sun with his flask in one hand and a cigar in the other. "Now that's all she'll want to eat for weeks."

Petting Heartbreaker's snout, Leiyara cooed, "Don't you listen to the big mean man. You're a nice horsey."

The mare snorted, then gobbled up another bloodfruit wedge.

The rest of the desert crossing was uneventful, save for a couple of close calls with the local wildlife. The salamanders generally came out at night, but they hissed at the travelers from their shaded dens if they passed too near. The only other danger presented as an over-anxious pit snake that Hrakar skewered, joking that it would be their dinner tonight. At least Esther *hoped* he was joking.

They crested a rise near evening, the sun burning low on the horizon to give the landscape a renewed flame, and saw the first settlement on the desert's border. It appeared to be a small clay hut, sun-bleached and sturdy. The doorway was arched, covered only with a sheer curtain. The windows were perfectly round, placed for optimum airflow (one could see straight through the house to the opposite window if one were so inclined). A small stable stood a few yards from the house where a dusty old milk goat drank out of a trough. A windmill near the barn worked the pump on a well built from fire-baked clay, giving off the pleasant creaking sound of civilization.

An Agi man – presumably the owner of the settlement – worked in a plot of small bushes. He was a stout, sturdy man with strong arms and a lean build. His flame-red hair was cropped close, his skin a burnt orange color, darkened by the sun. Every Agi developed a jewel-like dot in the center of their forehead, the darker and more faceted, the older the Agi. This man's was many-faceted and ruby red. Esther guessed him to around age sixty – middle-aged, given the life expectancy of his race.

At the sound of their approach, the Agi farmer squinted up at them, shielding his eyes from the sun. "*Bona saire*, pilgrims!" he called to them, bidding good evening in his native tongue.

"*Bona saire, maestra*," Esther replied in kind.

The older Agi smiled, shaking his head. "The respect is appreciated, *madelle*," he said in Sapien, "but it is not necessary. I am *Pah-ren*."

The Valet leaned over to Leiyara, whispering, "What sort of name is that?"

Leiyara giggled and Esther rolled her eyes. "What are you called?" she asked in Agish.

"My name is Emon," he replied, still in Sapien. "Your Agish is quite good."

"As is your Sapien," Esther said. She pulled her medallion from her shirt. "I am Peacekeeper Esther Triad of Ordo's Call."

Emon examined the medallion, but neither his smile nor his pleasant demeanor changed. "That would explain it. Well, I am sure it was a long journey through the desert and I am just finishing. Perhaps you would like to join me for *sairenfete*?"

"For what?" the Valet asked.

"Dinner," Hrakar replied. "He's asking us to join him for a meal."

The big man nodded his approval. "I could eat."

The inside of Emon's home was cozy and cool, helped along by the open floor plan and being dug a few feet into the ground. The main room was for leisure and dining – a small table that could seat four was placed near the stove in the corner; a couch and armchair crafted from richly dark wood with deep, soft cushions adorned the opposite corner. Emon's bed, a simple mattress with a metal frame, filled the last corner. At the back, another archway led to the washroom.

Emon showed them in. "Please make yourselves comfortable," he said. "I do not have much, but what I do have, I will share."

The Valet pulled up a chair, sat in the corner, and rested his dread blade against the wall. If Emon had noticed that the big man had remained armed, he paid it no mind. Leiyara went around the little hut, looking at and touching everything. Esther and Hrakar remained by the door. Tension still plagued the group, a kind of cautious cool that kept them on guard. Esther chalked it up to spending too much time in the Gray Marsh, having to constantly keep a lookout without allowing herself a moment's rest. She forced herself to relax.

"Thank you," she said to Emon. "You have a lovely home."

That phrase is typically used to describe homes that are well decorated or adorned with art and trinkets. Agi culture, however, was one based on utility; they saw beauty in a thing's function. As such, Emon had no paintings or portraits, no baubles. There were wooden utensils hanging on the wall by the stove, a shelf containing crockery and cookware. His table was scratched and pitted with use. Even the cushions on his furniture were a plain dun color, although they looked soft and inviting.

"It is functional," Emon said with pride. He moved to the stove to began preparing their meal. "Please feel free to relax and refresh yourselves." He gestured toward the back room, "The *lavarie* is back there. I have running water."

Leiyara jump at the chance before anyone else. She grabbed her knapsack, heading for the "lavarie" with a skip in her step. Esther dropped her things by the door before pulling up a seat next to the Valet. Hrakar chose the couch and, sprawled out decadently, snored softly within minutes.

Emon went about his meal prep silently, giving his guests time and space. He chopped vegetables and unwrapped stew meat. He filled a kettle and put it on the heat. All the while he hummed a tune to himself in his melodic native language.

When at last the stew simmered and the flatbread baked in the oven, Emon sat down with Esther and the Valet.

"You came from the northwest," Emon observed. "The Gray Marsh."

The Peacekeeper and the Valet nodded in unison.

Their host clucked his tongue. "There was news of an airship wreck a few days ago. Were you –" He didn't have to finish the question. Their expressions said it all. "I'm sorry. But let us speak of pleasant things."

The Valet took out one of his cigars, "Mind if I smoke?"

Emon smiled. "Only if I can join you," he replied, going to a small wooden box to find a cigarette. "Would you care for one, Peacekeeper? They are made from the aged Irami tobacco."

The Peacekeeper didn't know what Irami tobacco was, but a smoke sounded good. "Thank you," she said.

Emon brought over a large brown jug and three cups. "And perhaps some blood cider to seal our new friendship?" He poured the blood cider – made, of course, from the local bloodfruit – while they smoked their fine tobacco. Esther's cigarette produced a rich, aromatic smoke hinting at age and spices. The blood cider tasted at once sweet and sour, warming her insides.

"Do you make it yourself?" she asked, extending her cup for a refill.

Emon filled her cup once more. "I do. Every few weeks I make camp in the Arami and pick the fruit. I have a barrel out back I use to ferment it."

"It must be quite valuable," the Valet remarked, sipping it as if it were a fine Draconian Red.

Emon waved off the remark. "If one were so inclined. However, I don't sell much all the way out here."

The Valet nodded his understanding. "In other words, more for you."

Emon gave him a smile and wink while they clinked glasses. Their host's eyes flashed to the Valet's weapon, resting ominously against the wall. Up to this point, he'd been very careful to pointedly not notice it. "Is that what I think it is?"

The Valet glanced over, then nodded. "*Glaeve Pandaemonia,*" he said with both a touch of pride and foreboding.

Esther had been eager to ask about the greatsword herself, but hadn't found the time. She leaned forward involuntarily, listening intently.

"One of the eight Rune Blades," Emon said. "Forged by the Elders themselves from the husk of dead Pandaemonia."

"As you say."

Their host bit his lip, hesitating for the briefest second. "May I look at her?" he asked. "Close up."

A moment of hesitation from the Valet followed. Esther could sense his reluctance, his mistrust, but also something else. It seemed like the Valet wasn't trying to protect the weapon from Emon, but protect Emon from the weapon. She was already vaguely aware that the Rune Blade had some consciousness of its own – some eerie sense of watching and waiting – but it still made her jump in her seat when the Valet picked it up and its jeweled eye snapped open. He laid it on the table for Emon's hungry eyes. The Agish farmer hunched over it, examining every inch of it while taking care not to touch it. His eyes ran over the blade's black edge, then carefully read the runes etched into the side, then regarded the jewel on the hilt as it looked back at him.

"I've never seen its equal," the Agi said, breathless.

The Valet crossed his arms, as proud as if he'd forged it himself. "Even among the Rune Blades, it's considered superior. They say that it belonged to the Elder Xanos himself, also known as Alexander Wraithbane I."

Their host nodded, his eyes still fixed on the blade. "I have heard that," he said. "The runes here speak of blood, death, and war."

"From which she was forged."

Now, Emon put his ear to the blade. "It still retains some of the *Eteral's* – that is, the goddess's – *anima*. How do you cope with that?"

The Valet shrugged. "She and I generally agree on things."

Esther didn't know whether to be terrified or impressed. According to legend, it was because of the lasting echo of Pandaemonia that the Blades were locked away, lost to time and myth. To take up a Rune Blade was to challenge and master chaos itself. Having done that, the Valet became a frightening enemy or a dubious ally.

"And will it truly cut any substance in Morgarai?" Emon asked.

"Even black iron."

Whistling, Emon sat back in his chair, his curiosity sated. "You may take it away," he said. "I do not feel like she will tolerate any touch but yours."

The Valet nodded, lifting the weapon from the table. He propped it back up in the corner, whispering a few words to it so it could return to its slumber.

By now, Leiyara emerged from the washroom. She wore nothing but a black slip as she dried her fiery curls. Having only seen her fully clothed, Esther hadn't realized the girl had a shape to her or such long legs. The Valet appeared to notice as well.

"Well, hello there," he said with a sideways smile; he probably thought it was charming.

Noticing how they were staring, Leiyara froze, blushing a bright red. "What?" she asked, then looked down at herself. She hastily shielded her body with her towel. "Matron's blessing!" she swore. "This isn't, like, one of those propriety things is it?"

Emon just laughed. "No child," he said. "As craftsmen, we Agi appreciate the form given to a body as one of Virago's most blessed creations." He refilled the Valet's cup, regarding him wolfishly. "You are in for a real treat, my friend, when you see Agi women."

They clinked glasses again.

Esther rolled her eyes. *Men!* Then she gave Leiyara a reassuring glance. "It's fine," she said. "Nothing we haven't all seen before."

They ate their stew and flatbread while even Hrakar, who'd reluctantly woken from his nap, complimented the Agi's herbs and seasonings. The food tasted spicy, hot, and delicious. After the meal, the party sat back in their chairs, enjoying a full belly and a safe place. Esther, however, had business on her mind. It felt like it had been ages since she thought about her real mission: a possible spellcrafter making trouble in the Colonies.

"Is there a town nearby?" the Peacekeeper asked.

Emon stubbed out the end of his cigarette in a colorful, ornate glass ashtray. "The town of Patel is only about seven sects away. About twenty-four miles, by your measure."

He's quite educated for a Pah-ren, Esther noted. *Perhaps there's more to this Emon than meets the eye.*

"Is there a telegraph office there?"

Emon nodded. "There is. In fact, my nephew is the – how do you say? - 'tapper' there. I can get you a good price. I am taking some of my goods to Patel tomorrow if you would like to come along."

"I'd appreciate that," Esther replied. "We'll also need to arrange transport to the Colonies, if possible."

"I know the coachman, a Sapien like you. He will get you to Portalaine quickly."

Well educated and well connected, Esther thought.

"*Gracasa bacampa,*" she said.

Emon waved off the gratitude. He stood, clearing the table. Leiyara and Hrakar moved to help.

"You are, of course, tired from your journey," their host observed. "You may stay here tonight. I don't have much room, but if your man here –" he gestured to the Valet, "– wouldn't mind sleeping in the stable, your young lady can have the couch. You –" to Esther, "– and Hrakar may have the bed."

Esther reddened at the implication, mostly because it was true.

Emon leaned in, speaking confidentially. "It is a rare thing to win the affection of a Draconian," he said in a voice just shy of a whisper. "You should cherish that. Love is one of Virago's greatest works after all, for it is fire forged in flame."

She appreciated the sentiment, but the blushing Peacekeeper just wished everyone would stop looking at her.

••••

THE NEXT MORNING ESTHER awoke to the sounds and smells of breakfast being made, as well as the hushed voices of Hrakar, Leiyara, and Emon in the kitchen. Emon's bed was soft and comfortable, plus the pillow beside her head still smelled like Hrakar – the musk of a man mingled with spices and herbs. She thought about rolling over and getting some more shut-eye, but reason won out. It hardly became a Peacekeeper to spend all day in bed.

Having only worn her undergarments to bed, so she dressed quickly and discreetly. She was pulling on her boots that Leiyara appeared from the kitchen. Her secretary was wearing a dress made from light fabric, slit up the sides to show off her long legs and a pair of strappy sandals. Her red curls were piled on top of her head. Were it not for her lack of orange tone, she could have been Agi herself.

"Good morning," she said, flopping down on the bed where Hrakar had been the night before. "Or as the Agi would say, *bona mata*." She beamed at Esther, all good cheer.

Esther realized she hadn't had a "normal" morning with her secretary yet. It had been all travel and tragedy, air sickness and terror. Seeing her safe, healthy, and chipper – albeit provocatively dressed – was a nice change; it warmed the Peacekeeper's heart. Still, she had to keep up appearances.

"Is there coffee?" she grumbled.

Leiyara nodded emphatically. It took her a moment for the real reason for the question to sink in. "Oh, right!" she nearly cried. "I'll get you a cup. It's my job. I forgot!"

She pranced hurried into the kitchen.

"I have had bosses, too," Emon remarked with a laugh. Hrakar's hearty chuckle followed making Esther smiled in spite of herself.

Leiyara returned a moment later with a steaming ceramic mug. She handed it to Esther. "Just how you like it: milk and sugar. Although the sugar here is a little strange. It comes from vegetables. And the milk comes from some sort of desert animal I can't pronounce the name of. And it's blue."

Esther nodded, taking an experimental sip. The coffee tasted wonderful nonetheless. "Where did you get those clothes?" she asked.

"Oh these?" Leiyara replied, fingering the fabric. "They belonged to Emon's wife – well, his late wife. He gave them to me." She reddened a little, giving Esther an almost pleading look as if she'd be expected to return the gift.

Esther gave her a half-smile. "They suit you. I could almost mistake you for an Agi."

Leiyara beamed, twirling to show off more of her legs. "You think? I think the clothes are so beautiful! Agi women are so lucky!"

Thinking about corsets, petticoats, and stockings, Esther had to agree. It would be disappointing enough going back to her usual uniform after days in comfortable trousers and a loose linen shirt. She doubted she'd be comfortable in something so revealing as Leiyara's new dress.

And Emon's late wife? That added yet another layer to their mysterious host. Esther filed that away for another time when she would have a very frank conversation with the Agi.

At this point that the Valet came into the house. He looked well-rested and had his hair down, long golden locks cascading down to the small of his back, right above where his tight breeches told Esther a little more than she cared to know.

"I smell bacon," the big man said. He carried his coat inside – Esther imagined the day's heat had started by now – and tossed it unceremoniously on one of Emon's chairs.

"Not quite," Emon explained. "This comes from the maki, but it is very similar to bacon. Breakfast will be ready soon, and we are in for a treat: our friend Hrakar has provided us with spices from Draconia."

Esther took her mug, joining the men in the kitchen. She gave the Valet's coat a derisive glance and he moved it so she could sit. He made a face at her, then his eyes caught Leiyara. "Howling Void!" he swore, "Where have you been hiding all that?"

Under a gaze that seemed to be eating her all up, Leiyara blushed a brighter shade of red than Esther had ever seen. She turned her eyes down demurely, a smile touched her lips. "Um..." she said, the very definition of feminine mystique.

The Valet dropped into a chair next to Esther, pouring himself a glass of bloodfruit juice from a pitcher on the table. "You could take a lesson from her," he remarked to Esther. "You dress like a man."

Hrakar snorted, Emon laughed. Even Leiyara had to stifle a giggle. "I dress," Esther said, "like a Peacekeeper. And at least I don't keep a bow in my hair like some schoolgirl."

The Valet, who'd been putting his hair up into the aforementioned bow, grinned as the rest of the party burst into guffaws. "Feisty," he said. "I like that."

The rest of the morning they spent preparing for their trip to Patel. Esther took stock of what little she had left – her knapsack, the half-empty cask of wine she could never seem to get rid of – and the remainder of the money she'd taken out of the bank. Though it was a little frayed and crumpled, she also still had her check with the remaining three hundred royals on it.

Heartbreaker, already saddled, chewed idly on some scrub when they came outside. The Valet had secured his Rune Blade among the saddle straps where it appeared to be slumbering in the glare. Leiyara ran to the horse, cooing over her.

"I'm tempted to just give her the damned thing," the Valet grumbled.

Esther and Hrakar helped Emon hitch up his small, two-wheeled wagon to an abnormally large mountain goat (Esther later learned it was called a lapaco), then they went into the stables to help with loading up a few gunny sacks.

"What is it you grow?" Esther asked, hefting one of the bags over her shoulder. The activity hurt, as she just noticed how sore she was from all they had been through.

Emon took one sack beneath each arm deftly like the hundreds of times he'd likely done it before. "Beans, mostly," he said, "some brustel as well."

"Brustel," Hrakar asked, "what is this?"

Esther accessed her knowledge of Agi society. "It's a root vegetable that grows in the rocky desert soil. It needs very little water."

Emon seemed impressed. "They also taste good with raga butter and sea salt," he added.

"I will have to try some," the Draconian remarked, seemingly not convinced.

Once they loaded the wagon, they set off for Patel. Esther rode shotgun with Hrakar lounging among the sacks in the back. Leiyara rode tandem on Heartbreaker, clutching tightly to the Valet. He looked pleasantly smug to have the scantily clad redhead holding onto him.

The road to Patel was neatly trimmed and cobbled, a welcome change to the rocky pass through the Alcom mountains. Central Transit did a good bit of business in this part of the world, mostly thanks to Agi traders going back and forth regularly.

The sun was high and hot, making Esther miss her wide-brimmed hat. Behind her in the cart's bed, Hrakar seemed unaffected, dozing and snoring. The Valet wasn't wearing his signature great coat; instead, he kept it draped across Heartbreaker's shoulders. Occasionally, the big man would mop sweat off his brow and take a pull from his flask, making sure to offer a sip to Leiyara each time.

About halfway through their ride, they came to a toll booth staffed by an Agi man and a Sapien woman. The Agi had all the hallmarks of his race: orange-tinted skin, blazing red hair, and a ruby-like jewel in the center of his forehead. He was a young man of about thirty or so. The Sapien woman had the brown skin, dark eyes, and straight black hair that attested to her Kaij descent – the people of a desert sultanate in the west. Their uniqueness ended with the usual burgundy of Central Transit uniforms. Seeing them brought a little normalcy back to Esther's life.

"Blessings of Virago be with you," Emon greeted them, pulling the cart to a stop and taking out his purse.

"And to you," the Agi man said. He gave the party a sideways glance. "How many?"

"Five," Emon said, "but one is a Peacekeeper." He jerked his thumb at Esther as he said the last.

The Agi man – Laird, according to his name badge – looked Esther up and down, scrutinizing. "She don't look like no Peacekeeper," he said. His Sapien was good enough to be bad.

Esther produced her medallion, showing it to Laird.

"Good enough, then," the Kaij woman said, glancing over Laird's shoulder. Her name was Samara.

Once satisfied, Samara went around the cart, checking things off of a clipboard as she went.

"It's three royals per head," Laird counted. "Two more for the cart and one for the horse."

Samara finished with the cart, then moved on to examining Heartbreaker. “Is your horse shod?” she asked.

“Yes,” the Valet replied. He clucked his tongue and the mare lifted her front foot. Samara hunkered down to take a look.

“Does that matter?” Leiyara asked. “If they're shod or not?”

Samara checked a few more things off her list. “We have to have you sign waivers for an unshod horse, releasing Central Transit from liability if there's any damage to the animal.” Samara looked back at Laird. “They're good to go.”

Laird did some calculations on an adding machine. "So that's three per head – minus the Peacekeeper – two for the cart, one for one horse, shod. That comes to fifteen Royals."

Emon searched through his purse, counting under his breath. If the panicked, crestfallen look on the man's face was any indication, he didn't have enough. In the booth window, Laird scoffed, making some remark about Pah-ren under his breath. Esther clenched her teeth and reached into her side pouch, angered by the Agi's classism.

“I just remembered, we never paid you for the blood cider,” she said.

“Oh, that's not –”

Esther put a hand on Emon's shoulder. "I insist. Your hospitality to a Peacekeeper and her companions was more than generous already. I must pay you eighty royals, no less." She shoved a handful of silverbacks into his hand. As she spoke, she'd made sure to emphasize the words "Peacekeeper" and "blood cider". It left the Agi in the booth looking shamed.

Emon beamed as he counted out the fifteen royals, smugly handing them to Laird one at a time.

“We only take slips,” Laird grumbled. “Real silver.”

Esther went for her pouch again, preparing to exchange the money, when Leiyara chimed in. “That's not true!” she nearly shouted. “I worked for Central Counting since I was fifteen, so I know that anyone serving the Central Authorities is obligated, by policy, to accept all forms of legal tender. Section three, paragraph nine of the handbook. Look it up if you want, we'll wait."

Laird and Samara exchanged a look, the former miserable now with the humiliation. "She's right," Samara said.

Laird snatched the bills out of Emon's hand. "Do you want a receipt?" he asked grudgingly.

"Yes, please," Leiyara said, still on her roll. "And be sure to add your name and booth number. I'll be telegraphing your supervisor about how rude you've been to our gracious host."

Laird's eyes went as wide as Emon's smile. He hastily filled out a receipt, his stylus shaking as he did so. He handed it across delicately, politely. "Many blessings of Virago, *messire*," he said.

Emon took the receipt, sticking it in his purse with the silverbacks Esther had given him. Samara lifted the boom, and Emon, still grinning ear to ear, shook the reins, leading his goat through.

Once they were out of earshot, the Valet rode up to Emon's side of the cart. "What's that guy's problem?" he asked.

Emon shrugged. "I am Pah-ren," he replied as if that was all the answer he needed.

The Valet looked puzzled. Emon noticed. "I see. You must not know the word Pah-ren. In Agimonde, we have a system of..." to Esther, "...what is the word?"

"A caste system," Esther assisted.

"Ah! *Bona*! Yes, a caste system. Pah-ren is the lowest caste, not respected or well-liked."

The Valet nodded, satisfied with that answer, but Esther knew that, despite his nonchalance, Emon's lot was a difficult one. The Pah-ren were treated as second-class citizens, disdained and denied basic human rights. It was even acceptable to beat them publicly under certain circumstances. They were one step away from being slaves.

"Thank you," Emon said to Esther, then again to Leiyara. "Did you see his face? Never has a Pah-ren so embarrassed a Petrascel in such a way!"

The Peacekeeper smiled. "You have been more than kind to us," she said. "It was my pleasure."

"Yeah," Leiyara said, "that Petra-whatsit had it coming!"

Emon laughed heartily.

Chapter Thirteen: Patel, Agimonde

They reached Patel by mid-afternoon. Emon dropped them off at the town's entrance, bidding them a very fond farewell. "If you are ever in Agimonde again, you must come visit me."

"We'll do that," Esther said. "Thank you, Emon, and many blessings of Virago upon you and your crop."

Emon made a hand gesture that Esther didn't understand, then rode his cart toward the town center, leaving them to their business. The town of Patel was something larger than a village, but not quite large enough to be considered a city. Esther estimated it at somewhere between three and four thousand people. The buildings were all the same fired red clay as Emon's house, except that they were more expansive with additional rooms, terraces, and some with second or third stories.

The streets were brimming with people, Agi men and women going about their daily routine, dressed in light fabrics. Some drove carts pulled by etoxrin – beasts of burden that resembled oxen but with three horns and piebald fur, some rode in coaches pulled by clockwork horses. Esther noted that most of these coaches had a coat of arms resembling a hammer-and-chisel emblazoned on them. Petrascel, or stonemasons, were the cream of Agi society.

"He was quite pleasant," Hrakar remarked, looking after Emon's wagon.

"Quite mysterious," Esther said. The man had given her quite a bit to ponder, and she regretted that she wouldn't have the chance to ask him her myriad questions about him and his history. Perhaps one day, but on to business now. She turned to the group, temporarily dismissing their enigmatic host from her mind. "Right. So, as some of you may already know, the Agish economy works on a barter system."

"A what?" Leiyara asked.

"They trade goods and services instead of using money," the Valet explained.

"That's weird," the girl huffed.

Hrakar laughed, then waved a finger at her. "The Agi see value in their crafts. When we see silver, they see spoons. When we see gold, they see arm rings – you see many of the well-off women adorned with them. Money is for the Commerciers, or traders, to use when they're out in the world."

"But...how do we pay for anything?" Leiyara almost shouted.

"I was just getting to that," Esther said, putting up a hand to calm her. "What do we have that's worth trading?"

Hrakar reached about his person, producing a few pouches of Draconian spices, a couple of knives (Draconians were known for keeping multiple weapons about their person at all times), and a small bottle of healing salve.

"Are you sure?" Esther asked. "I don't know if I feel right taking things from you. I mean, we are all employed by various agencies, but..."

"I am paying my *echem*," Hrakar replied. "Unless you are saying that I am not, as you say, part of the team?" He feigned looking hurt, at least Ether hoped he was faking.

"No," the Peacekeeper cried. "I was only saying that we three are under an obligation."

The Draconian shrugged. "Then so am I," he said, forcing his haul into Esther's hands.

She turned next to Leiyara. "What about you?"

Her secretary searched through their belongings, riffling quickly through the bags. "Well, we've got some spare clothing, I have some jewelry I...borrowed from my mother," She turned bright red. "Not a lot else besides field rations."

Esther let her thievery slide for now, turning to the Valet, who didn't seem keen on contributing – he appeared to be looking anywhere but in Esther's general direction. "And you? Come on, pony up."

The Valet sighed theatrically, taking out his flask – he'd filled it with blood cider before leaving Emon's house – and his packet of cigars. He also produced a hunting knife. "I travel light," he said, shrugging. She knew he was holding out, but she spared herself the argument.

Stowing the bounty into her knapsack, Esther dug in her pouch for the rest of her cash. "Find us a *cassal* while you're at it. A decent place with running water and a tub. I need a bath." She saw Leiyara opening her mouth to protest, so she headed her off. "The *cassals* are like hotels. They're run by the Commercier caste, so our money's good there." She gave the money to Hrakar – she didn't trust the Valet not to blow it on wantons and wine.

"I could also use refreshment," Hrakar said, turning to the Valet. "We will see if they have a good wine – they will give me a good price."

The Valet grinned. "I knew I liked you for a reason."

Esther rolled her eyes. *Men!*

Leiyara slid down from Heartbreaker, giving a show of her legs again, and joined Esther's side as the two men ambled off. "What are we doing?" she asked.

"We have business," Esther answered.

The first stop was the smithy. Esther had lamented losing her weapons for too long and had every intention of rectifying that as quickly as possible. The smith's shop was clean and well lit by the desert sun. The floor was boarded with polished wood, the clay that made up the walls was a sun-bleached red that looked almost pink.

Display cases lined the walls showing fine pieces of metalwork – rapiers and sabers, rifles and pistols. Leiyara looked around wide-eyed, flinching now at the bang of steel on steel from the forge outside. Esther went to the counter to ring the small service bell she found there.

The banging of steel stopped and a moment later a burly Agi man with a shaved head and bushy red beard appeared from the back entrance. He wore a leather apron and pulling off a pair of thick padded gloves.

"*Bona jurnee*," he said, looking at once bemused and distressed at the appearance of two Sapien women in his shop.

"*Bona jurnee,*" Esther replied. "*Sapiana*?"

The smith shook his head. He did not speak Sapien. Esther switched to Agish. "I am a Peacekeeper," she said, producing her medallion. The smith looked at it, nodding his understanding. "I seek a weapon made," Esther went on, slowly and carefully drawing her revolver as to not cause alarm, "same to this." She spoke Agish conversationally – niceties and everyday talk – so her ability to communicate to the smith's technical proficiency wasn't perfect.

The smith looked down at the revolver. He picked it up in a pair of huge, callused hands, turned it over, looked down the sight, examined the bayonet's blade, opened the cylinder, spun it, listened. Then he nodded. "Return tomorrow," he said. "It will be done."

Esther reached for her bag. "I have a few items for trade. Will you take Draconian spices? Or container of blood cider?"

The smith just waved off the question. "Return tomorrow," he said, then went back outside to his work.

Esther holstered her revolver, turning to Leiyara, who admired a black iron combat knife. "Do you know how to use one?" she asked the captivated girl.

Leiyara reddened a little, taking on the persona of a child caught peeping. "No. I just like them."

Esther nodded, filing that away as a Midwinter present idea.

"Where to now?" her secretary asked.

The clothier was up next. The tailor's shop was less impressive than the smith's. It was all one big room with an earthen floor and walls of a rougher kind of clay. The racks hanging with trousers, coats, and dresses surrounded the tailor's measuring table; mannequins were poised throughout the shop like guards. The tailor was a young woman wrapped in purple satin, slit up one side to show off that all-too-much leg style fashionable in Agish society. Her red curls were done up in a messy bun held together by a knitting needle.

"*Bona jurnee,*" she said as the two women approached.

Esther returned the greeting, then asked, "*Sapiana*?"

"*Sai*," the tailor replied. Yes. Then, switching to a heavily accented Sapien, "How can I help you?" It came out as *'ow cahn aye 'elp yiu.*

Despite the heavy accent, Esther was pleased that she wouldn't have to muddle through clothing and fashion jargon in Agish. She presented her medallion. "I am Peacekeeper Esther Triad of Ordo's Call."

The tailor nodded her understanding, looking Esther up and down. "You have need of a uniform, yes?"

"Yes," the Peacekeeper replied, appreciating the no-nonsense way of doing business here in Patel.

The tailor's eyes gave Esther another scan, this time visually taking her measurements. "You come back tomorrow," the Agi tailor said. "I will have two uniforms for you."

"How much?" Esther asked, then corrected herself. "I mean, what would you take in trade?"

The tailor waved off the question in the same way the smith had, then went right to work on the new uniforms.

When they left the store, Esther was pleased to see Emon in the street with his goat and cart. With him were two very solid looking Agi men, their tunics emblazoned with the crossed hammer and chisel. The woman with them, garbed in a bright blue dress, adorned herself with golden arm rings, earrings, and a nose ring. Her hair was straightened by some Agi technique to tame the curls, pulled back into a tight, neat ponytail.

"This is the Peacekeeper," Emon said, keeping his eyes downcast. To see this lively man so subdued hurt Esther's heart.

"Ah, *gratis,* Emon Pah-ren," the Agi lady – a noble one if Esther had ever seen one – said. The Petrascel regarded Esther now. "Greetings from the Agi of Patel, and many blessings of Virago."

Esther gave a nod. "And to you," she said evenly.

The Agi lady approached Esther, ramrod straight and walking with a practiced grace. She wore high-heeled sandals with straps crisscrossing her well-shaped legs; they added at least three inches to her height, which already matched that of a grown Sapien man. The Peacekeeper knew her ilk instantly: this was a woman of wealth, position, and breeding. Her graceful beauty made her dangerous.

"I am called Cami Petrascel," she said, touching her upper arm in way of the Agish greeting. Between her arm rings, Esther could see a tattoo of the same hammer-and-chisel.

They greet one another by identifying their caste, Esther thought. *It certainly puts one in one's place, doesn't it?*

"I am Peacekeeper Esther Triad," Esther replied, presenting her medallion for inspection. "And my secretary, Leiyara –" she paused. She didn't know Leiyara's surname. *All we've been through, and it never occurred to me ask.*

The red-haired girl stepped forward. "Candish. Leiyara Candish."

Cami and the other Agi men eyed her uncomfortably, almost warily. The lady looked Leiyara up and down, but still addressed Esther when she spoke. "She is dressed like a woman of the Agi, and her red hair...is she *demigral?*"

It took Esther a moment to identify the word. She was too caught up by the insulting way that Cami wouldn't address Leiyara directly. Half-born, or half-breed. It was a slur used by people with archaic ideas about racial purity. In the Sapien world, it was equivalent to "mongrel".

"Not that I'm aware of," the Peacekeeper said, then, more pointedly, "and *she* can speak for *herself*."

Cami's eyes half-closed in amusement. "Forgive me," she said, "I did not mean to be insulting. In our world, is it considered polite not to address a Pah-ren without the, erm, master's permission."

Leiyara, the poor lamb, looked increasingly more uncertain of herself as the exchange went on. "Esther, what's going on?" she asked in a small voice.

Esther turned to Leiyara, her icy glare warming to one of caring concern. "A misunderstanding," she explained. "Cami here was under the impression that you were my servant." Then, to Cami, "Leiyara is my trusted companion, friend, and confidant. She also just happens to be in my employ. You will show her the same respect that you show me."

One of the Agi men standing by Emon's cart spat, grumbling an expletive under his breath. Cami, however, only looked more smug and amused. "Of course," she said, addressing Leiyara directly for the first time. "Forgive me, I allowed my prejudice to sway my speech."

"Um...okay," Leiyara said.

Cami clapped her hands. "Right," she said. "We are all friends. Now 'down to business' as the Sapien saying goes. I would like to invite you to dinner at my *cassenda* tonight to officially welcome you to Agimonde." She gave Emon a sideways glance. "Had we known that a Peacekeeper was among us, we would have welcomed you sooner instead of allowing a Pah-ren the honor."

Emon shifted uncomfortably where he stood; Esther had to wonder what it would be like to spend one day in his shoes. In her opinion, the treatment of Pah-ren was deplorable. They were the people who grew everyone's food, served their tables, and cleaned up their waste. They were just as worthy of respect and dignity as a builder or a smith, perhaps even more so. But the Unbound Law had strict guidelines on interfering with another culture's views, and she'd already pushed it at the toll booth earlier that day.

"Emon was a very kind and generous host," Esther replied. "It was a worthy enough welcome, in its way."

She saw Emon smile to himself, giving her a grateful look with his down-turned eyes.

"Well, that is good," Cami replied, giving a verbal brush-off. "However, I shall invite the heads of all the households and we will greet you properly. I insist."

The Peacekeeper nodded. "Then we accept. It will be myself, Leiyara, and my two male companions."

"Yes," Cami said. "The Pah-ren has told us about them: a Sapien and a Draconian. We would be honored to have you as our guests. At sun-fall I shall send my coach."

Esther nodded her assent. "We will be grateful."

Cami beckoned to her men and they left to prepare for their engagement. Emon stood by his cart, his eyes on his feet until his superiors were gone. When he looked up, he grinned. Esther could have been mistaken, but she swore she saw him wink.

• • • •

ESTHER SPENT THE REMAINDER of the day at Central Transit's telegraph office – actually, she'd *commandeered* the telegraph office on official Peacekeeping business. She sent reports of her journey so far, reassuring her superiors that she was alive and well, and would be on her way to the Colonies forthwith. She sent a report to Central Transit headquarters, informing them of the fate of their deceased crew members and the airship which had been reported missing. She allowed Leiyara to telegraph home to let her parents know she was alright and that she'd taken a new job.

"You mean you didn't tell them before we left?" Esther asked, tapping out the message.

She just shrugged. "I was in a hurry."

When they finished, the afternoon light diminished with sundown fast approaching. Their dinner engagement would soon begin. They left the telegraph office, heading for the small town's only *cassal*. To Esther's surprise, it was a large clay building three stories tall with terraces on each level under red tile roofs.

They went in via the cantina, where a crowd of travelers enjoyed a meal, a few drinks, and fanning themselves in the desert heat. In one corner, a guitar player plucked out a tune about racehorses. A bowler hat sat on the floor in front of him, filling slowly with slips and silverbacks. The bar had a tile floor and open archways in each wall, as well as large, round windows. Smoke from cigarettes, cigars, and pipes drifted out into the cooling breeze.

An already half-drunk Valet sat at a table in the corner, a fat cigar in one hand, bottle of cider in the other, and a young Agi woman in his lap. She must have been a progressive: her skirt was less than half as long as Leiyara's. Hrakar sat next to him with a bottle and glass of wine in front of him.

How much is their bar tab going to run me? Esther wondered. *Men!*

She pulled up a chair, sitting across from Hrakar, with Leiyara following suit. "I see you boys started without us," she said. "How much am I in the hole?"

The Valet flashed a gold imperial. "This one's on me," he announced, his grin even flashier than the gold.

"Ordo's name," the Peacekeeper swore. "Who did you rob?"

The Valet gave a look of mock offense. Hrakar answered in his stead. "There was a Taro game across the street. Our friend – how do you say? - 'sheered them'. It was very impressive."

"The correct expression is 'fleeced them'," the Valet replied, then, to Esther, "You know, your boyfriend here is quite a card player himself. Dropped the Tower on some hoity-toity teller so hard I thought the man was going to collapse."

The two men laughed, clinking their glasses chummily – Hrakar seemed to be getting the hang of this Sapien custom.

"Well, we should get ready," the Peacekeeper said. "We have a dinner engagement tonight. Patel's finest have extended an invitation."

Hrakar took a turn at being impressed. "You make friends very fast," he said. He pushed the bottle and a spare glass over to Esther. "Have you tried a Draconian red? It is the finest wine in all Morgarai."

Esther debated a moment, then poured. "Why not."

The scent of the wine was at once sweet and sour, giving off notes of fruits, nuts, and grains that Esther wasn't familiar with. The flavor was unlike anything she'd ever tasted, culminating in a nice oak finish that brought her back home. "It's very fine," she said. Then, to the Valet: "Who's your friend?"

The big man and the girl stopped their nuzzling and private whispers. "Her name is Ayala," he said. "Ayala..."

"Ayala Carpensi," she said, filling in the blank. At the same time, she touched the tattoo on her arm – a wooden board and saw.

Carpensi, Esther thought. Agish for Carver, a woodworker. As one of the higher castes in Agi society, Ayala must have been slumming it with Sapien men, sowing those wild oats while she could.

"Forgive me, Ayala," the Peacekeeper said, flashing her medallion, "but would you mind continuing this later? We're on official business."

Ayala pouted, but whispered something to the Valet, then climbed off his lap and sashayed over to the bar. Esther was surprised she didn't dislocate a hip with the way she was swinging them. The Valet looked after her a moment, then sulked. "Well, *that* was unnecessary."

Esther grabbed the cigar from his teeth, took a hearty puff, and stubbed it out in the table's ceramic ashtray. "We need to be fresh and on our best behavior. Do we have rooms?"

The Valet passed a key to her. "Two thirty-five," he grumbled.

Esther finished her wine in one gulp, ignoring Hrakar's visibly wince – Draconian Red should be *savored.* "Thank you. If you'll excuse me, I'll freshen up a bit."

The coach that picked them up was a lavish piece of craftsmanship, all white wood and purple satin drapes. It was drawn by two clockwork horses, painted to match. The coachman, of course, was Pah-ren, as all the serving staff would be, but he dressed in livery of purple and white – the caste's colors.

There was plenty of room inside for the four of them with plush cushions to make the ride very comfortable. The coach navigated the streets of Patel, taking them up the steep rise where Cami Petrascel's *cassenda* loomed. Instead of the typical sun-baked clay abode, the house was built from kiln-fired bricks with a pearlescent glaze, gleaming in the evening light. It consisted of the main house , walled in with a magnificent garden in the dooryard, and another wing extending out over the rest of the hillside. A great outdoor terrace overhung a steep drop-off; an onlooker could see all of Patel as it began to sparkle in the coming dark.

The party disembarked from the coach and were met by the house's porters, two more Pah-ren in livery, a man and a woman. Esther particularly noticed the high collar and long skirt of the woman; it appeared that only affluent members of society were allowed to show off their bodies.

The porters escorted them inside, ushering them into an enormous banquet hall. Like most structures in Agimonde, this one had multiple arched doorways, but the windows were wide and tall as well, a contrast to the small round portholes she'd seen everywhere else. Sheer purple drapes moved lazily in the cool night air. An assortment of Agi leaders waited in the dining room with their attendants in tow. The smith Esther recognized from her business earlier in the day, as well as the tailor, though they were both in finery now. The smith had traded his leather apron and linen shirt for an orange tunic embroidered with an anvil. The tailor was adorned with silver arm rings and bracelets, her yellow dress left one shoulder bare, exposing a tattoo of a needle and spool on her upper arm.

Cami sashayed across the room, her heels clicking on the polished tile floor. She wore a purple gown, her gold arm rings and bracelets gleamed, her long red hair cascaded down to the small of her back, having been straightened again. "Ah! Blessings of Virago upon you! Welcome, welcome."

In the custom of her people, she gave each of the party a kiss on the forehead where that little red jewel would've been had they been Agi. Esther passed on the ceremony and Cami allowed it, knowing full well that Peacekeepers were above local customs: they gave their greetings with Ordo's Seal, declining to bow to any king or god.

Once done, Cami addressed the room at large, tapping her wine glass with one of her many golden rings. "Our guests of honor have arrived!" she called. The room gave a general cheer in response. "Dinner will be served."

The next half an hour blurred together for Esther while she had trouble tracking everyone and everything. The Pah-ren serving staff came through, laying the table with all sorts of new and wonderful smelling dishes foreign to her. There was roast volwrath, something resembling couscous, dates and nuts, olives and bloodfruit.

They were served a wine made from desert flowers that was subtle, yet aromatic.

Cami introduced her to all the caste leaders in turn, noting that they were seated according to their station. Their hostess, representing the masons, sat the head of the table. Minos, the laconic smith, sat at her right hand. Beside him was Alder Carpensi, the fidgety, whip-thin head of the woodworkers. Down the line were Ilona, the tailor, Nairomi, the cobbler, and Saiyan, the tanner. Esther had already forgotten the names of the others, but she knew that next came the tinker (the newest caste, given the age of steam), the cooper, and the wainright. The last caste down consisted of the trader or Commercier.

Since the Agi valued craftsmanship, the importance of your craft determined your place in society. The masons built houses, providing shelter, so they were most revered. The smiths made tools and weapons, a means for crafting or defense, so they were second and so on down the line. The only one that didn't fit was the vizier, or priest, who seemed to hold a place apart from Agish custom. He sat where he pleased.

Esther pushed the thought aside. She couldn't get involved in their politics.

They ate, they drank, they talked in niceties. Were they finding their stay in Patel pleasant? Did they get all of the services they needed? How were the accommodations? And so on. Leiyara, seated between Ilona and Nairomi, chatted up a storm praising the Agi fashions and the shoes and the beautiful jewelry; the tailor and cobbler were practically puffing up with pride. Near the foot of the table, the Valet regaled the lower castes with some tale or another – Esther couldn't hear him, but she was sure it had something to do with fleecing a group of suckers at a Taro table. She didn't know if they were honestly amused or just humoring him. Hrakar appeared comfortable enough as he discussed matters of faith with the Grand Vizier, the ordained keeper of Virago's intangible crafts.

"So," the Vizier inquired, "the Avatar is believed to be the embodiment of your great dragon, who sleeps at the center of Draconia?"

Hrakar nodded. He had changed into fresh silks for the occasion, dark and rich, the colors of blood and chocolate. His bare, silvery arms rippled with lean muscle. Esther had watched him say a prayer to his dragon god before removing the veil from his mouth so that he could eat. "That is right," the Draconian affirmed.

The Grand Vizier, a fat man who wore a red robe emblazoned with a single yellow flame, puzzled over this, fascinated. "And your people believe that this man –"

"Woman, currently," Hrakar gently corrected.

"– that this woman is your dragon made flesh?"

Hrakar chuckled. "Well, some believe it more than others. I think it is symbolic, but I am paying my *echem,* so what do I know?"

They went on to discuss what the *echem* meant to the Draconians and the various forms of worship for the Agi – which mostly consisted of burning things. When the meal ended, the group dispersed out onto the terrace for cigars and more wine. Esther smoked in the company of Cami and Minos, the latter being no more pleasant or talkative than he'd been when Esther had been at his shop. This recalled to her mind the interactions at the shops earlier, particularly how the proprietors, including Minos, had refused her offer to trade with them.

"One thing I don't understand," she said after more pleasantries about the weather, "is when I tried to trade for services in town, they didn't seem interested. You have a barter system here, do you not?"

Cami and Minos exchanged a glance, clearly amused by the question. "I have heard that term, yes," Cami said.

Esther felt a cold stone drop into her stomach. "But you will not accept my offer to trade?"

Again Cami and Minos shared a glance, and Esther got the feeling she'd just stepped right into their trap. "You are a Peacekeeper," Minos replied. "You do not require payment."

"Indeed," Cami added. "To help a Peacekeeper is to help Agimonde."

Esther nodded, still wary. "I would still like to pay – or barter – for the goods. I wouldn't feel right taking advantage of your kindness."

That look again, the same non-verbal communication between the pair of them. Cami looked smug this time, Minos sour. Esther knew that sort of exchange: Cami had just won a bet. What she had won in a society that didn't believe in currency was beyond her. Perhaps a new arm ring or bracelet; Cami seemed to have a penchant for pretty things.

"Well," Cami said, not bothering to hide her clever little smile – she had a terrible Taro face. "If you insist on compensating, perhaps you could do us a favor."

Esther looked around for her friends, desperately wishing one of them was here to help – sometimes even Leiyara seemed more worldly than her. Hrakar still debated matters of faith with the Grand Vizier. The Valet played his seductive games with Ilona. Leiyara occupied herself fighting off Nairomi, who seemed to be all hands when he had one too many.

These are the kinds of situations, she told herself, *when a Peacekeeper must be capable of handling things.*

"What did you have in mind?" Esther asked, cautious of agreeing to anything prematurely.

For the first time since she'd met Cami, the woman seemed unsure of herself. She bit her lip, glancing at Minos. "Go on," the smith prompted, "this was your idea."

Cami took a deep breath. "How much do you know about our war with the Myrian?"

Esther thought back to her studies. According to myth, the Agi were born of Virago, the Prime fire elemental, while the Myrian were born of Myral, the chief water elemental. Since their countries bordered one another, they fought an endless war – two opposing primal forces made flesh, struggling for supremacy. They went back and forth for thousands of years, dealing horrific blows to one another. The Myrian had wiped out Agimonde's former capital of Allyrion, in return the Agi had crafted such a fierce weapon it wiped out the Myrians' corporeal forms, leaving them as living ghosts. In recent times, the two races appeared to be at a stalemate. Wards were constructed to keep the Myrian spirits out of Agimonde, and wraiths – those sad Myrian driven mad by their tragedy – patrolled the borders waiting to tear any Agi intruder apart.

"I know much of it," Esther replied.

Cami smiled. "Good. Then you will understand the gravity of what I'm about to tell you. Three days ago there was a breach in the wards near the southern road. The wraiths came and have been causing havoc to travelers and the food growers in the area."

Esther blanched. "You want me to stop an entire Myrian invasion?" she asked.

Giggling, Cami shook her head. "No, no. *Bona mé*, no. Our traders are only wanting someone to help escort goods to Portalaine. A guard, so to speak."

"We have the invasion under control," Minos added, obviously concerned with maintaining the Agi's good name. "Our wards are functioning again and the Mysthunters have driven back most of the encroaching force."

This was the most she'd heard the smith say since their first encounter. Perhaps he, too, had a mind for military matters – the Mysthunters were, essentially, Agimonde's army.

"The occasional band of rampaging wraiths has, as you say, slipped our nets," Cami went on. "We would like to know that our goods are kept out of Myrian hands."

Taken aback by the phrasing, Esther remarked, "And to be sure your people are safe."

Cami and Minos looked at each other again, this time puzzled. "They are Pah-ren," the leader of the masons said dismissively, "but if that's important to you, then yes."

Anger blazed in her heart. How could a people group matter so little to them? She bit down hard, putting on her best Taro face. "We are on our way to Portalaine ourselves, seeking passage to the Colonies."

Cami clapped her hands. "Ah! It is *çino*!"

It came to her: *çino*: a sign from Virago.

"We will guard your caravan," Esther committed. "Pray pardon me. I will need to consult with my team."

"Of course," Cami said. "*Bona noctus,* Peacekeeper."

••••

AFTER THE EVENTS OF the day, Esther finally took the hot bath she'd been longing for since being stranded in the Gray Marsh. The *cassal's* room had a full washroom, complete with a tub deep enough that Esther could lounge with her whole body submerged. Some salts and oils made the water fragrant and bubbly. She luxuriated there for at least an hour before she heard Hrakar rap on the arched door frame.

"Are you well?" he asked.

"I'm fine," Esther replied. "Will you bring me some wine?"

His hesitant silence radiated from the doorway. It lasted so long that Esther wasn't sure if Hrakar was still there or whether he had heard. Then he said, "I shouldn't. You are not dressed."

Esther chuckled. "Hrakar, we've shared a bed and braved death together. I think we'll be fine."

He came in a moment later carrying two wine glasses and a bottle of Draconian Red. He poured and they drank.

"You are quite beautiful," Hrakar said, unabashedly staring at her with those gorgeous amber eyes of his.

Esther smiled. When they were alone like this, she didn't blush. "Thank you," she said. "Now that I'm clean, I can start to start to believe it."

A smile touched his eyes as he reached out, caressing a loose strand from her messy bun. His hand brushed her cheek, the skin warm and smooth. Esther took his hand and held it there, filling up with that warmth he made her feel. She closed her eyes as his hand slid down her neck and across her collarbone and shoulder. When Hrakar's hand suddenly left her skin, she opened her eyes to find him undoing the silks about his face. She reached up, grabbing his hand. "Don't," she said. "You'll get in trouble."

That smile touched his eyes again. "I am already in trouble."

He moved her hand away gently and finished unwinding the silk, revealing a handsome, well-formed face with high cheekbones and a square jaw. His silver skin glistened in the light. His hair was a long mane of white, each strand was wispy, as delicate as a feather. When he smiled – his smile was *beautiful* – he showed a perfect row of white teeth with slightly elongated canines.

Esther couldn't stop herself. She sat up, kissing him deeply and hotly, parting her lips slightly to feel those sharp teeth brushing them. Hrakar leaned into her, twining his fingers into her hair, pressing his mouth to hers. She felt his strong arms wrap around her as he lifted her, still naked and wet, from the tub and carried her to the bedroom.

• • • •

THE NEXT MORNING ESTHER waited in her undergarments for Leiyara to retrieve her purchases. The caravan would be leaving at ten o'clock but Ilona and Minos assured her they would have her things ready in time. Hrakar and the Valet had gone to the general store to buy supplies. Esther already missed his warmth, his scent. She could still feel his hands moving over her expertly, touching all the right places. She warmed, smiled, then straightened. *No*. Today was about her official duties. She and Hrakar would be serving side-by-side, guarding the caravan, and nothing would be different between them in the execution of that task.

Would it?

Fortunately, Leiyara chose that time to enter her room. She carried two garment bags, a hatbox, and a bundle under her arm. She laid out the garment bags on the bed, then set the bundle gently next to them, then set the hatbox on top. Esther stood up from the dressing table where she had occupied herself with plaiting her hair. She eagerly went to her haul, opening the bags and boxes. The cassocks were blacker than her previous one, the hat was crafted from perfect felt. Lastly, she unrolled the bundle, amazed by what she saw.

Leiyara rattled on the whole time with "sorry I was late" and "carriage traffic" and the like. Now, she too looked into the bundle. "Minos said that he made them from the best parts he had on hand and that he specially forged the blades. I didn't know they they were *this* special!"

Surely they were one of a kind with grips were crafted from stonewood, smooth, polished, and hard enough to crack a skull. The cylinder, barrel, and bayonets were forged from black iron. They weighed almost nothing. On the blades were inscribed Force runes that would increase the power of the blow, the swiftness of a strike. It was a matched set, not just the one she had commissioned.

"They're beautiful!" Leiyara exclaimed.

Esther just nodded as she holstered the weapons in her gun belt. She tucked the old standard-issue revolver into her luggage. She hadn't been able to look at it the same since Dariana...

Casting a guilty glance back at her secretary, Esther couldn't help but admire her outfit. “A new dress?” she asked.

Leiyara blushed. “Yes. Miss Ilona gave me two new ones and a frock to replace the one I tore up. She said she would've given me a ball gown, too, if she'd had time to make one.”

Esther nodded her dubious approval; the Agi were being quite generous, perhaps *too* generous. She dressed in her new cassock then looked in the mirror, impressed. The fit was nearly perfect, despite the Agish artisan having only eyeballed her measurements; it even managed to make her backside look good. She put her gun belt on over her nicely hugged hips and settled her hat on her head. She looked like a real Peacekeeper again – a *woman* Peacekeeper.

“You look amazing!” Leiyara said. She stopped packing up their belongings long enough to admire the cut of the cassock.

Esther turned, looked, turned again, seeing herself from every angle possible in the room's full-length mirror. "No way Hrakar will mistake me for a man now."

Once packed they left the room, heading for the general store. Hrakar and the Valet were waiting for them outside with some sacks of beans and casks of fresh water. To Esther's complete surprise, Emon helped them load the fare into his cart.

“*Bona jurnee*,” he said, giving them a wave.

Esther tipped her had in response.

The Valet hefted up a sack into the cart, stopping dead when he saw the Peacekeeper. “Nice threads,” he said.

Esther didn't know what part of the world he'd picked up his idioms, but she thanked him for the compliment nonetheless. “I didn't realize you'd be joining us, Messire Emon,” she said.

Emon shrugged. "I have some goods to deliver to Portalaine." He finished loading two of the casks onto the cart, then hopped up onto the seat. "Would you care to ride with me, Peacekeeper Triad?"

Esther jumped aboard. "It would be my pleasure," she said. *Then perhaps,* she didn't add, *I can get some answers from you.*

The Valet looked at Leiyara. "I guess you'll be riding with me."

"Actually," Hrakar said, motioning to the stables. A Pah-ren stable boy who could be no more than fifteen came, leading Heartbreaker and a pair of clockwork horses. The freshly painted mechanical mounts shined in brilliant reds and yellows.

"I was asked to deliver these to you, Peacekeeper," the boy said. "As a gift from Ptolom, the tinker."

Esther got down from the cart, examining the pair of contraptions. As with all Agi work, the craftsmanship was perfect. The steel flanks were as hard as plate armor, the gears and cogs below well protected. The heads were sleek, hammered into the exact likeness of real horseflesh. They even had manes of soft, white hair and sightless eyes of fine-cut sapphire.

"They're beautiful," Esther said. "And we're deeply grateful, but there are only two and there are three of us."

The stable boy puzzled for a moment. "I was to understand that only three of our guests had any skill at riding, and one chose living horseflesh as a preference."

Esther looked about, seeing Leiyara redden and look away. *Another thing I'll have to teach you,* she thought.

"Do not despair, *mé flora,*" Emon said. "I need some company anyway – this old rickety cart gets quite lonely on long journeys."

Leiyara smiled but looked to Esther, as if for permission.

"Go ahead," Esther said. "Someone will need to keep an eye on our goods."

The red-haired girl excitedly hopped aboard, chattering to Emon about all she'd learned and seen in Patel. No doubt the poor Pah-ren farmer was in for an earful.

Hrakar joined Esther's side, standing pleasantly close while examining one of the clockwork horses. "It is no drake," he said. "But it will do."

They rode to meet the caravan at the edge of town. There were five covered wagons packed with crates, barrels, and sacks. A clockwork etroxin was hitched to each one, large and sturdy, built for hauling heavy loads. At the head of the group waited a woman dressed in a black wrap, adorned with bronze bracelets and arm rings. She stood out in stark contrast to the Pah-ren, who all wore dun-colored linens or khaki. Esther's best guess was that she was one of the Commerciers – a trader.

She greeted Esther by touching the tattoo on her upper arm – a coin with an anchor on its center. "Well met, Peacekeeper," the Commercier said, her Sapien fluent with only a trace of an accent. "I am Rae Commercier, the leader of this expedition."

"Well met, indeed," Esther replied. "I am Peacekeeper Esther Triad."

Rae smiled a little. "I know. Cami was quite adamant about you coming along."

Esther puzzled at this. She'd been expecting a warmer reception. "You don't fear the wraiths, or you don't believe we'll encounter any?"

The Agi woman just shrugged. "We have a Mysthunter, and I am handy with a blade myself." She examined Esther's features, then added, "We are grateful, however, for your company." This last was said as if rehearsed.

Grateful my eye, Esther thought. Either Rae was overconfident or Esther was being forced to waste her time. Either way, it galled her.

"And who are your friends?" Rae asked, a tactical change of subject.

Esther went around introducing each of her companions in turn.

Rae seemed quite impressed with the company she kept. "One hears much about *Le Valet des Coeurs* in the world. I look forward to seeing if you really are the greatest swordsman in Morgarai."

The Valet cracked a smile at her. "I look forward to exceeding your expectations," he said with a wink.

"And a Draconian Legionnaire," Rae continued. "Indeed you are an asset. You are paying your *echem* I assume?"

Hrakar gave a solemn nod. "You say true."

"Perhaps, after this journey, I will grant you a *kal* toward your honor."

A *kal*? Esther hadn't heard the term before. It meant stripe, didn't it? She filed it away to ask Hrakar later if they could be spared a quiet moment together. After last night, she very much hoped they could.

"A fire-touched girl as well," Rae observed, her red-brown eyes finally settling on Leiyara. "It is a rare thing among Sapien kind. Perhaps there is some Agi in you, as the legend goes?"

Poor Leiyara looked flustered. For one thing, she didn't know where to put her eyes. "Um...I don't...I don't know. Maybe."

Rae seemed as charmed with Esther's secretary as everyone else. "Well, to have one blessed by Virago is a boon to us." She glanced at Esther now, "Our route will take us near New Allyrion, but we must take a different path from there."

"Why is that?" the Valet interrupted.

"The city has an embargo on Central Transit within a certain radius," Esther replied. "They feel that the introduction of monetary wealth may threaten their economy."

Rae nodded. "It is so. Instead, we will go around the city and make for Alto Mecina, the nearest train depot. From there, we will use the railway to get to Portalaine." She looked up at the sky. "But, as you say, daylight is wasting. We must be off!"

The Commercier mounted her clockwork horse, shifting it into gear. The wagon train fell in behind her with Esther, the Valet, and Hrakar riding at its flanks. It didn't take long for Esther to pick out the Mysthunter among them: a young man dressed in dark grays and blues, a sharp contrast to his orange skin and red hair, but with his hood up he could blend seamlessly into the dismal landscape of Mystraam. He was armed with a longbow inscribed with runes and a quiver of arrows; at his side he wore a curved blade, also etched with runes. The young man had stern, scarred features that didn't pay the other guards any heed.

Such hubris, Esther thought. *But Ordo willing, they won't need us after all.*

Chapter Fourteen:
The Firala Riviera, Agimonde

They rode straight through the day, taking a lunch of flatbread and cheese on the go. The Valet was good enough to share his flask around. Leiyara and Emon spent their ride in pleasant conversation despite the blistering heat, while Esther and Hrakar passed the time by making eyes and flirtatious comments to one another. The Valet, seeing their fiery caravan leader as a new conquest, went back and forth to the head of the line to exchange pleasantries. Close to sundown – or sunfall as the Agi called it – they passed into the fertile lands along the Firala Riviera. Lining the roads were lush vegetation and tall palm trees heavy with gava melons and dekanuts. Once in a while they would snack on the fallen fruits, Esther reveling in the flavor of the dekanut milk and the cool, flaky flesh.

There were more farmers here than anywhere else in Agimonde, if Emon was to be believed, and they were able to grow corn and citrus fruits, as well as raise livestock. "This is the legacy of the Pah-ren," he said wistfully. "It is here that we are kings."

The boast would've gotten him a flogging by the upper castes, but Esther saw what he meant: unlike in Patel – or any city, she imagined – the Pah-ren here were hearty, healthy, and proud. They smiled and laughed even as they toiled. It seemed that peace and prosperity were as abundant here as their flora.

The caravan stopped to make camp at what the Agi called *prima nora*, or first dark, once the sun had vanished from the horizon. Rae also confided in Esther that it was bad luck to travel without Virago's Eye to guide them.

"In my faith," Esther replied, "it's similar, but we are guided by Ordo's chariot."

Rae seemed pleased with this answer. The Agi in general had a similar outlook on religion: both Virago and Ordo represented light and life, order among chaos. "Perhaps your god and my god should meet one day," she giggled, shooting the other woman a wink.

Esther wasn't one for blasphemy, but she smiled politely anyway.

They drove the wagons into a semi-circle with each group of wagoneers building a fire for the evening meal. Esther set up a perimeter and one of the guards would patrol it every hour, just to be safe. During Hrakar's patrol, Rae came to join the party. Leiyara labored over a pot of beans, sniffing at the seasonings Hrakar had given her while humming a tune to herself. The Valet lounged against Emon's wagon and smoked one of his fat cigars. Esther was watching their group of Pah-ren like a shepherd watches a flock.

"You needn't worry yet," Rae said, sitting next to the Peacekeeper. "The incursions are closer to the border, in the high desert. We will not see Myrian here."

Esther nodded. "Of course," she said, "but in Sapien, we have a saying: better safe than sorry."

Rae pondered this for a moment. "A wise policy."

Leiyara finally settled on the right flavors, allowing the pot to simmer undisturbed. In the firelight, one would mistake her for one of the Agi. "Pardon me, Rae," she said. "Can I ask you a question?"

"You may," Rae said.

Leiyara looked a little unsure of herself but urged herself on with her usual rapid-fire speech. "I noticed in town that whenever the...um...Pah-ren were around the other...well, the higher-up people that they always looked at their feet and didn't speak. But the Pahren here don't do that with you."

Rae nodded patiently. "And your question is why?"

"Um...yes."

"I was once one of them," Rae explained. "I worked in the house of one of the elder Commerciers. When he saw that I had a talent for money-counting and trade, he took me as an apprentice, raising me from Pah-ren."

"People can do that?" Leiyara asked, her eyes doubling in size. "I thought the Agi were born into their caste."

"Typically that is the case. But on occasion when a member of a caste – as you call it – recognizes a talent, they will take them into their *vamil* – or family, as you say – and train them."

"And the further up you go," Emon added, "the rarer that becomes."

Esther saw something peculiar here. She couldn't quite tell exactly what it was, but some tremor or vibration passed between Rae and Emon. She looked at him with something akin to caution, while he looked at her like a man desperate to keep a secret.

Secrets, Esther mused, *you have plenty of those, don't you Emon?*

Rae quickly recovered. "It is as he says. The Petrascels, for example, haven't taken an apprentice in nearly fifty years." She stood, rather more abruptly than she'd intended. "Pardon me. I must see to the others."

She disappeared among her people while Emon went back to tending his goat. Later that night Esther took watch while Hrakar, the Valet, and Leiyara slept. She walked the quarter-mile perimeter she'd established with ease among the sweet smells, the flow of the river, and the cool of the desert night. So much of this long journey had been pain and terror and blood that she had forgotten that there were still beautiful things in the world.

She topped a rise just behind the camp and found Emon with his back to her, relieving himself in the scrub.

"Beautiful night, isn't it?" he asked.

"That it is," Esther replied.

Emon did up his trousers, then lit one of his aromatic cigarettes. He breathed in the smoke and exhaled smoke rings into the still air. Esther felt compelled to keep up her patrol, but she and Emon were the only two awake. When else would she get this chance? "Who are you?" she asked.

Emon looked at her with feigned puzzlement. "Whatever do you mean?"

The Peacekeeper approached him and snatched the cigarette from his hand. She took a deep drag then handed it back. "You're no ordinary Pah-ren. I know that."

Now, the Agi smiled. "A test for your investigative skills, then. Who am I, Peacekeeper?"

"Well," Esther posited, "you speak Sapien fluently, although sometimes you pretend otherwise. You are quite educated, especially about matters outside your realm – runes and measures of distance and time. You know the history of the Elders and about the Valet's Rune Blade."

Emon nodded. "Go on."

Esther reached for his cigarette again, stealing another drag. "I take into account also that your average Pah-ren wouldn't have taken us in like you did, but would have summoned the nearest authority. You brought us to Patel, and then, in your way, led Cami Pretrascel to us by somehow planting the idea in her head that we would deliver them from the wraiths."

"My!" Emon exclaimed comically, thrilled by her analysis. "I do sound manipulative."

Esther returned his smile. "I imagine you used some brand of subterfuge to join the caravan as well. To what end, I'm not entirely sure."

"Your powers of observation are indeed keen, Peacekeeper," the Agi conceded with a grin. "Perhaps one day, I will answer your question." With that, Emon chuckled, pitched his cigarette, and returned to the camp.

••••

LEIYARA ONLY PRETENDED to sleep. Since the crash in the Gray Marsh and everything that followed, sleep hadn't come easy. Each time she closed her eyes the horrors assailed her again: watching that poor Freehold woman getting dragged away, seeing those things surrounding her with their whip-like fingers, watching Riggs being eaten alive by a daemonic fungus and killing Helena. Mostly, what she'd seen while she was alone haunted her, a sight both very real and entirely impossible all at once.

Primivite.

On the verge of sleep, the image of the creature's bony crown and eldritch eyes made her jerk awake. A constant whisper in an old, dead language rang in her ears for minutes, sometimes hours, after waking. She heard it now, those foreign tones that no living tongue could ever pronounce. Occasionally she thought she heard a word of Sapien sneak in. *But that's impossible,* she thought. *Isn't it?* Perhaps her brain just compansated for words it didn't understand.

She turned over on her side, away from the others. She didn't want them to see her silent tears or trembling hands. She wanted to be strong and not fall apart like everyone expected her to. But they were venturing into hostile territory again after so brief a period of rest and safety. Maybe Esther was right. It was so much more dangerous here than she ever could have imagined; she admonished herself for running off on her stupid adventure just to prove her mother wrong. Such a stupid, vapid girl, just like the old woman had said.

So Leiyara passed the night on the cusp of a nightmare.

Chapter Fifteen: The Highwaste, Agimonde

They had skirted around the Agi capital of New Allyrion to save time. Rae assured the party that taking the eastern bypass loop, although a few miles out of their way, would be shorter than trying to navigate the wagons and horses through the narrow city streets. "Besides," she joked, "we can't have every head of household asking you to dinner. We'd never leave!"

They crossed a sturdy stone bridge over the Firala Riviera. Hours later, Esther was disappointed to leave those beautiful green lands. By mid-day, they were working their way into up the rocky soil and winding, labyrinthine roads of the Highwaste. They urged their wagons up the steep inclines and meandering stretches, marveling at the sheer red cliff faces. Up here, the sparse vegetation grew spiny and waxen, evolved to hold in every last drop of moisture it could scrounge up.

At one point Esther went to touch one of the strange fronds and Hrakar gently caught her wrist. "You do not want to do that," he warned. "They call it painthistle. A single sting will put you in agony for days."

Esther withdrew her hand, glad he had stopped her. Hrakar loosened his grip, but his hand lingered on hers for a moment longer than necessary. Esther felt that warmth in her belly again, secretly longing for the moment when she and Hrakar were alone together.

The Highwaste leveled off by evening so they made camp on one of the bluffs overlooking the southwest. From up there Esther could see the road they'd taken, the riviera, and the widespread city of New Allyrion. There were clay structures that stood several stories, countless roads and streets, and an expanse that covered what seemed like half the desert.

"It's beautiful, isn't it?" the Valet asked from behind her.

Esther turned around to see him sitting on the back of Emon's cart, smoking another one of his cigars. The rest of the party built a fire as Emon regaled them with some story or another, making them guffaw. She wished she could be that jovial, but something had come over her since they'd entered the Highwaste: a sense of doom like a dark cloud even in the glaring desert sun.

"You feel it, too."

Esther nodded. "It feels like it did before the airship crash," she observed. "Or before we were attacked by those daemons in the Gray Marsh."

Leaving the card, the Valet joined her side. He offered her a cigar from a paper packet. She took one, he popped a match with this thumbnail, and lit it. The smoke formed a cloud in the still, dry air. They smoked in silence for a while, both trying to home in on the source of their shared dread.

"*Glaeve Pandaemonia* has been whispering of danger since we entered this Matron-forsaken place," the Valet said at last. "Not that it needed to. Every moment we spend here feels like someone walking over my grave."

Esther knew what he meant. That cold feeling hadn't left her stomach all day. "Could this be where the wraiths are waiting?" she asked.

The Valet shrugged. "I've encountered them so rarely that I couldn't say. I figure if its wraiths, they would have attacked us by now."

"We'll have a full watch tonight," Esther concluded. "You, me, and Hrakar, three hours each."

"I'm in total agreement," the Valet replied.

It was possibly the first time they'd agreed on anything since they'd met. If she hadn't already been worried, that alone would have been enough to put Esther on her guard.

• • • •

LEIYARA DREAMED, OR at least she thought so. In the dream, she was in another place, although she couldn't quite see clearly – it was as if she was looking at it through a translucent black veil, one that made the figures before her hazy, shifting shadows. *I'm invisible,* she thought, though her waking mind would have wondered where the thought had come from; to her dreaming self, it made perfect sense.

And there were voices, sounding warbling and *off* somehow, like the same invisibility casting a veil over her sight likewise affected her hearing.

...is approaching the canyon. Our forces are in place, one voice said. It sounded young, male. Perhaps a little older than her.

Wraiths and Sapiens, another voice said. This one deeper and older. *This operation will be highly suspect.*

A third voice, this one rich, velvety, feminine. *It is a means to an end.*

If all goes to plan, no one will live to tell about it. The young man's voice.

The older man: *Regardless, take the weather wizard with you. He may come in handy.*

There was a moaning sound, then the sound of chains rattling. It was followed by the hollow thump of a boot on flesh. *You heard the man,* the young man's voice said. *Get moving.* He sighed. *Translocation sickness again...*

A brief silence followed, then Leiyara felt a wave of power, like a strong gust of wind, push at her. It felt like she floated just above the ground, like she had to compensate by pushing herself forward. She sensed that the young man and another presence – this one larger and more imposing, although he was chained – had vanished.

Now, onto other matters, the older voice said. *I don't share our brother's confidence that this gamble will pay off. I want you to secure us a little insurance, just in case.*

She sensed rather than saw a predatory smile on a dangerously beautiful face. *I have just the thing. Leave it to me.*

After another wave of force the feminine presence disappeared.

That force swept against Leiyara again, then another wave of something else – like pressure on her chest. Her head swam, making her nauseous.

What's wrong? The older voice asked. *Don't tell me you don't approve of our methods.*

Then, she spoke. The voice that issued from her mouth wasn't hers, and she had no control over the words. It was raspy, whispering, the same voice she'd heard in the Gray Marsh. *Our little spy,* it said. *She's listening.*

How is that possible? The elder voice grinned, she could sense it. *Slipping in your old age, are you?*

A flash of anger. She swore at the owner of the older voice in a language she didn't know.

"Leiyara?"

The sensation of waking, staggering – she stood upright, which was unexpected. When she'd gone to sleep, she'd been lying on her bedroll by Emon's wagon. Now, it seemed, she'd walked a few yards from the camp to stand before a worn piece of carved stone that jutted up from the rocky ground. It differed from the red rock formations in the area, so it couldn't possibly have belonged here.

"Leiyara? Are you all right, child?" Emon's voice, soothing and familiar – not alien and malicious like the voices in her dreams.

She hugged herself, trying to curl up as much as possible while remaining vertical. "I...um...I think I was sleepwalking. I had a bad dream."

Emon put an arm around her, leading her back to camp. “Come away from the stone, child. They say it is cursed,” he said. “I'll make you some tea and you can tell me all about it.”

Chapter Sixteen: Alor Canyon, Agimonde

Rae had just informed them that they'd reached the halfway point of their journey when Hrakar came down from one of the crags to speak to the Valet in hushed tones. Once they'd passed out of the Highwaste and into Alor Canyon the terrain grew rockier, the road became gravel. The caravan rolled so slowly that Hrakar had taken to vaulting up the various crags and outcroppings to scout.

During one of these jaunts, Hrakar glimpsed something ahead then nimbly leaped down to meet with the Valet, who rode at the head of the caravan; Esther guarded the rear again. When the Valet raised a fist to halt the party, she rode ahead up the narrow road to find out what was happening. She found Hrakar and the Valet whispering, carefully glancing around a bend in the road.

"What's happening?" the Peacekeeper asked, dismounting and joining the men.

The Valet cocked his thumb around the bend. "Is it just me, or does that look like the perfect place for an ambush?"

Esther hugged the cliff wall, peering around the corner. Just ahead, the path narrowed further, framed by two high, sheer cliffs. She could see the Valet's point: anyone with bows or rifles could make a bottleneck out of the ravine.

"It would be the place I choose," Hrakar remarked.

Esther turned to them, falling back on her combat training. "If there are snipers, they're already positioned on each cliff."

"And probably a group lying in wait for us inside the ravine," the Valet added. "That's what I'd do."

Esther scanned the ravine again. "Is there a way to get to those cliffs without being spotted?" she asked Hrakar.

His amber eyes squinted in thought. "There is a goat herder's trail up the one side..." he indicated the southwestern cliff, "...and the other side is a sheer drop. One would have to climb quietly."

Esther nodded, turning to the Mysthunter. "What's your name, soldier?" she asked in Agish.

The young man, taken aback at being addressed in his language, replied, "Adon." He touched the tattoo on his upper arm as if in a salute – an ornate depiction of a bow notched with a flaming arrow.

"Good," Esther said, switching back to Sapien. "I hope you're feeling limber, Adon?"

They made a plan. Hrakar and Adon would climb the northwest cliff with all possible stealth while Esther and the Valet made their way up the goat herder's trail. The caravan would continue through the pass as if they didn't suspect an attack.

"You have a word for that in Sapien," Rae remarked drily. "It is called 'bait.'"

Nevertheless, the Commercier went back to relay the orders to the caravan. If there were any assailants on the ground on their side, Esther hoped that Rae and Emon could fight them off. They parted, executing their plans. Esther and the Valet climbed the rocky rise to a scrubby incline that curved around to meet the southwestern cliff, little more than a worn groove in the dirt. Esther looked across the way, catching a glimpse of Hrakar and Adon making their silent ascent.

The trail wound around the scrub, Esther and the Valet staying low to avoid detection. In anticipation of a fight, Esther drew her new pistol; she could feel the Force runes drawing in the kinetic energy of her movements. The Valet carried *Glaeve Pandaemonia* in one hand although the Rune Blade must have had some heft to it. If it did, his arm didn't appear to notice. Below, the caravan made its slow way toward the canyon, generating enough noise and dust with the creaking carts and Emon's braying alpaco to hide the defenders as they climbed.

They were right to be suspicious. Esther and the Valet caught sight of the first sniper as soon as they made the top of the cliff. He dressed in khaki, watching the caravan over the bead of his rifle. Esther raised her pistol, but the Valet put a hand up, then put a finger to his lips. *Quiet*. Esther nodded, circling behind the sniper. They were upon him before he knew they were there.

"Peacekeeper," Esther announced. "Lay down arms." She cocked her revolver to make a point.

The sniper hesitated, looking at her through the corner of his eye. Then, he went for his knife. The Valet's Rune Blade made a squishing sound as it pierced the man's back, then a horrible sucking sound as it lapped up his blood.

On the other side, Hrakar and Adon had dispatched their first sniper as well. One of Adon's arrows had pierced his belly while Hrakar skewered him through the throat.

Esther glanced down, finding that the caravan had nearly caught up with them. "We'd best move quickly," she told the Valet, who slid his sword out of the exsanguinated corpse. The Rune Blade's eye opened now, blazing the crimson of fresh blood.

And that's when all the Void broke loose.

The cliff walls behind and before the caravan exploded in a cacophony of dust and noise. The earth shook, dropping Esther and the Valet to their knees. Above them, thunder roared as storm clouds suddenly formed, unleashing a torrential downpour. The sound of shouting and screaming followed by the clash of metal erupted below.

"Wraiths!" someone shouted. Esther barely heard it over the ringing in her ears.

The Peacekeeper shook her head, trying to regain her senses, trying to see through the rain and the dust, trying to stand up in the thick red mud that soaked her boots. The caravan was under attack, the reports of encroaching gunfire were moving closer. She looked down, seeing the wagons blocked in by rubble and debris. Iridescent blue forms, cloaked and hooded, were closing on it. She felt a hand on her shoulder – the Valet, or at least she thought it was. She seemed to be looking at him from the bottom of a well.

"Pull it together, Triad!" he shouted. "We're moving. Back down the path. Come on!"

He wrenched her to her feet, half-dragging her down the mountain path.

• • • •

LEIYARA HAD BEEN HALF dozing in the seat next to Emon when the cliffs collapsed. The force of the explosion rocked the earth, shaking the cart and dumping her to the gravel. She landed hard on her hands and knees, scraping them. Beside her, the caravan came to an abrupt halt. Shouting erupted, the dust devolving into confusion while Rae, at the head of the line, barked orders to the Pah-ren in Agish. People scurried about, frightened and seeking safety under their wagons. A slight few armed themselves with whatever they could find. A woman clutching a mining pick guarded the wagon in front of Leiyara; others gathered around Rae with shovels, knives, and hatchets.

"Get up now, child," Emon said to her. He came to her aid, but his eyes scanned the sky.

Leiyara got to her feet, forcing her dread back down and trying to keep from shaking. She followed Emon's gaze to the clouds forming overhead, roiling and appearing out of nothing. It didn't take much to guess that it was spellcraft. Thunder boomed and, a moment later, the clouds burst, pouring rain over them. The dry earth swallowed it greedily, turning the pass into a gravelly mud.

Then someone shouted. "Wraiths!"

The group of Agi congregating around Rae scrambled, taking up defensive positions. Leiyara went for Esther's bag, frantically searching for her old revolver, but Emon grabbed her hand. "No, my dear," he said. "Conventional weapons do not work on wraiths." He reached inside his shirt, producing a knife whose blade glowed with red runes. "Take this and stay close to me."

Emon crouched down, drawing two long, slim blades from his boots; the pommels were fashioned into black serpents' heads giving Leiyara the sudden impression that Emon was no ordinary Pah-ren. More cries of alarm sounded from the line ahead. Leiyara turned her attention to the cliffside and her heart leaped into her throat. These things that could only be called wraiths were at once beautiful and terrifying; they floated down the cliffs, little more than cloaks and hoods rimmed with an incandescent blue light, billowing in a nonexistent wind. Ghastly pale faces with hollow eyes glared out and gnarled, corpse-like hands curled around sickles and scythes.

As the wraiths landed, a few Pah-ren struck at them with their makeshift weapons. Leiyara watched as a shovel passed right through a wraith; it shrieked, embedding its sickle into the Agi's guts. More attacks followed, the wraiths striking out at the Agi, the Agi clashing weapons with them, and swinging in futilely at their misty forms. Now and again one would become solid enough to take a blow and scatter into ash and shadow, but the wraiths had the obvious advantage.

Emon moved to engage the enemy, whirling and dodging their strikes with incredible speed. When he struck, the runes on his blade blazed with fire causing the wraiths to burst into momentary flames before turning to ash. Leiyara stayed as close as she could to Emon, unable to track everything happening around her. Wraiths screeched, Agi screamed, rifle shots rang out from above them, the rain poured down, making the ground slick and uneven.

In all the chaos, Leiyara lost track of Emon. Shaking and terrified, she put her back to one slick cliff side, clutching Emon's knife in front of her. She watched a wraith grappling with a Pah-ren, who screamed curses or prayers to Virago while the wraith stabbed him with a serrated dagger. As the fire faded from the Agi's eyes the wraith turned on Leiyara, staring at her through two empty hollows. Its mouth contorted into a vicious smile as it advanced on her.

It's so fast! Leiyara thought vaguely. And it was true: the wraith seemed to take a few loping steps, fade into mist, then reappear closer, then fade again. It set upon her before she could react, shrieking that horrible, metallic whine into her face. Its breath reeked of stagnant bogs and brackish mires.

Whispering a prayer to the Matron, she thrust Emon's knife at her attacker. She couldn't feel the blade make contact, as if stabbing the air, but she did feel the heat of the runes. The wraith screamed as it burst into a cloud of cinders, scorching Leiyara's hand and strands of her hair. The wraith's knife clanged as it struck the muddy rocks. Leiyara glanced down and recognized it as a fishing knife. Had the wraith been a fisherman once?

A shot rang out from above, splashing in the mud a few feet in front of her. Leiyara pressed herself back against the cliff, looking up. A man – a Sapien man – cocked his rifle to take another potshot at her when flaming arrow struck him in the side of his face. A few yards away, Adon stood with his bow notched with another arrow. He gave Leiyara a nod and drew his arrow in the direction of the wraiths. The arrow sparked on something – perhaps like a striking strip on a box of matches? – and it blazed with arcane red flame. The Mysthunter fired, reducing a nearby wraith turned into smoldering embers.

"Leiyara!" someone shouted. "To me!"

Leiyara glanced to her right, relieved to see Esther and the Valet running toward her. She was so filled with relief she nearly wept. On shaking and muddy legs, she ran.

••••

THEY MADE IT TO THE bottom of the cliff, slipping and sliding the whole way down the goatherd's trail. The Valet seemed to use the slick terrain to his advantage, skidding down huge swaths of the distance while using his greatsword for balance. Esther, on the other hand, wasn't as graceful: she held onto the scrub for leverage, falling more than once. One of the riflemen from the clifftop had pursued them, but Esther made short work of him by putting two bullets into his center mass. She marked him as the first Sapien she'd ever killed; somehow she felt little difference to slaying a daemon: a threat was a threat.

The wraiths swarmed the caravan, floating and misting about like ghosts. As they approached the spot where the cliff had collapsed, Esther took a shot at one. The bullet passed through it, a tiny wisp of mist trailing it. The wraith, unharmed, turned to shriek at her. Esther remembered just in time that wraiths – all of the Myrian race, for that matter – were semi-corporeal beings. Unless they made themselves solid by a monumental effort of the will, only magicks could harm them. That was why the runeguards of old Wraithbane had wielded the Rune Blades in the first place. As if to demonstrate, the Valet mounted the rubble, planting his Rune Blade in the wraith's skull. The malignant thing burst into a cloud of ash and dust, all that remained of a body it no longer possessed.

Esther followed him up the rubble pile and what she saw in the canyon was the stuff of nightmares. The wraiths closed in on the Pahren, who fought back impotently with their tools. Rae and Emon fought back-to-back with Runic weapons, trying to draw the wraiths off. Leiyara cowered against a cliff wall. Esther was about to shout, or move, or something, but Leiyara's attacker turned into a cloud of embers, revealing a rune-engraved knife in the girl's hand.

Good girl!

The Valet started down the rubble pile, swinging his Rune Blade at the wraiths surrounding Emon and Rae. Esther chased after him, thrusting a bayonet at the nearest wraith. The force runes activated with a hard recoil as the blade connected, scattering her target to the wind.

"Leiyara!" she shouted. "To me!"

The red-haired girl looked about wildly, then her huge eyes settled on Esther, filling with tears of relief. As she broke into a run a wraith swooped down, snatching her from behind. With a wave of its hand and a few arcane words, the wraith and Leiyara were lifted by a gust of wind. They were gone before Esther could do anything, spirited away above the canyon walls and moving southeast.

"Leiyara!" Esther cried after them.

The Valet grabbed her, spinning her around. "She's gone!" he yelled. "Focus on the fight!"

So she did. Blinded by her rage, Esther dove at the wraiths that assailed her companions. She swung her bayonets deftly and wildly, killing wraith after wraith. At one point – she didn't remember when – she holstered one revolver to summon glyphs, feeding her anger into the Source. Lights and luminous weapons flew from her hand, sending her enemies to their flaming end.

The Valet fought as fiercely, parrying the wraiths' weapon strikes, bouncing their magicks off of his dread blade, and cutting them down in turn. The rain mingled with ash and dust, covering them in a sooty paste. Their ferocity attracted the attention of other wraiths, who moved to charge when one of them cried out. Esther didn't catch all of what he said, but she did hear the Myrian for "Rune Blade". The wraiths turned their hollow eyes to the Valet, who brandished *Glaeve Pandaemonia* above his head. When they saw the weapon, the wraiths howled in rage and fear, then scattered. Within the span of a moment, the canyon quieted, the rain stopped, and the sky cleared, allowing the blazing sun to shine once again.

• • • •

"HOW DID YOU KNOW TO do that?" Rae asked the Valet after the fight was over.

They were going through the caravan, assessing the damage. Six of the Pah-ren were dead, four more wounded. One of the wagons was rendered unserviceable, having been crushed by the rock slide and looted for any salvageable goods. The caravan's cash box had also been stolen, drawing an Agish curse from Rae's lips. As if that wasn't enough, his Peacekeeper companion occupied herself with chomping at the proverbial bit to rush off to the southeast after Leiyara.

Howling Void, he silently cursed. *Something else I'm going to have to deal with.*

Rae still looked at him expectantly. The Valet forgot that she'd asked him a question. "The Blade once belonged to the Elder Xanos, the leader of the runeguards, also called Wraithbane. It remembers them," he replied. "It could sense their fear."

Suppressing a shudder, she looked at *Glaeve Pandaemonia,* saying something in Agish and drawing some religious symbols in the air. The Valet glanced over at Emon, who worked with an Agi priest – they called them "viziers", whatever that meant – to tend to the dead. The ritual consisted of removing the ruby-like stone from their brows, saying a few words dedicating their souls to Virago, and, of course, burning the stones – the Agi liked to burn things. The corpses were stacked and left to rot.

"Why do they just discard the bodies?" he asked Rae.

She glanced up at the vizier and Emon, caught the shifty Pah-ren's eye, then looked away quickly. *More than meets the eye, that one,* the Valet thought.

"The Agi soul resides in the *petravir* – firestone, as you would say. Once it is removed, the body is no longer Agi, but empty fired clay. It returns to the earth, while our spirits return to the Brazier of Life, waiting to be born again."

The Valet didn't buy into any of that religious hocus pocus, but he considered it a beautiful myth nonetheless. "What happens if the firestone is removed while the Agi is still alive?" he asked.

Again, Rae made that symbol in the air. "We do not speak of such things," she said curtly, returning to her business.

The Valet turned back to Esther, who spoke privately with Hrakar. He sauntered over to see what was happening, catching the Draconian appealing to Esther not to run off in search of Leiyara.

"She is important to us all," he pleaded, "but these people are important, too."

"He's right," the Valet interjected. "You have a duty to these people and your mission. By Ordo's word and the Unbound Law, these ideals must come first. Your vow as a Peacekeeper binds you."

Esther kicked the dirt, an act of impotent frustration. "Don't you think I know that?" she shouted. "You don't believe in anything! Who are you to lecture me?"

The Valet shrugged. "You're right," he said calmly. "I have no gods and I'm bound by no vows. Which is why *I'm* going to find her."

Both Esther and Hrakar looked shocked.

The Valet cocked a grin at them, trying to look more confident than he felt. "What? I can't resist a damsel in distress." He threw in a wink for good measure.

The truth was he liked Leiyara, and not just because she was a plucky redhead with long legs. Her bond with Esther, her ability to navigate the bureaucracy of the Central Authorities, and that strange ability of hers to rally the group made her its heart. She was an asset to the mission. Her being a plucky redhead with long legs didn't hurt, though.

"The wraith took her southeast," the Valet said. "I imagine its heading to Mystraam with her, although I don't want to guess why. I'll ride fast. In the meantime, take the caravan ahead to Alto Mecina. I'll catch up with you there."

Esther looked at Hrakar, who nodded his agreement. "Alright," she said. "Bring her back to us."

The Valet mounted Heartbreaker but didn't bother stowing his Rune Blade. With any luck, he'd soon be using it. "That's the plan," he replied. He nudged Heartbreaker and took off like a shot, riding hard to the southeast.

Chapter Seventeen:
The Standing Stones, Agimonde

Leiyara awoke with a start. The last thing she remembered was struggling to breathe as something in the darkness clutched at her with clammy, dead fingers. It felt like drowning. She didn't know what was happening. She moved to get up off the soppy ground but felt the pull of rope against wrists and ankles.

She was tied up.

Panic struck her as she thrashed against her bonds. Thick gray rope staked her to the ground. There were glowing blue symbols, ephemeral and misty, hovering over their carved likeness in the soil – she lay in some kind of rune circle.

Struggling did no good, so she laid back and forced herself to breathe. Deep inhale, slow exhale, the way she'd done when her mother locked her in a closet as a child. In, out. In, out. On the tenth slow breath she regained her senses. Yes, she was lying in some ritual circle; yes she was bound at the wrists and ankles. What else? The sky was still gray, but the rain had turned into a spitting drizzle. Large stone monoliths were sticking up from the earth, each carved with an arcane symbol, each symbol projecting a colored rune in ethereal light all the colors of the rainbow.

Standing stones. Leiyara had read all about them in her novels. They were old places of worship, old even when the Elders had arrived thousands of years ago. They were built on the intersections of leylines – veins of Source energy crisscrossing the planet, flowing like lifeblood. She never thought she'd see them close up, and wished to the Matron that it was under better circumstances.

Esther will come, Leiyara thought, prayed. *Esther will save me.*

Will she, though? That voice in her head that sounded like her mother. Or maybe that whisper that haunted her nightmares? Or both at once? *Why in the Void would she come for you? She has the*

Draconian and the Valet, Emon and Rae. She has useful people around that are worth protecting.

Leiyara couldn't help it: a tear trickled from the corner of her eye. It sparked when it touched the rune circle.

A rustling sound off to her left drew her attention. She looked up to see the wraith who had captured her. He knelt before a crude altar out of rocks, chanting his spellcraft over it. When he looked at her, his eyes were no longer hollow; they were the blue-green color of the sea. He had thin, blue-black hair and flesh the color of old grease, like a corpse.

"Sh sh sh," the wraith hushed then said something in his native Myrian, low and haunting, dirge-like.

"Please," Leiyara pleaded, "let me go."

For a brief moment she saw pity in those blue-green eyes, then the wraith's face contorted into one of hatred. He spat a curse at her in his dark brogue, then went back to chanting.

What would Esther do? Leiyara wondered. Easy, she'd twist up her fingers into one of those Light spells of hers, raining the Void down on this horrible creature. But Leiyara didn't know any glyphs, she couldn't channel the Source. She looked around for anything she could use, but she had left her knapsack in Emon's cart, the knife he'd given her dropped during her abduction. There wasn't even a sharp stone nearby; the circle had been cleared of all debris.

A useful girl could find a way out, that mixed voice said. *A useful girl wouldn't have to lay here and submit to this man. I always knew you'd end up dying spread-eagle with a man on top of you.*

The voice laughed, a mix of her mother's light tinkling titter and the whisper's shrill giggle. Unable to stop herself, Leiyara started to sob. She had no other options left.

The wraith stood, finishing his incantation. He held what looked like a double-bladed knife, etched with runes that glowed an eerie blue-black color. At the same time, the magick circle around her turned the same blue-black. Leiyara felt a cold feeling wash over her as her heart dropped into her stomach.

Shadow magick.

Shadowmancy was forbidden in Perdition – like in most parts of the world, as it was a close cousin to daemon magick – almost to the point of being outlawed. Growing up, Leiyara had heard terrible tales about Shadowmancers raising the dead, summoning horrors from the Outer Dark, and twisting the hearts of people. Now she faced a similar fate.

Entering the circle now, the wraith approached her, still chanting his dark arcana. Leiyara struggled feebly against her bonds, desperate and crying. Her captor positioned himself over her, straddling her midsection while holding his two-bladed dagger above her heart. She felt a surge of energy pulse through her, making her convulse. Feeling suddenly empty, her vision blurred, and she had the nauseating sensation of suddenly shifting perspective. When things came back into focus she stared down at herself – red hair, frightened face, but she had eyes the color of the sea; the wraith's eyes.

She felt hollow, cold. The wind and misty drizzle didn't touch her skin. The earth beneath her knees felt soft and spongy like in the Gray Marsh. The world had no color, no scent, no *life*.

Is this how it feels to be a wraith? She wondered idly. *Is this how they're forced to live?*

Leiyara closed her eyes, only vaguely aware of the cold tears running down her cheeks. She understood the wraith's hatred and hostility now, felt within her the need to shed blood just to feel something again. No longer could she discern which feelings were hers and which were the wraith's. She gripped the double-bladed knife now, incantations in a language she didn't understand issued from her lips, in her voice. She just needed to stop and it would be over, but she had to keep going. She needed to feel alive again.

No, she thought. *The wraith needs to feel alive again. I'm not a wraith.*

She closed her mouth, cutting off the incantation. Below her, the red-haired girl that she used to be stiffened and went blank somehow. Her eyes darkened from that sea-green back to the flame-flecked brown that she saw every day in the mirror. Somewhere inside her head another presence, *another mind*, raged at her, struggling for purchase; she felt its fear and confusion, its desperation for control.

How does it feel to be tied down? She thought at it. *How does it feel to be helpless?*

The raging mind stopped, now full of paralytic terror that she felt like a blast of snow in the face. *How are you doing this?* The wraith's mind asked. In her head, the wraith spoke Myrian, but the voice somehow echoed to her in Sapien at the same time. Blinking against the dissonance, Leiyara once again felt the prodding of that mind, hearing a single word. It didn't translate into Sapien.

Delkynian.

Before she could ask the wraith what that meant, she used his hands to try to unbind the hands of the red-haired girl that she was pretty sure was also named Leiyara. Seeing herself from the outside without the aid of a silvered glass was quite the experience, but she tried to bear with it and untie the knots. To her dismay, the fingers of that dreadful hand passed right through the rope.

What do I do? She asked the Wraith. *How do I make it so I can touch things?*

The knife. She held a knife.

She froze as a rush of power washed over her like a tidal wave, washed over the rune circle. Feeling wrenched aside, the world spun again and she found herself looking up at the sky, her hands and feet bound once again. There was warmth within her, a heartbeat, cold mist numbing her face and fingers. Taking a deep breath, Leiyara looked around, trying to gain some sense of what had just happened. The wraith who took her lay on the ground in a heap, trying to regain control of himself. The rune circle broke, disintegrating into the mist. To her right stood another figure: he, too, wore a wispy blue cloak that seemed to flutter and float on its own breeze. He, too, had those sea-green eyes. She would have thought he was another wraith were it not for his healthy-looking, blue-tinted skin and the softness of his features.

This must be a true Myrian, she thought.

Her rescuer spread his gloved hands, chanting an incantation in that melodic, dirge-like language. On her other side, the wraith trembled, outlined in an iridescent glow. With a deep, mournful howl the poor creature dispersed into the mist. The next thing Leiyara knew, someone was untying her.

"You are fortunate I am here," her rescuer said in a thick accent. *Ye're fartenate oi was 'ere.*

"Who are you?" Leiyara asked, rubbing at the wrists that were now free, but chafed to the Void.

"My name is Dal," her rescuer said as he worked the knots around her ankles.

Leiyara looked over to where the wraith had been. No ash or dust, no burning embers like the wraiths she'd seen die. Only his ritual knife remained. "Did you kill him?" she asked, her heart filling with pity for the poor, lost soul trapped in a living nightmare.

Dal finished with her bonds, helping her to her feet. His hands were cold and clammy as well, but at least they felt alive. "Would you object if I had?" he asked.

She looked at her feet, feeling ashamed for pitying someone who tried to do whatever it was the wraith tried to do to her. "I think maybe I would," she answered. "When he did...whatever it was, I felt what it was like living like that. It was awful."

Dal put a finger under her chin, guiding her eyes to his. "There's no shame in that, *lassai*. The Fallen are deserving of our mercy."

She nodded but looked away. Her rescuer was intense and beautiful, making her fear what she would feel if she looked too long, like something out of one of her novels. Instead, she tried to collect her thoughts.

"It was a spell to disperse him back into the Mist," Dal explained. "He'll awaken in our homeland in a few years, rested and relieved of his madness."

Despite what he had done to her, Leiyara took comfort that her captor would know some peace. "Is that what happens to your kind? Being taken by madness and hatred?"

Now Dal took his turn to look away. The question seemed to overwhelm him with sorrow. "*Aya*," he affirmed. "If we cannot have our rest. Since the Ruin, there is little respite for my people."

So many questions but no time. "I have to get back to my friends," she said. "Will you help me?"

Dal smiled. "I am at your service, *lassai*."

Chapter Eighteen:
On the outskirts of the Alor Canyon, Agimonde

The Valet stopped briefly at the edge of the cloud cover, dismounted, and examined the ground. Tracking a wraith wasn't easy, but there were telltale signs – a fresh misting over the earth, a twig of scrub bent against the wind. He touched the damp red earth, sniffed it: that dank stink of stagnant, brackish water. The wraith had been here, still moving southeast toward Mystraam. But there was something else, too, something that *Glaeve Pandaemonia* whispered to his unconscious mind.

"Why are you following me?" he asked his pursuer.

From one of the rock formations behind him, Adon appeared. The boy looked surprised that he'd been discovered, but even the Valet had to concede that he wouldn't have detected the Mysthunter's presence without help – the kid was *that* good. He was also fast. The Valet had ridden at a full gallop for nearly two hours now yet somehow he'd managed to keep pace. Some kind of sorcery, perhaps.

"I am pursuing the wraith, not you," Adon answered. "Or your friend."

The Valet chuckled. "And I'm pursuing a friend, not a wraith. Good thing we have our priorities straight."

Adon wasn't amused. "We should move forward."

Nodding, the Valet mounted his horse. "You're right," he said, "daylight's wasting."

Chapter Nineteen: Alor Canyon, Agimonde

The Pah-ren were arguing, huddled together in a group around Rae. Esther's Agish was serviceable, but they were going so fast and talking so out of turn that she had given up trying to listen. Emon, who managed the huddle, would fill her in later. In the meantime, she sat on the edge of Emon's cart, covered in dirt, feeling soggy and miserable. Defending the caravan had been her purpose and, once again, she'd failed. The mounting death toll, Leiyara being captured, even the money box being taken was her fault.

Hrakar, who had been keeping watch, sat down beside her. "You are doing it again," he observed.

"Doing what?" Esther asked absently, her eyes scanning the southeastern cliff face as if she could see through it.

"Blaming yourself for what happened," he took her hand, which forced her to look at him. "These Agi knew the risk in going this route, and they would have been here regardless of our escort. None of us expected the ambush to be so fierce."

Esther shook her head, dismissing his rationalizations. No, if she were better, stronger, faster to act, she could have saved them all.

Hrakar squeezed her hand while she clung to it like a life raft. "Think of it this way: how much worse would it have been if we were not here?"

That sunk in. Were it not for her, Hrakar, and the Valet, the snipers and wraiths would have wiped out the entire caravan and taken everything they had. Still, the fact that she had only minimized the damage instead of preventing it altogether hung heavy on her.

Wait...snipers? Sapien snipers?

She'd nearly forgotten about them in all the chaos and confusion. An alliance between Sapien men and Myrian wraiths was unheard of. Since they took opposing sides during the Daemon Wars, the Myrian and Sapien races still held old grudges. Sure, once in a great while one came across the Myrian out in the world, but they were neither trusted nor well-liked.

Esther stood, hurrying to the edge of the huddle. "What's going on?" she asked with all the authority she could muster. "Why aren't we moving?"

The group quieted, some of the Pah-ren instinctively looking at their feet while others glared their naked resentment at her. Rae and Emon broke off from the group and came to her. "The Pah-ren are still clearing the path ahead," Rae answered. "And the wraiths took our stake, the money to pay for food, lodging, and shipping our goods. Without it, we have nothing."

"So, we turn back?" Esther asked.

Emon scoffed. "If these Pah-ren return without completing their task, they will be imprisoned or flogged, or both. Rae will lose her status among the Agi and become Pah-vul – the 'not seen' – an outcast made to scratch a living from the wastes."

Rae nodded her agreement, chewing her lip in worry.

Esther took off her hat, mopping the sweat from her brow with a handkerchief. "Ordo's beard," she swore. *The stakes here are a lot higher than I imagined.* "Did you see who took your money and which way they went?"

Emon nodded. "I know the way."

Of course you do, Esther thought. *There's very little you don't know, you old snake.*

Next, she turned to Hrakar. "Can you get them moving?" she asked.

Hrakar nodded. "I will make a compelling case. I can keep them safe."

The way I couldn't, Esther thought. "Good." She turned back to Rae. "Emon and I will get your stake back. If we don't catch up to you on the road, then we'll see you in Alto Mecina."

This seemed to satisfy Rae. She took the proposal back to the Pah-ren and, after another heated exchange, they packed up to resume their journey. Hrakar mounted his clockwork horse, giving her a wave and a reassuring nod. "I will see you soon, *min voga*," he said.

As they rode away, Emon gave Esther a sly smile. Esther reddened a little. "My little bird?" he asked, effortlessly translating the Draconian phrase.

"Shut up and ride," Esther replied.

Chapter Twenty:
On the outskirts of Alor Canyon, Agimonde

They came upon the wraith camp about half an hour later. For the Valet, who had little experience with the Myrian, the sight was strange to behold. They were huddled around in a circle, no longer in their dread forms with hollow eyes and a blue sheen. They looked like ordinary folk now, men and women with sea-green eyes and hair the colors of ocean waves: one had a blue-black mane while another had the white of seafoam. Their flesh, or the illusion of flesh, was still a mottled gray-green, like that of a corpse. In the center of the huddle floated a large glowing orb emitting a soft blue light; the wraiths appeared to be basking in it, feeding off of its energy.

The Valet wiped the cold mist from his eyes; wherever the wraiths went, the weather seemed to follow. He and Adon hunkered behind a rocky outcropping, unseen by the camp at the bottom of a steep rise.

"We should execute them," Adon said, an edged enthusiasm in his voice.

The Valet had considered it. The wraiths were ferocious, mercilessly killing the Pah-ren he was meant to defend. Worse yet, they had kidnapped his friend. But seeing them now, not as hollow, ghastly shells, but as real people, he hesitated. What these poor, destitute people had to do to survive would be unimaginable torment to him.

"Or we could go around," he said to the Mysthunter, who had already notched one of his enchanted arrows.

Unflappable as usual, Adon drew his arrow back, igniting the Runic arrowhead with a red blaze of arcane flame. "What?"

"In case you didn't notice," the Valet said, masking his true intentions, "we're outnumbered. And we don't exactly have time for this." It wasn't exactly a lie, though the Valet had never really concerned himself with numbers when it came to a brawl, plus going around would cost them even more time than a straight fight.

Adon grinned a cruel grin. "My purpose is to hunt wraiths. Go and save your girl if you must. These are mine."

You're going to get your fool self killed, the Valet thought.

It was too late anyway – not that the Valet had any qualms about leaving the Mysthunter to his doom. The Myrian, probably some watch the wraiths had established, sounded the alarm; Adon's fiery arrowhead acted like a beacon, the damned thing was probably visible for miles. It sounded like breath through a conch shell mobilizing the wraiths at the camp as they assumed their ghastly shapes once again. Both the entire camp and the hills around it erupted with their shrieking.

Before the Valet could stop him, Adon loosed his arrow. It struck one of the wraiths, who had been a comely Myrian woman only a moment ago, in the face. She screamed, burning to ash while the others charged the hill.

The Valet leaped out from behind the rock, raising the Weapon of Wraithbane. Behind him, he heard Adon strike another arrow, filling the wet air with a phosphorescent red glow. "Cover me and don't shoot me in the ass," he ordered. He caught Adon's nod from the corner of his eye.

The wraiths surged up the hill, moving in their strange in-and-out, misty fashion, phasing through the drizzle from one step to another, and covering incredible swaths of ground with each movement. Three of them cast magicks to ride the wind, soaring over the surging throng. Adon quickly took out the first of the fliers, firing his arrows in rapid succession, working his sparking bow like mad. The airborne wraiths burst into flames, their ashes sizzling into nothing in the rain. The Valet, meantime, held his position, allowing the leading wraith the first strike. *Glaeve Pandaemonia's* response rent the attacker's sickle in two; a second slash did much the same to the wraith. Through the scattering of ashes, the Valet saw the remaining mob halt their advance, a momentary hesitation while the wave of fear moving through them turned to anger, then to hatred so strong that *Glaeve Pandaemonia* trembled; its runes blazed, its eye narrowed.

Another volley of Adon's fiery arrows made them forget their fear, and the wraiths surged forward again. The Valet struck another, but it faded into the mist, rematerializing behind him. He turned instead to strike down another one, clash blades with a third, and trust that the heat he felt at his back was Adon's arrow destroying the clever bastard.

It was neither a long nor particularly glorious battle. The Valet moved like water, despite his size, feinting and dancing around the wraith's simple weapons. He cut them down with ease, one after another. Adon covered him, blazing arrows loosed with blinding speed. Within the span of perhaps five minutes, the ten or so wraiths that the Valet had counted were reduced to dust in the wind.

Once the fight ended, the Valet nestled his Rune Blade back into Heartbreaker's saddle straps and took out a cigar, muttering curses on Adon's house the whole time. They didn't curse people's houses in Morgarai, but the big man thought they should start. Beside him, Adon still had an arrow readied. Glancing over, he saw a wraith cornered against a jut of rock. She had shed her dread form, looking like an ordinary woman now save for her greenish blonde hair and putrid looking flesh. Her large eyes were filled with tears. She repeated something in her funereal language.

"*Tocar,*" she sobbed. "*Tocar.*"

Adon loosed his arrow. It connected with her forehead, turning her into smoldering embers before she could even scream.

The Valet looked southeast once more, hoping they hadn't wasted too much precious time. He lit his cigar, a challenge in the damp air. "What does *tocar* mean?" he asked.

Adon paused as he pulled his arrow out of the ashes of the dead Myrian woman. "Mercy," he replied.

Chapter Twenty-One: The Panhandle, Agimonde

Among his other skills – those unbecoming of the average Pahren – Emon proved himself an expert tracker. The outlaws who escaped the fray were riding clockwork mounts (it hadn't occurred to Esther to count the horses back at the canyon, so she didn't discount them as stolen). The wraiths, on the other hand, he tracked in more arcane ways, using some stone he'd pulled from his person somewhere. He'd stop abruptly, sniff the uncharacteristically moist air, check the stone, and correct their course. Thus far, they were traveling due west.

"This is odd behavior for them," Emon reflected as they walked over the Panhandle, just outside of Alor Canyon.

It was a miserable, hot stretch of hardpan peppered with old oil derricks. According to legend, the Elders brought with them technology fueled by fossil-based energy. The oil pumped up from the earth powered horseless carriages and, some even said, flying machines. But that was before the Daemon Wars, before the advent of Runic power, steam, and clean-burning *teravir*. Now, the primitive tech stood like a vast, rusted ruin.

Esther marveled at them, Emon remained unfazed.

At the edge of the oil field, they could see clouds streaking the horizon, a clear sign of their quarry. Wherever the rain fell, the wraiths would surely follow. Esther felt her heart skip a beat, drawing her revolvers in preparation. Emon, in turn, drew his pair of thin, snake-headed knives from his boots.

"Is it normal for wraiths to team up with Sapiens?" Esther asked as they slowed their walk to a creep; the edge of the raincloud was close now.

Emon considered this for a moment. "It's not unheard of," he said. "But it's rare. Only when there is a common goal of great importance."

Esther didn't think robbing a caravan qualified, but she kept her opinion to herself. Perhaps this pursuit would get them more than just a money box.

As they moved into the spitting mist, they slowed further, the thirsty desert floor turning into a thick mud under their feet. Less than a quarter hour later they found a large crater cut into the desert by Esther knew not what. It was a perfectly round dust bowl with one sloping inlet. Four men stood guard, one for each direction. They were soaked to the bone, each holding a rifle. Esther felt grateful for the mist, as it obscured their approach and made it difficult for the men to aim.

She and Emon were moving in a crouch now. Esther holstered one revolver, folding her fingers into the Silent Night – a low-level hypnotic spell. The glyphs lit for a brief moment around her hand, then they circled the nearest rifleman's head like a halo. First, the guard sat down, yawned, then he lay back and fell fast asleep.

Emon gave her a look somewhere at the intersection of impressed and disappointed. "And I was just going to kill him," he whispered.

They crept to the edge of the valley, crawling on their bellies through the pungent, red mud. Down below Esther saw their camp: a few Sapien men huddled around sheltered cook fires trying to stay warm and dry. Nearby a group of wraiths gathered around a glowing blue orb of light, appearing to draw power or vitality from it.

"It's called a wavestone," Emon told her in low tones before she could ask. "It is a rune stone that gathers energy from the sea waves and the tides. It feeds them if such a term can apply. It also causes the rains."

Esther nodded. Emon was just full of useful information.

Down among the outlaws and the wraiths were a pair that didn't quite fit. One man dressed in finery – a ruffled shirt, black breeches, and a blue coat with tails. He had kinky black hair and absently shuffled a Taro deck. The other she mistook for an abnormally large man until she realized he was Gigan – one of the half-giants from the northlands. He wore a hooded gray robe that shone with blue runes, sleeveless to show off arms like rock formations. The rain diverted around the two men in an invisible semi-sphere as if glancing off of glass.

This must be the weather wizard who's been hounding my steps, Esther thought.

"Again you struck, and again the Peacekeeper survived?" the ruffled man in blue asked. The question was rhetorical. "She is the tenacious one, isn't she?"

The Gigan lowered his bearded face. "She has powerful friends," he said. "I thought blowing the cliff sides would distract them."

Ruffles shrugged and drew a card, looked at, put it back in the deck. "The ambush should have been enough. We've clearly underestimated her."

"They have the Weapon of Wraithbane," the weather wizard added. At its mention, the wraiths gathered around the wavestone let out a collective hiss.

This got Ruffles' undivided attention. "The Rune Blade, you say? Then the Meddlers have sent their Knight."

Meddlers? A knight? It was absurd to think of the Valet as any kind of knight, and, Esther thought, it was even more absurd that such an archaic term was being used outside of a militant kingdom like Kairal. Either these men were grossly mistaken, or Esther didn't understand a thing they were saying.

Ruffles reshuffled the deck. "This is news I'll have to take back to my colleagues," he said. "Will the Peacekeeper resume her mission to the Colonies?"

The Gigan nodded. "I have no doubt."

"Good. Allow the wraiths to return you there and keep up your rainmaking. I'll be in touch."

"And once the Peacekeeper is dealt with, my part in this is over?" the weather wizard asked.

The frilly one smiled. "We'll see," is all he said.

Then, Esther watched in amazement as a shadowy void enveloped Ruffles and he vanished into thin air.

"Impossible," Emon hissed. "Only the Corbeau can translocate."

Esther didn't know what a Corbeau was, but she did know that she had a chance to end this once and for all. She had a bead on the weather wizard, so it was time to dispense Ordo's Justice.

She stood to her full height, firing a warning shot into the air.

"Peacekeeper!" she shouted. "By the Unbound Law, I order you to lay down arms!"

She didn't hear Emon curse over the sound of gunfire.

Chapter Twenty-Two: On the outskirts of Alor Canyon, Agimonde

Leiyara didn't know how long they'd been walking, or in which direction – Dal could have been leading her straight into Mystraam. All she knew was that she was tired, and cold, and wet, and miserable. The Agish garment she wore was made from a light and airy fabric, designed for the heat of the desert. Now it clung damply, chilling her to the bone. Dal walked ahead of her, unfazed by the wind and the mist, but of course he was: being unable to feel anything had its advantages. A shiver went up Leiyara's spine thinking about that brief moment when she had been a wraith.

Mustering her courage, she asked, "Where are you taking me?" She didn't stand a chance of outrunning him – she'd seen how the Myrian could move – but if she didn't like his answer she'd run anyway.

Dal appeared to think, but Leiyara also thought he might be translating in his head. "Taking you back to your people," he said.

"Oh," Leiyara replied, feeling a little of her tension release. "Thank you."

The Myrian just shrugged.

They came upon some debris blocking their path, which Dal misted over, his movements flickering. He then reached across for Leiyara's hand to help her. As she reached for him, a shimmer of blue light danced across his body, limning him with a thin halo. When she grasped his hand it felt solid as any living being. She stumbled her way on top of the rubble, then Dal gently lifted her down by the waist. Being close to him felt like being close to nothing at all, like he wasn't even there. It was unlike when she'd been close to any other man – no warmth, no awkwardness, no sensation of either longing or revulsion, or that tiny twinge of fear any reasonable woman got around a strange man. No, Dal gave off an anti-presence, a void.

He let her go, shimmering again. Leiyara noticed he became translucent and somehow flat. Dal noticed that she noticed, looked down, and turned away.

After a moment, Leiyara started following him again. "You know," she said, mostly because she felt the need to say something, "it was lucky you showed up when you did. I don't know what that wraith was trying to do to me, but it felt really bad."

"It wasn't luck," Dal replied. "I was pursuing that wraith when I found you. He is my brother." Dal said it so matter-of-factly that it stunned Leiyara. "He was trying to possess you. Old magicks. I don't know how he learned them."

Leiyara hurried to catch up, walking at Dal's side. Even without doing the misty thing he still took long strides. "Is that why I could see myself through his eyes?" she asked. "Is that why I felt...what you feel?"

The Myrian kept a stern face, but she could sense a shift in his attitude, a sort of sinking. "You mean feeling nothing?" he asked. "Yes. If he had completed the ritual, you would have been discorporated like a Myrian and he would have your body."

Leiyara swallowed hard. To be that way forever would drive anyone mad. "How do you cope with it?"

"We don't have a choice. It is that or death," Dal's voice became solemn, almost mournful. "What separates the *Tocara* from the *Fuatha* is that the *Fuatha* – or wraiths, as you call them – don't care if they die. In fact, some long for it."

"That sounds like a terrible way to live," Leiyara clapped her hand over her mouth so hard that it hurt. "Matron's name! I'm so sorry!"

Her companion cracked a bit of a smile. "Some days are worse than others. We still have our wavestones and the sea to bring us comfort."

Leiyara didn't know what a wavestone was, but she thought she'd asked enough questions already. Instead, she just walked by Dal's side, puzzling over that eerie non-presence of his or how his hands felt wet and clammy even though the rain couldn't touch them. At least she didn't feel miserable anymore; wet and cold, yes, but not miserable.

At least not until Dal stopped abruptly, holding his arm out to halt her. "Wait!" he commanded in a hushed tone.

Before Leiyara could say anything, a fiery arrow pierced the mist in front of them. It just grazed the Myrian's robe, singing it slightly. With a flick of Dal's wrists, a silvery knife appeared in each hand, serrated and razor-sharp.

"Show yourself, coward!" he shouted.

That's when the Mysthunter – the same one who'd been protecting the caravan, Leiyara thought – charged.

"Adon! Howling Void, get back here!" another voice shouted. This one, Leiyara recognized.

• • • •

THE LAST BIT OF TERRAIN had been slow going. After passing the remains of the wraith camp, the path became rocky and craggy. The Valet led Heartbreaker by the reins over the loose, gravel-strewn road. Both he and the horse stumbled over the unsure footing, but Adon moved with grace, as if walking on air. The runes that sparked on his boots accounted for that. When they were at the last leg of Alor Canyon the path wound around a cliffside, obscured by rubble and fallen rock. More than once the Valet had to coax Heartbreaker over a pile of debris, careful not to injure the animal.

"Your horse is slowing us down," Adon pointed out. "I believe you would say it is ironic?"

"Don'tcha think?" the Valet sneered.

He wasn't in a joking mood. The stunt Adon had pulled at the wraith camp – his reaction to that wraith woman's pleas – had made him angry and more than a little wary about his company. He was by no means a moral man and wasn't one to readily turn down a fight, but even the Valet knew there were limits. Executing a helpless, unarmed enemy while she begged for mercy pushed those limits. In truth, he'd thought more than once about just killing Adon and going it alone, if not out of spite, then at least to eliminate the wild card the Mysthunter had become. Adon sensed this, he thought, taking care not to turn his back on the Valet. A smart move.

When they came to a bend in the road, Adon halted suddenly, notching an arrow.

"What is it?" the Valet asked, drawing his Rune Blade from Heartbreaker's saddle straps.

The Mysthunter held up a hand to silence him, cocking his head slightly, listening. Sure enough, there were faint voices on the air.

One of them he knew.

"Matron's name!" Leiyara exclaimed. "I'm so sorry!"

The other voice spoke in a dark brogue, lilted and dirge-like. "Some days are worse than others," it said. "We still have our wavestones and the sea to bring us comfort."

The Valet crossed to Adon's position as quietly as possible. At the last step, his boot caught a rock, skipping it over the gravel. The sound was negligible against the patter of the rains, but in the craggy pass and close cliffs, it resonated.

"Wait!" the brogue called out.

Adon grinned. "Now you've done it," he said.

The Mysthunter rounded the bend, ready to loose his arrow. As he drew back to light the arcane arrow, the Valet kicked one foot out from under him. He couldn't stop Adon from shooting, but it at least muddled his aim.* The flaming arrow sailed past Leiyara's companion – a robed man with dark, blue-black hair and sea-green eyes. It singed his clothing but did no other damage.

Adon wheeled on him, spitting something unpleasant in his native tongue. Having had enough of his shenanigans, the Valet punched him in the mouth. The Mysthunter hit the ground, going for an arrow. The Valet leveled *Glaeve Pandaemonia* at him. It must have been quite a sight for Leiyara and her new friend.

"Draw on me," the Valet said, "and I kill you in one stroke."

Adon cocked that grin at him. "Raise your blade, and I'll kill you with one arrow, wraith-friend!" he spat.

They stayed that way for what felt like hours, the Valet staring into those fiery, hateful eyes and Adon glaring back at his cool blue ones. Neither man seemed to take a breath the whole span, which lasted maybe a minute.

"Um...hi," Leiyara said, breaking their standoff.

The Valet didn't look at her. "You alright, honey?" he asked.

In his peripheral vision, he saw her nod. "Yes. Thanks to Dal, here."

Dal. He struggled to fathom a wraith having a name, a mother and a father to name him, relationships, thoughts and feelings. But the newcomer lacked the hallmarks of his tortured brethren; his skin didn't have that putrefied greenish hue. No, he was more likely a regular Myrian, uncorrupted by hatred and rage.

"I have returned your girl safely to your hands," the Myrian, Dal, said. His next line sounded rehearsed, almost ritualistic. "Away put your weapons, I mean you no harm."

Adon relaxed his grip on his bow, whispering a word of Runic. The flame on his arrowhead sputtered out. He said something in Agish that, although the Valet couldn't understand it, meant something to the effect of "you have no power here."

Dal nodded, crossing his hands over his chest. The Valet only now realized that they held two long, slim blades. Both the Myrian and the Mysthunter put their weapons away; the Valet, still baffled by the interaction, relaxed too. *Glaeve Pandaemonia* rested at his side, grumbling quietly for lack of blood.

Seeing the danger had passed, Leiyara ran to the Valet and threw her arms around him. Her body felt good against him, soft and supple curves, warm and inviting, and the way her dress clung to her...

The Valet stowed that line of thinking for later. "I'm glad you're safe," he said, putting an arm around her as she shivered.

He'd not forgotten Adon and Dal, who were having a tense, pregnant silence between themselves.

"You are lucky," Adon said. "I kill your kind."

Dal smiled wolfishly, producing a necklace from within his clothes. It had several ruby-like beads the Valet recognized as firestones, the very thing believed to contain the Agi soul. Dal had a collection. "And I yours," the Myrian said. "They speak to me sometimes."

Adon clenched his jaw, every muscle and sinew in his body tensed for a fight. But whatever ritual they had performed for their little cease-fire appeared to be inviolable; so they settled for just glaring daggers at each other instead of using them.

Leiyara left the Valet's side and went back to Dal, ignoring Adon completely.

"I have delivered you to your friend as promised," Dal said. "My obligation is fulfilled."

Leiyara reached out to him and the Myrian shimmered into physicality as she took his hand. "Thank you," she said, then went up on her tiptoes, kissing him on the cheek. "I hope you find rest or peace, or that you can feel something again soon."

Dal smiled a genuine smile. "Just that wish from you, *lassai*, warms me once more. Thank you." He looked up at Adon. "Go in peace," he said, his voice cooling. "Next we meet, I will surely kill you."

"Or I, you," Adon replied.

Dal shimmered, misted, and vanished.

The Valet shook his head. *Rituals and magicks and courteous threats*, he thought. *Howling Void, I need a drink.*

Chapter Twenty-Three: The Panhandle, Agimonde

She didn't hear Emon's cursing over the gunfire, but she could guess it involved Virago's undergarments in some way. Esther dropped as bullets and magicks whizzed by her, suddenly rethinking her decision to arrest the entire valley. There were shouts from the men and the screeching of wraiths. The two marksmen guarding the other side of the crater were rounding on them.

"Well," Emon shouted above the din, "this is a fine mess!"

Esther thought about playing it off as her intent to get them riled up, but there was no point. Instead, she took a shot at the nearest guard, winging him. He spun, falling from the cliffside. Below, a group of wraiths scattered as his body crushed their wavestone. Emon snatched her second revolver and fired on the other outlaws below. He turned out to be a crack shot: one of them fell dead for each of the six rounds. Meanwhile, Esther folded her fingers rapidly, casting bolts of light at the wraiths as they surged up the sheer rock face on conjured gusts of wind.

When a wraith made landfall, Esther cut it down with her bayonet, feeling the force runes connect with the misty form like a solid mass. It fell while Esther cast Ordo's Hammer at a second. She dodged a strike from a third, ducking under the scythe blade, and cast the Hammer again, breaking the wraith under a luminous sledgehammer.

Emon stood with his back to her, dropping the empty revolver back into her holster and taking up his Runic knives. He laughed maniacally as the wraiths surrounded them. The valley below had gone quiet, so Esther assumed they had emptied it. A red and yellow clockwork horse – one she recognized as belonging to one of her party – rode into the distance at a frenzied pace, carrying an oversized rider in a robe. The weather wizard.

Run while you can, Esther thought acidly, *I'll catch up to you soon enough.*

Turning her attention back to the circling wraiths, Esther saw that they were slowly closing in. She got a closer look at their weapons, realizing something for the first time: sickles, scythes, a trowel, a crudely forged sword, a pickax – these weren't warriors, these were farmers. She wondered idly, in that moment of calm before the onslaught, what had driven them so mad.

With a screeching battle cry, the wraiths engaged, closing their already tight circle. Esther folded her fingers into the Searing Light and, engulfing the wraiths to her left in white-hot fire. She then drew her other revolver, slashing one at the throat and another across the belly. The runes connected with a satisfying *thunk* as her bayonets tore through the ephemeral flesh, carving ashen, black gashes before reducing the wraiths to dust.

Behind her, she was vaguely aware of Emon. He ducked under a wraith's swing, stabbed it, slashed two throats with a single swing of each blade, feinted back, and sent both Runic weapons into another one's face. When they were finished, nothing remained but a cloud of soot whirling around them in the breeze. The fight took no more than a minute.

Esther instinctively moved in the direction in which the weather wizard had escaped, intent on giving chase. Emon's tight grasp on her arm halted her. "Where are you going?" he asked.

Esther shook off his grip. "That Ordo-forsaken weather wizard that's been dogging my heels," she said through clenched teeth. "I'm going to execute him."

She took another step toward her lofty goal when a brilliant burst of flame shot up before her. Flailing backward, she cried out while landing hard on her backside. Before the pillar of fire guttered out she saw the blazing red runes that had cast it, circling at the base of the flames. Without thinking, she wheeled on Emon, taking aim.

The runes were just fading from his hands. "To your duty, Peacekeeper!" he shouted at her. "Or have you forgotten you have a job to do?"

Esther blinked but kept a bead on her enigmatic companion. *We can add spellcraft to his list of unlikely skills,* she thought. "My job is to serve the Unbound Law. That weather wizard is in violation."

Emon lowered his hands, leveling both a stern and friendly gaze at her. He seemed to shrink as he took on the persona of the unassuming Pah-ren again. "Exactly," he said. "Your duty is to the law, not to your vendetta. In time, Virago's flame touches all."

As Ordo gives, Ordo takes, Esther thought. The phrase didn't just apply to the glyph magicks but everything. Including Justice. The Peacekeeper stood, holstering her weapons. "You're right, of course," she said. "I forgot myself for a moment."

Emon smiled sympathetically. "Happens to the best of us. Now, let us get Rae's lockbox and return to the caravan."

Chapter Twenty-Four: Alto Mecina, Agimonde

They met again at the crossing to Alto Mecina, just outside the train station. The Valet and Adon rode in from the northeast with Leiyara. The girl was soaking wet and shaken, but unharmed. Esther and Emon arrived on foot, lugging the caravan's cash box with them. Hrakar, ever vigilant, waited at the edge of the camp's perimeter, eyes on the horizon. The party rendezvoused with much rejoicing and relief. Emon tapped a keg of bloodfruit cider, so they drank and swapped stories. When Esther's turn came, she spoke of the shadowy dandy, the weather wizard, and their plot. Everyone but the Valet was astonished.

"Darwin," the big man said. Esther noticed his grip on his cup tighten. "The Mad Dandy."

"Like that game we used to play in the mirror as kids?" Leiyara asked. Under Esther's probing gaze, she reddened. "You stand in front of the mirror and say 'Mad Dandy' three times. He's supposed to tell your fortune. It's just an urban legend."

"One based in truth," the Valet said.

Esther scoffed. "You're telling me some children's story is trying to kill me? Who else is behind it? The Lullaby Lady?"

They sat for a moment in brooding silence.

"I knew the storm was no coincidence," he announced, almost triumphantly. "Didn't I say it was the work of a weather wizard?"

"You did, indeed," Esther conceded. "But why come after me? What makes me so important?"

The Valet cocked a finger in her direction. "And how did they know you were coming?"

Though the night was warm, Esther wrapped her arms around herself, suddenly feeling exposed, vulnerable, and betrayed. When she thought that the storm had been bad timing or bad luck, when she thought the airship crash and the horrors of the Gray Marsh were only unhappy circumstances, when she suspected their defense of the caravan from Myrian raiders unconnected, she'd been able to cope. Take one thing at a time and not be bothered. But when she ran that common thread – the arcanist – through the list, it was overwhelming. Every misfortune she faced had been leveled at her like a cannon, fired with precise intent. Who could be so malicious and why? What in the Void had she done to them?

Esther felt a steady, warm hand on her shoulder and looked up from the fire. Leiyara. "Don't worry, Esther," she said with an attempt at a reassuring smile, "as long as you have us, you can make it through."

The Valet nodded. "She's right," he said. "We'll find these bastards and dispense with the justice."

Hrakar took her hand, squeezing gently. "You are not alone."

The next day they mounted the platform at the train station. Rae paid their fare and the Pah-ren began unloading the wagons into the freight cars. While they busied themselves, Esther and her companions patrolled the tracks to ensure they had not been followed or another ambush wasn't laying in wait. By mid-morning, the train whistle blew sending them on their way to Portalaine. Although Esther vigilantly watched the tracks behind them, the trip was mercifully uneventful.

Chapter Twenty-Five: Portalaine, Agimonde

Rae thanked Esther and her friends for their help, then pulled Hrakar aside. While bidding farewell to the Pah-ren, Esther saw the Draconian hand Rae an ornate golden dagger. The two spoke some words in ritual, then Rae slashed Hrakar's forearm.

His stripes, Esther thought.

Once the caravan headed toward the waterfront, Esther and the others went into Portalaine. The city was Agimonde's major hub for trade. The harbor was filled with ships moving in and out of Firala Bay, airships filled the skies. The architecture here was more varied the rest of Agimonde: fired clay huts melding with Draconian black-stone spires and more traditional Sapien structures of wood with shingled rooftops. The people were as diverse as the cityscape with Draconians, Sapiens, and even a few Gigans mingled into the crowded streets, the latter towering a head and a half above the rest.

They came to a stop outside a run-down gambling den. The walls were splintered and worm-eaten wood, the roof a rotting thatch, the windows all broken out. Esther couldn't read the faded, pitted sign hanging above the door, but she did notice a tiny symbol in one corner – a stylized purple flower.

The Violet Rose, Esther thought. She knew they had satellite offices in seedy little places like this all over the world.

"This is where I leave you," Emon said to them, disembarking from his little cart.

They all shook hands, bidding farewell to the mysterious Pah-ren, wishing the blessings of Virago upon him. Emon was even good enough to give Hrakar another stripe for his assistance. While the Agi said goodbye to the Valet, she watched them on a hunch. While shaking, the Valet slipped him a gold imperial in the process.

You momerat bastard, the Peacekeeper thought. *You knew Emon and you played dumb the entire time.* It made her question even more the motives of her companion, and what the enigmatic Agi – this so-called Pah-ren – had really been up to.

With final farewells said, Esther and company went to the sky harbor to book passage, at last, for the Colonies. Esther sent a silent prayer to Ordo that the voyage would be uneventful.

Chapter Twenty-Six: An Undisclosed Location, somewhere in the Colonies

When one gets a feeling that there's a shadowy cabal manipulating events in their life, one should usually disregard it. But once in a great while it's true, like in Esther's case. Two members of said cabal waited in the abandoned banquet hall of an Iyon palace. One, a young, beautiful woman with raven locks and a stunning black ball gown, sat in the High Seat, looking elegantly regal. The other, a man who appeared to be in his fifties with close-cropped, salt-and-pepper hair wearing gray greatcoat, stood by the window that overlooked the Gray Marsh. He covered half his face with a peculiar plaster mask.

From the broken down doors – one propped against the wall, the other hanging feebly on one hinge – came the dandy and the weather wizard, escorted by two wraiths. They no longer wore their dread forms, so they appeared as two sallow Myrian men. Ruffles reached the center of the room, forcing the weather wizard to his knees. He drew a Taro card from his deck, turning it over to reveal the Hanged Man. The card floated above the arcanist, glowing an iridiscent white before its surface erupted into a mass of chains. The arcane bonds quickly immobilized the Gigan.

The masked man spoke first. "What news, Darwin?" he asked, not taking his eyes off the Marsh.

The Mad Dandy, Darwin, shuffled his Taro deck idly. "The arcanist has failed us again," he said. "The Peacekeeper and the knight have escaped."

The raven-haired woman tittered, the sound of tinkling crystal. She put a delicate hand to her corseted bosom. "I told you we should have just killed your little pet and executed her ourselves," she said, her voice as dark as tinted glass.

The masked man turned. Despite his middling height, he suddenly seemed taller, more imposing. "Lest you forget, my darling Celeste, our mission cannot be known to our enemies."

Celeste, cocked her head to one side, aiming her dark eyes at her companion. "I haven't *forgotten* anything, my dear Dalton, only I am saying that we need a more direct approach."

At this point, one of the wraiths stepped forward. "Enough of your squabbling," he commanded. "You've forgotten that you've promised my people warm bodies, to live again! Since you've failed, I say your bodies are forfeit."

The wraith presumed to draw a blade on them. His companion followed suit, putting his knife to Darwin's throat.

Dalton smiled. "Celeste," he said, dismissing the wraiths with a wave, "do away with them."

Celeste spread her arms beckoning the skirts of her gown to boil and seeth, liquefying around her delicate frame. A spike of pure darkness issued from within the morass, puncturing the wraith nearest her, while a black tendril snatched up the other, dangling him above the needle-toothed mouth that emerged from her bodice. As the first wraith disintegrated Celeste's gown devoured the other alive, he screamed as the jaws minced even his ethereal spirit.

When they were gone, Celeste's gown returned to its original, elegant form. She released a dainty little burp. "Pardon me," she said, a smile oozing over her crimson lips.

"Thank you, Celeste," Dalton said. He crossed the hall to the arcanist, whose eyes had widened with terror. "Mark what you saw, arcanist," he warned, "for it's your fate as well should we be discovered."

"Now, now," Darwin interjected, walking around Dalton while shuffling his cards theatrically. "No need to be rude, my brother. I'm sure Olen here will be very cooperative. Nod if you agree, Olen."

Olen the arcanist nodded.

"Very good," Darwin said. He snatched the Hanged Man card from the air above the Gigan and his bonds vanished. Olen dropped to all fours, pleading in his native tongue between ragged breaths.

Celeste looked at him with naked contempt. "Does it always blubber so?" she asked.

Darwin gave Olen a swift kick. "Silence!" he shouted. Then, to Dalton, "What shall I do with him?" he asked. "I've been wanting to find out what happens when you fuse a Gigan's spine with the head of a tortoise."

The arcanist sobbed but had the self-preservation instinct enough to stifle his protestations.

"Such a large creature whimpering like this," Dalton observed. "Perhaps you broke him overmuch." He turned back to the window with a theatrical flourish of his long gray coat. "No, he will make for good bait in drawing of our quarry. Keep him unspoiled until the time comes. Return to the Colonies and await them.

"Meantime," he looked at Celeste, "do you think you can succeed where our brother failed?"

Celeste clutched theatrically at invisible pearls. "Why, Dalton, you insult me. Of *course* I can!"

Back at his window now, Dalton clasped his hands behind his back. "I don't think the trouble is with any deficiency on Darwin's part, mind you. I think the trouble lies with our approach. Instead of unifying them as one target, we should focus on each of them individually. Divided they fall and all that."

Celeste and Darwin gave their wholehearted nods of agreement. Dalton cocked his head, listening to something unheard by any other. "Go now," he said. "To the task. I must apprise our silent partner."

With a wave of his hand, Darwin and Olen were engulfed in shadow, vanishing. In a similar vein, Celeste seemed to fold herself into her skirts, disappearing into the darkness. When they were gone,

Dalton turned back to the seemingly empty room. "You heard all of that, I assume?"

A powerful illusionist, Dalton could sense the things that were really there. The presence of their mysterious fourth cohort hovered somewhere near the back corner. It seemed even less human than Dalton himself.

"I was led to understand the Dark Magi were more effective," hissed a shrill, whispering voice.

"You've tied our hands with all this subterfuge," Dalton retorted. "Why is this Peacekeeper so important?"

The voice hesitated a moment and Dalton sensed reluctance. There seemed to be quite a bit of information that wasn't being shared with him. "She is the Meddlers' pawn," it said, "yet she does not know it."

The illusionist chuckled to himself. "The pawn and the knight," he mused aloud. "How appropriate."

Hostility from the back corner, danger. Glyphs he couldn't see circling, the pressure of old magicks long forgotten, an attempt at tapping a leyline that was fused long ago. "Are you taking this matter seriously?" the whisper asked.

"Quite," Dalton said, not bothering to raise his defenses. "Be patient and focus on breaking our prisoner. We'll deal with your Peacekeeper."

And just as suddenly as it had come, the presence disappeared.

Pawns, knights, thought Dalton, the Father of Lies, *we're approaching the endgame now.*

Chapter Twenty-Seven: Harbortown, Montblanc, the Colonies

The engines hissed and steamed as they powered down, adding to the clamor of the crew preparing the mooring while taking down the sails. The longboat lurched a little under Esther's feet as it the deckhands secured it to the dock and lowered a gangplank. The ship's captain, a bearded Gigan fellow with a jolly disposition, waited by the plank to see off his passengers and supervise the unloading of cargo. Esther and her companions were all waiting on deck with their luggage, waiting to disembark. The Valet, who had spent nearly the entire voyage vomiting over the side of the ship, was more eager than the others.

"About fisking time!" he exalted as he pushed his way to the gangplank. He took off like a shot, practically skipping onto the dock.

Leiyara and Hrakar followed, toting the remainder of the supplies they'd purchased in Portalaine. Leiyara, in keeping with the Colonies' more provincial attitudes, had changed into her plain black frock instead of the more risqué Agi dress. Adding that her red curls were piled professionally atop her head, Esther barely recognized her. Hrakar wore fresh silks of red and purple, his spear lashed to his back with a leather bandolier.

Esther paid the captain all that remained from her pouch. She made a note to stop at the first Central Counting house they found.

"You are here to see about the rains?" the captain asked, his voice a rich baritone with a thick, lilting accent.

Esther knit her brow. She'd finally had a chance to read through the file she'd been provided back at the Call and had learned that an arcanist, hired by the governor of Estrella Nova – one of the Colonies to the northeast – to deal with a drought, had instead caused great flooding with endless rains. He'd destroyed this year's crop yield, turning the farmlands of Estrella Nova into a swamp. His purpose, as yet, remained unclear and there weren't many more details provided. She'd been taken aback by the captain's direct question, but it wasn't all that strange: people in the area were obviously aware of what was happening, and a Peacekeeper could only conceivably be arriving for that reason.

"I am," she said.

The Gigan nodded. "Good," he said. "Flying back and forth to Frostgaard and Draconspire has been rough sailing since the storms began, and not much grain to haul."

"I'll do what I can," Esther replied.

She proceeded down the gangplank, meeting up with her friends. They were looking down the cobbled road at Harbortown. The sky harbor was built on a bluff overlooking Crystal Bay – aptly named as it sparkled a serenely in the sun – with a road built down to the town proper. There were more Kairulian structures here than anything: the stucco buildings with the blue tile roofs. The streets were laid out in a hard-lined grid, forming almost perfect square blocks. Parts of the town were allocated for commerce, some for industry, and some for residences, with a clear demarcation for each. The houses marked the northern part of the city; the smokestacks and harbor the south; the shopping centers and markets between.

It was quite a difference from what Esther was used to. Ordo's Call had been built hastily and piecemeal, builders throwing up whatever roughshod structure they could between attacks by the Cythraul. And it differed from what she'd seen in Agimonde, where industry melded seamlessly into living. The Peacekeeper acknowledged that these were the boundaries of Sapienkind, trying to shake the feeling that they caged her.

They started down the winding path, breathing in the salty sea air and enjoying a ray of sunshine that was neither hot nor glaring like the deserts of Agimonde. Esther felt a wave of relief wash over her: she had, at last, reached her destination and, despite the loss of life, she thanked Ordo that her friends were all okay. The change in scenery did the others good, too. With every breeze that rustled his silks, Hrakar breathed in deeply, drinking in the air like the fine wine of his homeland. The Valet, now on solid ground, smoked one of his big cigars while humming a tune; he had wrapped *Glaeve Pandaemonia* in a piece of tarp, carrying it over one shoulder. Leiyara smiled wide-eyed wonder, her pace quickening with her growing eagerness to see and experience everything Harbortown had to offer.

As they approached the city limits, the road widened into Market Row. An open-air bazaar filled the wide street with kiosks and vendor stands: fresh fruits, vegetables, fish, tools, weapons. They moved through a motley assortment of Draconians, Agi, and Gigans, and even the occasional group of Myrian, hooded and translucent in the sunlight. The Sapien people were as widely varied: there were people with dark skin, light skin, swarthy skin; people with angular eyes, or their hair plaited into braids, or their heads cleanly shaved, every variation appeared here. While going further inland would give way to more homogenous Sapien culture, these harbor towns tended to attract all sorts.

Market Row emptied into a square-edged with jewelry stores, a smithy, and the offices of the Central Authorities. Esther reminded herself that she had banking to do, as well as telegraphing the Call to let them know she had at last arrived. Before she could say this to her company, though, Hrakar's eyes narrowed.

"We are being followed," he said in low tones.

The Peacekeeper suppressed the urge to immediately look back. The Valet gently grasped Leiyara's arm to stop her from doing the same. *Not a moment's peace,* Esther thought. "Who?" she asked.

"Draconian, all dressed in black, a silver pendant about her neck."

The Valet grinned, reaching casually for *Glaeve Pandaemonia*. "Friend of yours?" he asked.

Hrakar gave him a warning look. "Most decidedly not! She is *schattenvander* – a shade walker."

"Dangerous?" Leiyara asked.

"She may even be beyond my skill," Hrakar admitted.

Esther felt that cold feeling drop into her stomach again, that mix of dread and danger. She swallowed it down. "Let's not tip her off," she said. "Does anyone know of good lodgings here?"

"The Wagon Wheel," the Valet said. "It's a quiet hotel and public house, just a little off the beaten path. I'd say it's perfect for our needs." He winked at Leiyara, who immediately reddened. "Pretty serving girls, too."

Under ordinary circumstances, the big man's lechery would have irritated Esther, but she'd learned by now that his good humor was fueled by his eagerness to meet danger head-on. In this case, she found it reassuring. "Good," she said. "We'll split up."

"What?" Leiyara squeaked.

"Are you sure that is wise?" Hrakar asked.

Esther nodded. "I don't know what a shade walker is, but it sounds like she won't attack in broad daylight with hundreds of people milling around."

Considering this for a moment, Hrakar nodded. "This is true."

"And I have business to attend to," Esther went on. "I want you and the Valet to secure our lodgings. Leiyara and I will go to the bank and Central Transit so I can telegraph the home office. We'll also have the added benefit of seeing which of us this shade walker follows – it may allow us to guess her intentions."

The Valet grinned. "Or we could just corner her and ask," he suggested, cracking his knuckles.

"That would not be wise," Hrakar advised.

The Peacekeeper held up her hand to stop the Valet's inevitable quip. "There will come a time for that. But we table it until we get the lay of the land. For now, we separate and see who she's after. We'll meet you at the Wagon Wheel by sundown."

They parted then, Esther and Leiyara heading for Central Counting while the Valet led Hrakar through the throng to find this off-the-beaten-path hotel. Esther had to admit she wary of separating, just as wary as Hrakar and Leiyara had been; that the Valet wasn't concerned only heightened her sense of caution. Since she'd hidden above that gorge with Emon hearing this was all some plot against her, she'd been looking over her shoulder. Everyone she'd spoken to was suspect, everyone she passed in the street a hidden assassin. It was no wonder she hadn't clocked the shade walker, she'd been suspecting everyone.

Resolving to get her head right, Esther mounted the steps to Central Counting.

• • • •

ESTHER WAS ACTING WEIRD. Leiyara first noticed it once they'd arrived in the Colonies and were walking through the crowds of people in the market: she kept looking over her shoulder, startled at small sounds, and watched the strangers' faces like they were all criminals. She'd told Leiyara and the others something about what had happened in Agimonde, although Leiyara couldn't quite wrap her head around it – it sounded too bizarre, like something out of one her novels: a vast, shadowy conspiracy, a dandy in frills, an evil wizard. Still, this was Esther she was talking about, and if Esther lacked anything it was imagination. The woman was the ultimate pragmatist.

Upon entering the Central Counting office Leiyara immediately felt a sense of comfort, a sense of *rightness*. Her books would have called the Central Authorities liminal spaces – they were all so standardized that one felt they could walk into a bank in Agimonde then turn around and walk out in the Duchies, across the world. They had the same marble floors, the same columns holding up the roof, the same blue carpet runner up the center aisle, the same richly varnished wooden cubicles. Even the offices of the bank manager and various VP's were in the same location, furnished with the same prefab furniture.

The strangely hushed environment, too, was standard. For some reason people are quieter around money and books. Customers spoke to the tellers in hushed tones, waited silently in line, and, of course, one could hear the occasional muffled cough or throat clearing that inevitably happened in places like that. Esther, too, was quiet, but that wasn't anything new. Unless she was issuing orders or making observations, the Peacekeeper tended to be more laconic. Not that she was particularly closed off, but if Leiyara wanted to know something personal about her, she often had to ask.

The line moved slowly, but eventually, they found themselves at one of the windows. Leiyara nearly cried out when the teller – a tallish man in the crisp blue Central Counting uniform with a pencil mustache, his greased hair flattened on his scalp – turned to greet them. For a moment, she wondered if it was the same pencil mustachioed man who had been so horrible to her back at Ordo's Call (Brad? Chad?), but he was older, with a bit of gray at his temples and a few distinguished wrinkles.

"May I help you?" he asked in the kind of voice that, if his nose hadn't been literally turned up in the air, then he made it clear it was rhetorical.

Leiyara stepped up to the teller, handing him Esther's check, taking up her role as Esther's secretary. "Peacekeeper Triad would like to cash the remainder of this check, please."

The teller – Thad, from his name badge – looked at the check dispassionately, then looked at Esther. "Does *Miss* Triad have identification?" he asked.

So it's going to be that way, is it? Leiyara wondered. She felt a little bit of anger rise into her throat, but she kept it down. *Fight bureaucracy with bureaucracy.*

Rummaging through her knapsack, Leiyara produced both her and Esther's passports as well as Esther's official Peacekeeper's license. "My name is Leiyara Candish, I am Peacekeeper Triad's secretary and authorized business representative," she said, then added, "before you ask."

Pencil-mustache (Leiyara couldn't bring herself to call him by name) looked over the documents, taking much longer than he needed to. Behind them, Leiyara heard a few people scoff theatrically. She thought about leveling one of Esther's hard stares at them but wasn't confident that she could do it right.

"Very well," Pencil-mustache sighed. He went about marking the check with his stylus, stopping when he saw Leiyara's initials, handwriting, and her Central Counting number. He glanced at it, then at her, then back at the check. At last, he stamped the document, slipped it into his lockbox, and asked, "Slips or silverbacks?"

Leiyara glanced back at Esther to get her opinion. The Peacekeeper shrugged. "Slips would be better," Leiyara said. "Silverbacks haven't caught on in the Colonies quite yet." Whether they did it out of defiance for their mother country of Kairal or because of the currency's newness was anyone's guess, but Leiyara left that part out.

"Slips, then," Esther said.

Leiyara nodded, turning back to Pencil-mustache. "You heard the lady," she said, suddenly feeling feisty in her natural element. She may not be much good in a fight and she couldn't ride a clockwork horse but she knew how to deal with bureaucratic red tape. She watched Pencil-mustache count out the remaining two hundred and fifty royals in varying denominations, but she felt herself redden as he came up a little short.

"There's only two hundred and twenty here," she pointed out. "Where's the rest?"

Pencil-mustache leveled a cold, stern stare at her. "Bank charges," he said. "For international checking." He said it as if Leiyara should have known this.

And she did. "I'm afraid you're mistaken..." she looked at his name badge now, deliberately, "...Thad. You see, according to the Central Counting policy, an international checking charge – *if* levied by the Central Counting house (and it is up to each house's discretion, mind you) – cannot exceed eight percent of the value of the check." She made it a point to give the stack of silver on the counter a quick count. "If I'm not mistaken, *sir*, you've taken twelve percent."

The teller kept leveling his stare at her, but Leiyara returned it with as much iron as she could fit into her wide eyes. "Now, you can either furnish the rest, or I can take this up with your manager, who I'm sure would be none too pleased that one of his tellers is trying to cheat a Peacekeeper." She then smiled, glancing back at Esther. "If I'm not mistaken, Peacekeeper Triad, Central Counting has a good relationship with the Call, is that correct?"

Esther nodded, looking a little stunned. "Yes. That's true." She cleared her throat and straightened, putting on a stern countenance. "I've met the representative for the Central Authorities – he was a friend of my mother's."

Pencil-mustache started to sweat now. He tugged at his collar, counted the silver slips again. "Oh! Do forgive me! I seem to have shorted you ten royals." He added it to the stack, then looked up, Leiyara's steely glare like a vice grip around his sensitive parts. "In fact, for the misunderstanding, let me waive the international checking fee. You are keeping us all safe, after all, aren't you Peacekeeper Triad? That is to say, *my* safety is important to you?"

Leiyara exchanged a glance with Esther, who nodded solemnly. "The safety of all citizens is of the utmost importance to the Peacekeepers, sir," Leiyara answered, gathering the money together. "Thank you, sir."

"And thank you," Pencil-mustache chirped. "Do please come again."

As they walked out, Esther looked at Leiyara with wide eyes, sparkling with pride. She cocked a thumbs up at her secretary, and Leiyara beamed.

• • • •

THE USUAL BUSINESS took up the rest of the day. At Central Transit, Esther had a telegram from the Call. *Good to hear from you (stop). Proceed to the Colonies with all haste (stop).* She sent a message in reply saying that she had arrived and was heading for Estrella Nova now. She made no mention of having spotted the weather wizard already, nor did she mention the apparent conspiracy to impede or end her journey. It still sounded crazy, even to her.

When they'd finished, Esther and Leiyara made their way to the Wagon Wheel, asking for directions a few times along the way. Most of the residents and Kairulian soldiers gave her an odd look when she asked for the place, those selfsame looks cluing her in on exactly what kind of place it was. Most importantly, Esther had also noticed the shade walker wasn't following them. Later, when she had a hot meal and at last settled into a hot bath, she finally asked Hrakar about her.

He knelt beside the tub, naked as the day he was born. They'd made love twice since Esther had comer-hithered him out of the casino downstairs. Since there was only one room available, they had to share, causing a moment of awkwardness when she dragged Hrakar into the washroom with her, locking the door behind them. Now, the Valet and Leiyara were in the other room, the former teaching the latter how to play Taro. They didn't seem too bothered by Esther's lack of propriety, nor did she – it had been a long journey and she would not be denied her satisfaction.

Hrakar hummed a tune in his native tongue, his voice a rich baritone that set Esther at ease as she luxuriated in the hot, robustly scented water. Whatever herbs Hrakar had added to her bath made her skin tingle pleasantly. "Tell me about shade walkers," Esther said.

Hrakar left off his tune mid-verse, looking at her with those beautiful amber eyes. "There were two great dragons," he recited. "Lumynos, the Dragon of Light, and Delkynos, the Dragon of Dark. Together, they spawned the dragon race, who later spawned my people. Lumynos, the Dragon of Light, is who my people worship. The shade walkers worship Delkynos."

Esther leaned forward, handing Hrakar the sponge. He began to wash her back with those strong, gentle hands. "Are there many of them?"

"No. Worship of Delkynos is forbidden – sacrilege, as you would say. In Sapien, you might call them a cult."

Outside, in the room proper, Leiyara slammed her hands on the table. "Taro!" she shouted.

The Valet muttered something in response. The sudden interruption of his voice into her intimate setting hit her like a bucket of ice water – were she a man, she would have shriveled. She focused instead on Hrakar's angular face, his perfectly sculpted chest and arms, those gorgeous eyes and that mouth that had surprised her with its skill.

"They are killers," Hrakar went on. "Assassins and arcanists, calling upon the shadows to do their will. They can even move from one shadow to another like this..." he snapped his fingers, "They are unworthy to be called Draconians."

Hrakar finished with her back, then ran his fingers through her hair. The feeling of his talon-like nails brushing her scalp gave her a pleasant chill. "But," Esther said, grasping wildly for her train of thought, "your holy men – your *arkons* – are trained as assassins, too, aren't they?"

He smiled, showing his pointed teeth. "That is, how you say, misconception. Our *a*rkons are fierce warriors, yes, and they are required to be trained in all aspects of the dragon – the tooth, claw, tail, and breath – but they are not assassins as you know them. That is, they are not paid to kill other men."

Esther nodded. "Thank you for correcting me," she said.

Waving off her misconception brought her eyes to the scars on his arm. They were already fully healed. "I want to give you one of those...what do you call them?"

"*Kal*," he replied, touching scar reverently. "The proof that I have paid the price of service. That I am once again worthy of my people."

She bit back a harsh remark about his culture's paltry idea of worthiness – to her, Hrakar was easily worth ten of them – but instead laid her hand on his. "I owe you many," she said. "I couldn't have done any of this without you at my side, and you're worthy enough to have won my heart." She smiled playfully. "Ask any of the boys at the Call and they'll tell you that isn't easy."

Hrakar smiled more beautifully than she'd yet seen. "You honor me," he said. "When your mission is complete and my service to you is at an end, you may grant me as many *kal* as you like."

"Service, huh?" Esther joked. "Is that what this is?"

Hrakar's long, skilled fingers slipped beneath the water and a rush of ecstasy filled her. "This?" the nimble Draconian said. "No. This, as you say, is a bonus."

• • • •

THE SOUND OF SPLASHING along with a few muted gasps snuck out of the washroom. The Valet, shuffling the Taro deck once again, grinned. *Get it, Triad!* he thought. He started dealing another hand of Taro, one to Leiyara, one to himself, and two dummies –

the game of Taro needed four players. Leiyara picked up on the game very quickly, doing quite well with the Valet stacking the deck in her favor. Failing to mention this fact seemed to make the girl happy, and Matron knew they could all use a little happy after what they'd been through.

He picked up his mug of Gigan beer, taking a long draft. Then, he looked solemnly at Leiyara. "You never did say what happened with that Myrian back at the canyon," he said.

Leiyara lowered her eyes, paling a little, and putting her cards down. "It...I don't remember much of it."

The Valet dropped a couple of silverbacks into the pot. "That Myrian man, Dal, he saved you?"

She nodded, bouncing her red curls. "Yes. The wraith was doing...something. Some kind of ritual, trying to take over my body."

"Ah," the Valet nodded, sagely putting up a finger. "Possession. I've met a few wraiths that actually pulled it off – it isn't pretty."

Leiyara looked at him with a knit brow and he realized he'd said too much. "Dal said that was old magick. But you're young."

He shrugged, hoping to curtail the subject. "I been around longer than you might think," he said. "And this Dal, what's his deal?"

"I don't know," Leiyara sorted through her cards, then raised him a few royals. "He didn't talk much while we were walking, and I mostly asked questions. Like, what is what like being Myrian, that kind of stuff."

"Touchy subject," the Valet said. He laid down his hand. "Retreat."

Bouncing up and down – which wasn't unpleasant to watch, he had to admit – Leiyara collected her winnings, dropping her cards on the table. "Haha! I had nothing. *Nothing*. I buffered you!"

He couldn't help but laugh. "It's called 'bluffing', young lady."

"Whatever. It's what I did and I won!" She started stacking the silverbacks into their respective denominations, a habit she'd picked up from Central Counting, no doubt. He'd already been regaled with the story of what she did to that swindler at the bank, and he had toasted her success.

Leiyara snickered at this, then grabbed his beer stein. She took a long swallow, then made a face. "Ew! What's *in* that?"

Taking another long draft of the beer, the Valet smiled. "In the Gigan world, there's a beast known as a bergha. Huge, shaggy things that provide everything for the Gigan people: you know, meat, fur, mounts, and, of course, milk." He shook his mug indicatively. "This beer is made from barley and fermented bergha milk." Leiyara made a face, swishing her blood cider around in her mouth. "It's not that bad. Puts hair on your chest."

She nearly spit out the cider. "I don't *want* hair on my chest!" she giggled.

Chapter Twenty-Eight: The Colonial Railway, the 9:15 to Four Corners, the Colonies

Leiyara had booked them passage on a train to a town called Four Corners in the Colony of Estrella Nova. From there, they would travel on horseback to the city of Meadowbrook, the apparent epicenter of the weather wizard's activity. Central Transit had been very accommodating, providing maps and literature about the Colonies, even going so far as telegraphing ahead to make for travel and lodging arrangements. Esther strongly suspected this had something to do with the little talk her secretary had with Pencil-mustache back at the bank.

They took a cozy first-class compartment with plush seats and a large window through which to view the passing scenery. At the Call, rail travel was limited to hauling cargo in heavily armored boxcars bristling with armed escorts. Esther couldn't help but feel a little exposed, thinking of all the different vulnerabilities that the train car left open to potential attackers. She had to remind herself more than once that they were in a civilized country now.

As they made their speedy way through the colony of Montblanc, the Peacekeeper couldn't keep her eyes off the alien landscape: rolling hills, pasture, and prairie; fields of wheat and corn stretching to the distant Whitecap mountain range. Having been raised in the desolation of Perdition, it was a dizzying, yet not unpleasant, experience. Leiyara appeared to be having a similar experience. Her huge eyes widened as they flicked across the panorama, her mouth forming unspoken words.

"So. Green," she barely manage.

The Valet and Hrakar, both being well-traveled men of the world, watched them with amusement, occasionally sparing the other a knowing look. More than once, the Valet inflicted one of his bawdy limericks on them, leaving Leiyara giggling and Esther rolling her eyes – they had to explain most of them to Hrakar, as the Sapien didn't translate well. Meanwhile, Hrakar would regale them with descriptions of the Vineyard in Draconia, home of the famous Draconian Red of which everyone was so fond.

"The hills there are filled with the largest, juiciest grapes," he said. "You can taste their sweetness just by looking at them. But you must not taste, no..." he wagged a finger at them, "...for if you do, that is one less grape given the honor of becoming something fine with age. You deprive it of its rest in the oaken barrel where it will become divine among its comrades."

The Valet scoffed. "By 'divine' do you mean squished under someone's toes and rotted until it becomes alcohol?"

Hrakar seemed deflated by this. "You, my comrade in arms, have no appreciation for poetry."

"Poetry is for wooing, wine is for drinking," the Valet replied philosophically.

Those amber eyes sank to the floor. "I think your tongue is as sharp as your sword," Hrakar grumbled.

The Valet shot a wink at Leiyara, "And as skilled."

This brought on another bout of blushing and giggling, endearing the Valet to Hrakar once more. *Men!* Esther thought.

They took their lunch in the dining car, sampling an assortment of Kairulian food. Meats and vegetables were cooked in rich, spicy sauces which were served with hearty flatbreads. They were served lamb, chicken, and some beast known as a bovul – the Valet said it was a cross between a bear and a boar, but Esther took the remark – not to mention the bovul meat – with a pinch of salt (she didn't much care for it). After lunch, they spent the remainder of their journey in the lounge car. The Valet stretched his long self out on one of the couches with a cigar, sipping a glass of the aforementioned Draconian Red – he conceded to Hrakar that it was, indeed, divine, putting the argument to rest – while Esther enjoyed a smoke and a pint of bloodfruit cider with Hrakar. Leiyara curled up in one of the armchairs, fast asleep. Kairulian soldiers in their crisp, charcoal gray uniforms passed in and out of the car, offering Esther a respectful salute.

At mid-day, they disembarked in the sleepy town of Four Corners, so named because it was built squarely on the border between four of the Colonies. That, however, appeared to be its only claim to fame. The town consisted of the railway station and a dusty high street with no name (the Valet joked that their one horse probably also had no name, but his humor failed to land). The Central Transit building was little more than a ticketing kiosk on the station platform, the few shops and storefronts, mostly catering to travelers passing through, were dusty stucco with those blue-tiled roofs one found in Kairulian architecture.

Esther and Leiyara retrieved their luggage on the platform, Hrakar and the Valet wrangled the mounts – Heartbreaker, of course, was still with them as well as the remaining clockwork horse from their caravan adventure. They were met outside the station by a stable boy – literally a boy, Esther clocked him at ten years old, at most – leading a rental mount with the Central Transit logo stamped on its rear. The Peacekeeper tipped the boy, sending him on his way.

As they mounted up, Leiyara fidgeted. "Who can I ride with?" she asked.

The Valet extended a hand. "Heartbreaker wouldn't forgive me if I refused," he said.

He helped her up, steadying her as she settled in the side-saddle fashion that propriety dictated in these parts. Esther and Hrakar shared a glance, betraying a discussion they'd had about Leiyara only that morning. She looked at them, abashedly puzzled.

Esther gave her a reassuring smile. “I think it's time we give you some riding lessons,” she said. “We'll begin when we make camp tonight.”

Leiyara tried to smile but only looked awkward, miserable. "Okay," she said.

Chapter Twenty-Nine: Outside Four Corners, Estrella Nova, the Colonies

Meadowbrook was a day and a half ride from Four Corners over a smoothly paved road. Good weather held, the fresh air blowing down from the mountains, bringing with it the smell of freshly tilled earth and growing things, each a new sensory experience for Esther.

About halfway into their ride, the Valet pointed southeast. “Over that way is a town called Turner. I was there when your airship went down. Just beyond those mountains is the Gray Marsh.”

The contrast fascinated Esther. The only thing separating these lush, fertile lands from that desolate horror show was the thin band of the Whitecaps. She imagined the boundaries there being as dramatically demarcated as the border in the Alcon mountains. Leiyara, however, just shuddered, looking miserable again at the memory. Esther felt a pang of guilt for all that the poor girl had been through but reminded herself again that she'd given Leiyara ample warning of the dangers that Morgarai presented. It did little to ease her mind.

They stopped to make camp near a circle of standing stones a little before sunset. The ancient holy place still hummed with leyline energies, the Source running through them like blood in the veins of the world. Esther could feel that living energy at the back of her mind, where she drew from it to work her glyph magicks. With the right tools or training, hypothetically, one could tap the leylines and draw upon the Source energies of the earth, creating the potential for unlimited power – legend had it that the Primivites did this during the Daemon Wars. Esther shuddered at the thought, unsurprised the practice had fallen out of favor.

While the Valet and Hrakar prepared the fire for their evening meal, Esther took Leiyara and her clockwork horse back to the road.

"I feel ridiculous," Leiyara complained, tugging at her breeches. The pants and shirt Esther lent to her were too big for her tiny frame – she practically swam in them.

Esther smiled. "You'll thank me later," she said. "You don't want to be riding in a frock."

"I don't want to be riding at all!" Leiyara protested.

The Peacekeeper just waved her off. She turned her attention to the clockwork horse, winding it up for what was likely going to be a rough ride. "Now, this unit is your standard four-speed, pedal-shift." She indicated the right stirrup. "To shift gears – that is, to make it go faster or slower – you press down on this stirrup, then..." she indicated the left stirrup, "...you'll press down on this stirrup. That will shift you from neutral to a walk, a trot, then a canter, then a gallop."

Leiyara nodded, still looking dubious.

"Now, you only need to hold down on the right stirrup when you're shifting, otherwise it'll play the Void with the crankshaft, and when you shift, you only need to press til you hear a click, then you let up on both stirrups."

"It seems like a lot."

Esther nodded. "It isn't easy at first. I won't tell you about my first experience riding one of these, but you'll catch on soon enough." She took hold of the reins, holding them up. "To steer, you only have to use the reins, but you'll pull right to go left and left to go right."

"That doesn't make any sense!" Leiyara complained, still tugging at her clothing with a pair of shaking hands.

"Think of it not as the direction the reins are going and more which way the mount's head is facing. That makes it easier. When you want to slow down, you pull back on the reins but do it gently or it'll stop suddenly and throw you. Also, don't forget to downshift."

"Downshift?"

Esther nodded. “Yes. You'll press the left stirrup upward to shift down from a gallop to a canter, or from a canter to a trot, or from a trot back to walk. Another shift and you're back in neutral.”

Looking wretched now, Leiyara threw her hands in the air wildly. "This sounds hard!"

“Just take it easy at first,” Esther said, patting the saddle to indicate where Leiyara should be. “Come on now, give it a try.”

Leiyara climbed up onto the clockwork horse, awkwardly shimmying into the saddle. She set her feet in the stirrups, taking the reins in both of her shaking hands.

“Don't be afraid, I'm right here,” Esther cooed reassuringly.

Giving a manic nod, Leiyara remained frozen on the mount.

“Now, push down with your right foot and shift into a trot.”

Leiyara pushed down on the right stirrup, then clicked the left one down once. She jumped a little when the mechanical horse lurched into a slow trot. Esther followed along beside her as her student beamed.

“I'm doing it!” Leiyara shouted. “I'm riding!”

“Good,” Esther instructed, “now pull the reins gently and bear to the right.”

Leiyara eased the reins over but instead bore left. She overcompensated, jerking to the right and nearly knocking Esther off her feet, then let out a small cry and tugged the reins too hard, bringing the horse up to an abrupt halt with the harsh noise of grinding gears.

“Downshift!” Esther reminded her.

Leiyara pressed down with her right foot but shifted up instead of down. The brakes screeched in protest, so she let up on the reins to ease them, which sent the clockwork horse off at a canter.

“Esther! Help!”

"Right foot down, left foot up," she commanded. Leiyara did so, easing the horse back into a slow trot. "Now, gently pull the reins." Leiyara did so, slowing down until the gears ground again. "Right foot down, left foot up," Esther reminded her, considering the repair costs if the crankshaft went out suddenly.

The mount came to a slow, easy stop. Leiyara sat frozen for a moment, pale and shaking. From the camp a few yards away Hrakar and the Valet were cheering her on.

"Not bad for a first-timer," Esther remarked. "My first time I wound up on my backside. How are you feeling?"

The stunned Leiyara let out a little giggle, then started laughing hysterically. "That. Was. Amazing!" she cried. "Let's do it again!"

Chapter Thirty: Meadowbrook, Estrella Nova, the Colonies

By the time they reached Meadowbrook, Leiyara had already taken to riding. Esther rode tandem with her, coaching her along the way. Before they reached the city limits, the party could also see the problem: to the northeast, as far as the eye could see, dark stormclouds poured rain down on the farmlands, drowning crops to create vast pools of stagnant water. To confirm the Call's suspicions, and her own, Esther reached out with her senses, touching upon her connection to the Source and allowing it to stretch out to the rainstorm. She felt a massive vibration, almost enough to throw her from her horse, certainly enough to shake her.

"Are you okay?" Leiyara asked, seeing her nearly tip over.

Hrakar and the Valet, on either side, reached out to steady her. "I'm fine," she said. "There's a massive amount of Source energy coming from that direction. It's our weather wizard."

As they rode on, Esther continued to feel the enormity of the magickal field like a low-level electrical current. It buzzed at the back of her head, making her fingers and toes tingle.

"How is he able to maintain it?" the Valet asked. "Wouldn't using up that much energy suck the life out of him?"

Scanning the horizon, Esther felt them: small areas where the Source pooled and eddied, flowing from singular, central points. "There are runes that compound and enhance the energy, like an echo chamber," she explained. "When positioned strategically, they can power spellcraft independent of the caster. It's what Wraithbane coined as 'Runic power', and it once lit up the whole empire."

As an agricultural center, Meadowbrook had the feel of a city that had once been alive, prosperous. The city center had a wide, open-air market filled with empty stalls where sellers once cried wares of fresh fruits and vegetables. The cobbled high street was flanked with shops and saloons, cafes and restaurants, all closed or boarded up. It appeared the city died along with its fields. They were met at the end of the lane by a contingent of Kairulian troops who were holding back a mob of citizens. The people were all shouting as they threw rotten food, moldy bread, even stones. They were crying out for their leaders to act, to end the flooding.

This is Sapienkind? Esther wondered. *They're so afraid that they're ready to lynch the man in charge.*

Behind the line of soldiers stood the governor's villa, a multistory building with two wings and a terraced garden on the top floor. It looked like a palace with arched doors and high windows. The grounds of the villa were wide and broad, filled with drowned, rapidly browning flora. A high, spiked fence wrought from black iron surrounded the property.

The Peacekeeper put her fingers to her lips, whistling loudly over the crowd, so loud that Leiyara had to cover her ears. The mob quieted, slowly at first, then all eyes were on Esther – the mob, the soldiers, her companions; Leiyara had to cover her ears. Esther dismounted, taking off her medallion to hold it high and try to keep her hands from shaking. If this went wrong...

"I am Peacekeeper Esther Triad," she shouted. "I've been sent by the Call to investigate the rains that are destroying your crops and your livelihoods. Please return to your homes and I will do everything in my power to restore your community."

The people of Meadowbrook all looked at each other, a susurration of hushed voices passed through them like a wave. They jostled, muttering to one another and, though it didn't immediately disperse, the mob's edges began to thin as it dissipated, parting for Esther and her company. As they rode to the gate of the governor's villa, Esther looked around at the faces. Men, women, even children, all frightened or angry, long past desperation. They weren't just holding rotted food, but farm implements as well: pitchforks, hoes, picks, shovels. Had the Peacekeeper not intervened, she wondered what kind of violence would have erupted.

A venerable soldier in a long gray coat met them at the gate. He had a well-kept beard and close-cropped hair that was going from black to white. His toasted skin was marked with age and a few battle scars, at his side he had a pistol and a sword – not the standard-issue rapier carried by Kairulian infantry, but a custom weapon with a broad blade and thick, black iron crossguard. He was no ordinary soldier.

"You are most welcome, Peacekeeper," the soldier said. "I am Sir Argas Swiftsteel, King's Justice and commander of the Royal Guard."

Esther put her medallion back on, touching her hand to it in return of Sir Argas's salute. Swiftsteel nodded to the guards on the other side of the gates, men also wearing gray coats, who opened the gates to admit the party.

"Do come in," Sir Argas said. "You are eagerly awaited."

Esther had read the word "posh" in books, but had only the vaguest notion of what it meant until she entered the governor's villa. The walls were painted in bright hues of yellow and red, the floors were stone tile polished to a brilliant shine; rich carpets were laid out here and there. They were escorted past sitting rooms – antechambers decorated with murals and varnished mission-style furniture – then led upstairs under a glowing crystal chandelier. Homes with electric lighting were not popular in these parts, most still using gaslights, but the villa appeared to have been retrofitted with wiring; lights shone everywhere in the house.

At last, they came to an antechamber with two heavy wooden doors closing off what Esther assumed was the governor's office.

Argas and his gray-coated escorts stopped them here. Sir Argas knocked on the door and a small, sweaty man peeked out. Everything about his appearance bespoke intellectual affectation: a pinstripe blue suit and waistcoat complete with a pocket watch, his thinning hair slicked back over a pallid pate, pair of pince-nez magnifying big, wet eyes. Despite his professional appearance, the man seemed sycophantic, nervous.

"Yes?" the balding man asked.

A momerat, Esther thought, reflecting on that fat, bushy-tailed vermin she'd idly executed as a young girl. *He reminds me of a momerat.*

Sir Argas indicated Esther and the company. "Our Peacekeeper has arrived," he said. "Esther Triad, of Ordo's Call."

The little rodent-man peered at the knight over his glasses as if he couldn't understand Sapien, then examined Esther. "Hm...I see," he said. "The governor will see you. Sir Argas, you as well, please."

The party made a move toward the door, but the little man held up a hand. "I'm sorry," he said with an awkward little chuckle, another affectation. "I meant the Peacekeeper and Sir Argas ...ah...exclusively. Delicate matters of national security, I'm afraid."

Esther looked about at her friends. The Valet glared at the tiny civil servant like he was a stone that needed kicking. Hrakar's expression matched hers in uncertainty. Leiyara just seemed lost among the rich décor and electric lighting; Esther wasn't even sure she was paying attention.

"These are my trusted companions," she ventured. "Anything your governor has to say to me can be shared with them as well."

The little bureaucrat removed his glasses to reveal that his eyes were small and beady. He smiled as though he had a private joke. "I'm sorry," he repeated, hesitating just long enough to give Esther hope. "It is...uncommon for a Peacekeeper to have trusted companions..."

he almost giggled over the term, "...and we uphold tradition in this house. You and Sir Argas may enter. Exclusively."

The little man put his spectacles back on, smiling like a person drunk on what little power they could scrape up – the expression at once amused, dismissive, and vicious. If a snake could smile, it would look like this.

"Triad, you can't possibly be considering..." the Valet began.

She put a hand up and, to her surprise, the big man stopped speaking. "It's alright," she said, leveling her gaze on the little bureaucrat. She unslung her knapsack, handing it to Leiyara. "Go to the hotel and get us settled in. I'll *fill you in* when this is finished." The Peacekeeper glared at the little man, putting a particular emphasis on the last. The momerat's smile was implacable.

No one moved. Turning to them, she saw clearly that they were about to protest. She considered telling the little man what he could do with "national security", refusing to oblige without her friends, but she also imagined how that would make her appear to her superiors, whom the civil servant would no doubt contact. "Please," she said. "I'll tell you everything when I get there. Trust me."

Her friends were not convinced but allowed themselves to be escorted out by Argas's attendants. Leiyara kept casting worried glances back, the Valet grumbled and muttered oaths under his breath, Hrakar's eyes were expressionless under his silks, but bristled with malice as sharp as his spearhead.

Once they were gone, the little bureaucrat clapped his hands. "Right, then. I am Mr. Douglas, the personal attaché to Governor Avalos." He opened the double doors behind him, which to Esther's surprise led to the terraced garden instead of the office. "The governor will see you now."

• • • •

"THAT SNIVELING, SUCKLING momerat whoreson of a two-bit, mangy fetch!" the Valet raged. "He's lucky I didn't plant my fist right in that smug little face."

They were on the streets now, relieved of their escort. The Valet's fists were clenched at his sides as he fumed, staring daggers up at the garden terrace on the villa's second level. "We slip in," he said. "Yeah. We distract the guards, hop the fence, and we hear what the governor has to say for himself. If we don't like his answers, we can cut our way out and wipe the grin off that smug little bastard's face in the meantime."

Behind him, Leiyara and Hrakar exchanged a glance. "I don't think that's a good idea," Leiyara said. "And Esther wouldn't approve."

The Valet wheeled on her, causing Leiyara to step back apprehensively. "And let the little-bureaucrat-that-could have his way?"

Hrakar stepped between them, holding up placating hands. "I agree with Leiyara," he said. "There are strict rules of conduct that Esther must observe. As her friends and compatriots, we should honor her in this."

The Valet appeared to calm a little. "I don't like it," he protested.

Hrakar shook his head. "I don't either," he said, his eyes flicking just over the Valet's shoulder. The shade walker followed them again. The Valet had spotted her the moment they'd left the villa, and *Glaeve Pandaemonia* had been warning him of her presence the entire journey to Meadowbrook. He didn't have to look to see her; she gave him the feeling of a net closing in around him.

"So what do we do?" he asked.

Leiyara spoke up, hefting Esther's knapsack over her already laden shoulder. "We do what Esther wanted: we find a hotel and wait." She started up the high street without waiting for them to follow.

Hrakar chucked the Valet on the shoulder. "Come," he said chummily, "I'll buy you a Draconian red."

The Valet took a deep breath. "You're right. I could use a drink about now." Then, as they caught up to Leiyara, "Sorry if I frightened you, honey. I get a little hot sometimes."

Leiyara smiled, but couldn't hide the wariness in her large eyes. "It's okay," she said. "Let's just get settled."

Settled, my eye, the Valet thought. *I'm going to get drunk.*

• • • •

ESTHER STEPPED OUT onto the terrace with Sir Argas and the obnoxious Mr. Douglas. She was met with myriad aromas: herbs, flowers, and all manner of other plant life. The sun sunk low in the east already, bathing the flagstones in a red-violet light. Among the trellises lined with winding thorn ivy, Governor Avalos stood with his back to them, hands clasped behind his back, feet spread shoulder length apart. A fit, bronze skinned man with a well-trimmed beard, he dressed in the standard-issue charcoal gray fiberweave of the Kairulian Royal Army, except that he had tasseled, sky blue epaulets to mark his status.

He's like something out of one of Leiyara's novels, Esther thought derisively, suddenly getting the impression that these theatrics of his were staged, but for whose benefit?

"You see what I'm up against, Peacekeeper," the governor said. "Six weeks of rainfall have destroyed my lands. My people, for fear of starving, revolt. The king, who no longer puts his trust in me, sends his judge and executioner to watch my every move. It's as though I'm part of some plot."

Glancing at Sir Argas at this last remark, Esther was impressed that he remained stone-faced. She moved forward, unbidden, but Mr. Douglas moved to stop her. She shot him a glare that shut that smart, grinning mouth of his. "I wouldn't know about that," she said. "I'm only here about your weather wizard."

Governor Avalos gave a humorless chuckle. "The weather wizard? Ah, the arcanist, of course. Yes, that seems to be the root of all of my present concerns." He turned now, gazing at her with dark, intense eyes. He looked tired. "I'm beginning to wish I'd never heard that word '*arcanist*'. Or spellcraft, or magicks. I should have rejected these things like the rest of my countrymen do."

I'd better get to the point before he starts a monologue, Esther thought. "Where is the arcanist now?"

Sir Argas answered. "We're not sure. My men tell me he may have fled into the Gray Marsh, suicidal as it may sound, while others report similar activity in Agimonde. I have contacts at Central Transit trying to verify those claims."

Esther turned to the knight. "You needn't look any further. I can verify them for you."

Silence from all parties. Swifsteel looked shocked, Avalos gobsmacked, and Mr. Douglas went on with that vapid grin, looking as though preoccupied with his own private joke.

"Mr. Douglas," Avalos said. "Bring tea for our guests. It would appear that we have much to discuss."

• • • •

HE DRANK AND HE DRANK. Then, he drank some more. It seemed as if no amount of wine could quench his rage or that unnerving feeling they had just been walked straight into a trap. And as any woman in Morgarai could tell you, the Valet was not the type to be trapped. Hrakar sat across from him at the table, his amber eyes tracking activity on the street. The hotel was a large hacienda-style building in the center of the city; a terrace outside of its cafe was peppered with travelers, but at sundown, the entire depressed place seemed to close up. A few people walked with trudging steps, a few closed their already desolate shops and restaurants, but the Valet knew not one of them piqued the Draconian's interest. His eyes were on the shadows.

"We should just take care of her," the Valet remarked. "Right here, right now. I'm spoiling for a fight."

Hrakar took a sip of his wine. It intrigued the Valet to find that the Draconians' staunch rules about modesty didn't appear to apply when they were at the table. They were allowed, after saying a certain prayer, to uncover their mouths. He'd watched Hrakar eat back in Patel having noticed the same thing. "She is beyond your skill," he said bluntly.

The big man hammered his fist on the table, his fury stoked once more. A few of the patrons jumped, a few gave him a warning glare. "There's no one *alive* beyond my skill!" he nearly shouted. "Draw steel and find out, *beschetna*!"

Hrakar's eyes narrowed dangerously. It was one of the few words in Drakkenspek that the Valet knew. It meant something close to "dishonorable" or "coward", or a combination of the two; he regretted saying it even as it left his mouth. *The stone is thrown,* he thought. *No use trying to retrieve it.*

"I will let that, as you say, slide, as a cost of your drunkenness," Hrakar said. "I did not mean to insult you. I have seen your skill as a fighter, attacking with all the fury of the *Untavalt*. But it is not a matter of strength and speed for a shade walker, but cunning. They fight...how do you say it?"

"Dirty," the Valet grumbled. "They fight dirty."

The Draconian clapped his hands. "Ah! Yes, that is the word. It is what makes the shade walker dangerous."

The Valet nodded, but the more his companion insisted the shade walker couldn't be beaten, the more he felt challenged to take that bet. As yet, he had not been defeated, dueling anyone foolhardy enough to challenge him or, sometimes, just to prove a point. The thought of being bested by some second-class, fringe Draconian fundamentalist stuck in his craw. Fortunately, the fickle heart of the Valet was not one to dwell. Of the three things he cared about most in the world – wine, fighting, and women – the third of the three stepped out onto the terrace.

She was tall and elegant, almost regal. Long, raven locks fell about her shoulders, framing her perfect skin. She wore a gown that was blacker than black, revealing just enough to whet the appetite. The woman glanced at him demurely, before sashaying to the edge of the terrace with her back to him.

The Valet finished his second bottle in a mighty gulp. "You'll have to pardon me, Hrakar," he said. "I'm going to see about a girl."

• • • •

HRAKAR DID PARDON THE Valet. Any man with a bruised ego that far into his cups wasn't good company anyway. He tried to let go of the fact that he'd been incensed about the Valet's slight on his dishonor, but that rage had passed from his unlikely companion into him. The shadows... Every one of them seemed to contain the shade walker, her yellow eyes peering at him, passing judgment upon him for his choice of company. As insular as Draconian culture was, the shade walkers were downright isolationist, believing the world would be better populated by a homogeneous Draconian species. They represented everything Hrakar was raised to stand against.

Making his mind up wasn't difficult. He returned to his room as the sun set, locked the door behind him, then opened his duffel bag. Removing its contents carefully, reverently, he laid them out on his bed one by one. His gauntlets, the claws of the dragon, spiked with wicked talons on each knuckle and fingertip. Next, his drakeskin coat, the wings of the dragon, a leather so durable it was all but bulletproof. Then, his helmet, an interpretation on the breath of the dragon, crafted from the skull of a drake, fired and bronzed. Last, the spearhead used by the Legion – far superior to the paltry weapon he'd settled for in his exile – the tail of the dragon, and had a long, curved blade on one side, a lethal pike protruding from the top, and a barbed hook sticking out from the back.

Hrakar removed his veil, unwrapping the silks with careful hands. He went down on one knee, holding up his hands, closing his amber eyes tightly. "Lumynos forgive me," he prayed. "I am not worthy to bear your gifts or take up your cause. In my disgrace, I beseech you to bless my hand, which is forced, and my soul, which is unwilling. I take up these gifts knowing I am most unworthy, but that the need is dire. Give me strength, grant me your light."

He stood, pulled on his coat, fastened his gauntlets, then changed his spearhead. Last, he pulled on his helmet, wrapping its long silk scarf around the lower half of his face. He took a deep breath, taking in the scent of leather, bronze, and steel. He was ready.

As Hrakar pulled the door closed behind him, a voice in the hall stopped him. "Hrakar, is that you?"

Leiyara. Of course, it was Leiyara. Truth be told, Hrakar liked Esther's young secretary, plucky and inexperienced as she may be, but over the last few days something about the girl made him uneasy. Something in the way she watched them made him wary, something in the way she didn't seem to ever sleep. It felt like spying. Since he had no proof of any misdeed, he'd kept the matter to himself, not even hinting at it during his time alone with Esther. Still, he did not completely trust her.

"It is I," he replied.

"You look...different," Leiyara remarked. Those big, round, Sapien eyes seemed to bore into him again.

"This is what Legionnaires wear into battle," he replied tersely.

Leiyara's expression changed to one of worry, her hands clasped together over her chest, but her eyes were still smiling. "The shade walker," she guessed. "You're going to fight the shade walker!"

"I am," he replied, "and I must go alone. I will not endanger my friends."

He'd expected her to protest – were she true to herself and her friends, she would have protested, suggest he wait for Esther and the Valet so they could face the threat together. She should have tried to reason with him. "There is an Iyon ruin to the north of here," she said instead. "It was a gathering place to settle disputes. You should lead her there."

Hrakar hid the suspicion from his voice. "A fitting place indeed."

The girl smiled, but it did not look like Leiyara's smile at all. It was wicked, sly. "May the blessings of Lumynos go with you," she said.

Hrakar thanked her and left the hallway, confident he was walking into a trap.

• • • •

LEIYARA WOKE FROM THE nightmare, finding herself standing outside her room. It wasn't the most peculiar place she'd woken up – the standing stones in Agimonde still held that title. She wasn't sure when exactly she'd taken up sleepwalking, but it worried her.

Had she been speaking to someone? It seemed like she had, but in the haze of the dream, she couldn't remember. There had been a man in the hallway, she'd only barely recognized him, and he was going somewhere. She felt like she needed to tell someone where he was going.

But the dream clung to her. In it, she'd been standing in what appeared to be an auditorium or arena – an ancient speaking place or maybe a place where disputes were settled. She remembered thinking it was north of Meadowbrook, even though she couldn't possibly know that. There were people in the speaking place, a man and a woman and a shadow. No, it had been the shade walker. They were talking, *she* had been talking, but not in her voice. In the dream, when she opened her mouth...or her mind, rather, since she didn't have a mouth (*none of this makes sense!*) that raspy, alien whisper came out.

What had they been saying? Something about a knight and a pawn? There'd been a fair amount of bickering between the elegant woman and the man shuffling his Taro deck. Eventually, they came to a compromise: the woman would handle the Knight of Cups (whoever that was) while the card shuffler would deal with the pawn. The question of someone called the drake rider was raised, but Elegant Woman said it was well in hand.

At that point, Leiyara shushed them. She explained in that creepy whisper that someone – a spy, apparently – was listening in on the converstion, that the connection worked both ways. After that a wave of force jolted her awake to find herself standing in the hallway outside here room.

The dream could be explained, she told herself. There had been a lot of talk in words she hadn't understood lately. Words like Pah-ren, *echem*, even her companions' names were foreign to her – she didn't know what language *Le Valet des Coeurs* was, for example. She'd just learned to play Taro, so the man with the Taro deck made sense. Her mother would tell her he represented sin. The woman was tall and dark and beautiful, like so many of the strong, beautiful women they'd encountered on their journey. The shade walker just represented the latest threat.

But that voice, she thought. *Why was I talking in that voice?*

She didn't know. Maybe that whisper had been invading her dreams for so long that it clung to her thoughts. Maybe because it spoke her mother's disparaging words, even taking over for her in Leiyara's memory. It had nearly replaced her own voice in her head by now.

What am I becoming? She wondered, panic clutching at her heart. *What if the wraith's spell worked and I'm becoming someone else?*

No, that couldn't be. The mysterious and strangely compelling Myrian named Dal had saved her. She'd been rescued, returned safely to her friends. It was just the nightmare compounded by her lack of sleep. Leiyara yawned, trying to dismiss the terror. She was safe now, she told herself in that whispering voice. She should sleep.

• • • •

ESTHER FINISHED HER tale, having recounted as much as she remembered about the attacks of the arcanist. Governor Avalos listened intently while the toad-like Mr. Douglas took detailed notes. Sir Argas bent an ear but seemed more concerned with spreading jam on his toast. Perhaps he had a better information network than they had in the Colonies, or perhaps such adventures held little interest for the mightiest – and only – knight on life.

"It doesn't make sense," Mr. Douglas protested. "After destroying our crop, what interest would he have in you?"

Esther shrugged. "That's what I'd like to know," she replied. "His finely dressed partner seemed like he was into something he didn't want a Peacekeeper to discover."

Avalos sat back in his wicker chair, lighting a pipe. "A peculiar tale, indeed," he said. "A rogue arcanist, a shadowy figure plotting with wraiths and outlaws. This Agi man you suspect of being more than he appeared. You've had quite your share of adventure."

"Thank you, Governor," Esther said, "but I would hardly call it adventure. We lost many good people – innocent people – on account of this arcanist. I would like to hear your account and any clues you may have to his whereabouts."

The governor nodded, his long, dark fingers forming a steeple in front of his nose. "Of course, but I fear there is not much to tell. These lands suffered from a drought only a few weeks ago. We made attempts to irrigate it, but to no avail. Our crops were in danger of dying and my people of losing their livelihoods. The arcanist was only passing through. As a last resort, I hired him to bring the rains. As you see, the rains have not yet stopped."

"And do you have any inkling as to the weather wizard's location?"

Spreading his hands, the governor shook his head.

Mr. Douglas turned his beady little eyes up from his notebook. "Recent reports suggest that he may have taken refuge in Plainview, but I haven't confirmed that."

Sir Argas finished his toast. "It sounds like a good place to start. Tell me about Plainview."

Avalos and Douglas exchanged a glance. "The first place abandoned after the flooding," Mr. Douglas said. "Or we assume it's abandoned. We've had no contact at all from within the floodplain."

The Peacekeeper grew exasperated by this news. "You mean you didn't send in rescue teams? Search parties? Medics?"

Avalos stood, pacing the terrace floor. "We haven't those sorts of resources here," he said. "Look around you! We are a small farming community on the edge of the Frontier. We have soldiers and a Peacekeeper now, but where were you when this spellcrafter flooded my colony?"

Esther put up a hand. "Calm down, Governor."

"No! I will not calm down!" Avalos shouted. "You come here with your accusations and hindsight about how I should run things, but you were not here when my people were forced from their homes, when they came in droves, soaked and starving. You were not here when a king who provided *no aid* passed judgment on me or when my people turned on me. Do *not* tell me to calm down!"

At this last, he slammed his fists on the small table, toppling it and spilling its contents onto the flagstones. Mr. Douglas moved swiftly to avoid the crashing teapot while Sir Argas stood, putting one hand on his sword-hilt. Esther, however, remained calmly seated.

"Are you quite finished, Governor?" she asked.

Avalos nodded, looking at his feet like a child ashamed of his tantrum.

Now, Esther stood. "Good. I do not envy you the burden of leadership, nor do I minimize your plight. I only meant to know all there is to know so that I can remedy your situation. I am charged with finding this...arcanist and bringing him to justice, and that's what I will do."

In response, the governor gave her a small nod then looked up at her, a glimmer of hope in his dark eyes. "Thank you."

Mr. Douglas stood with the cracked teapot fragments in his damp grip. "I can provide you the details of how to find Plainview, as well as any documentation we have on our dealings with the arcanist."

"That would be very helpful," Esther affirmed.

"I hope," Mr. Douglas added, "that we can resolve this unpleasantness yet tonight. Plainview isn't far."

Esther looked at each of the men in turn. Sir Argas with his steely gaze, Avalos with his miserable hope, Mr. Douglas with those dead eyes and haughty little smile. She had her friends to think about, but duty had to come first. "I will leave at once," she said. "If you don't mind sending word to my companions. They've sought out lodging in your city."

Avalos clapped his hands, letting out a triumphant laugh. "Simple!" he cried. "We have only one open hotel at present. Mr. Douglas will deliver the message straight away."

Esther stood, bid the governor farewell, and made for the door.

"Actually," Sir Argas said, "I wondered if I might accompany you."

Dubious, the Peacekeeper turned and looked at the knight.

Swiftsteel raised his hands plaintively. "I am charged by my king to get to the bottom of this mess..." he shot Avalos a pointed glare,

"...and, admittedly, I'd rather not do so alone. Spellcraft can be a treacherous business."

I wonder what he'd think if he knew I was guilty of spellcraft? Esther thought. Likely he made the distinction between Runic magicks and glyph magicks, "spellcraft" being his word for the former. While she wondered, she tried to appear that she was thinking things over; truth was she was relieved not to have to go it on her own. Mustering the stoic, solitary nature of every Peacekeeper she'd met, Esther put on a scowl. "Fine," she said. "But stay out of my way."

Chapter Thirty-One:
The Floodplain, the Colonies

The edge of the floodplain wasn't far from Meadowbrook. After less than an hour's ride northeast, Esther stared at the surreal sight: the rains had turned the fields into a wetland, drowned and dotted with large bogs; dead crops and trees poked up from the gray pools, the tops of the hills like islands in a vast lake. The rains cut off like a sheer wall before her, the clear night sky on one side, dense cloud cover on the other.

"We should go on foot," Sir Argas said. "Negotiating the bogs will be treacherous enough without our mounts."

Esther nodded, still aghast at the sight of the arcanist's work. They dismounted, Esther from her light and agile Agi horse, Sir Argas from his enormous mechanical charger. It was painted the color of Kairal – charcoal gray and gold – with heavily armored flanks and neck. She recalled that, as well as being a kingdom known for its martial strength, Kairal was well known for its engineering prowess.

Sir Argas waded into the water first; it came up to his knees. Esther followed, feeling the hem of her cassock drag in the swampy mire, the rain pattering on the brim of her hat. Everything stank of damp and mildew and decay. It was slow going and they were both soaked to the skin by the time they reached the first rise. The grass was dead, the mud black and slick. In the near distance, they could see the town of Plainview by the occasional flashes of lightning. No lights were burning, no chimneys belched smoke or steam. Looking at it, Esther could feel that cold stone settling into her stomach again, a sure sign that danger awaited her there.

"I don't suppose we can turn back and just tell Avalos that the town is abandoned," Esther remarked.

From beneath his hood, Sir Argas quirked a smile. "Would that we could. I'm soaked to the bone," he admitted. "But if the arcanist is there, we could put an end to this tonight."

Esther couldn't argue, though she no longer believed it was as simple as taking down one arcanist anymore. That dandy with the Taro deck had hinted at something much bigger at play here: these were people who not only had a powerful arcanist on their side, but had brought to bear the full fury of wraiths and daemons. It made Esther's skin crawl, the thought of so much trouble, so many lives lost, all on her account.

Perhaps it would have been easier just to die in the airship crash, she thought. Dismissing her despair as gloominess caused by the rain, she said a silent prayer to Ordo to grant her strength, then plunged ahead into the knee-deep bog. Sir Argas followed, trudging through the muck with about the same level of difficulty.

Half an hour later, they found themselves on a raised stretch of road, the paving stones soggy but very much above water. Half drowned at the side of the road were the decaying remains of a campsite. It was quite large with two pavilions, tables and chairs, and what appeared to be digging equipment. As well as shovels, pickaxes, and wheelbarrows, Esther also saw the rusted, toothed monstrosity that had been a steam-powered backhoe.

"A mining operation?" the Peacekeeper guessed. "This far from the Whitecaps?"

Sir Argas shook his head. The fact that he wasn't surprised led Esther to believe that he'd known about the camp – perhaps, even, it had been his goal to find it. "An archeological dig," he said. He glanced at Esther's dubious puzzlement, shrugging. "We received word that the Royal Archeological Society had found something of great significance in these parts. The rains came and communications were cut off before we could find out what."

Esther laughed bitterly. "So, your objective was never the arcanist. You came to survey this site among the ruins."

Swiftsteel reached up and touched his nose with one gloved hand, with the other he pointed at her. "The arcanist and his effect on the Colonies of Kairal is, officially, my primary objective," he explained. "However, if I can discover the nature of this significant find, I am ordered to do so."

As she squelched toward the camp, Esther felt both flattered and a little concerned with the knight's trust in her. "Well, let's get to it, then."

The campsite rested on the leeward side of the raised road, making the water only ankle deep. The first tent, a bunkhouse by the look of it, had started to collapse and mildew; one half of the rotted canvas had overturned the beds at the far end, while those on the near side were soggy and dripping, mold already eating away at them. There was a long table in the center accompanied by wooden benches, the remains of a half-eaten meal on it. Flies and larvae were making a feast of it now.

The second tent was barely the worse for wear, the canvas made from a sturdier oilcloth that kept the moisture out. Inside was an office with a makeshift bedroom at the back. A polished wooden desk stood to one side, covered with maps and grids, a diary, and books. The wet air moistened them, but hadn't degraded them further. It felt good to get out of the rain. Esther folded her fingers into the Lord's Lantern when Sir Argas lit a match, holding it to a lantern on the desk. It flared to life and, feeling a little embarrassed, Esther dispelled her magicks.

Probably better this way, she thought. Considering their opinions on spellcraft, there was no telling how a Kairulian would react.

The knight went straight for the diary and maps while Esther had a look around. There were crates situated around the tent acting as end tables and shelves for more books. She perused one such cache, finding *The Compendium of Iyon Ruins* by Professor Juli Rust, as well as *The Mysteries of the Marsh* by CJ Chaney. There was a copy of the *Libram ex Genisi*, which any man of faith would have, as well as a worn tome called *The Remains of Elder Days: A History of Lost Technology* by A. Figgins.

By the bed, another lantern stood next to a framed photograph. The photo showed a man with an impressive mustache – the archeologist, Esther assumed – dressed in a crisp white suit and hat, beside him sat a woman in finery, a fascinator pinned in her hair. It looked like a wedding portrait. This was a well educated man of means, the Peacekeeper deduced, with a new young bride and aspirations to uncover the history of Morgarai. Had his young wife traveled with him? Did they make it out alive?

"What's his name?" Esther asked.

"Hm?" Sir Argas said, deep in his own research. "Oh, Emerson Radcliffe."

Esther looked at the man in the photograph. He seemed almost jovial. "Emerson Radcliffe," she said to herself. "He doesn't look Kairulian," she added.

"He's from the south," Sir Argas replied absently. "They're fair-haired and pale skinned in the south."

Esther nodded, filing that information away. "And his wife?"

"What about her?" The knight's voice was tinged with annoyance now.

"Was she with him?"

Sir Argas looked up at her, his gaze softening as the direction of her inquiry sank in. "Yes. And no, I don't know if they made it out alive. There's been no contact, so naturally I assume the worst."

Solemnly, Esther put the photograph down. "Have you discovered what he found?"

The knight paged through the diary. "He doesn't say. He only describes it in terms of dimensions and location, referring to it in measurements I don't fully understand. He was planning to have sketches done or even a photograph taken, but the storms came soon after the discovery was unearthed." He laid down the diary and examined the grid. "It's near here. I should look into it, but..." he looked at her, almost pleadingly.

Esther nodded. "But Plainview," she said. "The town looks dead enough from afar. If the arcanist is lying in wait, he would have at least started a fire or lit a lamp. I'll check it out while you investigate Mr –"

"Doctor."

"– Dr. Radcliffe's findings. If you'll show me where it is, I'll join you there."

Sir Argas showed her a map with meticulous grid lines traced over it. A large, smudged X marked a spot only half a mile southeast of the camp. Esther took a glance, marking that Plainview was about equidistant. She headed for the exit, still unable to shake that cold sense of danger.

"Be careful," Sir Argas said, collecting Dr. Radcliffe's work.

Esther nodded and left the tent.

Chapter Thirty-Two: The Proving Ground, the Colonies

Hrakar moved slowly and carefully toward the Iyon ruin, checking behind him to ensure the shade walker still gave chase. Once or twice, he thought he'd lost her, her darkly veiled form melting into the shadows, but she would always be there a moment later, stalking him with feline grace. When he left the hotel he had spotted her and made a show of his armament, letting her know that he was a Legionnaire prepared for a fight. It had clearly piqued the shade walker's interest. As he moved along the moonlit cobbles at a deliberate pace, it once again dawned on him that he could be walking into a trap.

Trap or no, the shade walker belonged to him. Not only did he feel the burden of responsibility for a wayward kinsman pursuing them, but there were old scores to settle. He still remembered the fight that lost him his honor, watching his comrades getting dragged into the shadows to be slaughtered. He intended to pay this shade walker in kind for each one of those lives and for his honor.

He came upon the Iyon ruin abruptly. The road took a sharp bend around the structure, a high-walled semi-circle, like an arena. The stone was pitted and pockmarked with the scars of age, the arched entrances were crumbling and choked with debris. The wind whispered through its tall windows like long lost ghosts. A chill ran through Hrakar as he got the sense of exactly what function this place served: a killing place. Of Morgarai's native races it was said that the Iyon were the most civilized in the old times, but even a civilized culture needed entertainment and something to do with oathbreakers and criminals. Hrakar could practically smell the blood soaked into the stones.

Steeling himself, he entered the killing place, preparing to offer it one last sacrifice. Using the butt of his spear, he levered the rubble from the entrance, stone grinding on stone as the detritus cleared. He ducked through the crumbling arch and made his way to the place's center. All around him the auditorium benches of scarred stone rose to the starry sky. Hrakar could feel the excitement of the crowd, the Iyon people with their pallid skin and cat-like eyes, jeering and shouting. He could almost hear the cries of the prisoners as they were skewered and stabbed and torn limb from limb to the roar of some ancient, terrible beast. The ground beneath his feet thirsted for blood.

"You chose an appropriate place," the shade walker's voice echoed throughout the arena. She slunk up behind him.

Regardless of the circumstances, he felt a small comfort hearing his native Drakkenspek. The soft, ambivalent language of this strange Sapien land felt like yukar sap in his ear.

He turned, raising his weapon. The shade walker began circling him, almost casually. "No talk? Not even a greeting for an old friend?"

Hrakar's eyes narrowed. "I don't know you, blasphemer," he spat.

He could hear the smile in the shade walker's voice. "I would say we know each other intimately, Legionnaire, for I've seen your face."

The battle came back to him in a flash. The village on the edge of the Vineyard burning with blue-black flame, the shade walkers dancing in and out of the shadows, vanishing into one only to appear in another. Hrakar's unit hadn't stood a chance in the ambush. He remembered being wounded, pierced in the side with one of their needle-like *zahni* blades. Blood and pain pressed him to his knees. The shade walker who took his veil, who defiled him, was a woman; she walked with such grace. Such feline grace.

Hrakar took a breath, trying to calm the drake fire in his heart. "So. It was you."

The shade walker extended a hand, muttering a few words of Runic. A single lick of that blue-black fire appeared in her palm, reflected in her yellow eyes. With one more utterance and a flourish the braziers around the edge of the arena lit with dark fire. The flames devoured the stale heat and a cold wind rushed in, fluttering Hrakar's silks.

"I've come to finish the job," the shade walker said. "I am Zintana Retikov. Remember my name on your journey to the Undervault."

She struck fast, whirling her silks into a frenzy of darkness. Hrakar barely caught the glint of firelight from her *zahni* in time to deflect the blows. He swung his spear into the silken storm, but the Zintana dropped into her shadow. Hrakar pivoted right, away from his own shadow, and narrowly missed being skewered. He spun on the shade walker and struck, but she slipped down into his shadow. Less than a second later he felt the tiny impact of a throwing knife bounce off his coat. He spun as quickly as he could, hurling his spear.

Zintana sidestepped the weapon, but it struck one of the braziers, spilling the all consuming fire across the ground. The shade walker danced away from the flames, giggling all the while, providing the distraction he'd been wanting. Hrakar drew his boning knife and rushed her, shouting curses and allowing the raging drake's fire inside of him to consume his thoughts and actions. He got in close, just inside Zintana's reach, and slashed wildly. The first cut hit only silk, the second took a ragged chunk from her silver flesh, the third skimmed past her face, leaving the tiniest scratch.

Zintana feinted back, but was surrounded by the flames she had invoked; there were no shadows by which to escape now. She panted, clutching her side as the wound gushed silvery blood onto the thirsty dirt floor. Hrakar grabbed his spear from the ground and prepared for the final blow.

The sound of clapping hands echoed throughout the arena. At first, Hrakar thought he imagined it, but the sound got clearer and closer. From the corner of his eye he saw the shape of a man emerge from the darkness and pretend to warm his hands by another brazier. He very much fit the description of the ruffly-dressed man of whom Esther had spoken.

"The reputation of the Draconian Legion is well earned," the dandy said, shuffling his Taro deck idly. "The shade walkers are nothing to sneeze at, either."

Zintana made a move to strike, but Hrakar jabbed his spear at her. She moved back, almost touching the dark fire behind her. "Darwin!" she shouted in Sapien. "Help me!"

The frilly man – Darwin, apparently – flipped over the top Taro card. He clucked his tongue. "I'm afraid you oversold yourself," he said. "You said you could vanquish this Draconian pest."

The shade walker's eyes fell. Hrakar still held her at bay with his spear, kept his eyes fixed on her, but addressed Darwin. "Who are you?" he asked. "Why do you pursue us?"

Darwin circled around, stepping lightly and casually, shuffling his cards. "I am one of the Dark Magi," he said. "Some call us the Voidborn, the Fallen, devils. You can take your pick, really." He drew a card and smiled. "But for now, you can call me your captor."

He flipped the card, showing the Hanged Man. As soon as it turned, the card lifted from Darwin's fingers, surrounded by a halo of blue-white light. There was a flash and Hrakar felt heavy chains wrap around his arms and legs, dragging him to his knees. He shouted curses in his native tongue at the Mad Dandy all the way down.

Chapter Thirty-Three: Meadowbrook, the Colonies

Leiyara rolled over in her bed, half awake but still half dreaming. Her room was dark, lit only by moonlight, but she could see some other source of light – a blue-black ghost light – hanging just on the edge of her perception. Perhaps it was the dream. In it, she saw through those strange eyes, thinking whispered thoughts in that archaic language she couldn't understand. They were in the Iyon ruin she'd seen in the previous dream, surrounded by row upon row of stone seats. That dark firelight burned everywhere, from braziers and on the ground. Hrakar was there, and that shade walker woman with the well-dressed man from the other dream.

Darwin, she thought. At the same time, her own whispering voice intoned the name.

The well-dressed man (Esther had called him a dandy) turned and looked at her. She felt surprised that she had spoken his name, almost as if someone had done it in her own voice. As if it had been done against her will. She looked up and saw Hrakar wrapped in chains. The chains were coming from a Taro card hovering just above him. Leiyara knew that the sight should have shocked her, that it should have woken her with horror, a scream and a warning on her lips.

But all she could feel was delight.

It can't be me, she thought, in her own voice. *That feeling is someone else's.*

Darwin walked away from Hrakar and the shade walker. Leiyara felt compelled to put an arm out to stop him. She wasn't surprised to see her boney white hand, tipped with sharp claws etched with blue-black runes; tattered black cloth wrapped her arm, rising and falling on its own breeze. Where had she seen that hand before?

"You won't watch him die?" Leiyara asked in that raspy, whispering voice.

Darwin just waved her off. "The shade walker can have her way with him. I'll take what's left back to my workshop. I wonder what secrets a reanimated Draconian can impart." Leiyara felt herself – both her dream self and her real self – fill with disgust. "In the meantime I want to see how my experiment in Plainview is playing out. I'll see you back at the temple."

Leiyara's vision wavered and she felt as if some force tossed her backward. That whispering voice that no longer belonged to her groaned.

"Are you quite well?" Darwin asked, then chuckled and added, "You look somewhat pale."

The boney hand that was no longer hers covered the eyes that were no longer hers. Her vision was bathed in darkness. "That girl again," the whisper said.

She heard Darwin shuffle his cards, heard the amusement in his voice. "Want me to do away with her? I have an aberration for that."

A wave of force pushed her back further. Leiyara saw the scene as if from the back of a long tunnel. "No," the whisper said. "I have just the thing for her."

The whispering thing – the Primivite, Leiyara now knew – held out its hands and the sharp fingers began to form shapes. The glyphs flared into life in that blue-black light and spun around the pair of skeletal hands. That whispering voice chanted a few words in that dead language. As he invoked his spell, Leiyara jolted awake.

She could see only the ceiling of her room now, textured plaster and high vaults. She blinked and tried to sit up, but didn't. *I can't move,* she thought. Tentatively she tried to lift her arm, then her leg. Nothing. *I can't move!* She tried to scream, but no sound came out; her mouth wouldn't move either.

Matron help me, Leiyara prayed as tears welled up in her eyes, still fixed on the ceiling and unable to look elsewhere. She screamed again, but only in her head.

Chapter Thirty-Four: The Iyon Catacombs, the Colonies

He wasn't sure how long it had been since things went dark, or how long he had been wrapped in warm, soft cloth. The woman's lips were the last thing he remembered, soft and supple, warm as they brushed against his neck. She was a raven-haired beauty, he remembered that. Flawless skin showed through night-black ringlets as they spilled over her bare shoulders. The gown she wore was fine and dark, rich and sumptuous. It accentuated her curves, hinted at something so much sweeter underneath.

He didn't know her name. He'd wanted to call her Raven, but that resembled Corbeau – and even the Valet wouldn't dare invoke that ancient name. *The Valet,* he thought. *That's right. That's what they call me here. I have other names, but that's the one they call me. But hadn't the raven-haired woman called him something else?*

Yes. She'd whispered it in his ear before he blacked out. *Knight of Cups*. Well, she got it close enough, he supposed.

Surfacing from the darkness, he felt breath filling his lungs, although something bound his chest. He flexed his arms as if to stretch, but they were bound as well. These were like no ropes or chains he'd ever felt – no, they were fine and dark, rich and velvety, seeming at once both liquid and solid. Instantly he knew what they were, because it wasn't the first time he'd gotten himself tangled in a lady's garments.

Opening his eyes, he immediately regretted it. The raven-haired woman stood there, looking at him with wet, crimson lips, her eyes filled with hunger. Below that most kissable mouth was quite another, quite a bit less kissable mouth. From the bodice of her gown growled a needle-toothed maw big enough to swallow him whole. The gown's skirts extended out into tendrils that wound about his arms and chest. A whiff of the air brought with it the scent of not only her metallic, almost blood-like perfume, but also the stink of old bones and dry decay. Glancing around, he saw that they were in a narrow catacomb, the walls stretching out with alcoves filled with bones and musty rags.

The Valet turned back to face the raven-haired woman and her pet monstrosity/fashion *faux pas*. He quirked a smile and just couldn't help but say, "You're not gonna believe this, but I'm actually *not* going to ask you to dinner."

The raven-haired woman threw her head back and tittered a laugh. The Valet had read about women with laughter like the tinkling of silver bells, but he'd never heard it before until now. Unfortunately, those silver bells seemed to be tolling for him. "Even in death, you are a joker," she said. "How charming!"

He smiled his most winning smile. "More of a jack, really," he said. "So, what now?"

"Now, we devour you, body and soul," the woman said, her eyes twinkling with excitement. The saw-toothed maw at her belly snarled and drooled a blackish ichor that reabsorbed into the fabric around it.

The Valet reached out with his mind, feeling for the ominous, yet familiar, vibration of his Rune Blade. "Oooh, you don't want to eat me, honey. I'm too salty," he quipped, playing for time.

Again that tinkling giggle. "So funny. We shall enjoy that humor while we digest you time and again."

He had no retort, instead he stretched out with his consciousness hard now, reaching and reaching. *There! Glaeve Pandaemonia's* voice filled his head with that throaty whispering in words he didn't understand. No. There was one word in there that he caught, and he grasped it with the equivalent of white knuckles. "Celeste?"

The raven-haired woman's smile vanished. Her dark, gorgeous eyes narrowed. "How do you know my name?" she asked. *My* name, not *our* name.

Images now, not words, filled the Valet's consciousness. A young woman, pretty and perfect, bathed in light. A flash of whiteness. A cephalopodic monstrosity enveloping her, becoming one with her. *No, not one,* the Valet thought, *like me and* Glaeve Pandaemonia*, separate but same.*

Pain. He felt a jolt of it in his arms and shoulders, his breathing stopped. Celeste was squeezing.

"*How did you know my name?*" she demanded. This time, a deep-throated gurgling thing marred her words. The voice of the monster.

Separate, but same.

The tightness in his chest loosened and the Valet took a deep, ragged breath. "I know much about you, Celeste," he lied. "Until today I thought the Dark Magi were just a myth. To the Elders – those haughty, wannabe demigods – you were known by a different name. Do you remember it?"

The hungry jaws of her gown drooped and closed halfway. Celeste's eyes fell, looking downward toward her ample bosom.

"Say it," the Valet coaxed gently.

For a moment, he thought this would be the end. He expected that razor-toothed mouth of hers to snap him up and devour him over and over again for several eternities, like it had so many others. The Valet couldn't hear them screaming, thank the Matron, but *Glaeve Pandaemonia* was delighted by their suffering.

Where are you, anyway? The Valet thought at it. An impulse jerked at his neck on the lower right side, but he didn't look. The Rune Blade rested down among the sticks and bones, still wrapped in canvas. Somehow, even in his unconscious state, he'd had the presence of mind to cling to the Blade. Or perhaps it had clung to him.

Either way, Celeste appeared unconcerned about the weapon's presence. Advantage number two.

"The Fallen," she said at last, her voice thick with shame.

The Valet offered her a kind smile. He adjusted his voice to make it soft, soothing, giving the impression of compassion. He'd used that voice on countless women over the years, mostly to coax them into bed, but the trouble was, in Celeste's case, he didn't know if he was faking. "That's right," he said, "the Fallen. And how could they, after what you saw? After what *they* did to *you*? How hypocritical of them to pass judgment? After all you're the one who paid the price for their immortality."

A growl came from Celeste's gown and a ripple shot through it. The Valet could sense its impatience, its ravenous hunger. Celeste's eyes grew steely again, her mouth a cruel sneer. "Enough talk!" she shouted.

The gown pulled him closer, the maw snarled and snapped in anticipation, but the Valet didn't struggle. His eyes were almost level with hers now, and he pierced the darkness within them with his own bright blue. "Do you remember what it was like being a woman?" he asked.

The jaws about to close on his feet halted and hung open. The tendrils suspending him loosened slightly. "What?" she asked.

In her eyes, the Valet could see the two conscious minds at war – one moment hard and sharp, the next soft and solemn. He pressed his advantage. "Do you remember what it was like to be a woman? Young and free, before..." he indicated the monstrous evening wear with a nod, "...*that* took over. Do you remember the sunlight on your shoulders? The wind in your hair? The smell of flowers? Do you remember the touch of a man – or a woman, if you were into that? What it was like to be held through the night? Do you remember anything but rage and hunger?"

As a single tear welled up and spilled onto her smooth, perfect cheek, the Valet felt a pang of guilt. The feelings he exploited were genuine – the line between woman and monster more clearly defined than he'd dared to hope. *Separate but same.* He couldn't help but think about *Glaeve Pandaemonia*, when he first held her in his grip, the nights he'd nearly gone mad listening to her strange, ancient voice roaring in his head, when he thought the Blade would consume him. When at last, they *agreed.*

What makes me any different than her? He wondered. *Where is the line between monster and man?*

Ah, the Void with it, another part of him thought – the part he was far more accustomed to. *Too much is at stake to go soft now.*

In some languages of the Parallels, they would call it a *coup de grace*, and given the Valet's origins it would be appropriate. He looked at her with *those* eyes, smiled at her with *that* smile – the one that melted even the hardest and coldest of hearts and loosened the tightest of garments. He was close enough to her now that he could lean in for a kiss. Taking an enormous risk, he even shut his eyes.

The feel of Celeste's lips on his startled him. They were just as soft, warm, and inviting as they looked. The Valet could tell that it had been a long time since she'd been kissed and he could feel the desperate, hot passion behind her lips as her breath quickened and they parted for just an instant. He despaired because he knew he'd never be kissed like this ever again.

The monster in her raged, flailing its tendrils and shrieking, a sound like rusted metal being torn apart by lightning. The Valet felt the wisps of cloth release him and he dropped to the hard flagstones, turned the momentum into a roll, and grabbed his bundled Rune Blade. A twinge went up his arm as he grasped the gritty tarp and he dove to the left as an enormous, smashing arm came down, cracking the floor.

Celeste screamed as her gown undulated back and forth, tossing her about the catacomb. The scream turned from one of distress to one of pure, animal rage and she leveled a glare at him that might have killed a lesser man, literally. With a flick of his wrist, the Valet undid the canvas's slipknot and he brandished *Glaeve Pandaemonia*. The jeweled eye on the blade opened wide and glowed in the darkness, the edge of the Blade humming with an ominous bass tone.

"*What are you*?" Celeste and the monster screamed in that combined horror of a voice.

He grinned now, all his charm and games replaced with something dangerous, predatory. "I am *Le Valet des Coeurs*," he said. "My Blade is only one weapon in my arsenal, and hardly the most deadly."

Celeste roared, the gaping razor mouth opening impossibly wide. "How?" she cried. "How do you escape me?" It was more the monster than the woman, the Valet knew. It had been deprived of a meal, and it wasn't used to that – not with bait so tempting as Celeste.

"It ain't the first time a woman's had teeth down there," the Valet joked. He didn't realize that he shifted his gaze from the woman to the monster, but later thought that may have been significant. Then, he raised his Rune Blade. "Do you know what this is?"

Dark eyes fell on the sword, and a second later widened as the truth registered to the monster as well. "It's not possible," she said. "The Rune Blades slumber."

"Not this one, honey," he replied. *Checkmate.*

A spike of that black material shot out of the gown's skirts, as hard as steel and twice as sharp as any blade. Well, *almost* any blade. The Valet feinted right and struck it down with one swing. *Glaeve Pandaemonia* cut through the hardened fabric, sending a dead, harmless piece of velvet floating to the dusty floor. Both Celeste and the gown released a cry so loud and shrill that it shook the halls of the catacomb. Dust fell from the cracks in the ceiling, old bones quivered and crumbled. Celeste and her gown both shrank back, the cleanly cut tendril of cloth cradled to it like a hurt limb.

The Valet lost his smile. His blue eyes became devoid of humor, ruthless, dangerous. "Run along now, or I'll make this your final resting place."

Celeste looked at him with a mix of fear and uncertainty. Worse, somewhere in there lay the sadness of a lonely girl, lost to the ages. He didn't let it show, but the Valet felt a pang of sorrow for the poor woman. She'd gained the power of the Elders, but had become a monster in the process, one Void of a price to pay. Just when the Valet thought she was going to make a fight of it, the gown spilled out a mass of tentacles – like entrails from an eviscerated gut – and twisted around, retreating into the darkness with the woman's eyes still on him. The Valet watched it until it became a darker point in the already black tunnel, leaving him alone with the dead.

He breathed a sigh of relief. When he'd told the monster and, to lesser degree, Celeste that the catacomb would be their final resting place, he'd been bluffing. If she and the other Dark Magi were indeed fallen Elders, it meant they also possessed their immortality. It had been speculated that the Rune Blades could possibly kill an immortal, but that theory had never been tested – obviously. And despite his love of carnage and battle, he wouldn't try it out on Celeste. The monster, yes, but the woman? No.

You're going soft, you old fool, he thought, and shuddered because he wasn't sure if the thought came from him or the Rune Blade.

Catching his breath for a moment, he felt another vibration run up his arm and into his spine; *Glaeve Pandaemonia* communicating through sensation. "What's that, girl?" he asked. "Esther's in trouble?"

Chapter Thirty-Five: Plainview, the Colonies

Even up close the town of Plainview looked deserted. Esther walked cautiously up the high street, her revolvers drawn, the Lord's Lantern, a ball of incandescent yellow light, floating above her. She observed the decaying storefronts, the stucco houses that were crumbling into ruin under the constant downpour. Shattered blue roof tiles covered the cobbles. The high street emptied into a square, one of the open-air markets popular in the Colonies. All around the soaked wooden stalls and their wares were succumbing to rot, turning to mush, rusting, or sluggishly eroding away. She found a cart, a half legible sign advertising some sort of fruit.

At first only the hand was visible, white and bloated with decay. She turned the cart over to reveal a child, or least half of one. She wanted to turn away and retch, but Esther forced herself to look at the greenish, drowned face, the bulging blind eyes, the trail of gray innards. The kid couldn't have been older than five or six.

What could have done such a thing?

Esther took a few cautious steps backward and looked around. The square remained still and silent, there was no movement. Out of the corner of her eye she caught a glimpse of something that could be man under the overhang of the church, a mission-style building that towered over the rest of the town's squat architecture.

"Hello?" she called.

The figure under the overhang jerked, an awkward, almost inhuman, motion. Keeping her guns at her sides, Esther cocked their hammers back. The cold feeling in her stomach intensified as she glimpsed more movement, just to her right, the same shambling gait, then again to her left. Shapes emerged from the downpour from every direction, lurching and staggering.

"I am Peacekeeper Esther Triad of Ordo's Call," Esther called out to them. "Identify yourselves!"

The figures made no sound, they only kept lurching toward her. Esther took a few steps back, but halted when she heard wet, squelching footsteps behind her. She thought back to the Gray Marsh and being surrounded, but these didn't look like daemons to her. When at last one of the shapes stepped into the light, the Peacekeeper saw in horrible detail what they were. People, but not people. The one nearest her was a woman in a faded dress. A grayish-yellow growth covered half her face and most of her body; it bore a resemblance to some shelf fungus Esther had seen in one of her books. It had hardened and scaled over woman's flesh, marring her features and turning one hand into a hard, amorphous club.

The woman's one dead eye narrowed. What was left of her face contorted into an animalistic snarl and she raised her clubbed hand as if to strike. Instinct took over and Esther raised one revolver and fired, splattering the woman's head wide open – it made a sloppy noise and spurted a yellowish fluid stinking of putrescence. She fell, and Esther fired at the next closest, a man in overalls covered by the same creeping growths.

She advanced, firing again and again, cutting a hole through the assembling crowd. The infected bodies of men, women, even children fell before her. Instinct took each step, instinct pulled the trigger. Even as she watched them fall into splattered messes, Esther stored up her grief and guilt to be felt later.

I'm sorry, she thought as she gunned down a tiny form made featureless by the fungus. In one clubbed fist it held a doll.

When her cartridges were spent, Esther turned and put her back to the mission's wall. The remaining townsfolk were advancing, but they were neither fast nor responsive. It appeared their advantage was in numbers alone.

The Peacekeeper lashed out at a woman dressed in the habit of a Matron's maid – a holy woman dedicated to healing the sick and ministering to the dead. Her bayonet caught the woman across her gaping mouth; the force runes activated and a blast of kinetic energy sent the woman's body spiraling backward into the oncoming swarm of bodies, which toppled like tenpins. At the same time, Esther turned and unleashed Ordo's Hammer at a farmer with a pitchfork fused to one hand. The hammer of pure light struck him and, instead of tossing him back, blew his decrepit corpse into chunks of wet yellow mush.

Moving quickly, Esther reloaded her revolvers, jamming the cartridges into the cylinders with nimble, automatic fingers. She slammed the second cylinder shut just in time to put one of the fresh bullets into a teenage girl in her Season gown. One of the advancing townsfolk, this one an old woman, lunged. Esther twisted out of the way just in time to dodge the spray thick grayish vomit she spewed. The Peacekeeper put her down, then turned her guns on the rest of the thinning crowd.

She got two head shots, ducked under a swollen, flailing fist, took a potshot at an infected chaplain, and sent another Matron's maid sailing with a strike from her bayonet. She unloaded her revolvers, hacked away with her blades, reloaded, fired on the infected townsfolk again. When she ran out of bullets this time, she turned to her spells: Ordo's Hammer crushed the frail aberrations, the Lash of Light cut them into spongy, quivering pieces, the Searing Light reduced them to ashes.

By the time the last inhabitant of Plainview fell, the Peacekeeper dry fired into the rain, screaming and crying, but wasn't sure how long she'd been doing that. When reason finally caught up with her, she holstered her weapons and looked over the bodies of Plainview's population. In places, the fungus eating away at them still pulsed, rising and falling as if it was drawing breath, but none of the bodies stirred. She knelt over one of the Matron's maids she'd cut down and examined the hard, slick infection, a shelf of which burst through the maid's skull on one side. She dared not touch it.

What is this? She asked herself, sorting through all the knowledge of parasitic or carnivorous mycology she could think of. *I've never heard of anything like it.*

There were, of course, certain spores that infected small animals and insects – spores that spread and changed the very makeup of the poor creature being infested. There were even some that could take over brain function with the sole purpose of spreading those spores to others. The Watchers in the Gray Marsh had the ability to spread to Sapiens, but this fungus didn't appear daemonic in nature: it lacked that strange membrane and the twisted reflection of Sapien life, like eyes and random limbs or teeth. Nothing from the natural world that she recalled could do something like this, as if she'd stumbled upon a new and horrible form of life.

I must report this, Esther thought, falling back on protocol to avoid breaking down into hysterics. *And Sir Argas may also be in danger.*

She turned and headed back toward the town limits. She thought about all the people that had once lived here, what it must have been like when the infection first took hold. She imagined parents watching their children suffer and be consumed, husbands and wives losing their beloved while they yet lived. Parents, priests, and friends all being devoured by the mysterious parasite, and being cut off from any help by the rains and the flooding. How terrified they must have been, how isolated.

Esther clenched her fists at her sides until they trembled and her knuckles turned white. She would add these people's lives to the scales when if came time to pass judgment on the weather wizard. Esther would see him broken on the wheel for this.

But for now, we take care of the dead.

Taking a deep, slow breath, the Peacekeeper drew in as much Source energy as she could muster. She folded her fingers carefully, reverently, into the glyphs for the Sacred Flame. She uttered a silent prayer to Ordo that they would be judged fairly. When she released the spell, white hot flames engulfed the whole of Plainview, taking with it the bodies of the townsfolk and their sickness. From outside the town, Esther watched it burn, allowing herself to lament the dead. There was no one else to cry for them.

Chapter Thirty-Six: The Elder Gate, the Colonies

"Is that what I think it is?" Esther asked, staring up at the enormous, monolithic ruin that had been unearthed.

It had been a mournful, wet, and miserable walk from Plainview. Esther had taken the road instead of cutting across the drowned floodplain, even though it added an hour to her journey. The whole way she had been debating on what to tell Sir Argas about Plainview, what she had done to its inhabitants, but when she arrived at the dig site her mind was wiped clean of it all. The archeological team had dug an enormous crater in the earth with a single path leading in. The muddy gravel was treacherous as she made her way down, but at the bottom the soil was hard-packed with wooden planks making a rough boardwalk through the site. Trenches had been dug and the rainwater poured away from the find in great rushing streams.

At the back of the crater stood the discovery that Esther could not believe, even for seeing it. It must have been a hundred yards long and a hundred feet tall. It was carved and sculpted meticulously from some hard and ageless stone. In the center was an enormous arch, behind it nothing but the sheer crater wall. Six god-like figures were carved beside it, three on each side. Esther recognized them all from engravings and iconography she had seen before, and named them off as she climbed the massive stone stair led to the Elder Gate.

Nearest the arch stood Aisha, better known in Elderism as the Matron: tall and regal with long curls cascading down her shoulders, her gown something any maiden wore at her wedding – long skirts, off-the-shoulder straps, sequined bodice. On the other side stood Alastar, known by the Church as the Patrus Superior, the father of the Exorcists. He was also tall and imposing, with a stern gaze under a bald pate. His statue was hewn in a plain robe and held the Crux of Alastar, a heavy, rune-carved staff with the shape of a T at the top. Esther knew that in life, the staff had been said to be made of black iron and infused with powerful magicks.

Beside Alastar were Duuren and Graham, the Champion and the Spymaster. Duuren, cursed to life as living stone by the same power that granted them immortality, a hulking stone knight with a T-shaped visor his only facial feature. The stone likeness of the already stone knight leaned on a massive war hammer. Graham the Spymaster, Graham the Sly, was garbed in a cloak whose hood hid his face. By tradition, icons of Graham never portrayed his face, and it whispered rumor had it he still walked the Parallels, hatching his various schemes.

On Aisha's other side were the statues of Xanos and Caprecia, although Esther thought the latter's dimensions might be exaggerated. Caprecia, the smallest and youngest – if such a term can be applied to beings that live forever – of the Elders looked like a young woman, her hair cut short and stone skin carved with protection runes. In one hand, she held a scroll, in the other a scimitar.

The icon of Xanos bore a familiar item: a great sword with a broad, flat butcher's blade, an eye-like jewel at the hilt. Esther guessed that the statue had been retrofitted after the forging of the Rune Blades, after the Daemon Wars. Xanos himself, the father of Wraithbane, bore all the hallmarks of the royal bloodline: high cheekbones, a heavy brow, and long, strong limbs. The only thing missing from his likeness were his dark skin and gray eyes.

Esther marked the obvious lack of the seventh Elder, Rayan the Gatekeeper, who never appeared in any iconography, supposedly to protect the secrets of the Gates.

She met Sir Argas Swiftsteel at the top of the stair. The knight gaped at the structure. Esther couldn't blame him: this legendary find represented a piece of mythical folklore brought into full life, legitimizing an entire faith system. An Elder Gate, used to usher the Sapien race into Morgarai.

When he didn't respond to Esther's half forgotten question, she looked over at Sir Argas and felt like something wasn't quite right. The chill and thrill tingling in her spine from seeing the Gate turned into the cold stone in her stomach again. This was very wrong. The knight's eyes were wide and vacant, his mouth open and a trail of spittle running into his beard. Esther noticed a card sticking out of the lapel of his coat, the Fool card.

She sensed Darwin behind her before she even heard him. She spun about, drawing steel on him. He wasn't alone. With him were the Gigan arcanist, shackled and chained, and another man. This new addition had short, graying hair and a plaster mask covering the left half of his face. He wore a gray greatcoat and hefted a heavy, flanged mace.

"I see you discovered out little secret," Darwin said.

The other man scoffed. "It appears our Mr. Douglas wasn't as effective as he claimed. We've been oversold again."

Douglas! Esther knew the odious little toad couldn't be trusted. She cocked the hammer of her revolver. "Peacekeeper Esther Triad of Ordo's –"

"We know who you are," the masked man said, holding up a hand to halt her. "You've been quite a thorn in my side since I heard of your coming. The Gray Marsh couldn't vanquish you, the wraiths we put in your path were little more than straw dummies, and our arcanist proved a complete failure."

Esther thought back to each event that had brought her to this moment: the zeppelin crash, the Gray Marsh, the Agi convoy, the inciting incident of an arcanist causing trouble in the Colonies. The paranoia she'd felt about some shadowy figure behind it all coalesced into the form of this masked man that stood before her. The plot was simple: cover up the discovery of the Elder Gate at all costs. But to what end? What possible secrets could be uncovered from such an artifact?

"So, you're the one behind it all," she said, shifting her aim to the masked man instead.

He smiled. "Your investigative skills are impeccable," he mocked. "Yes. I am Dalton, known as the Deceiver, Father of Lies, and I lead the Dark Magi."

Dark Magi? Esther wondered. *Who in the Void are they?*

"What do you want?" Esther asked. "What's the point of all this?"

At this, Dalton laughed. "The point, Peacekeeper?" he said. "The point is to sow chaos. To undo what our former brethren have done."

"You speak overmuch, brother," Darwin cautioned.

Dalton waved him off. "Our captive has given up his secrets. It's too late for her to stop us now."

"What brethren? What captive?" Esther demanded. She understood nothing of what these obnoxiously formal-speaking strangers were saying. "*You speak overmuch*". *Who the Void talks like that?*

Dalton and Darwin exchanged a baffled glance. It would appear that she'd taken them by surprise. "You mean, you really don't know?" Darwin asked.

Feeling impotent and angry, Esther drew her second revolver. She pointed this one at Darwin and trained the bead of the first trained on Dalton. "Tell me!" she shouted.

Darwin laughed hysterically, Dalton just grinned. "This whole time you've been undermining us," Dalton mused. "And you have no idea what plot you're foiling."

"Her colleague sent the right Peacekeeper alright," Darwin remarked. "A real – how did he say it? - greenhorn? At least *he* came through for us."

My colleague? Esther thought, a cold sweat breaking over her. She'd been a pawn in this from the beginning, moved about the board like an insignificant piece, chosen for her lack of field experience. But chosen by whom?

"You may as well surrender now, Esther Triad of Ordo's Call," Dalton said, spreading his hands. "Your friends are divided and neutralized, we have taken what we need from the Gate, and soon our goals will be within reach. You have lost a game you didn't even know you were playing."

Esther's hands began to shake. She didn't bother trying to stop them. "My friends?" she asked. "What have you done to them?"

Darwin casually checked his pocket watch, a monstrous and unwieldy antique. "By now they are either dead or begging for it."

"Surrender, Peacekeeper," Dalton said. "We will allow you to walk away. We'll simply add your friends to the cost of this venture and we can forget the whole ordeal."

The Peacekeeper clenched her teeth. "No," she said. "I will not surrender."

Dalton shrugged. "Very well, then. Darwin?"

At Dalton's prompt, Darwin gestured to Esther's left. Before she could react or resist, Sir Argas drew his sword. He struck at the revolver in her left hand, sending it spiraling down the stair. He grabbed her right hand and twisted it behind her back. She fired one wayward shot, but it only splintered the plank walkway inches from Dalton's feet. Argas's strong hands forced her to her knees. With her left hand she began shaping the glyphs for Ordo's Hammer, but Argas grabbed her two middle fingers and twisted them until they issued a dry crack and a surge of red-hot pain. Esther cried out in rage and agony, but could do nothing else.

Dalton turned to the Gigan arcanist now, raising a hand to his face. "Let me show you, Peacekeeper, the cost of defiance."

He removed his mask. Light burst from the side of his face, an eerie, purple-white light, and the arcanist screamed. All around him a cloud that looked like a starry night sky coalesced and enveloped him. The cloud became something else then, something roiling with purple and indigo and black; something that screamed with the voices of a thousand tortured souls.

The Howling Void.

The weather wizard's screams added to the discord as the Void closed about him, leaving behind only a pillar of ash to mark his earthly remains.

Esther went limp in Sir Argas's grip. *He can summon the Howling Void itself,* she thought. *What chance do I stand against such power?*

Dalton replaced his mask and turned away. "Dispose of her, Darwin," he said. "Permanently. I don't want to see her face on any of your creations."

Darwin, the Mad Dandy, smirked. "As you command, my brother."

With a glance back over his shoulder, Dalton gave Esther a smile and a nod, then vanished into a cloud of darkness.

Chapter Thirty-Seven: The Floodplain, the Colonies

The old Iyon catacomb emptied out onto the floodplain. As the Valet emerged from the darkness of that place, the moon's silvery glow almost blinded him. The rains had stopped. He took that to mean Triad had neutralized the weather wizard. Had this been any ordinary mission, he would have been relieved and congratulated himself on a job well done, but the presence of the Dark Magi meant that the wine would have to wait. There was more work to do tonight.

The Valet stepped to the edge of one of the stinking, stagnant pools, trying to ignore the bloodflies that buzzed around him, occasionally nipping at his skin. He knew Esther was in danger from the strange sensation, the instinct, fed to him by *Glaeve Pandaemonia*. Putting aside the fact that the Rune Blade relished this knowledge, he tapped into that vibration at the back of his mind. He felt what the remnant of the dread goddess felt, brushed at it ever so slightly with his own consciousness.

Reluctant to give up her secrets, the Valet had to coax something out of her. One word: *northeast*. Wishing he had his horse, the Valet set off across the soggy plains at a run.

Chapter Thirty-Eight: The Elder Gate, the Colonies

As soon as the weather wizard died, the rain stopped. Whatever power the arcanist used to maintain them appeared to be linked bodily to the arcanist who'd been banished to the Void. Within seconds the downpour receded to a trickle, then stopped altogether as the clouds overhead dissipated and the Elder Gate was bathed in pale blue moonlight. The Gate took on a certain ethereal quality as bits of quartz and other minerals glimmered, creating eldritch fireflies all about the graven images.

The sudden change in the weather offered some small comfort. Esther almost barked hysterical laughter when she thought about it: here she was, the target of some secret and deranged plot, wrestled to the ground by an enthralled ally, staring her own impending death in the face, and she felt relieved by a change in the weather.

That bitter, sardonic thought alone kept her from falling into despair. Right from the start, from the very moment she left the Call, she'd been used and deceived and bushwhacked into something much larger than she could ever imagine. The conspiracy involved not only officials of the local governments and bands of raiders and thieves, but people in the highest tiers of the Call, all done to keep her from getting to the very place she now knelt, being held down by a knight turned puppet by Darwin's maniacal will. She couldn't help but feel a bitter pride at her own tenacity, her talent for foiling a plot she didn't even know needed foiling. Marveling at the absurdity of it all, Esther started to laugh, a harsh and humorless sound that rebounded off of the god-like images carved into the ruins.

The sound piqued Darwin's attention. "What's so funny, Peacekeeper?" he asked, idly shuffling his Taro deck.

The Peacekeeper didn't reply, but instead her chest filled with a sudden rush of defiance – looking back later, she would attribute her reaction to the smug look on the Mad Dandy's face. She threw back her head, once hanging in defeat, and felt the shock of pain as her skull connected with Sir Argas's nose. After an audible crunch, the baffled knight released an involuntary cry. His grip on her arm slackened and she twisted out of his hold, simultaneously taking a swing with her bayonet.

It was a gamble, really. Members of the Kairulian Royal Army habitually wore the textile known as fiberweave, offering the flexibility of cloth with the durability of steel. The bayonet skidded across the knight's coat, severed the Fool card on his lapel in two, and the added kick of the activated force runes delivered Sir Argas a punch that sent him sprawling.

Esther wheeled on Darwin, firing madly. Her revolver's range was sketchy and her aim, through both madness and the pain of her broken hand, was untrue. The boardwalk beneath Darwin's feet splintered and popped. One bullet pierced his thigh, another blew a chunk out of his shoulder. Darwin danced backward, screaming some forgotten obscenity through clenched teeth. He nearly lost his footing in the mud as he skidded to a stop.

Calmly, with a deep breath to steady herself, the Peacekeeper holstered her revolver. A feeling of peace came over her that only losing all hope could allow. Immersed in the ring of gunfire, the blood, and the battle now, everything else became peripheral. She folded her fingers into the glyphs for the Prayer of Mending and, when they shone in brilliant yellow light around her hand, she held the light over her twisted fingers. Wincing as the bones snapped back into place, Esther felt the pain rapidly drain away, the spell leaving her whole again.

Darwin was down on one knee, spitting curses at her in some dead language, giving her enough time to almost casually reload her revolver. She eyed the second of the pair, sitting on the fourth step of great staircase, the runes glittering in the moonlight. It was too risky to move to for it now; she would bide her time.

"Why?" she asked, speaking over Darwin's endless stream of obscenities. "That's the one thing I can't work out. Why all this: the coverup, the subterfuge, the lies and the manipulation? It can't just be for the Gate. What's your endgame here?"

Resuming his smug smile and standing straight – though he favored his injured leg – Darwin shook his head. "It's too late for that, Peacekeeper. Our objectives are met. You ask me what the endgame is even as the game ends. We've extracted untold secrets from our captive. The only thing left to do is to bury you with the Gate and let you both fade into obscurity. After that, Morgarai will fall to chaos. We've already won, and yet you fight."

"Who is it, this 'captive' of yours?"

Darwin threw out his hand in a dramatic flourish. "No! Enough talk!" He shuffled his Taro deck vigorously, no longer hiding any agitation. "The cards will speak your fate now!"

Esther sensed movement at her side. She risked a glance and saw Sir Argas there, his nose bloodied and crooked, his broadsword in hand. "I stand with you, Peacekeeper," he said. "And I'm sorry about your hand."

Allowing herself a sliver of hope, the Peacekeeper smiled. "Sorry about your nose."

"We're even, then," the knight replied, smiling in his turn.

They charged together down the stair, some collective warrior's spirit driving them in unison. Darwin shuffled his cards and drew one, casting it in Sir Argas's direction. As the knight's feet hit the mud-caked boardwalk, the card flashed and from its face six swords extended. Sir Argas skidded to a halt, parrying and feinting away from the animated blades as they sliced and stabbed at him.

Esther drew on Darwin and fired, but with a flick of his wrist and an uttered word, the bullet deflected off of a translucent semi-sphere of Force in front of him. Esther fired again, to much the same effect. Darwin, laughing, threw another card in Esther's direction. She shot it down and rushed him, swinging her bayonet. The Dandy slickly danced around her frantic strikes, giggling all the while. With another wave of his hand and another word in Runic, Esther felt like she'd been hit in the chest with with a sledgehammer. The force magick knocked her off her feet and planted her in the mud.

"I've not had this much fun in half a century!" Darwin declared through his giggle fits. "But you haven't chosen a card."

Trying to catch her breath, Esther grabbed her dropped revolver, glancing in Sir Argas's direction. The knight still fenced with the swords that projected from the Taro card. She didn't have time to count, but she was sure there were fewer of them now. She snapped her head back and fired on Darwin, but again the slippery man pranced backward, the clumsy shot kicking up the mud to his left.

He drew a card. The surface of the Champion card lit with incandescent light and the ground erupted in front of it. A stone construct twice the size of a man rose up from the disturbed earth, shaped like an ancient gladiator – a bare chest chiseled with muscle, a plumed helmet on his stone head, a heavy war hammer in one hand.

He came out swinging.

Esther rolled out of the way as the boulder-sized hammerhead splintered the boardwalk. As she dodged, she managed to fire two rounds into the champion's stone body. They succeeded in only chipping out two round holes in the torso. The champion took no notice, but instead pivoted and swung again.

The boardwalk shattered into splinters as Esther barely leaped out of the way, nearly losing her footing in the mud. She formed Ordo's Hammer and cast it at the automaton; the hammer of light flashed from her hand and collided with the champions arm in an explosion of dust and rubble. Its arm and the hammer gone, the champion still took no notice, instead it used the momentum of the blow to spin and deliver a punch that knocked her off her feet and cracked a few ribs.

She tucked painfully and rolled as she hit the ground, preparing another strike with her left hand. Nearby, Sir Argas struggled against the ghostly swords. One slash bounced off his fiberweave coat, another sheared a small cut in his cheek. He wheeled about and with a heavy swing broke the offending blade in half. Only three blades remained.

Behind the champion, Darwin watched the fights with glinting eyes, shuffling his Taro cards with a hungry, sadistic smile.

Esther regained her footing and cast another Hammer at the automaton. In response, the champion brought his hand down on it, smashing it into the boardwalk. Shrapnel of wood and stone showered Esther, biting into the skin of her neck and cheek, snapping her head back and filling the night with a choking cloud of dust. She didn't realize she was on her back until a patch of starry sky cleared its way through to her vision.

To her right, something red streaked past, a blaze in the night. Red and yellow.

The Valet? What is he doing here?

"Shoot down the cards!" a voice she vaguely recognized shouted.

The unexpected appearance of her companion shocked the Peacekeeper back to her senses. Instinctively, she rolled away as the stump of the champion's wrist – as thick as the columns at the Call – smashed down. Mud spattered, Esther let out a ragged, bloody breath, and she managed to get to one knee.

The Valet wrestled Darwin to the ground. *Glaeve Pandaemonia* stuck halfway into the stone champion's skull. The automaton thrashed, striking at the Rune Blade with the shattered stump of his hand. Sir Argas feinted past one of the remaining arcane swords and delivered a strike at the card itself – the pasteboard split and floated to the mud, instantly dispelling the ghostly blades.

Esther followed suit, cocked her revolver, and aimed a shot at the Champion card. With a guttural cry of rage, the stone champion flickered out of existence. *Glaeve Pandaemonia* clattered to the boardwalk with the Valet landing next to it, victim of one of Darwin's force spells.

Silence and stillness fell upon them.

The three of them closed on Darwin, the Valet in the center, Esther and Sir Argas circling his flanks. The mad dandy, ruffled now from his tussle with the Valet, brushed a lock of curly black hair from his face. His eyes were wild, searching for an out or another route of attack. They had him cornered and knew it.

"It's your play," the Valet said, a wolfish smile forming on his lips. "Draw your own fate, Darwin. Those are the rules of your sick little game, aren't they?"

Esther shot him a glare. "What in the Void are you doing? Have you seen what those cards can do?"

The Valet held up a hand and shot her a wink.

Darwin looked at him warily, but followed the rules. He drew a card from the top of the deck and looked at it. His eyes widened with instant terror. At the same time, the card erupted into a cloud of shadow, darker than the night around them. Darwin fell back, stumbling in the mud and landing on his backside; he kept scrabbling backward, dragging his tails through the trenches of water, whimpering all the way. The black cloud surrounding the card took shape, forming a cloaked and hooded figure with a hideous, skeletal face. A boney hand emerged holding a deadly looking scythe. Even in Morgarai they recognized the figure of Death, the reaper.

"No!" Darwin shouted at the dread form. "No! We defeated you! We beat you back into the Void! You can't take me, I'm immortal now! Please!"

The reaper raised his scythe and cut Darwin in half. Blood sprayed up from his chest and gut, mingling with the stream flowing through the trenches and painting the mud red as he emitted a gurgling, pleading scream. When the reaper finished his macabre work, he grabbed Darwin's leg and hauled him bodily into the shadows from whence it came. As it went, Death looked at them each in turn, Sir Argas, the Valet, Esther. His gruesome smile, the unblinking hollows of his eyes. Before he vanished, he gave them a nod.

Esther drew an excruciating breath and fell to the ground, hacking up her own blood. At a guess, one of her broken ribs had pierced a lung – she could feel it filling with fluid. She started to form Ordo's Mercy, channeling what little Source energy she could. She'd have to bear the wounds on her face and they would probably leave scars, but Esther had never been a vain woman. Peacekeepers had scars, that was the way of it.

Sir Argas glared at the Valet openly. "That was a dangerous gamble, friend," he scolded.

The Valet grinned. "It wasn't a gamble at all," he replied. "I stacked the deck during our little tussle."

As the glyph light surrounded her and snapped her ribs back into place, Esther couldn't help but laugh.

• • • •

YOUR FRIENDS ARE DIVIDED and have been neutralized. Dalton's words in her head. Esther set about reloading her revolvers, using the last of the bullets in her gun belt. *Our Mr. Douglas isn't nearly as effective as he says.* She mentally reserved a bullet for that little toad, too. Her stomach rumbled, but she ignored it – one of the costs of tapping the Source was having it tap you in return. She felt tired, cold, wet, and now ravenously hungry. Esther decided to let that make her dangerous.

Meanwhile, Sir Argas and the Valet were marveling at the Elder Gate.

"This has enormous significance for Kairal's faith," Sir Argas marveled.

The Valet, a man who put little stock in faith, shrugged. "It's certainly something. Think it's one of the first?"

"Not likely," the knight replied. "Legend has it the Elders first arrived in the west. The first Gates are probably scattered throughout the gray wastes of Alastar's Wrath."

Esther holstered her guns and grabbed the Valet by the shoulder. The big man wasn't easy to move, but she managed to turn him. "Where were Hrakar and Leiyara the last time you saw them?" she asked, her voice edged with urgency.

The Valet looked at her with wide eyes and, if Esther didn't know better, she'd say she intimidated him. "At the hotel. Safe and sound," he said, rattling off the words with as much urgency. "Leiyara went to bed. Hrakar was having a drink and grumbling about the shade walker."

The shade walker! Of course, Esther thought, a cold sweat breaking out as it dawned on her. The mysterious assassin had been bait for Hrakar all along.

"We have to go, now!" Esther commanded, starting toward the crater's exit.

The Valet hurried to keep up, despite his long legs. "What's the rush?" he asked.

"Something Dalton said. The masked man, one of the Dark Magi. He said our friends are divided and neutralized."

"That would explain my little encounter with the queen of darkness," the big man reflected. He'd already given Esther his short version of what happened with Celeste. "So they tried to take us out one by one. Clever."

"And Mr. Douglas was party to the plot."

"That little momerat!" he spat. They were beginning their ascent from the dig site when the Valet finally noticed that Sir Argas didn't join them. "What about the mightiest-knight-on-life back there?"

Esther glanced back. Sir Argas stood guard at the Gate, his sword drawn and waiting. He gave Esther a salute, she returned it, despite her training. "Leave him. He's found what he's looking for."

Moving with a sense of urgency was nearly impossible on the floodplain. Even without the rain it was still slow going, wading through the pools and the mud. Esther breathed a sigh of relief when they finally made it back to the horses. Esther wound hers quickly, then mounted and shifted it into a gallop while the Valet fumbled with the controls. He was a quick study and was running Sir Argas's warhorse alongside her in no time.

The pre-dawn chill was just settling over Meadowbrook when they arrived at the hotel. They hurried up the stairs, toppling one of the poor chamber maids in the process. When they found Leiyara in bed, Esther breathed a sigh of relief, but when she didn't stir, her fear settled back in. That was odd for a girl who had barely slept since their ordeal in the Gray Marsh. When she did finally lay down, Leiyara had terrible fits and night terrors. She thought Esther hadn't noticed, but it hadn't escaped any of her companions, especially not the Peacekeeper.

"She's barely breathing," the Valet said, bending over her. "Leiyara!" he called, cradling her head and looking into her eyes. "Leiyara, can you hear me?"

Esther came to their side. Leiyara's eyes were wide open, tears streaming down her cheeks and temples. Her mouth opened and closed as if she was trying to speak. Or scream.

"What's wrong with her?" Esther asked.

"I don't know," the Valet said. He lifted the girl out of the bed gently, as if she weighed nothing. "Maybe Mr. Douglas can shed some light. Where's Hrakar?"

Esther crossed to his room, but found it quiet and dark. Hrakar wasn't in his bed, but his duffel bag was, open and half empty. His spear's head lay abandoned next to it. "He's gone to take on the shade walker," Esther said, already knowing it to be true.

The Valet nodded. "I'd stake my reputation on it."

She thought about remarking on the quality of the man's reputation, but left it for later. She only thought about Hrakar, a man unafraid of anything they'd yet encountered, warning them off the shade walker as if she was the thing he feared most. She thought about him going against his ancestral enemy alone with no backup, and risking dying without the people he cared for by his side.

"Hrakar, you prideful fool!" Esther shouted, kicking the bed with all her impotent rage.

"Save it," the Valet snapped. "We'll see what Douglas has to say, and make him answer for this."

Seldom had Esther ever, in the course of their entire acquaintance (for you couldn't call them friends, per se), agreed with the Valet, but on this point they were precisely in sync. She would face Mr. Douglas, that horrible little man, and be his judge, jury, and executioner.

Their next stop was the governor's villa. They rode as hard and as fast through the waking town as they had from the floodplain. Early risers and a few laborers had to make way for them, hastening to clear a path for the two wild riders. Curses and speculation followed in their wake. The Valet held Leiyara as they rode, whispering soothing things to her. Esther, in the meantime, stoked the fires of her rage with each hoofbeat, waiting for the moment when she could unleash her fury on the man responsible for endangering her friends. She had to remind herself not to put a bullet between his eyes before she knew where he'd sent Hrakar to die.

A bullet if he's lucky, Esther thought. She was dismounting before her horse came to a complete stop, thinking about sentencing the bureaucrat to be drawn and quartered, or broken on the wheel, or any other of the hundred terrible methods of execution they taught her at the Call.

Though she hadn't stopped to consider his company, the Valet shouted after her, "Go! I'll tend to her."

The men guarding the gates stood down when she showed her medallion. "Where's Douglas?" she demanded.

One of the guards was struck dumb by the ferocity with which she'd questioned him. The other guard, sensing trouble for the little toad, tried to hide a smirk. "Garden," he said, opening the door for her.

Esther took the stairs two at a time, invoking her medallion to get past the guards at the garden entrance. She burst through the doors and instantly drew her revolver. Governor Avalos sat at his small table, holding a cup of coffee mid-sip. Mr. Douglas sat across from him, a stack of ledgers opened in front of him. They both looked dumbfounded. The absurdity of the situation wasn't lost on Esther, even through her blind rage. Here the governor enjoyed his breakfast, discussing the day's business with his trusted attaché, when a mad Peacekeeper, soaked to the skin and covered in mud and blood, burst in locked and loaded. She almost laughed in spite of herself.

"You sniveling little momerat!" she shouted at Mr. Douglas, leveling her pistol at him. "I'll see you hang for this!"

Douglas flew out of his seat so fast that it toppled backward. Avalos shot to his feet, too, putting himself between her and her prey, although not in the weapon's sights (*Smart man,* Esther thought). Having heard the ruckus, the guards rushed in with blades and pistols drawn.

Ever the diplomat, Avalos stayed them with a gesture. "What is the meaning of this, Peacekeeper?" the governor demanded.

"Your attaché has betrayed you," Esther replied. "And he walked my friends and I right into a trap."

Avalos scoffed; Douglas sniveled. "I don't know what you're talking about," whined the latter.

"So you had no idea Plainview was a deathtrap? You had no idea that an Elder Gate was discovered just outside the town? And you certainly didn't threaten the weather wizard to make him cover up the discovery with the flood?"

Douglas went pale, a greasy cold sweat broke out over his greasy pallid pate. He stammered what might have been protest, if he'd had the *petralets* to speak at all.

Avalos turned a pair of dark, dangerous eyes on the bureaucrat. "Is any of this true?" he asked.

Mr. Douglas's legs shook so badly that he fell to his knees. He began to sob. "They made me do it!" he cried, his beady little rodent eyes filling with tears. "The three! The Magi!"

Esther felt the edge come off of her rage the moment the poor little man urinated himself. She'd seen with her own eyes what the Dark Magi were capable of, and even with all her training she'd barely stood a chance against them – *still* might not stand a chance against their leader, Dalton. She holstered her revolver and took a deep breath.

"I'll deal with you later," she said. "Tell me what's become of Hrakar."

The little man peered at her with those wet, beady eyes, almost as though he stared right through her. "Who?" he asked.

"The Draconian who was traveling with me. Tell me!" she shouted, slamming her fists on the little table. The governor's coffee cup tumbled over, shattering on the flagstones. Esther's renewed fury blazed hotter in her eyes that it ever could from her guns.

The bureaucrat shrank back as if he'd been struck. "The proving ground!" he sobbed. "They wanted him at the proving ground so the shade walker could take him."

Avalos gasped. "Shade walker? By the Matron, man, what have you gotten yourself into?"

"Where is this proving ground?" Esther asked.

"To the northwest, a short ways. An Iyon ruin."

Esther nodded and stood straight. She leveled her glare at the governor; he visibly winced when she did it. "Governor Avalos," she said, taking a formal tone. "I charge this man with infractions to the Unbound Law. I command you to bind him and keep him until my return..." her glare settled back on Mr. Douglas, "...when he will be judged."

Avalos nodded and beckoned to his guards. "Take this traitor to the cells," he ordered. "Don't let him out of your sight. And take away his belt and boot laces. I'll not have him taking the easy way out."

The guards moved to take Mr. Douglas away, but Esther was already halfway down the stairs before they laid hands on him. She left the villa at a half-run, but stopped when she reached her mount. The Valet had Leiyara laid out on a bench near the gate. He held *Glaeve Pandaemonia's* jeweled eye up to her, allowing the Rune Blade to examine her. The poor girl still stared and mouthed her silent scream.

"This is old magick," the Valet said, opening his eyes. "The Rune Blade doesn't even know it."

Esther looked between her mount and Leiyara, torn.

"Go," the Valet said. "I'll see to her."

With barely a thought, Esther climbed into the saddle. "What will you do?"

The Valet quirked a smile at her. "See a man who knows about these things."

Esther wondered briefly what cryptic and arcane things he had in mind, but she and the Valet were bound in blood and battle, so she trusted him. She shifted her horse from a dead stop to a full gallop, playing the Void with the crank shaft, and took off to the northwest.

Chapter Thirty-Nine: The Proving Ground, the Colonies

The sun barely touched the western horizon when Esther reached the proving ground. Having lived in the sunless wastes of Perdition her whole life, she was still awed by the orange and rose and purple tones of the sunrises and sunsets in this part of the world. Had she the time, she would have stopped to admire this one.

When she saw the proving ground, she didn't have to wonder if she'd found the right place. The semi-circle of stone walls towering over the landscape was unmistakable. Esther had read about places like this, ancient arenas where slaves and prisoners fought for their lives or were fed to vicious animals. It was a barbaric practice put to rest once the Elders came, or so the stories went. Esther pulled her horse up to an arched entrance that looked freshly cleared of debris. She dismounted and drew her revolvers. She could already sense Hrakar as she passed into the corridor – the scent of his skin and those exotic smelling spices lingered. It spurred her steps.

The corridor opened onto an auditorium, a full circle of stone seats rising up to the top of the wall, an altar-like stone structure at its center: a place of sacrifice. Hrakar knelt before this altar, chained by a famliar looking Tarot card – the Hanged Man. They'd stripped to his waist, his silvery skin striped with ragged lashes, his back bloody and shredded. The shade walker had even removed his veil, leaving him both tortured and dishonored.

At the sight of him, Esther's heart broke. This powerful man – friend, confidant, and lover, a man with more strength and spirit than any she had known – had been beaten and broken and left for dead. *No,* she thought as that cold stone settled into her stomach. *She hasn't left at all. I've only interrupted her.*

"Hrakar," Esther said, taking conscious effort to keep her voice from cracking. "Hrakar, speak to me."

For one heart-stopping moment, his still form didn't stir. Esther held her breath until she saw Hrakar lift his head, take a ragged breath. "Esther," he managed to whisper in a hoarse remnant of his once rich baritone. "Esther, leave me. Get away."

Renewed rage filled the Peacekeeper's heart as she caught the slightest movement out of the corner of her eye. The shadows of the columns were coalesced, undulated, then took form. The shade walker. "Not a chance," Esther said through a bitter, blood-thirsty grin.

She pivoted and fired into the pooling shadow. For the briefest moment she caught a glimpse of the shade walker's darkly veiled form before it vanished. Instinct took over and Esther spun, slashing with a bayonet. The blade clashed with the shade walker's needle-like knife, the force runes activated, and the Draconian woman's weapon rebounded with a piercing vibration. Instead of being thrown off balance, she used the momentum and swung her hooked boning knife at Esther, almost too quickly for her to catch. Esther bounced the blade off the barrel of her other revolver and fired on the shade walker.

Quick as could be, the shade walker dropped into her own shadow, the bullet sending up an impotent puff of dust a few yards away. Esther wheeled again, but the shade walker didn't appear behind her.

"Your woman is quite a match," a dark, feminine voice said. The shade walker spoke in Sapien with a thick Draconian accent. "I can see why you like her."

"Come out!" Esther shouted. "Fight me, you coward!"

Movement to her left. Too fast. Esther pivoted and fired, but the shade walker whirled around, deflecting her revolver. The bullet opened a pockmark in the aging stone of the auditorium. She twisted again and Esther fell back, barely in time: she watched the gleaming blade skirt within inches of her eye.

Esther stabbed out at the shade walker, but caught only a trail of whirling silk. She feinted away from another strike, dropped into a roll under the needle-like weapon's stab, and fired. Once more, the shade walker vanished. Turning quickly, the Peacekeeper saw no sign of her foe. She kept her eyes moving, holstered one revolver, and folded her fingers into the Lord's Lantern. If she timed this just right...

There!

She fired at a gathering shadow near a fallen brazier. The shade walker dropped into the shadow of a column. Esther felt the slightest change in air pressure behind her and released the Lord's Lantern with all the Source energy she could muster. A brilliant white light burst above her, filling the auditorium, reducing every shadow to nothing like the noonday sun. Esther shielded her eyes, momentarily blinded and realizing that if her gamble didn't pay off, she was a dead woman. After a second passed without a knife in her back, she turned cautiously.

Nothing could have prepared her for what she saw.

She cast her spell at the very moment the shade walker was half-in, half-out. Her head, arm, and part of her torso were protruding from the ground. The rest of her was fused to the earth, flattened and glistening like half congealed tar. The shade walker uttered stifled, gurgling screams, her entrails now flattened and buried.

"Mercy," she begged.

Esther smiled, bitter and cold, and took aim at the shade walker's head. "Where can I find Dalton?" she asked.

Her enemy hissed some obscenity at her. "Why do you seek the Father of Lies?"

Esther shrugged and fired a shot into the half congealed shadow. The shade walker howled in pain as her silver blood bubbled up from the earth. "Where can I find Dalton?" she asked again. "I've got a few scores to settle."

Another hiss of pain and impotent rage. "Leave it, Peacekeeper. Your friends yet live. Just leave it."

With a sigh, Esther put another round into the shade walker's squashed guts. The woman howled in agony again. "Where can I find Dalton?" she repeated.

The shade walker spat blood into her veil as she spoke. "A temple, just beyond the drowned fields. The Iyon worshiped there. On the edge of the Gray Marsh." She coughed and made a horrid, ragged groaning noise. "Now please show mercy. Kill me."

Esther cocked the hammer of her revolver back and trained the bead on the shade walker's head. "One last question: if you had killed Hrakar in his dishonor, what would his fate have been?"

"The Undervault. You would call it the Void."

"That's what I thought," Esther replied. Then, she tore the shade walker's veil from her face and, before the Draconian assassin could cry her lament, Esther put a bullet in her brain. Silvery blood and gore spattered the ground. The part of the woman's body still above ground slumped forward. When Esther dispelled the Lord's Lantern, the remainder of the shade walker's twisted, dishonored corpse seeped back to the surface in the ensuing shadow.

The Source took its due and Esther dropped to one knee, feeling it drained all of her life force. *As Ordo gives, so Ordo takes.* Her vision blurred and her heart pounded for fear of passing out. Ordo be praised that she didn't. After a few deep breaths, the Peacekeeper rose to shaky feet and went back to the center of the arena. She slashed Darwin's Hanged Man card out of the air and the chains binding Hrakar vanished. He dropped to the ground unceremoniously.

Esther went to him, put her arms around him, and hauled him to his feet. For a man of his size, he weighed surprisingly little. Chalk it up to being born of the air.

"You should not..." he gasped. "You should not have come."

"Save it," Esther scolded. "We'll get you better and then we can talk about how you're going to thank me."

Hrakar began to pant in a wheezing breath. Esther was alarmed until she realized he was laughing.

Chapter Forty: Meadowbrook, the Colonies

The Horsehead was a seedy gambling joint even by seedy gambling joint standards. The walls were bowed and caving in, the ceiling creaked and leaked, the air a toxic cloud of acrid smoke, stale beer, and urine. The floors were caked with filthy sawdust, the bar was no more than a plank laid across two sawhorses, and the tables and chairs were cast-off crates and barrels of worm-eaten wood, strewn with bent cards and silver royals.

To the Valet, it felt like home.

He wasn't terribly comfortable with leaving the helpless Leiyara outside, propped up on his horse, but it was far better than letting her get pawed at by the raw, savage folk that frequented this place. The patrons were dirty and pockmarked, some with the oozing sores of whatever love bug was going around that week.

The Valet went to the bar, the man behind the tap giving him a nod of his bald, heavily bearded head. He started to pour a dirty mug of swill for the Valet. "Don't see you in these parts often," he said.

"I'm on business," the Valet replied. "No way I'm coming to this snoozefest colony for pleasure. And no brew this morning, I'm afraid."

The bartender stopped pouring and gave him a flat look. "Must be urgent."

"It is," the Valet confessed. "I'm looking for the World Walker."

When he told it later, going for the full-on dramatic effect, he said that all activity and conversation in the bar ceased and all eyes turned, gaping, to the Valet. In reality the weary, reddened eyes that had gotten no sleep shot wary glances and glares at him. The prickling on the back of his neck tipped the Valet off to a few who were looking for a fight. He hoped they knew better: he didn't have that kind of time.

"He was killed in a knife fight a few hours ago," the bartender said casually. "But the sun's coming up, so he should be good as new any minute now. You'll find him out back with the rest of the trash." He spat on the floor in a charming display of emphasis.

The Valet nodded and slipped a few silverbacks across the counter. The bartender took them and gave him a parting nod.

Out back, the Valet found a pile of refuse with a corpse plopped on top of it. The corpse bore a resemblance to a man of average height, long limbs, and stark white hair that splayed across the trash. He was wearing a long black coat and his wide-brimmed hat was lying crumpled beside him. At his side lay a particularly nasty-looking sword with the skull of some horned daemon decorating the pommel. A great, gaping wound seeped a yellow-tinted blood that could not possibly be Sapien.

In life, he'd been known as Ashe, and would be again soon. The Valet stood by and waited, his second least favorite activity.

The moment the sun came over the horizon, something remarkable happened. The wound on Ashe's throat closed up, the flesh seeming to knit itself back together. The man's skin darkened to an olive tone and even his white hair gained back some luster. He took a deep, snoring breath and, just like that, he lived again.

Immortals, the Valet thought, *they have all the fun.*

He delivered a light kick to Ashe's torso. The man sat up and drew his nasty looking sword – the Valet noted that the blade was black iron fused to the daemon's spine. Ashe opened a pair of yellow cat's eyes and looked at the Valet through their narrow, vertical slits. "Sweet mother of Chaos," he grumbled in perfect Sapien. "What the Void do you want?"

"I have a job for you," the Valet replied.

Ashe turned over on his side, making himself comfortable on the trash heap. "I don't need a job."

"Really? Can you afford to buy drink tonight? Sleep in a bed?" the Valet asked, baiting him. "I'm sure your cutthroat friend wasn't shy about lightening your purse."

The immortal grumbled something and shrugged it off, but then sniffed at the air. The Valet thought for a moment that he had finally realized where he'd slept, but Ashe sat bolt upright, looking around wildly. "I sense old magicks here," he said. "Magicks I haven't encountered since the Daemon Wars. Who is it that got cursed?"

The Valet had him now. "A very sweet young woman. There's a gold imperial in it for you."

Ashe stood up and donned his hat, dusted himself off, and was, just like that, alert and ready. "Let's get to work, then."

• • • •

THE HOTEL LOUNGE WAS closed at this early hour, but the cook and a serving girl were there already, preparing for the few guests that would soon come to breakfast. When Esther burst through the door, hoisting Hrakar along with her, the pair were shocked and a little put-out; she cleared one of the trestle tables of its condiments and accoutrements and laid out Hrakar face down, they didn't argue; they already knew who she was.

"You, girl," Esther barked at the petrified serving girl. "Fetch a Confessor." When the girl only gaped at her Esther shouted, "Go! Now!"

The young girl, still wide-eyed, ran out the door, whose latch Esther had broken. Meanwhile, the Peacekeeper stood over Hrakar's ragged back, the wounds seeping out his silver lifeblood and swollen to a deep gray at their edges. He muttered something in his native tongue, perhaps a prayer, but Esther was too concerned to listen. She focused and drew upon whatever Source energy she had left, making the glyphs for Ordo's Mercy. Her hands filled with a faint, undulating light, the torn flesh on Hrakar's back twitched and the gaps between the skin and muscle inched together briefly.

Unable to hold out for long, Esther collapsed into a nearby chair, exhaustion threatening her with unconsciousness again. Taking a deep breath, she stood and prepared the spell again, drawing on power she didn't have. The glyphs sparked and crackled about her cramped fingers, but the spell failed. Her vision swam and went gray at the edges. She dropped back into the chair.

At the same time, she became vaguely aware of the Valet rushing in, carrying Leiyara with him. The girl's wide eyes were still unmoving, but she no longer wept, no longer mouthed those unheard screams. If Esther had had any presence of mind, she would have seen a glimmer of hope in those huge, flame-flecked eyes. There was a stranger with the Valet. The newcomer dressed in a tattered black coat and a wide-brimmed hat. He had white hair and olive toned skin, his eyes dark yellow and cat-like.

On the periphery of her conscious mind, one word registered to Esther: *Iyon*. Although they'd all died out thousands of years ago, there was a myth around Morgarai that the last of their kind still walked the earth, but until this morning she hadn't put any stock in it. Given what her journey had thrown at her so far, nothing could surprise Esther now.

The cook, a stocky, middle-aged woman in an apron and cap, rushed forward at the entry of the second wounded. "Now see here!" she shouted. "This is a restaurant, not an infirmary. I've got half a mind to..."

The newcomer raised a hand and formed glyphs so quickly and nimbly that Esther could barely follow them. Deep blue-black symbols circled his gloved hand and the cook went silent and slack, her eyes vacant. Another word hovered at the edge of Esther's thoughts: *Shadowmancy*. It was another thing she'd heard of at the Call, something talked about in hushed tones, something she and other servants of Ordo were trained to be wary of. The Shadowmancers, using daemon magicks, were a rare form of Exorcist that turned darkness against darkness. The Eldrist Church accepted them as a necessary evil: where there is light, there is shadow, and all that, but it was still widely believed that the Void awaited them after death.

"I need herbs," the Iyon said to the cook. "All the herbs you have." He turned those cat's eyes on the Valet. "This requires ritual magick."

The newcomer patted down his coat, reached into a pocket, and found what he was looking for: a stub of black chalk. The Valet laid Leiyara out on another table and the newcomer drew glyphs – older and more arcane than any Esther had ever seen – at her head and feet. He hastily went about toppling chairs around the table, scribbling glyphs in a wide circle around the afflicted girl. As he did so, he looked up at the Valet. "How long since she encountered the Primivite?" he asked. The Valet was stricken into silence. His eyes widened at the mention of the supposedly extinct race. "How long?" the newcomer demanded.

"Days," Esther said. "Weeks. I'm not sure." She tried to count them, the days in the Gray Marsh, their trek through Agimonde, the voyage to the Colonies. It seemed like years.

The Shadowmancer shrugged. "It'll have to do," he said, etching something more in chalk.

The serving girl returned with the gray robed Confessor on her heels. The man was older, sporting a bald head and bushy beard. He carried with him a medical bag. When the pair saw what the Iyon was doing, the girl gasped and the Confessor cruxed himself. "Matron be praised!" he exclaimed. "What is the meaning of this?"

Esther stood and flashed her medallion. "Never mind them," she ordered. "Your patient is over here."

The Confessor uttered a few prayers and something about blasphemy under his breath, but tended to Hrakar anyway. He opened his bag and took out an apparatus that looked like a pair of spectacles lined with clockwork mechanisms, a telescopic contraption on one lens. He extended the scope and examined the wounds on Hrakar's back. "Lacerations are one-half inch deep," he said to himself. "Flesh is torn and ragged, as if whipped by a barbed instrument." The Patrus removed his glasses and produced a sewing kit and a bottle of wood alcohol. "I need a bowl or a glass," he said, turning to the serving girl, who had drawn the short straw for nursing duty this morning. She was shaking and stark white, her unblinking eyes staring at the torn skin and blood.

"Quickly now," the Confessor gently coaxed, putting a hand on the serving girl's shoulder. She looked at him, registered what he'd said, then ran off to comply. Meantime, the Confessor threaded a hooked needle with a suture. "What's your name?" he asked.

"Esther Triad."

The Patrus nodded his approval. "Esther," he said. "A good name. I am Patrus Colvin Winkle, recently transferred from Turner. Do you know it?"

It dawned on Esther this was the Confessor's version of bedside manner. He got her to talk to ease her worry and keep her from succumbing to hysterics. Little did he know that at this point Esther was beyond any emotion, especially histrionics. She carried on automatically. The name of Turner rang a bell vaguely somewhere in her awareness, perhaps she was supposed to meet someone there once.

"I don't."

The Patrus smiled as the serving girl brought over a large basin – much larger than Winkle would need. Still, the old man smiled at her kindly. "Thank you, child. Now, perhaps you could boil me some water. The largest pot you can find."

The poor, shaken girl nodded emphatically and rushed off to do as she asked.

"Why do you need boiling water?" Esther asked.

Patrus Winkle flashed her that kind smile again, this time tinged with amusement. “I don't, but the poor child needs something to occupy her.”

In spite of herself, Esther laughed.

The Confessor poured a measure of alcohol into the basin and dipped in the needle and thread. He went about stitching the lacerations with the steady hand of an expert while, with the other hand, he formed glyphs and cast spells. While he sewed the wounds, the needle and thread glinted with light and they began to heal rapidly.

This glyph magick is so subtle, Esther thought. It made her feel like her magick was blunt and blundering.

Turning her attention to Leiyara, she saw that the girl still lay on the table at the center of the wide ritual circle. Esther had to refocus her eyes on the glyphs, thinking for a moment she was seeing double, then realizing that hovering over each of the drawn glyphs was an ethereal afterimage in that same blue-black. The Shadowmancer had bundled together a variety of herbs and burned them, producing an acrid and strange smelling aroma. The cook he'd enthralled stood at the edge of the circle, her head down, hands folded demurely over her apron. The Valet sat at a table with a bottle of wine, watching intently.

"It's called the Silent Scream," the Shadowmancer explained to the room in general as he waved the burning bundle of herbs through the air. "They used to use it on us when we were unruly. It traps the victim inside their mind, unable to move or speak. I can't tell you how many days I spent wallowing in my own filth, staring at a decaying ceiling somewhere." He glanced at the Valet and quirked a smile. "It doesn't take long for the madness to set in."

The stranger dropped the bundle of burning herbs to the floor. He went to Leiyara, put a hand on her brow, and looked deep into her eyes. He hesitated a moment, thinking, then looked into her eyes again. "This one is Delkynian," he said. "When the Primivite got into her head, she was able to swing the door the other way. Remarkable."

He wasn't making sense. Esther didn't know what these words meant.

"Judging by her flame-flecked eyes, I'd say part Agi, too," the Shadowmancer went on. "A half-Agi delkynian. You are a treasure, indeed, my dear." He stroked her cheek gently. "Don't you worry about a thing. I'm going to get you out of there."

He stood straight and raised both of his hands, the fingers of each moving rapidly to form forbidden glyphs older than any in Esther's reckoning. The lights in the lounge dimmed as the blue-black symbols intensified. A slight vibration emanated from the circle, shaking the glasses and bottles stacked behind the bar. Esther felt a massive influx of Source energy, like a giant taking a deep breath, and then she felt its release – a blinding shock that nearly toppled her.

Just how powerful is this man? She wondered.

When he finished, the lights came back up and the ethereal glyphs winked out of existence, leaving only smoke and chalk to mark the spellcraft. Leiyara took a deep breath and blinked, like a sleeper who's suddenly been roused. She held her hand up to her eyes and opened and closed it twice. Then, she began to weep in relief. "Thank you," she whispered.

The Shadowmancer ran his fingers through her hair delicately, then turned to the Valet. "A gold imperial, as promised." He held out a gloved hand and quirked a malicious grin. "And don't think this makes us even."

The Valet raised his glass to the Shadowmancer. He produced a gold slip from an inner pocket and flicked it to the stranger. "Wouldn't dream of it."

The strange man, dark and frightening and gentle, the last of his kind, headed for the door. He gave Esther a nod on his way out. The whole exchange left questions boiling in her weary head. Who was this man? What had his words about Delkynian and doors opening both ways meant? How did he and the Valet know each other and what was this apparent rivalry between them?

Patrus Winkle cleared his throat, calling Esther's attention to him. He had finished his work and Hrakar's back was clean and stitched, the wounds already closing seamlessly. The Draconian breathed easily and steadily – he was asleep. Winkle hastily packed away his things. "He'll need rest," the Confessor instructed. "In a couple of days, he should be good as new. Draconians heal fast." He finished packing and glared at the remnants of the Shadwomancer's work. "We at the Church believe that there is no light that does not cast a shadow, but to *work* that magick is heresy. You'll excuse me while I pray to the Matron that she cleanse me of what I have just witnessed."

The Patrus left, also sparing the Valet a nod on his way.

That's quite a peculiar set of friends you have, Esther thought.

• • • •

WITHIN THE HOUR HRAKAR slept soundly in his bed, Esther vigilantly seated beside him. The Valet and Leiyara sat at the room's small table, an untouched pot of coffee and a plate of uneaten pastries between them. Leiyara twirled a fork idly, now and then shuddering at the thought of what she'd been through. She'd only stopped crying fifteen minutes ago.

Esther and the Valet had let her cry. They could offer the girl little comfort from the vantage of their pensive pondering. They exchanged troubled glances between Leiyara's sobs and Hrakar's snores, knowing that there were plans to be discussed, a final mission upon which to embark. Dalton had to be dealt with and whatever remained of his plans crushed. Justice, or in the Valet's mind, vengeance, must be served.

But first, Esther needed to know that her friends were safe and on the mend. She also needed ammunition and sleep. *How long has it been since I've slept?* She wondered. She knew it was only the night before last, but the night before last seemed like an eternity ago.

"What was that thing he called me?" Leiyara asked suddenly, startling Esther out of her dark musing.

"A delkynian," the Valet replied. Esther didn't know the word either. "It's an old Drakkenspek term, from before they merged their language loosely with Sapien. It means 'shadow kin.'"

Leiyara's flame-flecked eyes widened in fear. "What's that mean?" she asked, looking like she was on the verge of tears again.

"It's not an evil word," the Valet reassured her, "except to the staunchest Draconians. You see, when Sapienkind brought livestock and other fauna over from their Parallel, they found that Morgarai had a way of changing the life forms. It's where we get the dromedon, the momerat, and the volwrath – a sort of rodent that lives in the desert – mighty fine eating, too, I might add.

"They later discovered it had a similar effect on people. Certain people, especially those mixed with native Morgarian races, are born with remarkable abilities, like seeing the future or bi-location. These are the Delkynians, or so the legend goes."

Leiyara looked down at her hands as if seeing them for the first time. "So when that Primivite...got into my head, or whatever, that's how I could get into his? To see through his eyes?"

The Valet nodded.

"Oh," Leiyara said. "And about me being part Agi, do you think it's true?"

Esther took her turn now. "You have all the hallmarks of a Sapien-Agi crossbreed. The fire-touched hair, the flame-flecked eyes."

"My dad used to say that I turned orange when I tanned." Leiyara chewed her lip for a moment, then looked up at Esther pleadingly.

"Could it be that my mother isn't my real mother? Is that why she does...does things to me?"

Esther tried to give her a reassuring smile, but Leiyara's lineage was the furthest thing from her mind. "It's possible."

Suddenly, the girl brightened. "So I'm part beautiful Agi woman who can control people's minds?" She squeaked. "That is so amazing!"

The Valet burst into laughter, Esther was dumbstruck. It was hardly the reaction either of them expected. After a moment, Leiyara blushed – Esther could almost see the hint of orange in her skin, now that she looked for it – and turned her eyes down. "What?" she asked.

• • • •

IT WAS LATE AFTERNOON. Hrakar still slept and Leiyara curled up on the floor next to the bed. She'd fallen asleep a few hours ago and, as near as Esther could tell, was at peace for the first time since her encounter with the Primivite – that impossible creature that had put an impossible curse on her. Before she slept, Leiyara had confessed to acting, unknowingly, as the Primivite's spy and begged Esther to forgive her; she said that she had betrayed and divided them. It broke Esther's heart as she reassured the poor girl that it wasn't her fault, that there was nothing to forgive. She added it to the debt she owed to Dalton, a debt that would be paid in holy light and hot lead.

While the Valet dozed in his chair – strategically placed by the door and watched over by *Glaeve Pandaemonia* – Esther got to work. She changed out of her torn, soiled, and bloodied cassock and into her fresh one. She plaited her damp, dirty hair into a tight braid. She cleaned and loaded her revolvers. With steady and precise fingers she filled the loops on her gun belt with cartridges, and then unpacked her bandolier, strapped it on, and filled it as well. Lastly, she pulled her medallion from under her shirt and polished it to a mirror finish. She left it hanging out, shining and brilliant in the afternoon light.

As she stood in the washroom, looking at her bruised and shrapnel-torn face, she realized it marked the first time since she'd left the Call that she had no doubts. It seemed odd to her. After seeing what Dalton and the other Dark Magi could do – *had* done – she should be terrified. After the arcanist had met his end, her mission had been completed. She should have been thinking about letting things rest and returning to the Call but somehow her path was clear; something drove her to this confrontation with Dalton, and for the first time, she felt Ordo's will wash over her.

"Bless my hand, O Lord," she whispered in prayer, "may it balance your scales. Bless my heart so I may mete out your justice. Bless my eye, so I may see your will." She turned her eyes down, clenched a fist at her side. The prayer was standard for a Peacekeeper entering into their duties, until now. "Bless my guns, that they may shoot down my foe."

She touched her medallion reverently, then looked at her face again in the mirror. Shrapnel marred the right side; there were small cuts and bruises everywhere, some more healed than others. A knot formed on the back of her head where it had met with Sir Argas's nose. But it was her eyes that most caught her attention. They had a steely look to them, hardened; a stranger's eyes.

Have I really seen so much? She wondered, then looked away before the memories of the Gray Marsh or the ambush at the canyon could resurface. *Look ahead,* she reminded herself. *Always look ahead.*

The Valet still dozed by the door when Esther came out of the washroom. She thought for a moment that she could creep past him without him noticing, but as soon as she reached for the door latch, he spoke.

"You're going to face him?" he asked rhetorically. "I'm coming with you."

Esther shook her head. "No, you're not."

The big man's blue eyes narrowed at her dangerously. "Why not?"

"I need you to stay here and watch over them," the Peacekeeper replied, gesturing to Hrakar and Leiyara. "If the Magi decide to take another shot at them, they'll be helpless without at least one of us."

The Valet appeared to think it over. "Then wait. When Leiyara is rested and Hrakar is healed, we'll all brave the hazard together."

Esther had to admit it was tempting, but she couldn't risk it: she may have missed her shot at Dalton already. "There's no time. Dalton could be on the move as we speak."

For a moment she thought he was going to protest, but instead, he just leaned back in his chair. "You should have said something heroic like 'this is something I have to do on my own,'" he joked, but his eyes were devoid of humor. "Be careful."

Esther gave him a nod and walked out the door.

Chapter Forty-One: The Frontier, the Colonies

The Peacekeeper made good time, riding hard and testing the limits of her clockwork horse. The floodplain was already starting to dry up, but there had been places where she'd had to lead her mount through waist-deep water and ankle-deep mud. She passed the dead archeologist's camp within an hour and the Elder Gate only a short while later. By now the site swarmed with Kairulian soldiers; Esther didn't stop to greet them. The terrain had changed in the northeastern corner of Estrella Nova, turning from low lying fields to rolling hills and bluffs. By nightfall, she'd reached the Frontier, an uncharted stretch of land not yet held by Kairal.

She stopped to rest by a spring, partaking of its cool waters. The spot she'd found was a small lowland wedged between two bluffs with the spring cutting through the cleft, flowing from the White Caps. All around her were green grasses, saplings, and strange fern-like plants with serrated, red-black leaves. She started a small cookfire and, as her beans warmed, looked up the plant in her *Journal of Flora*. It was called waspweed for the stinging spines on each serrated edge. The sap, the *Journal* said, was something akin to honey. While she ate her dinner, Esther vaguely played with the notion of tasting some but dismissed it as unnecessary frivolity.

Deciding she should get some rest – she was still so very tired, despite the catnap she took that afternoon – Esther undid her bedroll and laid it out on the grass. She lay down and, with the bubbling of the spring so close by lulling her to sleep. She woke once during the night, rolling away from the embers of the cook fire. A strange feeling danced at the edge of her awareness, a tingling sensation in the back of her mind where she stored her Source energies. It felt like being watched, but from the inside.

"Leiyara," she muttered. "Is that you?"

She sensed hesitation, a slight pulling back as the tension at the back of her head eased momentarily. *Oh...um...hi Esther.*

Leiyara's words in her head. It was strange, yet familiar all at once. "What's wrong?" Esther asked. Since she shared no feelings of panic with the girl, she wasn't alarmed.

Nothing. I was just worried about you.

Esther quirked a smile. After all that this young girl had been through, she still worried about her friends. "I'm fine. I haven't even reached the temple yet. Is the Valet still with you?"

Yes. He's guarding the door. I don't think he knows I'm awake yet.

Oh, he knows, Esther thought. *We both knew about your sleep disturbances the entire time.*

That hesitation again. Esther rolled her eyes at herself: if the girl was in her head, then she could read her thoughts.

I see, Leiyara said. *Why didn't you say anything?*

I must look quite the madwoman, lying here talking to myself, Esther thought. "We thought you were just dealing with everything. We had no idea it was something more arcane."

A slight pause, almost like a searching feeling. Leiyara probed her mind, probably without knowing it, perhaps to ascertain if Esther told the truth.

We're going to need some ground rules for this psychomantic thing, Esther said in her mind, catching on that she didn't need to address Leiyara verbally.

As soon as she did, the searching stopped. *I'm sorry,* Leiyara said. *I'm just scared.*

You're being guarded by the greatest swordsman who's ever lived. Well, self-proclaimed anyway. You'll be safe.

I'm not scared for me, I'm scared for you.

Esther opened her eyes again, giving her invisible companion a dubious look. "Why?" she asked out loud.

That hesitation again, but this time the psychomantic force increased. Esther's mind strained to hold both her and Leiyara's consciousness at the same time. *Dalton is powerful. When I was in Scioxeles's mind – that's the name of the Primivite – I could sense enormous power in him. Even he was afraid of Dalton, but he wouldn't dare show it.*

Scioxeles. So our enemy has a name. Esther thought.

Oh yeah, his name is Scioxeles, Leiyara said, filling in the obvious blanks. *I forgot to tell you that. He's been alive for eons, since before the Daemon Wars. He's really powerful, too, but I felt a limit on that power, almost like he was chained up by something – something invisible. Mostly he has to use lies and influence.*

Esther nodded her understanding. *I won't underestimate him. Now, leave me be while I rest.*

She felt that pressure pull back and dissolve. She was just sighing with relief when it surged back. *You'll be careful, won't you?* Leiyara asked hastily.

Smiling again – the girl's concern warmed her heart – Esther replied, *Of course.*

The pressure dissipated again. Esther rolled over and slept.

Chapter Forty-Two: The Iyon Temple, the Frontier

The Iyon temple wasn't what Esther had expected. Up until now, when she thought of temples, she imagined small shrines or cozy little chapels, but this massive, domed structure before her was mind-blowing. The dome itself must have been a hundred yards wide with spires and towers bristling over its surface. Enormous portholes had been hewn into the sides at each cardinal point of the compass. The one that Esther faced had an ancient rune carved above it, and after a moment she recognized it as an archaic dialect of Runic – the element of Fire. She surmised that the others would represent Air, Earth, and Water, respectively; the Iyon had worshiped the Prime Elementals, physical embodiments of the elemental forces that had once lived among the people.

As she entered the structure, she haunting images welcomed her. The temple was sized so that an entire community could live within its dome, and the crumbling remains of homes and shops surrounded her with broken walls and decaying archways. Here and there, she even caught a glimpse of tables and chairs, the wood petrified by time, and ancient crockery and metal dinnerware still set neatly in place. It gave the Peacekeeper the chilling sense that the inhabitants of this place had left in a hurry.

In the center of the structure stood the temple proper – someone familiar with modern churches would probably call it a sanctuary. She entered and walked up an aisle of stone benches where the mummified remains of parishioners still bowed in prayer. They were veiled in desiccated cloth and covered in a thick layer of dust. The stone benches formed a circle around a large open space. The rising sun shined through a skylight to form a circle of illumination – a sort of pulpit of light. She found Dalton there.

"I had expected a more hostile welcome," the Peacekeeper said, instantly drawing steel on the man. Dalton looked up at her from behind his plaster mask but said nothing. "Any last words?" Esther asked.

Before she could pull the trigger, she felt a massive pressure drop onto her. She thought for a moment that the ceiling had collapsed, but there was no impact of falling rock, no sharp blows about her head and shoulders. As some heavy force drove her to her knees, she saw that she stood in a rune circle. Brilliant white force runes hovered just above their carved likeness in the stone. She'd walked into a trap.

"Thank you, Scioxeles," Dalton said.

Beside him, the Primivite materialized, long bony arms and that skull-like head crowned with ivory horns. Glowing eyes glared at her from otherwise empty sockets. The creature appeared to be wearing a tattered black robe and floated half an inch above the floor. It was the first good look Esther had at the archaic life form, once thought to be extinct. "It is with reluctance that I do this, illusionist," Scioxeles said in his raspy, almost disembodied voice.

Dalton waved him off. "We'll have every opportunity to dispatch her," he told his comrade. "First, allow me to enlighten her. Perhaps she'll be sympathetic to our plight."

Esther laughed derisively and pressed against the invisible bonds, trying to raise her revolver. A wave of pain shot through her as the runes hammered at every nerve in her body, turning her laugh into a scream. When she was still again, the pain ceased. "Turn me to your side," she sneered. "*That's* your plan?"

The Primivite looked from her to Dalton. "Kill her, Dalton. This is folly."

Folly? Esther thought idly. *What is with these people?*

Dalton, however, persisted. He raised his hand and a blue-white flame of magick appeared in his palm. "Allow me to paint you a picture, Peacekeeper."

The flame expanded and rippled around them, drawing glowing blue-white lines in the air. They wove together to show her a phantom chamber filled with phantom instruments, like an alchemy lab, only the contraptions were nothing like Esther had ever seen before. The flames drew together at the spectral room's center to form a large machine. It consisted of a circular platform and four mechanical half-arches reaching into the center, covered in runes and buttons and flashing lights.

"Behold," Dalton said, walking through the illusory image, "the Eternity Engine, the Elders' most terrible and marvelous achievement. This is where they were given the gift of immortality."

With another casual wave of his hand, ghostly images of the Elders appeared. All seven figures, the first five of which she recognized from the Elder Gate, appeared before her. The sixth she imagined was Duuren before he was entombed in living stone, tall and massively broad. The seventh must have been Rayan, the Gatekeeper, young and lean looking with a mop of hair and a babyface. Esther couldn't judge the color of his hair or eyes – the images were all drawn in that incandescent blue-white light.

All of the Elders in the image were gathered in a circle around the machine – the Eternity Engine – but Esther saw that they were unevenly spaced; three figures appeared to be missing.

Three, she thought, *the same number as the Dark Magi.*

Cold settled over her as she realized the horrible truth: they had been Elders once. The look on her face betrayed her revelation. "You've guessed it," Dalton said. "In the beginning, there were not seven Elders, but ten."

At his words, the remaining three figures appeared among the Elders, filling in the circle. Darwin was unmistakable, dressed even then in ruffles and frills, and the image Dalton stood just as straight and proud as he stood before her now – minus his plaster mask. The last of the Magi, whom Esther hadn't met yet, Celeste, stood tall and regal in a beautiful gown.

Dalton continued to pace around the room. "I sometimes envy the naïve fools we once were," he said, gazing at his illuminated double. He stroked a hand across the image's face, on the side that was not yet marred. "With all our science and magicks, with all of the quantum universe at our fingertips, we forgot the cardinal rule: as above, so below."

At the center of the Eternity Engine, a great orb of energy spun into existence, kicking up waves of force that caused Elders and Magi alike to hunker down and hold onto something. A growing sound emitted from the energy orb, a crackling, high-pitched whine.

Then it exploded.

The images in the illusory room went into slow motion as a shock wave washed over them. Dalton moved among the ghosts as he spoke.

"As above, so below," he repeated. "For five to be blessed, five must also be cursed."

Dalton gestured to Alastar, the robed, bald man holding his rune staff before him, screaming in defiance of the energy trying to overtake him. He looked just as severe and fierce as advertised in all the holy writ. "Alastar knew, of course, but he...neglected to mention it. His heretical quest for knowledge and power forsook all others."

He spat at the image, then walked around to the big, bearded man, who was slowly soaring backward, an afterimage of an already illusory image, leaving his body and being thrown toward a sculpture of a stone knight. The image of the body turned to dust.

"Duuren's body was sacrificed, leaving him in cold and unfeeling stone for eternity," Dalton explained. He went around next to Celeste, whose beautiful gown morphed into some horrible, tentacled monster that appeared to be consuming her. "Celeste was fused with one of the netherkind, a being from the Outer Dark, forever cursed with an insatiable hunger for the bodies and souls of men."

Next, Graham, who screaming in agony as his right eye burst into flames. "They say that Graham was gifted with one eye that could see into all the Parallels at once, but he once confessed to me that looking upon three superimposed worlds was a torment."

Now Darwin. The blue-white flame formed into skeletal hands, reaching for him. "My blood-brother, Darwin's curse was more inside than out, something you can't easily see."

"The cards," Esther guessed. She'd never seen magick like it before.

Dalton looked amused, but also sad. "Everyone thinks its the cards. I wish every day that was true, but the Taro trick is a magick of his own invention – he's brilliant, my brother – but no. His powers are necromantic. He can reanimate dead flesh." Dalton stroked the cheek of his brother's image. "A gift, you might say? Perhaps, but it twisted his mind and his appetites. He uses this so-called gift to sew together the dead and give them life as aberrations, unnatural monstrosities. He was once such a sweet child."

The illusionist now came to the image of himself. The image's face appeared to be cracking and imploding, collapsing into nothingness. The image of Dalton screamed, hands like claws clutching at the wound. "Then," he said, "there's me. Without the mask, the Void takes whatever I look upon, my eye constantly transfixed on the howling, tortured souls within it."

Dalton waved his hand and the phantom images vanished, leaving them in the tomb-like temple once more. "Immortality, you see, is not meant for Sapienkind. This is the sin of the Elders. Once our dark powers were revealed, we were ejected from their company, forced to suffer an eternity of exile in the Outer Dark."

Esther nodded, unable to stop the pang of remorse for the three would-be Elders. “How and why are you here?” she asked.

Dalton looked over at Scioxeles. “We were taught the ways of World Walking by Corbeau. It was then we escaped the Outer Dark and met Scioxeles here, who has a rather brilliant plan.”

Esther could already guess. “You want to destroy Morgarai,” she said, “as revenge on your former brethren.”

Dalton laughed. Scioxeles scoffed. “On the contrary!” the Primivite spat. “We wish to restore my world, to undo the damage these meddlers have caused.”

“Damage?” Esther asked. “What damage?”

Dalton looked amused. He glanced at his accomplice. “She doesn't know,” he remarked. “History, as they say, is written by the victors.”

The Primivite growled something in his old, dead language; to Esther, it sounded like an ancient form of Daemoniac. "Get on with it. She will join us, or die."

Esther moved cautiously under the weight of the spell that bound her. She inched her revolver's bayonet toward one of the runes on the floor. At the same time, she drew upon the Source energies within her. She wasn't familiar with Runic magick – it was outlawed or at least discouraged in many parts of the world, courtesy of the Wraithbane empire – but she thought that if she could just activate the Force runes on her blade...

“Peacekeeper,” Dalton was saying, “my associate and I are engaged in a noble undertaking. Surely, as a woman of the Unbound Law, you understand the need to right this grave injustice.”

Injustice? Esther wondered. *What injustice could be made right with all this blood and pain and death?*

The illusionist looked at her closely. "I understand your hesitation. In our fervor, I'm afraid we've done great harm to you and yours, but you've proven a worthy foe. A foe that would serve us better as a friend.

"Morgarai is wounded, hurting under the strain of a bondage imposed by my former brethren. You've seen it yourself in the Gray Marsh: a land scarred and scorched by their war, unable to heal." Dalton went to one of the stone benches and hefted his heavy, two-handed mace, already prepared for Esther to tell him no. "So, Peacekeeper Esther Triad of Ordo's Call, what is your answer? Will you help us save the world?"

Esther allowed the Source energy within her to trickle into her hand, charging the runes on her bayonet. The rune circle masked their eldritch glow. She thought of all the people she'd lost on her mission, all the people hurt or corrupted by this man before her. The whole time she had blamed herself for their misfortunes: the deaths of the airship crew, the Agi in the ambush, even to some degree for the deaths of the tortured wraiths she'd taken with her own hand. She'd blamed herself for Hrakar's injury and dishonor, for Leiyara's curse and the horrors she'd experienced. She even felt somewhat responsible for the Valet's shenanigans.

But in a flash, all that blame and inner rage shifted. This thing that was once a man, the Dark Magus and former Elder, had arranged it all. He'd expertly navigated the political climate of three or more nations, manipulating events that led to each misfortune to either deter or eliminate her. He'd even corrupted someone at the Call and arranged for her, a newly-minted Peacekeeper (a "greenhorn", as this mystery person had put it), to be assigned to the mission. Perhaps they'd thought that Esther would be an easy target, but she had grit, and she'd proved it.

In spite of herself, Esther smiled. "My answer?" she said.

The word and the will came easier to her than she'd expected. Für, the Runic word for Force. She focused all her rage into that word, all her pain. The blade of her bayonet rang out and gave a violent jerk, blasting a crater in the floor. The rune circle snapped and Esther felt that great weight lifted from her. She wasted no time.

Springing up, she fired on the Primivite. It wasn't a well-aimed shot by any means, but the bullet blew a hole in Scioxeles's shoulder. Milky white blood burst from the wound and the specter whirled with the force of the blow, cursing in his dead language. He vanished in an instant, retreating.

Esther fired two rounds at Dalton, but they passed through him as his image faded into blue-white flame. She spun about, expecting the same trickery she'd gotten from the shade walker, but Dalton was nowhere in sight.

"I see," Dalton's voice echoed off the walls. Esther couldn't put a bead on it. "Then we are truly enemies. You serving Order and me, Chaos. Very well, then, Peacekeeper. I shall miss our game."

She picked up movement to her left, near one of the four sanctuary entrances. Esther turned and fire, but the image of Dalton flashed away in that ghost light of his. "Face me, coward!" she shouted into the seemingly empty room.

"Very well," Dalton replied. He sounded amused.

His image appeared at the pulpit again, translucent and outlined in flame. The image blurred before Esther could take a shot, then Dalton's phantom circled her, leaving spectral motion trails. When it finished, nine Dalton copies surrounded her, each one sporting that malevolent mace, each one deadly.

"A fair fight, I'd say," the Dalton images all said at once. "Nine foes for nine bullets. Choose your target wisely, Peacekeeper."

They engaged her all at once. Esther turned and shot at the two on her left, the copies bursting into flame and vanishing. A third struck at her with its mace, but she feinted left and fired on it; Number Three followed its brothers into oblivion. She felt an impact on her back as it thrust her forward at Number Four. The Dalton copy choked upon his mace and swung it like a calibri bat. Thinking fast,

Esther dropped to her knees and, propelled by the force of the blow to her back, slid under the swing (Dalton hadn't known she'd played in the Peacekeepers' calibri league four years running). She fired a shot through Number Four and whipped around, still in the slide, putting a bullet in the one that struck her: Number Five.

Esther tried to get to her feet as the pain set in – two broken ribs – but screamed in pain as Number Six smashed her right knee with a mighty swing. A wet cracking noise echoed through the temple as Esther fell. She wheeled right and aimed at Number Six, but he swung his mace at her revolver, effectively breaking her hand in the process. The force runes on the revolver's bayonet activated, giving her a glimmer of hope, but they only bounced the mace backward hard enough to throw Number Six off balance. She formed the glyphs for Ordo's Hammer and aimed it at the copy, but Seven delivered a hard punch to her jaw. Eight fell upon her, too, kicking her hand out of sequence and dispelling the magick. The specter delivered a swift kick to her flank, jostling her already busted ribs.

As she cried out, she spat blood.

Seven, Eight, and Nine surrounded her, all wearing the same smug expression. "Did you really think you could defeat me?" they asked in unison, echoing Dalton's smug cadence.

Then the real beating started.

Chapter Forty-Three: Meadowbrook, the Colonies

Leiyara sat bolt upright from where she lay on the floor, uttering a cry of pain. It hadn't been her pain, but Esther's. She'd acted as a passenger in the Peacekeeper's mind, seeing the Primivite and that Dalton character. She'd watched the images of the Elders play out in their ghostly way. And she watched through Esther's eyes as she took a horrific beating.

The Valet sprung from his seat, raising *Glaeve Pandaemonia* to strike. When he saw her crying on the floor, he relaxed. "Another nightmare?" he asked.

Leiyara shook her head. "It's Esther," she sobbed. "She's dying."

The big man hunkered down and looked at Leiyara with those soft blue eyes. "She's facing Dalton?"

"And she's losing!"

The Valet nodded. "Is the Primivite there?" he asked.

Leiyara bobbed her head again, bouncing her red curls urgently. Even riding along in the back of Esther's mind she could still sense Scioxeles. His malevolence felt as bitter as a winter's breeze. He too watched, giddy with pleasure.

Now, the Valet quirked a smile. "Think you can get back into his head?"

Horror filled Leiyara and she felt her eyes widen. "I won't go back there. I don't want to."

"For Esther," the Valet said. He took her hand gently and laid it on *Glaeve Pandaemonia*. "Take this with you, in your consciousness. Let it ride along."

As her fingers brushed the jeweled eye, she felt something else, a vibration in the back of her head, like another conscious mind. She felt hunger, rage, an overwhelming need to kill. *Is this what the Valet feels all the time?*

She tried to pull her hand away from the Rune Blade, but the Valet held it firm. "Take that feeling with you and use it on that son of a fetch," he said.

Leiyara's heart pounded in her chest, a cold sweat breaking out all over her, but she closed her eyes and focused on the icy, hateful presence of the Primivite. She felt his mind, heard his thoughts in that terrible archaic language. They soon formed into thoughts she could understand.

Just in time for Scioxeles to recognize her.

How? He asked her. *How are you once again in my mind?*

She felt enormous pressure, and at the same time felt as though she was putting that pressure on an invader – feeling both her mind and Scioxeles's simultaneously. Pushing back, she felt her own pressure against the Primivite's will. It was like a wrestling match, Scioxeles grappling with her mind, her slipping out of his grasp and reasserting her psychic strain on him. A massive wave of vertigo overtook her as she and the Primivite spun in the darkness, reaching, grappling, fighting for control. At last, Leiyara felt a push like a cold, bony hand on her throat. Her body, far away and sitting on the floor of the hotel room, struggled to breathe.

What are you? Scioxeles demanded, his shrill voice filled with the kind of rage only born from fear.

Leiyara gripped that fear, merged it with her, and closed her mind around *Glaeve Pandaemonia's* alien consciousness. It felt heavy and dangerous, an almost physical sensation in this place of the mind. As soon as she held the weapon, an image struck her for just one second.

She was alone and cold, in her body again, or at least a projection of it. A frozen wind whipped at her from the starlit void all around her. She stood on some alien gray rock, a piece of debris suspended in the empty sky. All around her, other rocky detritus floated. To her left, the world of Morgarai floated far away, spinning on its lopsided axis, the atmosphere swirling with a hundred different colors. *The moon,* Leiyara thought. *I'm on the moon.*

Then, she felt another presence. It was alike to both the Primivite and *Glaeve Pandaemonia* in its outright malice and hunger, but it was infinitely greater in scope. The mind behind it raged with myriad lunatic thoughts. Leiyara turned her spectral eyes to her right and what she saw made her knees buckle.

The woman sat on a swirling black throne. She wore a purple gown that seethed as it were made from a hundred silken serpents. Her skin was stark white, her lips and fingernails blacker than the void around her. Her opalescent eyes kept shifting color. Suddenly, all of Leiyara's pain and struggle from her first adventure subsided, minimized by the terror of this one moment.

The goddess Pandaemonia, on her throne of dead souls, *looked at her.*

Her horror propelled her backward into the dark again. She felt Scioxeles's psychic grasp, she felt the heavy fury of the Rune Blade. Without a moment's hesitation, Leiyara brought to bear *Glaeve Pandaemonia's* insatiable will and swung.

Chapter Forty-Four: The Iyon Temple, the Frontier

Esther was only aware of pain. The Dalton copies crowded around her, kicking and punching and stomping. She bled in more places than she cared to know, had more broken bones than she could count. Still struggling to get a grip on one of those striking limbs, her fingers passed straight through the illusions. She tried to form glyphs, frantically folding her fingers, but each time a foot stomped on them. Each time she went for one of her revolvers, they dragged her back.

So, she thought idly on the edge of consciousness, *this is how it ends.*

Then, the beating stopped. Esther opened her eyes to see the Dalton copies all looking across the room. Scioxeles had rematerialized and was thrashing through the air, holding his clawed hands to his bony head. Hope sprang back into Esther's heart. *Leiyara*!

With their attention diverted, Esther dragged herself across the floor and grabbed her revolver. She turned and took aim at the Dalton copies, thinking that one of them must be the genuine article and praying to Ordo she had enough bullets left. But as she aimed with a swollen and bloodied eye, her weapon cocked in a throbbing and bruised hand, the Primivite looked straight at her.

"Count the shadows!" Leiyara cried through Scioxeles's voice.

The Dalton copies looked around at each other as if trying to discern the Primivite's meaning. Esther eyes frantically searched the room, noting the shadows from the morning light. The benches, the columns supporting the roof, her own, the Primivite's thrashing shadow on the floor. Then, she spotted it: the Dalton copies cast no shadows. How could they, being made of pure light?

At the same time that she noticed this, the copies turned on her. When they saw her holding a gun they converged once more, rushing the few feet between her and them. While she waited for the torment to once more commence, Esther's eyes shot around the room wildly, searching for any sign of the true Dalton. She almost didn't see it – and thank Ordo she did – as it looked very much like the shadow of one of the broken columns. But eight columns were supporting the structure, and nine shadows.

Without thinking, Esther fired.

The bullet connected with something in mid-air and the Dalton copies vanished. The illusionist materialized again, holding his face and crying out. His plaster mask was cracked and broken at his feet, having deflected Esther's round. Dalton's screams turned into maniacal laughter. "Idiot woman!" he shouted. "You've only doomed yourself!"

Esther fired again, hearing nothing but a dry click. In the space of a second Dalton was upon her, flitting in and out in bursts of his illusory magicks. He kicked her gun away and grabbed her by the collar, hoisting her up to eye level.

"Are you prepared for the Void, Peacekeeper?" Dalton asked. "Your paltry god can't hear you there."

As his hand moved away from the ruined side of his face, as Esther watched the Void itself claw its way through him, she thought of her friends and hoped they would finish this for her. She prayed Ordo would show mercy and pluck her from the torment of the Howling Void. She wished she had passed sentence on that quivering toad Douglas. Now, all they would find of her would be a pillar of ash. Not even her medallion, polished to a mirror shine, would survive to tell anyone that she had died serving the Unbound Law. No one would...

Wait.

A mirror shine.

She had no weapons left, her fingers were too swollen or broken to form her glyphs; all she had was her medallion and a tiny shred of hope. Esther shut her eyes tight and looked away, raising her badge of office to Dalton's face. She didn't see what happened next. She didn't see Dalton's wide-eyed expression. She didn't see the Void bounce off of his reflection in the medallion, and all she heard were Dalton's screams and curses as the shadowy torment ushered him into the Howling Void, a prison to which he'd condemned so many others.

When all was quiet, Esther opened her eyes. A pair of wide, dead eyes stared back at her. Dalton, former member of the Dark Magi and late illusionist, was no more than a sculpture of ash. Esther touched the hand that still held her up, and it crumbled and dumped her painfully to the floor. Bruised, beaten, with no more will to fight and no magicks by which to heal herself, Esther just lay there and bled, awaiting the sweet release of death.

• • • •

A BLINDING LIGHT WOKE her. It was brighter, somehow, than the daylight shining through her swollen eyelids. Esther fully expected to open her eyes and see Ordo awaiting her, taking her into his arms and ushering her to her final reward. She felt an unexpected stab of disappointment when she instead saw two figures haloed by that brilliant white light.

I'm still alive, she thought.

As the light faded, the pair of figures came into focus. One was an old man with a bald head and bushy beard. He wore a white robe and leaned on a staff carved with runes. The second was a woman, tall and regal, with bronze-toned skin and long black curls. She wore a gown that shimmered with an opalescent wave of color. The two looked familiar to Esther, but it took some time to dawn on her that she'd recently seen their likeness carved in massive stone splendor at the Elder Gate.

"I had my doubts, but she came through for us," Alastar said.

Aisha nodded. "I knew she would."

The old man tapped his staff on the floor and that brilliant white light surrounded Esther. She felt an overwhelming wave of relief as all her pain suddenly vanished. "Be healed, child," Alastar's voice said.

When the light faded, Esther stood once more among the ruins of the Iyon temple. Patting herself down, she felt like she was whole again – no more broken ribs and fingers, no more cuts and bruises; they'd even put her revolvers back into their holsters.

Aisha approached and took her arm as Alastar led the way to the back of the sanctuary. "Come, child," he called back over his shoulder. "I want to show you what this has been about. You deserve to know."

Puzzled, Esther looked into Aisha's dark eyes. Was this a dream?

The Matron gave her a reassuring smile. She was as radiant and beautiful as all the stories said.

Alastar led them into a room at the back, a sort of rectory for whatever holy man had preached in this ancient place. The room was empty of any furniture or debris. A series of concentric rune circles had been drawn on the floor, which glowed with undulating blue-black light – the hallmark of Shadow magicks. In the center of the rune circles, a man hung chained to the ceiling by one arm, his other stripped of flesh, bloated and putrefied. He was a wisp a man, shirtless, with a shock of shaggy red hair.

Rayan the Gatekeeper, Esther thought, recognizing him from Dalton's light show.

"Foul magicks," Alastar spat, "begone!" He rapped his rune staff on the floor and the oily rune circles melted away. With another tap of the weapon the chain binding Rayan snapped. Aisha rushed to catch him as he fell. She guided him to the floor and held him like a child while he wept.

While she comforted him, Alastar went to join her. "I am sorry you had to be involved in all this, my child," he said.

"And what exactly is *all this*?" Esther asked.

Alastar and Aisha exchanged a glance. "There is a war brewing," the old Exorcist said, "between Order and Chaos. The very soul of Morgarai and the fate of its people hang in the balance."

Esther nodded. Dalton, in his sanctimonious diatribe, had said as much. "What must I do?" she asked.

The Matron answered. "Your part in this is done for now. You may return to your life with our thanks."

Esther was taken aback, feeling a pang of anger. *I may return to my life, that's* all, she thought. She didn't have to wonder who had orchestrated this whole nightmare. *What did Dalton call it? The sin of the Elders?*

"And Rayan?" she asked. "What happens to him?"

"We will take care of him," Alastar replied, almost curtly.

"Why were the Magi interrogating him? What did they want to know?" she asked, her Peacekeeper instincts kicking in, despite the absurdly surreal moment she experienced.

The old man put a hand up to cease her questions. "In time, child, all will be revealed."

Alastar tapped his staff on the floor again and that white light began to encroach on them. Aisha helped Rayan to his feet and led him into the light. Alastar began to turn away.

"One last question," Esther called after him. "Is what Dalton said true? Did you know you were sacrificing them for your immortality?"

He stopped dead, then looked over his shoulder, his hard gaze melting into what looked like remorse, regret. "As above, so below, my child. As Ordo gives, Ordo takes." Esther took his meaning and clenched her fists at her sides, filled with impotent rage. "Only remember, my child, that Dalton is called the Father of Lies for a reason, and the greatest lies are often little more than twisted truths. Go in peace."

Before she could retort, Alastar and the light vanished, leaving her alone in the empty rectory.

My child, she thought as a shiver went up her spine. The graven image of Alastar hadn't captured his eyes, but in reality, they were familiar to her. She'd looked at them in her reflection many times.

Chapter Forty-Five: Ordo's Call, Perdition

Two months had passed since Esther had returned to the Call. She filed a full report on her experiences, leaving out certain details that would make her look insane. She omitted any mention of the mysterious Emon Pah-ren, for if her suspicions were correct, the Agi spy wouldn't want his name brought into it. She'd also kept out any reference to the Dark Magi or her encounter with the Elders – omitting any involvement of mythical figures was probably wise, she thought. She still wasn't sure if that last part had been real – as if walking out of the Iyon temple without a scratch hadn't been evidence enough.

As for Hrakar, when she returned from defeating Dalton, she gave him his remaining *kal*, thereby allowing him to return to his people. Esther would never admit it, but it was a tearful goodbye. She was thrilled to receive news later that, for his deeds of valor, Hrakar had been appointed as liaison and ambassador to Ordo's Call. He'd be moving to this desolate rock within a fortnight.

The Valet had concluded his business with her with a drink to their honor, and then he'd vanished into the night with a random serving girl. The next morning he'd gone, although it wouldn't surprise Esther in the least if their paths crossed again.

Leiyara, having discovered her Agi heritage, had come home to have a frank discussion with her father and the woman who turned out to be her stepmother. She'd managed to shame them into paying her fare back to Agimonde to learn about her birth mother and her heritage.

Esther waited at the sky harbor now, looking over Ordo's Call and marveling at not having missed it. The desolate place presented quite a change from the arid beauty of Agimonde and the lush green of the Colonies, and she longed to once again leave that barren rock and return to the world. Unfortunately, that took longer than expected. She'd initially been given leave after filing her report, but the Magister had needed more time to review it, so she'd been put on guard duty, patrolling the town. The days had turned into weeks, the weeks into months. At first, she had been content with the mundane work, but she became restless too soon.

Leiyara's airship pulled into the harbor and Esther waited impatiently as the craft moored and the gangplank lowered. The truth was that she'd become accustomed to – even fond of – the girl's company throughout their adventure, and she had to admit that she missed her bouncy little secretary.

When Leiyara disembarked, Esther gaped at a whole new woman. Her hair was longer now, reaching the small of her back in a cascade of fiery curls. She dressed unabashedly in one of those thin Agi dresses that showed entirely too much leg for Sapien society. Her skin had been toasted to a faint orange color by the desert sun. To the untrained eye, one would mistake her for a full-blood Agi woman. She even wore those strappy sandals that were in fashion in the desert nation.

When she saw Esther, Leiyara lit up. She ran across the platform and hugged her fiercely. "Esther!" she cried.

Esther returned her embrace, then drew her back and took a good look at her. "I barely recognized you."

The blushing was hardly noticeable under her new hues. "I know. I changed a lot."

"For the better," Esther said. She noticed something on Leiyara's upper arm, just below the copper arm ring that adorned it. "And they even gave you one of those."

Leiyara showed off the tattoo – a coin with an anchor at its center. "I'm Leiyara Candish-Commercier now," she said. "There was a ceremony and everything."

"Did it hurt?"

"A lot," Leiyara admitted. "But I had a lot of Emon's blood cider, so I hardly remember it."

"Very impressive."

"Oh! And you'll never guess. Remember Rae from the caravan?" Esther remembered. Rae, the confident Commercier who had fought bravely during the wraith ambush. She told Leiyara she did. "Well, it turns out, she's my cousin!" Leiyara announced.

Esther took her affectionately by the arm and led her down the stairs. Meanwhile, Leiyara chattered on about meeting her extended family, getting her tattoo, and learning everything she could about her birth mother. It turned out Laryssa Commercier had died in childbirth, but Leiyara's father had shipped her body back to Agimonde to have her firestone returned to flames. "They say I'm just like my mom," the girl added. "Which I think is a compliment, but I guess she talked a lot, too, so who knows? Why are you smiling that way?"

Esther hadn't realized it, but she beamed at her friend. "Nothing," she said. "It's just good to have you home."

• • • •

THE SUMMONS CAME TWO days after Leiyara's return. Esther had just gotten off a long, dull night of patrolling and sat outside Gallowschurch, waiting. She looked out over the Barrowlands and counted the cairns, just like the day she'd been given her first assignment. It seemed such a long time ago, like she'd been a whole different person then.

At last, the doors opened and Secretary Morgis came to greet her. "Esther, my child, it's good to see you!" he said in his usual cheerful manner.

Esther clapped the chubby man on the shoulder. "And you, Secretary."

Morgis took her by the arm and led her inside. "Now, don't worry about a thing," he said. "This is all just a formality."

In truth, Esther didn't worry until he told her not to, but she kept it to herself. As they walked down the hall and passed the pillars depicting the Aspects of Ordo, Esther felt that she now had a deeper understanding of their true meaning. The Scales, a balance between Order and Chaos. The Lion, courage and nobility. She pondered them as they proceeded to the High Seat.

Magister Pontus waited in his high seat, looking over the lengthy report she had submitted months ago. He didn't look pleased, but that wasn't unusual for the scarred old man. Esther stood squarely in the center of Ordo's Seal and clapped her hands behind her back, remembering a long gone, insecure girl standing on this exact spot.

"Peacekeeper Esther Triad reporting as ordered, Your Honor," she said.

The Magister looked up at her with his one dead eye. Esther remembered how that eye had frightened her the first time she saw it before she knew what real fear was.

"Good to see you're well," Pontus said. "Let's get started, shall we?"

"Yes, Your Honor."

Pontus shuffled through his papers. "Well, for starters, you completed your mission. The arcanist has been neutralized and the Colonies are ready to restore their lands next planting season. The king of Kairal sends his compliments."

Esther nodded. "Thank you, Your Honor."

"However," the Magister said, going stony, "you involved a civilian, this..." he searched his documents, "...Lee-air-a girl, who had no training whatsoever, even going so far as to employ her as your secretary."

"I apologize for the misstep, Your Honor, but *Lay-ara...*" she put a bit of emphasis on the correct pronunciation, "...proved invaluable to the mission."

The Magister looked at her severely and cleared his throat – a telltale sign that he was displeased with her intercession. "Yes, indeed," he grudgingly admitted, "which is why, in light of her connections to the Agish people and her abilities as a delkynian, we've concluded that she's an asset to the Call. She will be permanently assigned to you as your attache, should she so choose."

Oh, she'll be thrilled to death, Esther thought.

"Furthermore," Pontus continued, "you showed great leadership in assisting the Central Transit crew in the Gray Marsh, even though they were tragically lost. Central Transit has pledged a gold imperial per month as a donation to the Call. Also, the caste leaders of Agimonde send their compliments, as well as a shipment of black iron munitions to aid in our fight. They've also agreed to fashion weapons in the likeness of those..." he gestured to her revolvers, "...as standard issue." Pontus raised his gavel. "Overall, I'd say this mission was a success and a job well-done Peacekeeper Triad." He banged his gavel. "Now, report to Commander Tyrell for your next assignment."

Esther turned and allowed Secretary Morgis to escort her outside. Once they were back in the open air, Esther lit a cigarette. After all those long nights patrolling and cuffing drunkards, smoking was becoming her vice, though she'd soon be adding a large Draconian man to that list. "That went surprisingly well," she said.

Morgis chuckled. "Not all *that* surprising," he said. "You accomplished your mission and made a few valuable friends for the Call in the process. Not bad for a greenhorn."

Freezing with her cigarette halfway to her lips, Esther's other hand dropped to her revolver. "What did you say?" she asked, that cold feeling dropping into her stomach again.

"I said, not bad for a greenhorn," the secretary repeated. "It means a new recruit."

"I know what it means," Esther said, flicking her cigarette over the railing. "It's just that a little bird told me that their spy in Ordo's Call used that same word to describe me." She folded her fingers into the Seal of the Confessional, just in case she'd need to use it.

The secretary went ashen and started shaking, wobbling a little, too. "I don't...I didn't..."

"What did Dalton offer you for your soul, Secretary Morgis?" the Peacekeeper asked. "Never mind. I don't want to know."

"So, what now?" Morgis asked, flop sweat starting to form on his brow.

"What now," Esther replied, "is that you resign from service – *today* – and you run back to your masters. The Dark Magi's plot isn't over yet, so you tell them Esther Triad is coming, and the Void is coming with me. Then, you hide. You find whatever hole you can and you hide there. And never forget that I have a Delkynian and a Draconian who will do anything for me. Do you understand?"

Morgis nodded his quivering jowls.

"Good," Esther said. "Go. Now."

When the secretary was out of sight, bounding down the steps to the village, Esther removed her hand from her weapon. Morgis was the last loose end she'd needed to tie up, but so many questions remained. What was the Dark Magi's ultimate goal? How did they intend to "restore" Morgarai? And what was the secret they were trying to torture out of Rayan?

Acknowledgments

Wow, lots of people to mention here. First, my wife and Queen of Darkness Sarah for backing me up on this crazy gambit, and for putting up with hours-long ramblings about Morgarai and her strange cast of characters. Also, special thanks to my mother-in-law Juli Kautzmann for being my #1 fan and first beta reader; my thanks go out to Charity Chaney for beta-ing as well and for being, like, half as obsessed with this stuff as I am. Thank you to Jess, Mandy, and Susan over at Shadow Spark Publishing for taking a shot on a hapless rogue like me, and for their editorial help along the way. Here's to what I aim to be a long and lucrative career. I have to give credit where credit's due and mention the best writing assistant kitties a guy could ask for: Furryosa, Scarface, and Captain George Tiberius Snuggles (gods rest him). Thanks, too, to the Twitter #writingcommunity, who backed me every step of the way.

Credits

Cover Design—Jessica Moon
Cover Design—Chad Moon
Editing—Susan Floyd
Formatting—Mandy Russell

Dalton had said that they had achieved their goals, and the possibilities frightened her. A war between Order and Chaos. Esther left Gallowschurch to find Commander Tyrell, uttering a silent prayer that she would be there whenever this war started.

About the Author

andrew slinde is a writer, film geek, and a decent cook. He lives in des moines, Iowa, and cohabitates with three apex predators. He is definitely not a dozen squirrels in a raincoat.

six-gun sorcery, the first installment of his fantasy steampunk series, *The Sins of the Elders,* will be released in february 2021.

he can be found on twitter @andrewslinde

Made in the USA
Columbia, SC
17 March 2021

34224841R00190